EROTICA

Women's Writing from Sappho
to Margaret Atwood

EROTICA

Women's Writing from Sappho
to Margaret Atwood

EDITED BY
MARGARET REYNOLDS
with a foreword by
Jeanette Winterson

Fawcett Columbine
New York

A Fawcett Columbine Book
Published by Ballantine Books

Compilation and Introduction Copyright © 1990 by Margaret Reynolds
Foreword © 1990 by Jeanette Winterson

Library of Congress Cataloging-in-Publication Data

Erotica : women's writing from Sappho to Margaret Atwood / edited by
    Margaret Reynolds ; with a foreword by Jeanette Winterson.
    —1st American ed.
        p.   cm.
    Includes bibliographical references and index.
    ISBN 0-449-90616-7
    1. Erotic literature—Women authors.   I. Reynolds, Margaret.
    PN6071.E7E685   1991   91-70538
    808.8′03538′082—dc20   CIP

Manufactured in the United States of America

First American Edition: October 1991

10   9   8   7   6   5   4   3   2   1

For J., who explains.

And for the bright days:
when the sun diminishes the pupils to pinpricks
and we can hardly see.

CONTENTS

EROTICA

CONTENTS

EROTICA

CONTENTS

CONTENTS

ACKNOWLEDGEMENTS

Thanks to all those who have shared their secrets.

Thanks to Candida Lacey, Philippa Brewster, Ginny Iliff and Debbie Licorish at Pandora.

The Editor and Publisher would like to thank the following for permission to reproduce material in this anthology:

the extract from *Sexing the Cherry* by Jeanette Winterson reprinted by kind permission of Bloomsbury Limited, Atlantic Monthly Press and Lester & Orpen Dennys © 1990; from *The Passion* by Jeanette Winterson by kind permission of Bloomsbury Limited and Atlantic Monthly © 1987; from 'The Laugh of the Medusa' by Hélène Cixous, translated by Keith Cohen and Paula Cohen, from *L'Arc* and published in *Signs* (1976), by kind permission of the author, the translators and the University of Chicago Press; extracts by Luce Irigaray and Annie Leclerc from *New French Feminisms* ed Elaine Marks and Isabel de Courtivron (Amherst: University of Massachusetts Press, 1980), copyright © 1980 by the University of Massachusetts Press; from *Dreams of the Woman Who Loved Sex* by Tee Corinne reprinted by kind permission of the author and Banned Books; from *Mrs Dalloway* by Virginia Woolf reprinted by kind permission of the Executors of the Virgina Woolf Estate, The Hogarth Press and Harcourt Brace Jovanovich Inc (copyright 1925 and renewed in 1953 by Leonard Woolf); from *The Women's Room* by Marilyn French reprinted by kind permission of the author, Andre Deutch Ltd and Summit Books, a division of Simon & Schuster Inc; the story 'A Dash of Vanilla' and the extract from *The Calyx of Isis* by Pat Califia reproduced by kind permission of the author and Alyson Publications Inc; 'My Subway

translated by Elaine Feinstein; the poems by Marilyn Hacker from *Love, Death and the Changing of the Seasons* published by Onlywomen Press Ltd and Arbor House (a division of Wm Morrow & Co) reprinted by kind permission of the author; 'Self' by Marilyn Hacker from *Going Back to the River* by Marilyn Hacker reprinted by permission of the author and Random House Inc; 'Laustic' and 'Les Deus Amanz' from *The Lais of Marie de France* translated by Glyn S Burgess and Keith Busby (Penguin Classics, 1986), copyright © Glyn S Burgess and Keith Busby 1986 reproduced by permission of Penguin Books Ltd; extract from *Breathing Water* by Joan Crate (Nunatak Fiction Series) reprinted by permission of the author and NeWest Press, Edmonton, 1990; the extract from 'Putting the Great Mother Together Again' by Sarah Murphy from *A Mazing Space* ed Shirley Neuman and Smaro Kamboureli, published by NeWest Press, Edmonton, reprinted by kind permission of the author; the extract from *Working Hot* by Mary Fallon reprinted by kind permission of the author and Sybylla Co-Op Press, Melbourne; 'Aria for Midsummer's Eve' by Maureen Duffy from *Collected Poems 1949–84* by Maureen Duffy reprinted by permission of the author © 1971 by Maureen Duffy; extract from *Wide Sargasso Sea* by Jean Rhys reprinted by permission of Andre Deutsch Ltd (1966); extract from *The Millstone* by Margaret Drabble printed by permission of Weidenfeld & Nicholson Ltd; 'Oppenheim's Cup and Saucer' by Carol Ann Duffy from *Standing Female Nude* by Carol Ann Duffy (1985) reprinted by permission of Anvil Press Poetry Ltd; 'The Pleasure of Children' by Margaret Drabble reprinted by kind permission of the author and the Peters Fraser & Dunlop Group Ltd; the extract from *Lifting Belly* by Gertrude Stein from *Bee Time Vine and Other Pieces* by Gertrude Stein reprinted by permission of the Estate of Gertrude Stein and David Higham Associates © 1959 Alice B Toklas; extract from the Preface to *A Book Of Mediterranean Food* by Elizabeth David (Penguin Books, Second Revised Edition, 1965) copyright © Elizabeth David 1965, reprinted by permission of Penguin Books Ltd; poems from *The Flowering of the Rod* by H D (Hilda Doolittle) published as *Trilogy* by kind permission of Carcanet Press Ltd and New Directions; the extract from 'The Adult Life of Toulouse Lautrec by Henri Toulouse Lautrec' by Kathy Acker from *Young Lust* by Kathy Acker reprinted by permission of Unwin Hyman Ltd and Grove Weidenfield © 1975 Kathy Acker; 'Loving for Two' by Jill Dawson reprinted by kind permission of the author © Jill Dawson 1990; the extract from *The Lover* by Marguerite Duras reprinted by permission of Collins Publishers and Pantheon Books (a division of Random House Inc); 'Love in three movements' by Elizabeth Jennings from *Extending the*

FOREWORD

by Jeanette Winterson

Some years ago a magazine asked me if I would agree to be photographed naked. They were about to run a detailed interview on my life and times and wanted, I suppose, to make the most of their centre spread. At first I was amused, then aghast, but I agreed. My decision was a mixture of curiosity and bravado. I have always admired Gloria Steinem for her stint as a Bunny Girl (the best weapons are the ones you take from the enemy) and I thought that on a humbler scale I might have something to add to the endless Page Three debate.

In a lofty studio in London, West One I took off my clothes. The photographers, both men, were far more interested in their equipment than they were in me and I felt comfortably invisible. I had been made up to look like a faun. This didn't worry me because I feel kinship with woodland creatures. What it did do was to remove successfully any question of Jeanette Winterson herself, as a writer or as an individual, relating to the camera. There was a body, there were props, there was an idea and there was a photograph, none of these had anything to do with me.

The common image of sex photography, or sex writing, or sex shows, is one of lustful enthusiasm. Men must have access to all this stuff because they are wild about women. She is central, urgent. She has the power, as body or muse. They are obsessed with her, both as art icon and bedroom fantasy. *Playboy* boss Hugh Heffner has said that pornography celebrates women.

The truth, I think, is quite different. There is no engagement with the woman either at the level of production or consumption. She is the sum of her parts and these parts are discussed, manipulated and packaged in much the same way as a set of machine tools.

Whilst undergoing my exposure, I had the opportunity to talk to a few of the glamour models coming in and out. Like me, they were pleased with the business-like way their bodies were treated. Most cited the courtesy of an electric fire. One pointed out that she had put up with a lot more hassle as a secretary. They were all in it for the money, making the most of their assets before gravity took its toll. The question of invisibility was not, to them, an important one. They had already learned to cut themselves up, split themselves off, in order to do the job at all. The ritual of dressing and undressing had become the doorway from one world into another; from the world of ordinary concerns where they went shopping and saw their friends, to the hyperbole of soft porn, where the simplest things are overstated.

In the stories of oppressed peoples you will find stories of disappearing. Plantation slaves made magic potions to render themselves invisible and thus to escape the whip, heat and humiliation of their lives. In modern-day Brazil, some rain-forest tribes have elected not to exist. Each member simply turns away from their ancestral lands and walks on until she or he meets death.

Linda Lovelace, infamous star of numerous porn films including *Deep Throat*, was first hypnotised and then learned self-hypnosis in order to cope with the various sex acts she was required to perform. Interestingly, this technique of hypnosis is now being used on chimpanzees and other wild animals to make them more amenable to being photographed with tourists.

In her books, *Ordeal* and *Out of Bondage*, Lovelace talks a lot about being invisible. Her 'keepers' had no interest in treating her as a human being with a particular identity, and she soon learned that to assert that identity fired their sadism and increased her humiliation. The body was there, the woman inside disappeared. Which of us wouldn't when the day started with a beating and climaxed with a penis in the gullet?

Erotica seeks to return women to their bodies by offering a looking glass and not a distorting mirror. Here women can speak for themselves and by doing so deliver a valuable counter-argument to the lies, secrets and silences that typically pass for a woman's sex life. Re-defining the erotic in terms of female rather than male experience is crucial to the pornography debate, not only to introduce some truth telling but also to remind those who want to protect and sanctify, that censorship may replace one kind of gag with another. We don't want men to package us but we must have the freedom to describe ourselves. This desire is not modern. One of the pleasures of *Erotica*, is that it chooses work across the centuries. Work

that has been overlooked in the current fad for contemporary sex anthologies.

This broad historical perspective allows us to think about women's sexuality as a developing continuum rather than as a series of fragments. Men have been devotedly recording the vagaries of their lust for centuries and they have left a vast library for consultation. Naturally that library is held to be the A–Z of female experience too. Any good scholar will tell you that when we talk about 'he' we include 'she'.

Women have thought otherwise, and not just recently. In spite of the prohibitions on women writing at all, we have managed to document ourselves even in the forbidden area of sexual self-expression.

Women's history is not an easily traceable straight line. Women's concerns do not make the stuff of history. Following us is to watch for the hidden signs, to look in the gaps and be prepared for strange ziz-zags. *Erotica* is a wild plunge into mostly overlooked territory. It accepts that women will not always have been able to write directly about sex or desire but that they will have done so through nuance, suggestion, poetic device and allegory. The *Lais of Marie de France* are a good example of this and what else was Christina Rossetti doing in *Goblin Market*? Dr Reynolds is not so simple-minded as to assume that the authors of her extracts will, in every case, have been aware of what they were doing. Most of us, even now, do not have that kind of self-knowledge. We are full of sub-texts.

Some will argue that if a text was not conceived as erotic it should not now be interpreted as such. But reading is not a passive act. We bring ourselves to a text and in that moment the text is changed. Shakespeare survives because he is able to admit any number of readings. There are always new ways of looking at his work.

It is right, then, that we should see what we can find in the body of our written heritage. It will nonetheless bob up over the wash of all our theorising and present itself fresh to a new generation. We need not be too delicate with art, it is much tougher than we are.

If anyone is worried that Margaret Reynolds has demonstrated by her selection that everything and anything can be considered erotic, they should recall that men have no difficulty in sexualising the most banal encounters and unlikely objects. A whole range of hardware is commonly put up for sale wrapped around a woman's body. Add to this every woman's experience of a lewd exchange when she has asked a perfectly simple question and it will not be difficult to see that men are licensed to picture the whole world as a giant reflection of their prick.

In fact the world is round. In fact it is women, not men who are intimate with their bodies; who bleed and bear children and have, as Dr Reynolds has pointed out, the one organ that has nothing to do with reproduction or peeing. The clitoris is for pleasure only and yet we are told that vaginal orgasms are 'real' sex. Real sex is whatever a woman says it is. No one but she should decide where pleasure lies or how desire is drawn. Some women will find the more oblique passages in this book very exciting. Others will not. Women, unlike men, do not agree on the broadstream of what is sexy. I do not know whether this is a fact about women *per se* or whether it is a result of our fragmented inheritance. I do know that such lively dispute takes us away from the monolithic tedium of male pornography. Most men do not like to think about women in all their variety, much less in all their glory; they prefer the stereotype. *Erotica* has women of all sorts busy with all kinds of bodily delight. The range is huge. The only way to read it is as a personal document; take what works for you and respect the rest as someone else's pleasure. Or indeed someone else's pain, for there is both.

Much of life is got through the senses. Mind and spirit that we are, we are also in these bodies for good or ill, and it might as well be good. There is nothing shameful about wanting sex and there should be nothing disgraceful in enjoying titillation. I have said that my objection to pornography is that it renders women invisible, stripping them of their independent identity and self-respect. It is very hard to respect what is always being cheapened, and women who have nothing to do with the sex industry still suffer from it in this way. Can women who write about sex do it differently? Can women arouse and engage without exploitation? I think so, and I think this book shows clearly that we can.

The three most striking elements of male pornography are that it is utterly man-centred, that it avoids contact with real women, preferring its own fetishised versions, and that it is all the same. Through the evidence of *Erotica* and, should anyone care to look, those magazines produced by women for women, we can see that our own versions of desire are quite different.

I have already talked about variety. It is also important to talk about the value of putting a woman back at the centre of her own sexuality. The stories and poems and songs that you will find in this anthology are absolutely to do with women. Men occupy an incidental role; incidental in that, although they may pleasure a woman, they do not become the focus of the piece. Whilst men are removed from the central role they so covet, they are not objectified or humiliated. It is salutary that women know how to turn the tables without falling into the same traps. It is

not necessary to devalue half of the species in order to manufacture pleasure. Men may not like their walk-on parts, but at least we let them do it on their own two feet, not in spiked stilettos, wearing a dog collar and a gag.

Naturally, the lesbian pieces in this book, and there is a representative amount of it, leaves out men altogether. Giving birth, breast-feeding and bleeding leaves them out too, but many women find these experiences sexy. It is right that they should appear, not only as part of womanhood, but also as a challenge to the complacent, male-directed canon of what turns us on.

Pornography is not a simple issue and it does not stand apart from the rest of our cultural heritage. Those women who believe that porn reinforces the common male-to-female attitudes of violence and contempt are right. But porn is a reinforcing symptom not a fundamental cause of those attitudes. We will have to do a lot more than dismantle the top shelf and send home the Bunny Girls if we really are to change the way that men think about women.

Crucially, we need to remake the language of sex. Language is power and as women we have plenty of abuse words waiting for us. We will have to refuse them, to refuse ourselves as sluts, whores, cunts, holes, ground-sheets, slags, nymphos, frigid spinsters. But in the two-fold image of the goddess Kali, as we destroy with one hand, we will have to build with the other.

Iris Murdoch, in *The Sovereignty of Good Over Other Concepts* tells us that human beings cannot give things up, they can only replace them. This seems to be true. We should then be working towards re-drawing the sexual landscape so that it is a place where violence can be repudiated, not affirmed, and where, irrespective of gender or gender preference, we can meet as equals. Women have the power to do this.

In a lofty studio in London, West One, I put on my clothes. There was still faun gel in my hair and I fancy that my ears were pointier than usual. A former stripper once said to me, 'Naked is the best disguise' and in that strange half-world, I was glad to find she was right. How much better, though, to put out your hand and find skin that is only itself; warm, articulate and unafraid.

London, 1990

INTRODUCTION

When Anaïs Nin was writing erotica for a dollar a page, she and her fellow contributors were irritated by their patron's insistence that they 'leave out the poetry' and 'concentrate on the sex'.[1] This emphasis, she said, turned them all into saints producing porn. For what they found most moving were not the clinical gestures, the precision lists of bodily parts, but the varieties of feeling and context surrounding the eternal repetitions of the sexual act. 'Poetry' became their aphrodisiac. Colours, textures, exotic scenes, bizarre variations, perverse violations, became their addiction. Curiosity excited. Ideas turned them on.

Without invention and surprise Nin and her companion writers felt that their writing about sex could only be barren, crude, dull. 'The language of sex', she wrote, 'had yet to be invented.'

In particular, the language of sex for women had to be invented. Even while she was writing erotica in the 1940s Nin worried that she was not writing about women's sensuality, which she felt was different from a man's. Deriving her style from a reading of men's works, Nin believed that she had compromised her 'feminine self'. When she eventually decided to publish her erotica in 1976, she was surprised to find that there were here elements of what she named her 'feminine'. Conscious of a difference between men and women, she attributed the male with explicitness and gusto, the female with ambiguity and poetry.[2]

This is a simplified and essentialist notion of the difference between men and women in their attitudes to sex and their idea of the erotic. But it is a common one. The reason for its persistence is that reiterated

[1] Anaïs Nin, Preface (December, 1940), *The Delta of Venus* (1976), pp. xi–xii.
[2] Anaïs Nin, 'Postscript', *The Delta of Venus* (1976), p. xvi.

expectations have encouraged women (and men) to believe in this differential.

When a teenage boy focuses his attentions on his first girlfriend, he is licensed to regard that encounter as one rooted in uncluttered sexual need. For him, it is allowed to be pure sex. But the girl (still too often denied any explicit sexual advice about her own capacity for pleasure) is trained to think of romance, to believe in love, to imagine that she alone, and by some mysterious power, has excited this astonishing reaction.

The cultural betrayal is the same wherever you find it. There is always the same discrepancy between the sexes. In the most 'romantic' of operatic love duets, Puccini's Butterfly sings of the night, the moon, the stars, her love; Pinkerton sings 'Come to bed'.[3] As long ago as 1696, Delarivier Manley made the same point when one of her male characters cynically advised another on love and gender difference:

> Our sex can never bear themselves too bold
> Provided still we lay the stress on love,
> For when we warmest urge our fierce desire,
> The self–conceited she mistakes the cause,
> Nor nicely weighs the influence of temper,
> But thinks them all strong arguments of passion
> Which nothing but her beauty could inspire.[4]

Women and men do feel differently about sex. In part, this is due to the differing expectations and licences which the sexes bring to their experience of desire. But part of the discrepancy may also be a mirror of biological fact.

Woman's sensual life has always seemed mysterious to men because it is hidden. Her sex is discreetly concealed; her arousal is difficult to detect; her coming – unless she chooses to claim it – is hard to verify. As a result, the confused male has no way of understanding women's sexual pleasure. He cannot be certain it is there.

Furthermore, because he is encouraged to focus on the penis as the instrument of sexual satisfaction, he, quite literally, obscures the evidence of woman's bodily pleasure with the phallus. His mission of exploration wipes out the native landscape. All he can hear and see are words, expressions and gestures. It is no large step to believe that these

---

[3] Guiseppe Puccini, *Madam Butterfly* (1907), Act I. Libretto by Giacosa and Illica.
[4] Delarivier Manley, *The Royal Mischief* (1696), Act II, Scene 1.

evanescent signs are the first and only constituents of women's sensuality. All too much 'poetry' is present in this version.

And yet, set against this, is another biological fact. Women are the possessors of the only anatomical part which serves no other function than the simple one of bodily pleasure. No wonder that the ordinary man is frightened. He can't see any exact physical evidence of woman's excitement, and at the same time, he knows that she owns a large capacity for pleasure.

No wonder he fears for the safety of his member. No wonder he invented the myth of women as asexual beings. No wonder he reinforced it with social prejudices.

The taboo on women's physical sexual feeling is solid enough. For a woman to write about that feeling is similarly scandalous. Virginia Woolf thought that prohibition was a handicap for all, but especially for the female artist. In her essay 'Professions for Women', she described the current of the creative mood:

> She was letting her imagination sweep unchecked round every rock and cranny of the world that lies submerged in the depths of our unconscious being... And then there was a smash. There was an explosion... The imagination had dashed itself against something hard. The girl was aroused from her dream. She was indeed in a state of the most acute and difficult distress. To speak without figure she had thought of something, something about the body, about the passions which it was unfitting for her as a woman to say. Men, her reason told her, would be shocked. The consciousness of what men will say of a woman who speaks the truth about her passions had roused her from her artist's state of unconsciousness. She could write no more.[5]

I was often reminded of Virginia Woolf's awareness of this prohibition on speaking during the process of compiling this anthology.

Many writers on female sexuality agree that, for the most part, women have not been permitted (been able?) to write about the body, or about their sexual lives until the 'liberation' of the twentieth century. But women have always known sexual experience. And women have always been able to write. It is true that throughout history both these activities have been limited for women. And yet, women broke through the one set of laws to feel desire. Why not the other? Where might women, however secretly, have been attempting to write out, to express their experience of the erotic? This anthology grows out of that investigation.

[5] Virginia Woolf, 'Professions for Women' (1931).

It is a book about love.

Love recognises the existence of something beyond the self. It takes many shapes. But as our physical shape is rounded by the body, love must always be known on the skin.

After that, comes imagination. After that, comes tenderness, passion, cruelty, lust, mystery, pain, abandon, surrender.

Eros, the blind boy. Under one tradition he was the son of Aphrodite and Hermes. Love, realised in the body of a woman rising out of the sea, unites with speech and exchange in the winged messenger of the gods. These are the two strands in the erotic. The body's craving and the mind's release.

This definition is not an accepted one. You will not find it in any dictionary. But it is the understanding of 'erotica' which best explains the choices in this book.

Women have always been beggars at the erotic feast. Men have eaten their fill. Of course, there have been obstacles and prohibitions. Yet for the most part male desire is legitimate, 'natural'. Women's desire has been forbidden, purified, regulated, by laws, by conventional assumptions, by chastity belts and other instruments of torture.

In thrall to the rule of silence, women began to believe that the sexual life was a subject on which they should be quiet. Those that didn't, and wished to speak, were silenced. Virginia Woolf saw this in the past. It still happens. Some extracts included in the draft for this collection are not here, because their copyright holders refused permission. The women who wrote were not embarrassed. Others were embarrassed for them.

Today women can reclaim their right to speak. Feminism has given back woman's voice. And yet today women are again holding their tongues. Rightly angry about sexual exploitation, rallying organisations are sweeping up the erotic with the pornographic and clearing them all off the shelf.

It is easy to see the arguments against the trivial and everyday exposures of the tabloids, the more glamorous Vaseline of the glossy magazines. But where does this leave the desiring woman? Is she not being shackled as securely as ever to the image of high-minded saint and puritan moralist? Folk mythology is just that, even when it is a feminist mythology.

For women, the place where that debate continues most fiercely is in the area of lesbian erotica. Satisfactory images of men as objects of desire have rarely been produced. The best are those created by men for men, but few straight women would think to look there. In the meantime, heterosexual women are stuck with heterosexual porn which makes a

fetish of woman and leaves many female viewers confused. Art, literature, convention and popular opinion all declare that women's bodies are most beautiful.

With lesbian pornography, images and accounts of women produced by and for women, a feminist position becomes very fraught. (It is also more exposed and self-critical than in debates around the heterosexual, for many lesbians are also feminists.) While this material is being consumed by the women for whom it is produced, in the loving spirit in which it is produced, then all is well. When it is used by others – by voyeurs in effect – then ugly questions arise. Are women thus licensing the excesses of heterosexuality from which they have suffered for so long? Worse, are women making themselves the exploiters they deplore?

This is a difficulty. Without defusing the problem, I can only suggest some questions that may assist in providing answers.

If desire is always with us (and it is) then clearly it is a suitable subject for representation, whatever the character of the product, whoever produces it. So, why not for women as well as men?

If men have misused something for centuries, does that mean that the thing itself is tarnished? Should women deny themselves all that has been corrupted by misuse? Should cultural assumptions of what is a 'male' activity and what 'female', govern our actions, our choices?

If asked to categorise, how would you rank the offensiveness of *Playboy* and *On Our Backs* as against the virgin sacrifice which functions as a frontispiece to that quintessentially English magazine, *Country Life*?

Two things are clear. It will always be difficult to legislate on the production of erotica and pornography. And it will always be – perhaps should always be – impossible to legislate on the consumption of erotica and pornography.

I use the two terms, erotica and pornography, together. Many writers throw up their hands and throw down their pens, saying that they cannot distinguish between these two thorns. Perhaps the usual focus on production is misleading. Could it be that the clue to discrimination depends rather on the reading?

In this way pornography consists of those depictions of sexuality which are used exploitatively and selfishly. Erotica consists of those portraits which are used honestly and with love. This explains why one woman's pornography is another woman's erotica.

The organisation of this anthology is designed to confess a creative process of reading. I hope that the themes suggested here will make readers examine my reading principles – and their own.

Each of the eleven headings offered themselves as selections were made. At the start I knew that I would begin with 'Invitations' and end with 'Consummation'. Other themes developed from there as I began to think about what – in the largest sense – might be the categories of the 'erotic'. 'Consumption' was included because I found food and sex together as I knew I would. 'Taboo' and 'Danger' were easy to compile because, through history, so much of women's sexual life has been subject to regulation and threat. Most of the extracts in 'Danger' turned out to have a heterosexual orientation. This was not deliberate, but I think it is telling. By contrast, several of the pieces in 'Consummation' turned out to be lesbian in character, suggesting that women could often only discover security in sexual love when it was found between women. 'Voyeurism' was another problematic section because looking has always been a male prerogative. Oddly, 'Desire' proved a difficult section because frank speaking for women is uncommon. 'Romance' and 'Fantasy' were uncomplicated because these have always been the categories of erotica permitted to women.

As I worked, I found that I had left-over selections which were about women loving themselves or each other. So 'Loving Self' was added. I was pleased to discover that this yielded eleven sections in all. One more than the ten which is the law of Moses. One less than the twelve which is the unit of order and value. A small indication of the largeness of a task which attempts to escape old laws and evade conventional formulas.

I have said that the use of themes admits to a creative reading. A chronological arrangement would have been a more obvious system. I rejected that method because it might have implied that there was some discreet tradition in women's erotic writing. There is indeed a well established tradition for erotic writing which influences what women think of as erotic and what women write about. That is, erotic writing by (and for?) men. Obviously this tradition cannot be ignored. 'Feminine writing' is not determined by the sex of the author. This is why Anaïs Nin worried that she may have betrayed her sex by using a male-oriented tradition of the erotic. As readers, what we can try to do is to distinguish the character of that which is conventionally and 'malely' erotic from that which may be more tellingly connected to the feminine.

But there is also a recognisable 'women's line' in erotic writing. Those wanting to find it have known where to look and it is visible in this collection. The good-time grandmothers are Sappho or Aphra Behn, George Sand or Colette. Naughty then and naughty now.

The gleaning for these voices need not be wearisome. Nor need the harvest be meagre. I hope that this anthology makes some beginning.

The selection is subjective. With a subject of this character it can hardly be otherwise. Some extracts will appear erotic to one reader, pornographic to another – and altogether unsexy to a third.

But here they are. By women, for women, for you to use as you will.

INVITATIONS

Invitations take many forms, but they are always of one kind. They are ideas rather than actions. Imagined, anticipated, framed, for the suspended moment invitations postpone the fulfilment which they propose.

Invitations are rich with words, signs, metaphors. But because the end they envisage is always in another time, always in another place, they are paradoxically impoverished. Faced with that teasing balance, the invitations in this section often draw attention to their character as a language. That language may be made up of mouth-watering images as in Elizabeth David's Preface; it may be made of a surprising code, as in Margaret Atwood's game of Scrabble; or it may be made up of signals, discreet disclosures, detours and half promises inscribed across Jeanette Winterson's map of Venice. At the same time, the invitation envisages another language – the silent language of mouths, of flesh against flesh, of hands, lips and eyes.

Writing about food, like writing about love, involves the extremes of deprivation and excess. Elizabeth David's Preface to the 1955 Penguin edition of *A Book of Mediterranean Food* reveals this contradiction. It reiterates a litany of good things against the counterpoint of rationing. Her vocabulary ('deadly boredom' and 'frustration' as against 'ingenuity' and 'stimulation') emphasises the physical nature of the experience she renders. Her preface ends with an invitation as her recipes promise 'the warm, rich, stimulating smells of genuine food'.

Extremes appear in other extracts. Brews, Anne Boleyn and the speakers in Sappho's poem, in 'O Would I Were', in Kath Fraser's 'Song (October 1969)' and in Marilyn Hacker's sonnets, all play upon the absence which is presently felt as against the abundance which will be theirs in the future. Margery Brews, Hacker and Fraser imagine an uncomplicated pleasure in the granting of their desire (Brews will be 'the

1

meryest mayden on grounde'). Anne Boleyn, however, employs a complicated rhetoric which invites through competitive challenge: 'if you recompense so slight a conversation by gifts so great, what will you be able to do for those who are ready to consecrate their entire obedience to your desires?'

Competition, gambling and commerce often figure in invitations to play the game that takes two. This happens quite literally in those historical periods where sexual exchange is governed by market forces. In different circumstances, Margery Brews, Anne Boleyn and Harriette Wilson offer wares in anticipation of recompense. In other texts, these forms of exchange are used metaphorically; in Dickinson's poem where the beggar's request receives an overwhelming response, or in Atwood's sensuous re-working of that most innocent of games, Scrabble.

Who invites? Who is invited? Some of these invitations are addressed directly to the beloved who holds the power to fulfil or deny. Others are more oblique. Aphra Behn plays with conventions of female passivity to seduce her lover into action; Jane Austen's Mary Crawford and Edmund Bertram exchange a mutual flirtation, but the real invitation to feeling is extended to the onlooker in the person of Fanny Price; Emily Brontë's speaker is besieged by an invitation she would rather reject, but which she cannot resist; and Harriette Wilson, most discreet in her indiscretion, seduces her reader with tales of seduction which at once reveal and conceal. By hinting, but not saying, she enacts a textual striptease. As she removes the layers of cocoa trees and nightcaps which leave all – and nothing – to the imagination, she still invites the reader on, drawing her further and further in hope of the promised exposure.

Sappho
I Beg, You, Gongyla
(c. mid C7th BC)

[...come here tonight,] I beg, you, Gongyla,[1]
take up your lyre [and sing to us;]
for once again an aura of desire
hovers around

your beauty, your dress thrills all those who see you
and the heart in my breast quickens;
once I too poured scorn on Aphrodite,
goddess of love,

but now I pray [that you will soon be here...]
I wish [we were never apart...][2]

Anonymous
O Would I Were the
Salt Sea-wind (BC)

O would I were the salt sea-wind
And you upon the beach

---

[1] *Gongyla*: generally described as 'one of Sappho's companions'. There is still some
scholarly dispute over the nature of Sappho's sexuality, ranging from the judgement of
George Devereux who declares her a 'masculine lesbian' (see 'The Nature of Sappho's
Seizure in fr. 31LP as Evidence of Her Inversion', *Classical Quarterly* n.s. 20 [1970], pp.
17–31), to Judith Hallett who argues that her relations with women were confined to a
social context where women were segregated for most activities (see 'Sappho and her
Social Context: Sense and Sensuality', *Signs* 4 [1979], pp. 447–64). See *Sappho: Poems
and Fragments* translated by Josephine Balmer.
[2] Translation by Josephine Balmer, *Sappho: Poems and Fragments* (London, 1984),
fragment 22. For the Greek, see *Poetarum Lesbiorum Fragmenta*, ed. Edgar Lobel and
Denys Page (Oxford, 1955), fr. 22. The text of this poem is corrupt.

Would bare your breast and let me blow
Until your heart I reach.[3]

Margery Brews

Unto my ryght welebelovyd Voluntyn, John Paston, Squyer, be this bill delyvered, &c. (1477)

From Selections from the Paston Letters *as transcribed by Sir John Fenn (arranged and edited by Alice Drayton Greenwood [London, 1920]). Margery Brews was the daughter of Sir Thomas Brews, and John the son of Sir John Paston (d. 1503) and Margaret Mauteby. Arrangements for a marriage settlement between the families were long drawn out. In June 1477, John's mother succeeded in finalising matters with Elizabeth, Margery's mother, and the couple were married later that year.*

Right reverent and wurschypfull, and my ryght welebeloved Voluntyne, I recomande me unto yowe, ffull hertely desyring to here of yowr welefare, whech I beseche Almyghty God long for to preserve un to Hys plesur, and yowr herts desyre.[4] And yf it please yowe to here of my welefar, I am not in good heele[5] of body, nor of herte, nor schall be tyll I her ffrom yowe;

For there wottys[6] no creature what peyn that I endure,
And for to be deede, I dare it not dyscure[7]

---

[3] From the Greek. Translation by F. A. Wright, see *The Oxford Book of Greek Verse in Translation*, ed. T. F. Higham and C. M. Bowra (Oxford, 1938), fr. 670.
[4] This letter in February 1447 was sent with the approval of Margery's mother. It accompanies an encouraging note from Elizabeth Brews addressed to John Paston and describing Margery's enthusiasm for the match: 'ye have made her such [an] Advocate for you, that I may never have rest night nor day, for calling and crying upon me to bring the said matter to effect, &c.'.
[5] Health.
[6] Knows.
[7] Discover.

And my lady my moder hath labored the mater to my ffadur full delygently, but sche can no mor gete then ye knowe of, for the whech God knowyth I am full sory. But yf that ye loffe me, as I tryste verely that ye do, ye will not leffe me therefor; for if that ye hade not halfe the lyvelode that ye hafe, for to do the grettest labur that any woman on lyve myght, I wold not forsake yowe.

And yf ye commande me to kepe me true wherever I go,
I wyse I will do all my myght yowe to love and never no mo,
And yf my freends say, that I do amys,
Thei schal not me let so for to do,
Myne herte me bydds ever more to love yowe
Truly over all erthely thing,
And yf thei be never so wroth,
I tryst it schall be better in tyme commyng.

No more to yowe at this tyme, but the Holy Trinite hafe yowe in kepyng. And I besech yowe that this bill be not seyn of none erthely creatur safe only your selffe, &c.
And thys letter was indyte[8] at Topcroft,[9] with full hevy herte, &c.
By your own, MARGERY BREWS.

To my ryght welebelovyd cosyn, John Paston, Squyer, be this letter delyveryd &c. (n.d., 1477)

Ryght wurschypfull and welebelovyed Volentyne, in my moste umble wyse, I recommande me un to yowe, &c. And hertely I thanke yowe for the lettur whech that ye sende me be John Bekarton, wherby I undyrstonde and knowe, that ye be purposyd to come to Topcroft in schorte tyme, and withowte any erand or mater, but only to hafe a conclusyon of the mater betwyx my fader and yowe; I wolde be most glad of any creatur on lyve, so that the mater myght growe to effect. And ther as ye say, and ye come and fynde the mater no more towards you then ye dyd afortyme, ye wold no more put my fader and my lady my moder to no cost ner besenesse, for that cause, a good wyle aftur, wech causyth myne herte to be full hevy; and yf that ye come, and the mater take to none effecte, then schuld I be meche mor sory and full of hevyneese.

8 Written.
9 The home of the Brews family.

And as for my selfe, I hafe done and undyrstond in the mater that I can or may, as Good knowyth; and I let yowe plenyly undyrstond, that my fader wyll no mor money parte with all in that behalfe, but an *Cli.* and I, marke, whech is ryght far fro the acomplyschment of yowr desyre.

Wherfore, yf that ye cowde be content with that good, and my por persone, I wold be the meryest mayden on grounde; and yf ye thynke not yowr selffe so satysfyed, or that ye myght hafe mech mor good, as I hafe undyrstonde be yowe afor; good, trewe, and lovying volentyne, that ye take no such labur uppon yowe, as to come more for that mater, but let is [*it?*] passe, and never more to be spokyn of, as I may be yowr trewe lover and bedewoman[10] duryng my lyfe.

No more un to yowe at thys tyme, but Almyghty Jesus preserve yowe, bothe body and sowle, &c.

Be your Voluntyne,
MARGERY BREWS.

Anne Boleyn
Letter Addressed to Henry VIII (n.d., 1527)

*F*rom Letters of Royal and Illustrious Ladies of Great Britain, from the Commencement of the twelfth century to the close of the reign of Queen Mary, ed. Mary Anne Everett Green [Wood], 3 vols (London, 1846), II, pp. 14–16. After her return from France in 1522, Anne Boleyn attracted the attention of King Henry who installed her as maid of honour to the Queen, Katherine of Aragon. This letter, written relatively early on in the development of their relationship, suggests Boleyn's dependence upon his goodwill. Henry divorced Katherine and married Anne Boleyn in 1533.

Sire,
It belongs only to the august mind of a great king, to whom Nature has given a heart full of generosity towards the sex,[11] to repay by favours so extraordinary

---

[10]   One who is bound over to pray for another.
[11]   Women.

an artless and short conversation[12] with a girl. Inexhaustible as is the treasury of your majesty's bounties, I pray you to consider that it cannot be sufficient to your generosity; for if you recompense so slight a conversation by gifts so great, what will you be able to do for those who are ready to consecrate their entire obedience to your desires? How great soever may be the bounties I have received, the joy that I feel in being loved by a king whom I adore, and to whom I would with pleasure make a sacrifice of my heart, if fortune had rendered it worthy of being offered to him, will ever be infinitely greater.

The warrant of maid of honour to the queen induces me to think that your majesty had some regard for me, since it gives me the means of seeing you oftener, and of assuring you by my own lips (which I shall do on the first opportunity) that I am,

Yours majesty's very obliged and very obedient servant,

without any reserve,
ANNE BOLEYN.

Aphra Behn
In Imitation of Horace (1684)

*F**rom** Poems Upon Several Occasions: With a Voyage to the Island of Love (London, 1684), pp. 98–100. Behn refers to Horace's Ode I.v where the speaker chastises the beautiful Pyrrha for her heartless seduction of youths whom she later abandons. By making the speaker a woman Behn simultaneously teases with conventional ideas of woman's passive role in the sexual encounter, while allowing her text the bold reclamation of the unabashed expression of female desire. See* Kissing the Rod: An Anthology of Seventeenth Century Women's Verse, *ed. Germaine Greer, Jeslyn Medoff, Melinda Sansome and Susan Hastings (Virago, 1988), pp. 248–9.*

I
What mean those Amorous Curles of Jet?
For what heart-Ravisht Maid
Dost thou thy Hair in order set,
Thy Wanton Tresses Braid?

---

12 Exchange, or relationship.

And thy vast Store of Beauties open lay,
That the deluded Fancy leads astray.

II

For pitty hide thy Starry eyes,
    Whose Languishments destroy:
And look not on the Slave that dyes
    With an Excess of Joy.
Defend thy Coral Lips, thy Amber Breath;
To taste these Sweets lets in a Certain Death.

III

Forbear, fond Charming Youth, forbear,
    Thy words of Melting Love:
Thy Eyes thy Language well may spare,
    One Dart enough can move.
And she that hears thy voice and sees thy Eyes
With too much Pleasure, too much Softness dies.

IV

Cease, Cease, with Sighs to warm my Soul,
    Or press me with thy Hand:
Who can the kindling fire controul,
    The tender force withstand?
Thy Sighs and Touches like wing'd Lightning fly,
And are the Gods of Loves Artillery.

Jane Austen

FROM

Mansfield Park (1814)

*F*anny *Price has been brought up at Mansfield Park as an act of charity on the part of her uncle and aunt Sir Thomas and Lady Bertram. While Sir Thomas is in Antigua seeing to his plantations there, Henry Crawford and his sister Mary come to stay, much enlivening the everyday boredom of Fanny's cousins Maria and Julia. Although Maria is engaged to Mr Rushworth, she and Julia compete for Henry Crawford's attention. Meanwhile Mary Crawford is proving all too attractive to*

Edmund, the younger Bertram son and Fanny's particular friend and confidant. Matters come to a head when the young people resolve to perform a play for their own amusement.

Lady Bertram seemed quite resigned to waiting.[13] – Fanny did not share her aunt's composure; she thought of the morrow a great deal, – for if the three acts were rehearsed, Edmund and Miss Crawford would then be acting together for the first time; – the third act would bring a scene between them which interested her most particularly, and which she was longing and dreading to see how they would perform. The whole subject of it was love – a marriage of love was to be described by the gentleman, and very little short of a declaration of love be made by the lady.[14]

She had read, and read the scene again with many painful, many wondering emotions, and looked forward to their representation of it as a circumstance almost too interesting. She did not *believe* they had yet rehearsed it, even in private.

The morrow came, the plan for the evening continued, and Fanny's consideration of it did not become less agitated. She worked very diligently under her aunt's directions, but her diligence and her silence concealed a very absent, anxious mind; and about noon she made her escape with her work to the East room, that she might have no concern in another, and, as she deemed it, most unnecessary rehearsal of the first act, which Henry Crawford was just proposing, desirous at once of having her time to herself, and of avoiding the sight of Mr Rushworth. A glimpse, as she passed through the hall, of the two ladies walking up from the parsonage, made no change in her wish of retreat, and she worked and meditated in the East room, undisturbed, for a quarter of an hour, when a gentle tap at the door was followed by the entrance of Miss Crawford.

'Am I right? – Yes; this is the East room. My dear Miss Price, I beg your pardon, but I have made my way to you on purpose to entreat your help.'

Fanny, quite surprised, endeavoured to show herself mistress of the room by her civilities, and looked at the bright bars of her empty grate with concern.

'Thank you – I am quite warm, very warm. Allow me to stay here a little while, and do have the goodness to hear me my third act. I have brought my book, and if you would but rehearse it with me, I should be *so* obliged! I came

[13] For the performance of the play, Kotzebue's *Lovers' Vows* (1791). Elizabeth Inchbald's translation was published in 1798 and remained a popular favourite in the theatre.

[14] Mary Crawford plays the part of Amelia, and Edmund the part of her tutor, Anhalt. Amelia persuades her father to allow her to marry the man she loves and her self-determination in sexual matters matches Mary Crawford's own. The disposal of all the parts in the play reveals a sub-text for the personal relations among the inhabitants of Mansfield Park.

INVITATIONS

here today intending to rehearse it with Edmund – by ourselves – against the evening, but he is not in the way; and if he *were*, I do not think I could go through it with *him*, till I have hardened myself a little, for really there *is* a speech or two – You will be so good, won't you?'

Fanny was most civil in her assurances, though she could not give them in a very steady voice.

'Have you ever happened to look at the part I mean?' continued Miss Crawford, opening her book. 'Here it is. I did not think much of it at first – but, upon my word – . There, look at *that* speech, and *that*. How am I ever to look him in the face and say such things? Could you do it? But then he is your cousin, which makes all the difference. You must rehearse it with me, that I may fancy *you* him, and get on by degrees. You *have* a look of *his* sometimes.'

'Have I? – I will do my best with the greatest readiness – but I must *read* the part, for I can *say* very little of it.'

'*None* of it, I suppose. You are to have the book of course. Now for it. We must have two chairs at hand for you to bring forward to the front of the stage. There – very good schoolroom chairs, not made for a theatre, I dare say; much more fitted for little girls to sit and kick their feet against when they are learning a lesson.[15] What would your governess and your uncle say to see them used for such a purpose? Could Sir Thomas look in upon us just now, he would bless himself, for we are rehearsing all over the house. Yates[16] is storming away in the dining room. I heard him as I came up stairs, and the theatre is engaged of course by those indefatigable rehearsers, Agatha and Frederick,[17] if *they* are not perfect, I *shall* be surprised. By the bye, I looked in upon them five minutes ago, and it happened to be exactly at one of the times when they were trying *not* to embrace, and Mr Rushworth was with me. I thought he began to look a little queer, so I turned it off as well as I could, by whispering to him, "We shall have an excellent Agatha, there is something so *maternal* in her manner, so completely *maternal* in her voice and countenance." Was not that well done of me? He brightened up directly. Now for my soliloquy.'

She began, and Fanny joined in with all the modest feeling which the idea of representing Edmund was so strongly calculated to inspire; but with looks and voice so truly feminine, as to be no very good picture of a man. With such an Anhalt, however, Miss Crawford had courage enough, and they had got through half the scene, when a tap at the door brought a pause, and the entrance of Edmund the next moment, suspended it all.

Surprise, consciousness, and pleasure, appeared in each of the three on this

---

15 The East room was once the nursery.
16 Mr Yates plays Baron Wildenhaim, Amelia's father.
17 Two of the characters in *Lovers' Vows*, played by Maria Bertram and Henry Crawford. Frederick is Agatha's illegitimate son by Baron Wildenhaim.

unexpected meeting; and as Edmund was come on the very same business that had brought Miss Crawford, consciousness and pleasure were likely to be more than momentary in *them*. He too had his book, and was seeking Fanny, to ask her to rehearse with him, and help him prepare for the evening, without knowing Miss Crawford to be in the house; and great was the joy and animation of being thus thrown together – of comparing schemes – and sympathising in praise of Fanny's kind offices.

She could not equal them in their warmth. *Her* spirits sank under the glow of theirs, and she felt herself becoming too nearly nothing to both, to have any comfort in having been sought by either. They must now rehearse together. Edmund proposed, urged, entreated it – till the lady, not very unwilling at first, could refuse no longer – and Fanny was wanted only to prompt and observe them. She was invested, indeed, with the office of judge and critic, and earnestly desired to exercise it and tell them all their faults; but from doing so every feeling within her shrank, she could not, would not, dared not attempt it; had she been otherwise qualified for criticism, her conscience must have restrained her from venturing at disapprobation. She believed herself to feel too much of it in the aggregate for honesty or safety in particulars. To prompt them must be enough for her; and it was sometimes *more* than enough; for she could not always pay attention to the book. In watching them she forgot herself; and agitated by the increasing spirit of Edmund's manner, had once closed the page and turned away exactly as he wanted help. It was imputed to very reasonable weariness, and she was thanked and pitied; but she deserved their pity, more than she hoped they would ever surmise. At last the scene was over, and Fanny forced herself to add her praise to the compliments each was giving the other; and when again alone and able to recall the whole, she was inclined to believe their performance would, indeed, have such nature and feeling in it, as must ensure their credit, and make it a very suffering exhibition to herself. Whatever might be its effect, however, she must stand the brunt of it again that very day.

Harriette Wilson

FROM

Memoirs of Harriette Wilson, Written by Herself (1825)

*H*arriette Wilson decided to write her Memoirs when the Duke of Beaufort reneged on his promise of an annuity of £500 – the

price of her ending a three-year liaison with his son Lord Worcester. Blackmail, as much as literary fame and fortune, was the end she had in view, but she was not very successful in this respect; it was the imminent publication of the Memoirs *that was said to have provoked the Duke of Wellington's phlegmatic response 'publish and be damned'. The* Memoirs *were published by J. J. Stockdale and went through thirty reprintings in the first year – earning publisher and author sufficient to offset the cost of a number of awards as a result of prosecution by men named in the work.*

I shall not say why and how I became, at the age of 15, the mistress of the Earl of Craven. Whether it was love, or the severity of my father, the depravity of my own heart, or the winning arts of the noble Lord, which induced me to leave my paternal roof and place myself under his protection, does not now much signify: or if it does, I am not in the humour to gratify curiosity in this matter.

I resided on the Marine Parade, at Brighton;[18] and I remember that Lord Craven used to draw cocoa trees, and his fellows; as he called them, on the best vellum paper, for my amusement. Here stood the enemy, he would say; and here, my love, are my fellows: there the cocoa trees, etc. It was, in fact, a dead bore. All these cocoa trees and fellows, at past eleven o'clock at night, could have no peculiar interest for a child like myself, so lately in the habit of retiring early to rest. One night, I recollect, I fell asleep; and, as I often dream, I said, yawning, and half awake, Oh, Lord! oh, Lord! Craven had got me into the West Indies again. In short, I soon found that I had made but a bad speculation by going from my father to Lord Craven. I was even more afraid of the latter than I had been of the former; not that there was any particular harm in the man, beyond his cocoa trees; but we never suited nor understood each other.

I was not depraved enough to determine immediately on a new choice, and yet I often thought about it. How, indeed, could I do otherwise, when the Honourable Frederick Lamb was my constant visitor, and talked to me of nothing else? However, in justice to myself, I must declare that the idea of the possibility of deceiving Lord Craven, while I was under his roof, never once entered into my head. Frederick was then very handsome; and certainly tried, with all his soul and with all his strength, to convince me that constancy to Lord Craven was the greatest nonsense in the world. I firmly believe that Frederick Lamb sincerely loved me, and deeply regretted that he had no fortune to invite me to share with him.

Lord Melbourne, his father, was a good man. Not one of your stiff-laced moralising fathers, who preach chastity and forbearance to their children. Quite

---

[18] The fashion for sea bathing and the presence of the court at the exotic Brighton Pavilion made this resort a desirable place of residence.

the contrary; he congratulated his son on the lucky circumstance of his friend Craven having such a fine girl with him. 'No such thing,' answered Frederick Lamb; 'I am unsuccessful there. Harriette will have nothing to do with me.' – 'Nonsense!' rejoined Melbourne, in great surprise; 'I never heard anything half so ridiculous in all my life. The girl must be mad! She looks mad: I thought so the other day, when I met her galloping about, with her feathers blowing and her thick dark hair about her ears.'

'I'll speak to Harriette for you,' added His Lordship, after a long pause; and then continued repeating to himself, in an undertone, 'Not have my son, indeed! Six feet high! A fine, straight, handsome, noble young fellow! I wonder what she would have!'

In truth, I scarcely knew myself; but something I determined on: so miserably tired was I of Craven, and his cocoa trees, and his sailing boats, and his ugly cotton nightcap. Surely, I would say, all men do not wear those shocking cotton nightcaps; else all women's illusions had been destroyed on the first night of their marriage!

I wonder, thought I, what sort of a nightcap the Prince of Wales[19] wears? Then I went on to wonder whether the Prince of Wales would think me so beautiful as Frederick Lamb did? Next I reflected that Frederick Lamb was younger than the Prince; but then, again, a Prince of Wales!!!

I was undecided: my heart began to soften. I thought of my dear mother, and wished I had never left her. It was too late, however, now. My father would not suffer me to return; and as to passing my life, or any more of it, with Craven, cotton nightcap and all, it was death! He never once made me laugh, nor said nor did anything to please me.

Thus musing, I listlessly turned over my writing-book, half in the humour to address the Prince of Wales. A sheet of paper, covered with Lord Craven's cocoa trees, decided me; and I wrote the following letter, which I addressed to the Prince.

BRIGHTON.

I am told that I am very beautiful, so, perhaps, you would like to see me; and I wish that, since so many are disposed to love me, one, for in the humility of my heart I should be quite satisfied with one, would be at the pains to make me love him. In the mean time, this is all very dull work, Sir, and worse even than being at home with my father: so, if you pity me, and believe you could make me in love with you, write to me, and direct to the post-office here.

By return of post, I received an answer nearly to this effect: I believe, from Colonel Thomas.[20]

---

[19] The Prince Regent, later George IV.
[20] An equerry to the Prince.

Miss Wilson's letter has been received by the noble individual to whom it was addressed. If Miss Wilson will come to town, she may have an interview, by directing her letter as before.

I answered this note directly, addressing my letter to the Prince of Wales.

SIR,
To travel fifty-two miles, this bad weather, merely to see a man, with only the given number of legs, arms, fingers, etc., would, you must admit, be madness, in a girl like myself, surrounded by humble admirers, who are ever ready to travel any distance for the honour of kissing the tip of her little finger; but if you can prove to me that you are one bit better than any man who may be ready to attend my bidding, I'll e'en start for London directly. So, if you can do anything better, in the way of pleasing a lady, than ordinary men, write directly: if not, adieu, Monsieur le Prince.

I won't say Yours,
By day or night, or any kind of light;
Because you are too impudent.

Emily Brontë
Ah! Why, Because the Dazzling Sun (1844)

Ah! why, because the dazzling sun
Restored my earth to joy
Have you departed, every one,
And left a desert sky?

All through the night, your glorious eyes
Were gazing down in mine
And with a full heart's thankful sighs
I blessed that watch divine!

I was at peace – and drank your beams
As they were life to me
And revelled in my changeful dreams
Like petrel on the sea.

Thought followed thought – star followed star
Through boundless regions on,

While one sweet influence, near and far,
Thrilled through and proved us one.

Why did the morning rise to break
So great, so pure a spell,
And scorch with fire the tranquil cheek
Where your cool radiance fell?

Blood red he rose, and arrow-straight
His fierce beams struck my brow
The soul of Nature sprang elate,
But mine sank sad and low!

My lids closed down – yet through their veil
I saw him blazing still;
And bathe in gold the misty dale
And Flash upon the hill.

I turned me to the pillow then
To call back Night, and see
Your worlds of solemn light, again
Throb with my heart and me!

It would not do – the pillow glowed
And glowed both roof and floor
And birds sang loudly in the wood,
And fresh winds shook the door.

The curtains waved, the wakened flies
Were murmuring round my room
Imprisoned there, till I should rise
And give them leave to roam –

O Stars and Dreams and Gentle Night.
O Night and Stars return!
And hide me from the hostile light
That does not warm, but burn –

That drains, the blood of suffering men
Drinks tears, instead of dew –
Let me sleep through his blinding reign
And only wake with you![21]

---

[21] This poem appears in a manuscript in Emily Brontë's hand entitled 'E. J. B. Transcribed February 1844'. It was one of the few poems which Brontë herself prepared for publication in *Poems*, by Currer, Ellis and Acton Bell (Aylott & Jones, 1846). In that edition and in some later editions this poem is named 'Stars'.

Emily Dickinson
As if I Asked a Common Alms (c. 1858)

As if I asked a common Alms,
And in my wondering hand
A Stranger pressed a Kingdom,
And I, bewildered, stand –
As if I asked the Orient
Had it for me a Morn –
And it should lift its purple Dikes,
And shatter me with Dawn![22]

Elizabeth David
A Book of Mediterranean Food (1955)
Preface to the Penguin edition

This book first appeared in 1950,[23] when almost every essential ingredient of good cooking was either rationed or unobtainable.[24] To produce the simplest meal consisting of even two or three genuine dishes required the utmost ingenuity and devotion. But even if people could not very often

---

[22] Written c. 1858 and preserved in manuscript by Dickinson until her death in 1886, this poem was first published in 1891 in *Poems, Second Series*, edited by Mabel Loomis Todd and Thomas Wentworth Higginson (Roberts Brothers, Boston, 1891). This text is taken from *The Complete Poems of Emily Dickinson*, ed. Thomas H. Johnson (London, 1970) where the punctuation and line arrangement of the manuscript is reproduced.

[23] *A Book of Mediterranean Food* was first published by John Lehmann Ltd in 1950.

[24] After the war, rationing remained in force in Britain until 1952.

make the dishes here described, it was stimulating to think about them; to escape from the deadly boredom of queuing and the frustration of buying the weekly rations; to read about real food cooked with wine and olive oil, eggs and butter and cream, and dishes richly flavoured with onions, garlic, herbs, and brightly coloured Southern vegetables...

So startlingly different is the food situation now as compared with only two years ago that I think there is scarcely a single ingredient, however exotic, mentioned in this book which cannot be obtained somewhere in this country, even if it is only in one or two shops. Those who make an occasional marketing expedition to Soho or to the region of Tottenham Court Road can buy Greek cheese and Calamata olives, Tahina paste from the Middle East, little birds preserved in oil from Cyprus, stuffed vine leaves from Turkey, Spanish sausages, Egyptian brown beans, chick peas, Armenian ham, Spanish, Italian, and Cypriot olive oil, Italian salame and rice, even occasionally Neopolitan Mozzarella cheese, and honey from Mount Hymettus. These are the details which complete the flavour of a Mediterranean meal, but the ingredients which make this cookery so essentially different from our own are available to all; they are the olive oil, wine, lemons, garlic, onions, tomatoes, and the aromatic herbs and spices which go to make up what is so often lacking in English cooking: variety of flavour and colour, and the warm, rich, stimulating smells of genuine food.

Kath Fraser

Song (October, 1969)

I love you, Mrs. Acorn. Would your husband mind
if I kissed you under the autumn sun,
if my brown-leaf guilty passion made you blind
to his manly charms and fun?

I want you, Mrs. Acorn. Do you think you'll come
to see my tangled, windswept desires,
and visit me in my everchanging house of some
vision of winter's fires?

I am serious Mrs. Acorn, do you hear?
Forget your family and other ties,

17

Come with me to where there is no fear,
where we'll find summer butterflies.
I am serious Mrs. Acorn, are you deaf?[25]

Margaret Atwood

FROM

The Handmaid's Tale (1986)

O*ffred is a 'handmaid' in the house of the Commander in the future state of Gilead. Her function is to produce babies in a world where fertility is an increasingly precious commodity and where women are both enshrined and exploited, their assigned roles – as Wives, Handmaids or Marthas – depending upon their social status and reproductive potential. She has been unexpectedly and surprisingly summoned by the Commander.*

The clock in the hall downstairs strikes nine. I press my hands against the sides of my thighs, breath in, set out along the hall and softly down the stairs. Serena Joy[26] may still be at the house where the Birth took place; that's lucky, he couldn't have forseen it. On these days the Wives hang around for hours, helping to open the presents, gossiping, getting drunk. Something has to be done to dispel their envy. I follow the downstairs corridor back, past the door that leads into the kitchen, along to the next door, his. I stand outside it, feeling like a child who's been summoned, at school, to the principal's office. What have I done wrong?

My presence here is illegal. It's forbidden for us to be alone with the Commanders. We are for breeding purposes: we aren't concubines, geisha girls, courtesans. On the contrary: everything possible has been done to remove us from that category. There is supposed to be nothing entertaining about us, no room is to be permitted for the flowering of secret lusts; no special favours are to be wheedled, by them or us, there are to be no toeholds for love. We are two-legged wombs, that's all: sacred vessels, ambulatory chalices.

So why does he want to see me, at night, alone?

---

[25] Published in *One Foot on the Mountain: An Anthology of British Feminist Poetry 1969–1979*, ed. Lilian Mohin (London, 1979).
[26] The Commander's Wife.

18

If I'm caught, it's to Serena's tender mercies I'll be delivered. He isn't supposed to meddle in such household discipline, that's women's business. After that, reclassification. I could become an Unwoman.[27]

But to refuse to see him would be worse. There's no doubt about who holds the real power.

But there must be something he wants, from me. To want is to have a weakness. It's this weakness, whatever it is, that entices me. It's like a small crack in a wall, before now impenetrable. If I press my eye to it, this weakness of his, I may be able to see my way clear.

I want to know what he wants.

I raise my hand, knock, on the door of this forbidden room where I have never been, where women do not go. Not even Serena Joy comes here, and the cleaning is done by Guardians.[28] What secrets, what male totems are kept here?

I'm told to enter. I open the door, step in.

What is on the other side is normal life. I should say: what is on the other side looks like normal life. There is a desk, of course, with a Computalk on it, and a black leather chair behind it. There's a potted plant on the desk, a pen-holder set, papers. There's an oriental rug on the floor, and a fireplace without a fire in it. There's a small sofa, covered in brown plush, a television set, an end table, a couple of chairs.

But all around the walls there are bookcases. They're filled with books. Books and books and books, right out in plain view, no locks, no boxes. No wonder we can't come in here. It's an oasis of the forbidden. I try not to stare.

The Commander is standing in front of the fireless fireplace, back to it, one elbow on the carved wooden overmantel, other hand in his pocket. It's such a studied pose, something of the country squire, some old come-on from a glossy men's mag. He probably decided ahead of time that he'd be standing like that when I came in. When I knocked he probably rushed over to the fireplace and propped himself up. He should have a black patch, over one eye, a cravat with horseshoes on it.

It's all very well for me to think these things, quick as staccato, a jittering of the brain. An inner jeering. But it's panic. The fact is I'm terrified.

I don't say anything.

'Close the door behind you,' he says, pleasantly enough. I do it, and turn back.

'Hello,' he says.

It's the old form of greeting. I haven't heard it for a long time, for years. Under the circumstances it seems out of place, comical even, a flip backward in time, a stunt. I can think of nothing appropriate to say in return.

I think I will cry.

---

[27] A criminal category, subject to execution or exile.
[28] The security force.

He must have noticed this, because he looks at me, puzzled, gives a little frown I choose to interpret as concern, though it may merely be irritation. 'Here,' he says. 'You can sit down.' He pulls a chair out for me, sets it in front of his desk. Then he goes around behind the desk and sits down, slowly and it seems to me elaborately. What this act tells me is that he hasn't brought me here to touch me in any way, against my will. He smiles. The smile is not sinister or predatory. It's merely a smile, a formal kind of smile, friendly but a little distant, as if I'm a kitten in a window. One he's looking at but doesn't intend to buy.

I sit up straight on the chair, my hands folded on my lap. I feel as if my feet in their flat red shoes aren't quite touching the floor. But of course they are.

'You must find this strange,' he says.

I simply look at him. The understatement of the year, was a phrase my mother uses. Used.

I feel like cotton candy: sugar and air. Squeeze me and I'd turn into a small sickly damp wad of weeping pinky-red.

'I guess it is a little strange,' he says, as if I've answered.

I think I should have a hat on, tied with a bow under my chin.

'I want. . .' he says.

I try not to lean forward. Yes? Yes yes? What, then? What does he want? But I won't give it away, this eagerness of mine. It's a bargaining session, things are about to be exchanged. She who does not hesitate is lost. I'm not giving anything away: selling only.

'I would like – ' he says. 'This will sound silly.' And he does look embarrassed, *sheepish* was the word, the way men used to look once. He's old enough to remember how to look that way, and to remember also how appealing women once found it. The young ones don't know those tricks. They've never had to use them.

'I'd like you to play a game of Scrabble with me,' he says.

I hold myself absolutely rigid. I keep my face unmoving. So that's what's in the forbidden room! Scrabble! I want to laugh, shriek with laughter, fall off my chair. This was once the game of old women, old men, in the summers or in retirement villas, to be played when there was nothing good on television. Or of adolescents, once, long long ago. My mother had a set, kept at the back of the hall cupboard, with the Christmas-tree decorations in their cardboard boxes. Once she tried to interest me in it, when I was thirteen and miserable and at loose ends.

Now of course it's something different. Now it's forbidden, for us. Now it's dangerous. Now it's indecent. Now it's something he can't do with his Wife. Now it's desirable. Now he's compromised himself. It's as if he's offered me drugs.[29]

'All right,' I say, as if indifferent. I can in fact hardly speak.

---

[29] Women of the status of Handmaid are supposed to be illiterate; as the revolution has only taken place recently, Offred retains many illicit memories and skills.

He doesn't say why he wants to play Scrabble with me. I don't ask him. He merely takes a box out from one of the drawers in his desk and opens it up. There are the plasticised wooden counters I remember, the board divided into squares, the little holders for setting the letters in. He dumps the counters out on the top of his desk and begins to turn them over. After a moment I join in.

'You know how to play?' he says.

I nod.

We play two games. *Larynx*, I spell. *Valance. Quince. Zygote.* I hold the glossy counters with their smooth edges, finger the letters. The feeling is voluptuous. This is freedom, an eyeblink of it. *Limp*, I spell. *Gorge.* What a luxury. The counters are like candies, made of peppermint, cool like that. Humbugs, those were called. I would like to put them into my mouth. They would taste also of lime. The letter *C*. Crisp, slightly acid on the tongue, delicious.

I win the first game, I let him win the second: I still haven't discovered what the terms are, what I will be able to ask for, in exchange.

Finally he tells me it's time for me to go home. Those are the words he uses: *go home*. He means to my room. He asks me if I will be all right, as if the stairway is a dark street. I say yes. We open his study door, just a crack, and listen for noises in the hall.

This is like being on a date. This is like sneaking into the dorm after hours.

This is conspiracy.

'Thank you,' he says. 'For the game.' Then he says, 'I want you to kiss me.'

I think about how I could take the back of the toilet apart, the toilet in my own bathroom, on a bath night, quickly and quietly, so Cora outside on the chair would not hear me. I could get the sharp lever out and hide it in my sleeve, and smuggle it into the Commander's study, the next time, because after a request like that there's always a next time, whether you say yes or no. I think about how I could approach the Commander, to kiss him, here alone, and take off his jacket, as if to allow or invite something further, some approach to true love, and put my arms around him and slip the lever out from the sleeve and drive the sharp end into him suddenly, between his ribs. I think about the blood coming out of him, hot as soup, sexual, over my hands.

In fact I don't think about anything of the kind. I put it in only afterwards. Maybe I should have thought about that, at the time, but I didn't. As I said, this is a reconstruction.

'All right,' I say. I go to him and place my lips, closed, against his. I smell the shaving lotion, the usual kind, the hint of mothballs, familiar enough to me. But he's like someone I've only just met.

He draws away, looks down at me. There's the smile again, the sheepish one. Such candour. 'Not like that,' he says. 'As if you meant it.'

He was so sad.

That is a reconstruction, too.

Marilyn Hacker

FROM

Love, Death and the Changing of the Seasons (1987)

L ove, Death and the Changing of the Seasons *uses the traditional form of*
the sonnet-sequence to trace a year-long affair between the poet-speaker
and her younger lover, Rachel.

Didn't Sappho say her guts clutched up like this?[30]
Before a face suddenly numinous,
her eyes watered, knees melted. Did she lactate
again, milk brought down by a girl's kiss?
Its documented torrents are unloosed
by such events as recently produced
not the wish, but the need, to consume, in us,
one pint of Maalox, one of Kaopectate.[31]
My eyes and groin are permanently swollen,
I'm alternatingly brilliant and witless
– and sleepless: bed is just a swamp to roll in.
Although I'd cream my jeans touching your breast,
sweetheart, it isn't lust; it's all the rest
of what I want with you that scares me shitless.

First, I want to make you come in my hand
while I watch you and kiss you, and if you cry,
I'll drink your tears while, with my whole hand, I
hold your drenched loveliness contracting. And
after a breath, I want to make you full
again, and wet. I want to make you come

---

[30] See Sappho's poem, 'It Seems to Me that Man is Equal to the Gods', p. 51.
[31] Proprietary medicines for gastric ailments.

in my mouth like a storm. No tears now. The sum
of your parts is my whole most beautiful
chart of the constellations – your left breast
in my mouth again. You know you'll have to be
your age. As I lie beside you, cover me
like a gold cloud, hands everywhere, at last
inside me where I trust you, then your tongue
where I need you. I want you to make me come.

Future Conditional

After the supper dishes, let us start
where we left off, my knees between your knees,
half in the window seat. O let me, please,
hands in your hair, drink in your mouth. Sweetheart
your body is a text I need the art
to be constructed by. I halfway kneel
to your lap, propped by your thighs, and feel
burning my hand, your privacy, your part
armour underwear. This time I'll loose
each button from its hole; I'll find the hook,
release promised abundance to this want,
while your hands, please, here and here, exigent
and certain, open this; it is, this book,
made for your hands to read, your mouth to use.

Jeanette Winterson

FROM

The Passion (1987)

*I*n 1804 Venice is ruled by France having fallen to Napoleon
Bonaparte. Villanelle is a Venetian girl, born, because of a mistake
made by her mother in the superstitious rituals which should precede
childbirth, with the webbed feet peculiar to the boatmen of the city. She

earns her living as a croupier, her pocket money as she can, and cross-dresses for her own amusement.

Nowadays, the night is designed for the pleasure-seekers and tonight, by their reckoning, is a *tour de force*. There are fire-eaters frothing at the mouth with yellow tongues. There is a dancing bear. There is a troupe of little girls, their sweet bodies hairless and pink, carrying sugared almonds in copper dishes. There are women of every kind and not all of them are women. In the centre of the square, the workers on Murano[32] have fashioned a huge glass slipper that is constantly filled and re-filled with champagne. To drink from it you must lap like a dog and how these visitors love it. One has already drowned, but what is one death in the midst of so much life?

From the wooden frame above where the gunpowder waits there are also suspended a number of nets and trapezes. From here acrobats swing over the square, casting grotesque shadows on the dancers below. Now and again, one will dangle by the knees and snatch a kiss from whoever is standing below. I like such kisses. They fill the mouth and leave the body free. To kiss well one must kiss solely. No groping hands or stammering hearts. The lips and the lips alone are the pleasure. Passion is sweeter split strand by strand. Divided and re-divided like mercury then gathered up only at the last moment.

You see, I am no stranger to love.

It's getting late, who comes here with a mask over her face? Will she try the cards?

She does. She holds a coin in her palm so that I have to pick it out. Her skin is warm. I spread the cards. She chooses. The ten of diamonds. The three of clubs. Then the Queen of spades.

'A lucky card. The symbol of Venice. You win.'

She smiled at me and pulling away her mask revealed a pair of grey-green eyes with flecks of gold. Her cheekbones were high and rouged. Her hair, darker and redder than mine.

'Play again?'

She shook her head and had a waiter bring over a bottle of champagne. Not any champagne. Madame Clicquot.[33] The only good thing to come out of France. She held the glass in a silent toast, perhaps to her own good fortune. The Queen of spades is a serious win and one we are usually careful to avoid. Still she did not speak, but watched me through the crystal and suddenly draining her glass stroked the side of my face. Only

[32] An island in the Venetian lagoon famed for the delicacy of its glass, so fine that it was said to shatter if poison were poured into it.
[33] Veuve Clicquot, an independent woman who, at the beginning of the nineteenth century, made her contribution to the refinement of champagne production by inventing a method of removing sediment without losing sparkle. Old-fashioned in the maturity of its texture and substance, her fine champagne is still the best.

for a second she touched me and then she was gone and I was left with my heart smashing at my chest and three-quarters of a bottle of the best champagne. I was careful to conceal both.

I am pragmatic about love and have taken my pleasure with both men and women, but I have never needed a guard for my heart. My heart is a reliable organ.

At midnight the gunpowder was triggered and the sky above St Mark's[34] broke into a million coloured pieces. The fireworks lasted perhaps half an hour and during that time I was able to finger enough money to bribe a friend to take over my booth for a while. I slipped through the press towards the still bubbling glass slipper looking for her.

She had vanished. There were faces and dresses and masks and kisses to be had and a hand at every turn but she was not there. I was detained by an infantryman who held up two glass balls and asked if I would exchange them for mine. But I was in no mood for charming games and pushed past him, my eyes begging for a sign.

The roulette table. The gaming table. The fortune tellers. The fabulous three-breasted woman. The singing ape. The double-speed dominoes and the tarot.

She was not there.

She was nowhere.

My time was up and I went back to the booth of chance full of champagne and an empty heart.

'There was a woman looking for you,' said my friend. 'She left this.'

On the table was an earring. Roman by the look of it, curiously shaped, made of that distinct old yellow gold that these times do not know.

I put it in my ear and, spreading the cards in a perfect fan, took out the Queen of spades. No one else should win tonight. I would keep her card until she needed it.

Gaiety soon ages.

By three o'clock the revellers were drifting away through the arches around St Mark's or lying in piles by the cafés, opening early to provide strong coffee. The gaming was over. The Casino tellers were packing away their gaudy stripes and optimistic baize. I was off-duty and it was almost dawn. Usually, I go straight home and meet my stepfather on his way to the bakery. He slaps me about the shoulder and makes some joke about how much money I'm making. He's a curious man; a shrug of the shoulders and a wink and that's him. He's never thought it odd that his daughter cross-dresses for a living and sells second-hand purses on the side. But then, he's never thought it odd that his daughter was born with webbed feet.

34 The cathedral in the Piazza San Marco.

'There are stranger things,' he said.

And I suppose there are.

This morning, there's no going home. I'm bolt upright, my legs are restless and the only sensible thing is to borrow a boat and calm myself in the Venetian way; on the water.

The Grand Canal is already busy with vegetable boats. I am the only one who seems intent on recreation and the others eye me curiously, in between steadying a load or arguing with a friend. These are my people, they can eye me as much as they wish.

I push on, under the Rialto,[35] that strange half-bridge that can be drawn up to stop one half of this city warring with the other. They'll seal it eventually and we'll be brothers and mothers. But that will be the doom of paradox.

Bridges join but they also separate.

Out now, past the houses that lean into the water. Past the Casino itself. Past the money-lenders and the churches and the buildings of state. Out now into the lagoon with only the wind and the seagulls for company.

There is a certainty that comes with the oars, with the sense of generation after generation standing up like this and rowing like this with rhythm and ease. This city is littered with ghosts seeing to their own. No family would be complete without its ancestors.

Our ancestors. Our belongings. The future is foretold from the past and the future is only possible because of the past. Without past and future, the present is partial. All time is eternally present and so all time is ours. There is no sense in forgetting and every sense in dreaming. Thus the present is made rich. Thus the present is made whole. On the lagoon this morning, with the past at my elbow, rowing beside me, I see the future glittering on the water. I catch sight of myself in the water and see in the distortions of my face what I might become.

If I find her, how will my future be?

I will find her.

Somewhere between fear and sex passion is.

Passion is not so much an emotion as a destiny. What choice have I in the face of this wind but to put up sail and rest my oars?

Dawn breaks.

I spent the weeks that followed in a hectic stupor.

Is there such a thing? There is. It is the condition that most resembles a particular kind of mental disorder. I have seen ones like me in San Servelo.[36]

---

[35] A bridge over the Grand Canal bearing small shops, and the centre of commercial exchange for centuries.

[36] An asylum for the insane on an island in the lagoon. The fashionable world took excursions to the island to view the inhabitants.

It manifests itself as a compulsion to be forever doing something, however meaningless. The body must move but the mind is blank.

I walked the streets, rowed circles around Venice, woke up in the middle of the night with my covers in impossible knots and my muscles rigid. I took to working double shifts at the Casino, dressing as a woman in the afternoon and a young man in the evenings. I ate when food was put in front of me and slept when my body was throbbing with exhaustion.

I lost weight.

I found myself staring into space, forgetting where I was going.

I was cold.

I never go to confession; God doesn't want us to confess, he wants us to challenge him, but for a while I went into our churches because they were built from the heart. Improbable hearts that I had never understood before. Hearts so full of longing that these old stones still cry out with their ecstasy. These are warm churches, built in the sun.

I sat at the back, listening to the music or mumbling through the service. I'm never tempted by God but I like his trappings. Not tempted but I begin to understand why others are. With this feeling inside, with this wild love that threatens, what safe places might there be? Where do you store gunpowder? How do you sleep at night again? If I were a little different I might turn passion into something holy and then I would sleep again. And then my extasy would be my extasy but I would not be afraid.

My flabby friend, who has decided I'm a woman, has asked me to marry him. He has promised to keep me in luxury and all kinds of fancy goods, provided I go on dressing as a young man in the comfort of our own home. He likes that. He says he'll get my moustaches and codpieces specially made and a rare old time we'll have of it, playing games and getting drunk. I was thinking of pulling a knife on him right there in the middle of the Casino, but my Venetian pragmatism stepped in and I thought I might have a little game myself. Anything now to relieve the ache of never finding her.

I've always wondered where his money comes from. Is it inherited? Does his mother still settle his bills?

No. He earns his money. He earns his money supplying the French army with meat and horses. Meat and horses he tells me that wouldn't normally feed a cat or mount a beggar.

How does he get away with it?

There's no one else who can supply so much so fast, anywhere; as soon as his orders arrive, the supplies are on their way.

It seems that Bonaparte wins his battles quickly or not at all. That's his way. He doesn't need quality, he needs action. He needs his men on their feet for a few days' march and a few days' battle. He needs horses for a single charge. That's enough. What does it matter if the horses are lame and the men are poisoned so long as they last so long as they're needed?

I'd be marrying a meat man.

I let him buy me champagne. Only the best. I hadn't tasted Madame Clicquot since the hot night in August. The rush of it along my tongue and into my throat brought back other memories. Memories of a single touch. How could anything so passing be so pervasive?
But Christ said, 'Follow me,' and it was done.

Sunk in these dreams, I hardly felt his hand along my leg, his fingers on my belly. Then I was reminded vividly of squid and their suckers and I shook him off shouting that I'd never marry him, not for all the Veuve Clicquot in France nor a Venice full of codpieces. His face was always red so it was hard to tell what he felt about these insults. He got up from where he'd been kneeling and straightened his waistcoat. He asked me if I wanted to keep my job.
'I'll keep my job because I'm good at it and clients like you come through the door every day.'
He hit me then. Not hard but I was shocked. I'd never been hit before. I hit him back. Hard.
He started to laugh and coming towards me squashed me flat against the wall. It was like being under a pile of fish. I didn't try to move, he was twice my weight at least and I'm no heroine. I'd nothing to lose either, having lost it already in happier times.
He left a stain on my shirt and threw a coin at me by way of goodbye.
What did I expect from a meat man?
I went back to the gaming floor.

November in Venice is the beginning of the catarrh season. Catarrh is part of our heritage like St Mark's. Long ago, when the Council of Three ruled in mysterious ways, any traitor or hapless one done away with was usually announced to have died of catarrh. In his way, no one was embarrassed. It's the fog that rolls in from the lagoon and hides one end of the Piazza from another that brings on our hateful congestion. It rains too, mournfully and quietly, and the boatmen sit under sodden rags and stare helplessly into the canals. Such weather drives away the foreigners and that's the only good thing that can be said of it. Even the brilliant water-gate at the Fenice[37] turns grey.
On an afternoon when the Casino didn't want me and I didn't want myself, I went to Florian's[38] to drink and gaze at the Square. It's a fulfilling pastime.
I had been sitting perhaps an hour when I had the feeling of being watched. There was no one near me, but there was someone behind a screen a little way off. I let my mind retreat again. What did it matter? We are always watching or

---

[37] The theatre in Venice.
[38] A café in the Piazza San Marco, established in 1720 and the resort of the rich and the idle. The present interior dates from 1858.

watched. The waiter came over to me with a packet in his hand. I opened it. It was an earring. It was the pair.

And she stood before me and I realised I was dressed as I had been that night because I was waiting to work. My hand went to my lip.

'You shaved it off,' she said.

I smiled. I couldn't speak.

She invited me to dine with her the following evening and I took her address and accepted.

In the Casino that night I tried to decide what to do. She thought I was a young man. I was not. Should I go to see her as myself and joke about the mistake and leave gracefully? My heart shrivelled at this thought. To lose her again so soon. And what was myself? Was this breeches and boots self any less real than my garters? What was it about me that interested her?

You play, you win. You play, you lose. You play.

I was careful to steal enough to buy a bottle of the best champagne.

Lovers are not at their best when it matters. Mouths dry up, palms sweat, conversation flags and all the time the heart is threatening to fly from the body once and for all. Lovers have been known to have heart attacks. Lovers drink too much from nervousness and cannot perform. They eat too little and faint during their fervently wished consummation. They do not stroke the favoured cat and their face-paint comes loose. This is not all. Whatever you have set store by, your dress, your dinner, your poetry, will go wrong.

Her house was gracious, standing on a quiet waterway, fashionable but not vulgar. The drawing-room, enormous with great windows at either end and a fireplace that would have suited an idle wolfhound. It was simply furnished; an oval table and a *chaise-longue*. A few Chinese ornaments that she liked to collect when the ships came through. She had also a strange assortment of dead insects mounted in cases on the wall. I had never seen such things before and wondered about this enthusiasm.

She stood close to me as she took me through the house, pointing out certain pictures and books. Her hand guided my elbow at the stairs and when we sat down to eat she did not arrange us formally but put me beside her, the bottle in between.

We talked about the opera and the theatre and the visitors and the weather and ourselves. I told her that my real father had been a boatman and she laughed and asked could it be true that we had webbed feet?

'Of course,' I said and she laughed the more at this joke.

We had eaten. The bottle was empty. She said she had married late in life, had not expected to marry at all being stubborn and of independent means. Her husband dealt in rare books and manuscripts from the east. Ancient maps that showed the lairs of griffins and the haunts of whales. Treasure

29

maps that claimed to know the whereabouts of the Holy Grail. He was a quiet and cultured man of whom she was fond.

He was away.

We had eaten, the bottle was empty. There was nothing more that could be said without strain or repetition. I had been with her more than five hours already and it was time to leave. As we stood up and she moved to get something I stretched out my arm, that was all, and she turned back into my arms so that my hands were on her shoulder blades and hers along my spine. We stayed thus for a few moments until I had courage enough to kiss her neck very lightly. She did not pull away. I grew bolder and kissed her mouth, biting a little at the lower lip.

She kissed me.

'I can't make love to you,' she said.

Relief and despair.

'But I can kiss you.'

And so, from the first, we separated our pleasure. She lay on the rug and I lay at right angles to her so that only our lips might meet. Kissing in this way is the strangest of distractions. The greedy body that clamours for satisfaction is forced to content itself with a single sensation and, just as the blind hear more acutely and the deaf can feel the grass grow, so the mouth becomes the focus of love and all things pass through it and are re-defined. It is a sweet and precise torture.

When I left her house some time later, I did not set off straight away, but watched her moving from room to room extinguishing the lights. Upwards she went, closing the dark behind her until there was only one light left and that was her own. She said she often read into the small hours while her husband was away. Tonight she did not read. She paused briefly at the window and then the house was black.

What was she thinking?

What was she feeling?

I walked slowly through the silent squares and across the Rialto, where the mist was brooding above the water. The boats were covered and empty apart from the cats that make their homes ander the seat boards. There was no one, not even the beggars who fold themselves and their rags into any doorway.

How is it that one day life is orderly and you are content, a little cynical perhaps but on the whole just so, and then without warning you find the solid floor is a trapdoor and you are now in another place whose geography is uncertain and whose customs are strange?

Travellers at least have a choice. Those who set sail know that things will not be the same as at home. Explorers are prepared. But for us, who travel along the blood vessels, who come to the cities of the interior by chance, there is no preparation. We who were fluent find life is a foreign language. Somewhere between the swamp and the mountains. Somewhere between

fear and sex. Somewhere between God and the Devil passion is and the way there is sudden and the way back is worse.

I'm surprised at myself talking in this way. I'm young, the world is before me, there will be others. I feel my first streak of defiance since I met her. My first upsurge of self. I won't see her again. I can go home, throw aside these clothes and move on. I can move out if I like. I'm sure the meat man can be persuaded to take me to Paris for a favour or two.

Passion, I spit on it.

I spat into the canal.

Then the moon came visible between the clouds, a full moon, and I thought of my mother rowing her way in faith to the terrible island.

The surface of the canal had the look of polished jet. I took off my boots slowly, pulling the laces loose and easing them free. Enfolded between each toe were my own moons. Pale and opaque. Unused. I had often played with them but I never thought they might be real. My mother wouldn't even tell me if the rumours were real and I have no boating cousins. My brothers have gone away.

Could I walk on that water?

Could I?

I faltered at the slippery steps leading into the dark. It was November, after all. I might die if I fell in. I tried balancing my foot on the surface and it dropped beneath into the cold nothingness.

Could a woman love a woman for more than a night?

I stepped out and in the morning they say a beggar was running round the Rialto talking about a young man who'd walked across the canal like it was solid.

I'm telling you stories. Trust me.

ROMANCE

Romance tells a story. This is the simplest element of the dictionary definition which relates the form to medieval chivalry and the elaborate rituals of courtly love.

Everyone likes stories. Lovers like stories about themselves. Their stories are of three kinds: they are set in the past – 'the first time I saw you...' and 'do you remember...?'; in the future – 'and then we'll go there and do this...'; and in the present. Lovers' stories told in the past tense are for leisurely and indulgent retrospect. Lovers' stories told in the present are for more urgent purposes – told in bed, doubling pleasure, one to another, voice and mouth, telling and acting, imagined and real:

> Kiss my lips. She did.
> Kiss my lips again she did.
> Kiss my lips over and over and over again she did.

Some stories suppose a large audience and are displayed in public places. The anonymous inscription at Corinth is one; a public story of a private love at which we can only guess. Erinna's poem is also an epitaph, but the public character of that literary form conceals a very secret erotic presence. Only with the last line, 'She was always at my side', and the knowledge of the poet's continued loyalty as she composes the life of Baucis, can we make sense of the precise and felt regret which comes with the contemplation of the funereal jar holding 'the little ash that now is I'.

Stein's *Lifting Belly* tells a personal story of love, speech and acted response. In Sand's *Lélia* Pulchérie tells of desire arriving in a moment and colouring her life thereafter with its potent recognition of beauty in another. Edith Thompson revives the moments of surrender and

vulnerability in her tale of a shared past; 'I finished with pride Oh a long time ago – do you remember? when I had to come to you in your little room – after washing up.' Margaret Drabble's heroine recalls the first moments of a love affair in the romance between mother and child.

The courtly love model for erotic romance yields other patterns suggested in these texts. Edith Thompson asks her lover not to elevate her to a pedestal where she will have to 'strive to remain'. But chivalry supposes the knight and the lady, the lover who aspires to the unobtainable mistress. Charlotte Brontë's letters woo Ellen Nussey who is out of reach, not by choice, but because of economic, social and conventional constraint. Stephen Gordon woos Angela Crossby from the straight and narrow only to fail in her quest. In *All Passion Spent* Mr FitzGeorge takes up the most stereotyped of all chivalric patterns as he worships the married lady, quite out of reach in a long silence stretching over the plains and across the desert years.

Against that emptiness, the conventional garden setting for romance is the self-consciously chosen background for Stephen's seduction of Angela; it is the place of Pulchérie's approach to Lélia; and Lady Slane's recollection blends doves, monkeys and the emerald flight of the parakeets with the moment of her exposure to Mr FitzGeorge. Roses and fruits provide the imagery for Stein's love poem. Even Brontë's cottage and Adrienne Rich's 'forests just washed by sun' and 'rose red cave' are related to the garden of romance. In that place of safety, of ideal bliss, love can be savoured and contained, or even rationed, as in Drabble's extract.

In the walled garden of her memory Lady Slane tells Mr FitzGeorge that he is 'a romantic'. Time, memory and nostalgia figure in the creation of romance. Rosy with distance, loss and regret focus poignant concentration upon the fugitive moment of erotic recognition. In the two Greek love poems, that time is gone, to be recalled in a very different present. The same happens in Sand's text, in Vita Sackville-West, and in Thompson's letter to Bywaters. But Charlotte Brontë's 'nostalgia' is for a future which can never be realised. And Adrienne Rich looks into a future which she imagines loaded with loss and regret. Yet even in that future she provides for the return of the physical present through the powerful story of romance as told and re-told by the erotic memory:

> Whatever happens with us, your body
> will haunt mine...
> ...whatever happens, this is.

Erinna
Baucis (fl. 350 BC)

*A*ccording *to Greek legend, Baucis and Philemon entertained Zeus
and Hermes when they visited the earth in the guise of poor travellers.
As a reward, Zeus made their cottage a temple where they acted as priests.
At their death, Baucis was transformed into a linden tree, while her
husband became an oak, and their branches intertwined. Their names
became synonyms for faithful lovers.*

Ye Columns and my Sirens, and thou funereal jar
  Holding the little ash that now is I,
To all who pass give greeting, no matter if they are
  My countrymen or from another sky:
'My father called me Baucis', say: say 'Telos was my home.'
  And tell them I was buried here, a bride,
That all may know: and name the friend who thus inscribed my tomb,
  Erinna; she was always at my side.[1]

Anonymous
*On a Stone at Corinth
(c. C4th BC)*

So this, my good Sabinus, is the one
Record of our great love, this little stone.[2]

[1] Translated by William Marris. From the *Oxford Book of Greek Verse in Translation*,
ed. T. F. Higham and C. M. Bowra (Oxford, 1938).
[2] Translated by R. A. Furness. From the *Oxford Book of Greek Verse in Translation*,
ed. T. F. Higham and C. M. Bowra (Oxford, 1938).

George Sand

FROM

Lélia (1833)

L *élia is on a passionate quest. After many affairs she is loved by Stenio,*
ten years younger, who she sends away. In the desert she spends some
time alone in meditation. Returning to society, she attends a fabulous
costume ball where she finds her sister Pulchérie, now a fashionable
and notorious courtesan. The dialogue between the two sisters is the
centre of the novel.

'You are right, my dear sister, we were not alike. Wiser and happier than I,
you lived only for enjoyment; I, more ambitious and perhaps less obedient
to God, lived only to desire. Do you recall that sultry summer's day when we
rested on the bank of a brook under the cedars of the valley, in a mysterious,
dark retreat where the murmur of water falling from stone to stone mingled
with the sad song of the cicadas? We lay down on the grass, and as we looked
up through the trees at the burning sky above our heads we were overcome
by a deep untroubled slumber. We woke up in each other's arms unaware
that we had slept.'

At these words Pulchérie started and squeezed her sister's hand.

'Yes, I recall this better than you, Lélia. It stands as a glowing memory in
my life, and I have often thought of that day with emotion full of charm, and
maybe also of shame.'

'Of shame?' said Lélia, drawing back her hand.

'You have never known, you have never guessed this,' said Pulchérie. 'I
would never have dared to tell you of it then. But now I can confess all,
and you can learn all. Listen, dear sister, it was in your innocent arms, on
your virgin breast, that God revealed to me for the first time the power
of life. Please do not withdraw this way. Put aside your prejudices and listen to me.'

'Prejudices!' exclaimed Lélia, drawing closer again. 'If only I had prejudices! That at least would be some kind of belief. Speak, tell me all, dear
sister.'

'Well,' said Pulchérie, 'we were sleeping peacefully in the warm, moist grass.
The cedars gave off their exquisite, sweet-smelling scent and the noon wind

fanned our damp foreheads with its burning wings. Until then, carefree and merry, I had greeted each day of my life as a new blessing. At times sudden, deep-reaching sensations would stir my blood. A strange ardour would seize my imagination; the colours of nature would seem more sparkling; youth would throb more vivaciously and more cheerfully in my breast; and if I looked at myself in the mirror, I found myself flushed and more beautiful at such moments. I felt like kissing my own reflected image which inspired me with an insane love. Then I would start laughing, and I would run, stronger and lighter, over the grass and the flowers; for nothing was ever revealed to me through suffering. I would not, like you, tire myself out trying to divine things; I would find because I did not seek.

'On that day, happy and calm as I was, the hitherto impenetrable and calmly unquestioned mystery was revealed to me through a strange, delirious, extraordinary dream. Oh, dear sister! you may deny the heavenly influence! You may deny the sanctity of pleasure! But had you been granted this moment of ecstasy, you would have said that an angel from the very bosom of God had been sent to initiate you into the sacred mysteries of human life. As for me, I dreamed simply of a dark-haired man bending over me to brush my lips with his burning red mouth; and I woke up overwhelmed, palpitating and happier than I had ever imagined I could possibly be. I looked around me: the sun was glinting on the depths of the wood; the air was good and sweet and the cedars were lifting their majestic, spreading branches like immense arms and long hands stretching up towards heaven. Then I looked at you. Oh, my dear sister, how beautiful you were! I had never considered you as such before that day. In my complacent girlish conceit I preferred myself to you. I thought that my glowing cheeks, my rounded shoulders, my golden hair made me the more beautiful. But at that moment the meaning of beauty was revealed to me in another creature. I no longer loved only myself: I felt the need to find an object of admiration and love outside myself. Gently I raised myself and I gazed at you with strange curiosity and unusual pleasure. Your thick black hair was sticking to your forehead, its tight curls twisting and intertwining, clinging as if endowed with life to your neck, velvet with shade and perspiration. I ran my fingers through it: your hair seemed to tighten around them and to draw me toward you. Tight over your breast, your thin white shirt displayed skin tanned by the sun to an even darker shade than usual; and your long eyelids, heavy with sleep, stood out against your cheeks which were of a fuller colour than they are today. Oh, how beautiful you were, Lélia! But your beauty was different from mine, and that I found strangely disturbing. Your arms, thinner than mine, were covered by an almost imperceptible dark down which has long since disappeared under the treatment that luxury imposes. Your feet, so perfect in their loveliness, were dipping in the brook, and long blue veins stood out on them. Your breast rose and fell as you breathed with a regularity that seemed to betoken calm and strength; and in all your features, in your posture, in

your shape more clear-cut than mine, in the darker shade of your skin, and especially in the proud, cold expression on your sleeping face there was something so masculine and strong that I scarcely recognised you. I felt that you looked like the beautiful dark-haired child I had just been dreaming of, and trembling I kissed your arm. Then you opened your eyes and their expression filled me with an unknown shame; I turned away as if I had done something shameful. And yet, Lélia, no impure thought had even crossed my mind. How did this happen? I was totally ignorant. I was receiving from nature and from God, my creator and my master, my first lesson in love, my first sensation of desire. Your eyes were mocking and severe as they had always been. But never before had they intimidated me as they did at that instant. Do you not recall my confusion and the way I blushed?'

'I even recall a remark that I could not explain,' replied Lélia. 'You made me bend over the water and said: "Look at yourself, dear sister; do you not think that you are beautiful?" I answered that I was less so than you. "Oh, no! much more so," you continued. "You look like a man."'

'And that made you shrug your shoulders contemptuously,' Pulchérie went on.

'And I did not guess,' replied Lélia, 'that destiny had just been achieved for you, while for me no destiny would ever be accomplished.'

'Begin your story,' said Pulchérie.[3]

Charlotte Brontë
Letters to Ellen Nussey (1836–46)

C *harlotte Brontë's friendship with Ellen Nussey began at school as an adolescent attachment, but developed into the most important relationship of her life, always a source of strength and support.*

6 December, 1836

I wish I could come to Brookroyd for a single night but I don't like to ask Miss Wooler.[4] She is at Dewsbury and I am alone at this moment, eleven

---

[3] Translated by Joseph Barry. From *George Sand in Her Own Words*, ed. Joseph Barry (London, 1979).

o'clock on Tuesday night. I wish you were here. All the house is in bed but myself. I'm thinking of you, my dearest.

[n.d.] 1836

Last Saturday afternoon being in one of my sentimental humours, I sat down and wrote to you such a note as I ought to have written to none but Mary Taylor[5] who is nearly as mad as myself... I will not tell you all I think and feel about you Ellen. I will preserve unbroken that reserve which alone enables me to maintain a decent character for judgement; but for that I should long ago have been set down by all who know me as a Frenchified fool... Ellen, I wish I could live with you always. I begin to cling to you more fondly than ever I did. If we had but a cottage and a competency of our own, I do think we might live and love on till Death without being dependent on any third person for happiness.

20 February, 1837

What shall I do without you? How long are we likely to be separated? Why are we to be denied each other's society – I long to be with you. Why are we to be divided? Surely, Ellen, it must be because we are in danger of loving each other too well – of losing sight of the Creator in idolatry of the creature.[6]

26 July, 1839

Your proposal has almost driven me clean daft.[7]... The fact is, an excursion with you, anywhere, whether to Cleethorps or Canada, just by ourselves, would be to me most delightful. I should indeed like to go... Must I give it up entirely? I feel as if I could not. I never had such a chance of enjoyment before. I do want to see you and talk to you and be with you. I must...I will...I'm set upon it...I'll be obstinate and bear down all opposition.

4   Miss Wooler ran the school at Roe Head where Brontë worked as a teacher.
5   Mary Taylor was a close mutual friend. The three women met at Roe Head in 1831.
6   Compare *Jane Eyre*, Chapter 24: 'My future husband was becoming to me my whole world; and more than the world; almost my hope of heaven. He stood between me and every thought of religion, as an eclipse intervenes between man and the broad sun. I could not, in those days, see God for his creature: of whom I had made an idol.'
7   Ellen had suggested a brief holiday together. Difficulties with transportation threatened the proposal but, through Ellen's ingenuity, the two did manage to go to Bridlington in September 1839. Charlotte was later to describe that holiday as 'one of the green spots that I look back on with real pleasure'.

28 December, 1846

[I feel] ... a haunting terror lest you should imagine I forget you ... that my regard cools with absence – nothing irritates and stings me like this. It is not in my nature to forget your nature – though I daresay I should spit fire and explode sometimes if we lived together continually and you too would be angry now and then and then we should get reconciled and jog on as before.

Gertrude Stein

FROM

Lifting Belly (1917)

*S*tein's Lifting Belly *is a long poem written during the years 1915–17. It was begun on Majorca and partly documents her life there with Alice B. Toklas. It was first published in 1953 in* Bee Time Vine and Other Pieces. *This extract is from Part II.*

Lifting belly. Are you. Lifting.
Oh dear I said I was tender, fierce and tender.
Do it. What a splendid example of carelessness.
It gives me a great deal of pleasure to say yes.
Why do I always smile.
I don't know.
It pleases me.
You are easily pleased.
I am very pleased.
Thank you I am scarcely sunny.
I wish the sun would come out.
Yes.
Do you lift it.
High.
Yes sir I helped to do it.
Did you.
Yes.
Do you lift it.
We cut strangely.
What.
That's it.
Address it say to it that we will never repent.
A great many people come together.

Come together.
I don't think this has anything to do with it.
What I believe in is what I mean.
Lifting belly and roses.
We get a great many roses.
I always smile.
Yes.
And I am happy.
With what.
With what I said.
This evening.
Not pretty.
Beautiful.
Yes beautiful
Why don't you prettily bow.
Because it shows thought.
It does.
Lifting belly is so strong.
A great many things are weaknesses. You are
pleased to so. I say because I am so well pleased.
With what. With what I said.
There are a great many weaknesses.
Lifting belly.
What was it I said.
I can add that.
It's not an excuse.
I do not like bites.
How lift it.
Not so high.
What a question.
I do not understand about ducks.
Do not you.
I don't mean to close.
No of course not.
Dear me. Lifting belly.
Dear me. Lifting belly.
Oh yes.
Alright.
Sing.
Do you hear.
Yes I hear.
Lifting belly is amiss.

This is not the way.
I see.
Lifting belly is alright.
Is it a name.
Yes it's a name.
We were right.
So you weren't pleased.
I see that we are pleased.
It is a great way.
To go.
No not to go.
But to lift.
Not light.
Paint.
No not paint.
All the time we are very happy.
All loud voices are seen. By whom. By the best. . . .

II

Kiss my lips. She did.
Kiss my lips again she did.
Kiss my lips over and over and over again she
did.
I have feathers.
Gentle fishes.
Do you think about apricots. We find them very
beautiful. It is not alone their colour it is their seeds
that charm us. We find it a change.
Lifting belly is so strange.
I came to speak about it.
Selected raisins well their grapes grapes are good.
Change your name.
Question and garden.
It's raining. Don't speak about it.
My baby is a dumpling. I want to tell her some-
thing.
Wax candles. We have bought a great many wax
candles. Some are decorated. They have not been
lighted.
I do not mention roses.
Exactly.
Actually.
Question and butter.
I find the butter very good.

Lifting belly is so kind.
Lifting belly fattily.
Doesn't that astonish you.
You did want me.
Say it again.
Strawberry.
Lifting beside belly.
Lifting kindly belly.
Sing to me I say.
Some are wives not heroes.
Lifting belly merely.
Sing to me I say.
Lifting belly. A reflection.
Lifting belly adjoins more prizes.
Fit to be.
I have fit on a hat.
Have you.

Edith Thompson
Letter to Frederick Bywaters
(n.d., 1922)

*E*dith Thompson and her young lover Frederick Bywaters were executed in January 1923 after Bywaters murdered Thompson's husband Percy in October 1922. Thompson had not assisted in the murder, but she was found guilty of conspiracy partly on the evidence of her letters to Bywaters which seemed to contain reference to a plan to poison her husband. She had destroyed all of her lover's letters. When her mother asked, 'How could you write such letters?', Thompson replied, 'No one knows what kind of letters he was writing to me.'

[Envelope] – Mr F. Bywaters P.O. R.M.S. 'Morea' Marseilles France.
[On back] – I burnt this sealing it. – PEIDI.
[Stamps – Three 1.1/2d.]

Well let us accept it then – and bear the hard part as willingly as we enjoy the natural part.[8] Darlint, I didn't think you wanted to go into the other carriage – but I suggested it because I felt there would be less temptation there – not

---

8 The beginning of the letter is missing. 'Peidi' is Thompson's pet name.

only for you but for me too – do you think it is less pleasure to me, for you to kiss me & hold me, than it is for you to do so? I think its more pleasure to me than it can possibly be to you – at least it always feels so & darlingest, if you had refrained from doing these things (not perhaps last night – but at some time before you went) I am not above compelling you to – darlint I could, couldn't I, just the same as if the position was reversed – you could compel me to – because we have no will power. I felt thats how it would be darlingest lover of mine – I was strong enough in spirit, until I was tempted in the flesh & the result – a mutual tumble from the pedestal of 'Pals only' that we had erected as penance for ourselves. No darlint, it could never be now – I am sure that you see that now dont you? intentions – such as we had – were forced – unnatural – & darlingest we are essentially natural with each other – we always have been, since our first understanding. Why should we choose to be as every other person – when we're not – is every other person such a model that you & I should copy them? Lets be ourselves – always darlingest there can never be any misunderstandings then – it doesnt matter if its harder – you said it was our Fate against each other – we only have will power when we are in accord, not when we are in conflict – tell me if this is how you feel. As I said last night, with you darlint there can never be any pride to stand in the way – it melts in the flame of a great love – I finished with pride Oh a long time ago – do you remember? when I had to come to you in your little room – after washing up. I wonder if you understand how I feel about these things – I do try to explain but some words seem so useless. Please please lover of mine, dont use that word I dont like it – I feel that Im on a pedestal & that I shall always have to strive to remain there & I dont ever want to strive to do anything anything with or for you –.thats not being natural & when you use that word – thats just how I feel – not natural – not myself. Would you have me feel like this just so that you could use a term that pleases you & you only? Tell me.

Do you remember me being asked if I had found 'The Great Lover'? Darlingest lover of mine – I had & I'd found 'The Great Pal' too *the best pal a girl ever had*. One is as much to me as the other, there is no first and second they are equal.

I *am* glad you held me tightly when you went to sleep darlint, I wanted comforting badly – I cried such a lot – no I wasnt unhappy – I look a sight today.

Darlingest – what would have happened had I refused – when you asked me to kiss you? I want to know.[9]

from

PEIDI.

9   From *The Trial of Frederick Bywaters and Edith Thompson*, ed. Filson Young (London, 1923). Bywaters was a ship's writer on board the ss *Morea*.

Radclyffe Hall

FROM

The Well of Loneliness (1928)

*S tephen Gordon has recently met a young married woman, Angela
Crossby, and has invited her to see her house at Morton.*

On a beautiful evening three weeks later, Stephen took Angela over Morton.
They had had tea with Anna and Puddle,[10] and Anna had been coldly polite to
this friend of her daughter's, but Puddle's manner had been rather resentful –
she deeply mistrusted Angela Crossby. But now Stephen was free to show Angela
Morton, and this she did gravely, as though something sacred were involved in
this first introduction to her home, as though Morton itself must feel that the
coming of this small, fair-haired woman was in some way momentous. Very
gravely, then, they went over the house – even into Sir Philip's[11] old study.

From the house they made their way to the stables, and still grave, Stephen
told her friend about Raftery. Angela listened, assuming an interest she was
very far from feeling – she was timid of horses, but she liked to hear the
girl's rather gruff voice, such an earnest young voice it intrigued her. She
was thoroughly frightened when Raftery sniffed her and then blew through his
nostrils as though disapproving, and she started back with a sharp exclamation,
so that Stephen slapped him on his glossy grey shoulder: 'Stop it, Raftery,
come up!' And Raftery, disgusted, went and blew on his oats to express his
hurt feelings.

They left him and wandered away through the gardens, and quite soon poor
Raftery was almost forgotten, for the gardens smelt softly of night-scented stock,
and of other pale flowers that smell sweetest at evening, and Stephen was
thinking that Angela Crossby resembled such flowers – very fragrant and pale
she was, so Stephen said to her gently:

'You seem to belong to Morton.'

Angela smiled a slow, questioning smile: 'You think so, Stephen?'

And Stephen answered: 'I do, because Morton and I are one,' and she
scarcely understood the portent of her words; but Angela, understanding,
spoke quickly:

---

[10]   Anna is Stephen's mother; 'Puddle' is Miss Puddleton, at one time Stephen's
governess.
[11]   Stephen's father, now dead.

44

'Oh, I belong nowhere – you forget I'm the stranger.'

'I know that you're you,' said Stephen.

They walked on in silence while the light changed and deepened, growing always more golden and yet more elusive. And the birds, who loved that strange light, sang singly and then all together: 'We're happy, Stephen!'

And turning to Angela, Stephen answered the birds: 'Your being here makes me happy.'

'If that's true, then why are you so shy of my name?'

'Angela – ' mumbled Stephen.

Then Angela said: 'It's just over three weeks since we met – how quickly our friendship's happened. I suppose it was meant, I believe in Kismet. You were awfully scared that first day at The Grange; why were you so scared?'

Stephen answered slowly: 'I'm frightened now – I'm frightened of you.'

'Yet you're stronger than I am – '

'Yes, that's why I'm so frightened, you make me feel strong – do you want to do that?'

'Well – perhaps – you're so very unusual, Stephen.'

'Am I?'

'Of course, don't you know that you are? Why, you're altogether different from other people.'

Stephen trembled a little: 'Do you mind?' she faltered.

'I know that you're you,' teased Angela, smiling again, but she reached out and took Stephen's hand.

Something in the queer, vital strength of that hand stirred her deeply, so that she tightened her fingers: 'What in the Lord's name are you?' she murmured.

'I don't know. Go on holding like that to my hand – hold it tighter – I like the feel of your fingers.'

'Stephen, don't be absurd!'

'Go on holding my hand, I like the feel of your fingers.'

'Stephen, you're hurting, you're crushing my rings!'

And now they were under the trees by the lakes, their feet falling softly on the luminous carpet. Hand in hand they entered that place of deep stillness, and only their breathing disturbed the stillness for a moment, then it folded back over their breathing.

'Look,' said Stephen, and she pointed to the swan called Peter, who had come drifting past on his own white reflection. 'Look,' she said, 'this is Morton, all beauty and peace – it drifts like that swan does, on calm, deep water. And all this beauty and peace is for you, because now you're a part of Morton.'

Angela said: 'I've never known peace, it's not in me – I don't think I'd find it here, Stephen.' And as she spoke she released her hand, moving a little away from the girl.

But Stephen continued to talk on gently; her voice sounded almost like that of a dreamer: 'Lovely, oh, lovely it is, our Morton. On evenings in winter

these lakes are quite frozen, and the ice looks like slabs of gold in the sunset, when you and I come and stand here in the winter. And as we walk back we can smell the log fires long before we can see them, and we love that good smell because it means home, and our home is Morton – and we're happy, happy – we're utterly contented and at peace, we're filled with the peace of this place – '

'Stephen – don't!'

'We're both filled with the old peace of Morton, because we love each other so deeply – and because we're perfect, a perfect thing, you and I – not two separate people but one. And our love has lit a great, comforting beacon, so that we need never be afraid of the dark any more – we can warm ourselves at our love, and we can lie down together, and my arms will be round you – '

She broke off abruptly, and they stared at each other.

'Do you know what you're saying?' Angela whispered.

And Stephen answered: 'I know that I love you, and that nothing else matters in the world.'

Then, perhaps because of that glamorous evening, with its spirit of queer, unearthly adventure, with its urge to strange, unendurable sweetness, Angela moved a step nearer to Stephen, then another, until their hands were touching. And all that she was, and all that she had been and would be again, perhaps even tomorrow, was fused at that moment into one mighty impulse, one imperative need, and that need was Stephen. Stephen's need was now hers, by sheer force of its blind and uncomprehending will to appeasement.

Then Stephen took Angela into her arms, and she kissed her full on the lips, as a lover.

Vita Sackville-West

FROM

All Passion Spent (1931)

A fter the death of Lord Slane, Lady Slane, now in her eighties, decides to live alone in a small rented house in Hampstead. She forbids her children and grandchildren to visit her and takes up with an elderly friend of her son, the eccentric millionaire collector Mr FitzGeorge. One day, Lady Slane recalls a forgotten meeting with Mr

VITA SACKVILLE-WEST

FitzGeorge which took place many years ago while her husband was Viceroy of India.

' **W**hy don't you come with us to Fatihpur Sikhri?'[12]
... The broken puzzle in Lady Slane's mind shook itself suddenly down into shape. The half-heard notes reassembled themselves into their tune. She stood again on the terrace of the deserted Indian city looking across the brown landscape where puffs of rising dust marked at intervals the road to Agra. She leant her arms upon the warm parapet and slowly twirled her parasol. She twirled it because she was slightly ill at ease. She and the young man beside her were isolated from the rest of the world. The Viceroy was away from them, inspecting the mother-of-pearl mosque, accompanied by a group of officials in white uniforms and sun-helmets; he was pointing with his stick, and saying that the ring-doves ought to be cleared away from under the eaves. The young man beside Lady Slane said softly that it was a pity the ring-doves should be condemned, for if a city were abandoned by man, why should the doves not inherit it? The doves, the monkeys, and the parrots, he went on, as a flight of jade-green parakeets swept past them, quarrelling in the air; look at their green plumage against these damask walls, he added, raising his head, as the flock swirled round again like a handful of emeralds blown across the Poet's House. There was something unusual, he said, in a city of mosques, palaces, and courts, inhabited solely by birds and animals; he would like to see a tiger going up Akbar's steps, and a cobra coiling its length neatly in the council chamber. They would be more becoming, he thought, to the red city than men in boots and solar topees. Lady Slane, keeping an ear pricked to observe the movements of the Viceroy and his group, had smiled at his fancies and had said that Mr FitzGeorge was a romantic.

Mr FitzGeorge. The name came back to her now. It was not surprising that, among so many thousands of names, she should have forgotten it. But she remembered it now, as she remembered the look he had given her when she twitted him. It was more than a look; it was a moment that he created, while he held her eyes and filled them with all the implications he dared not, or would not, speak. She had felt as though she stood naked before him.

'Yes,' he said, watching her across the fire at Hampstead; 'you were right: I *was* a romantic.'

[12] A deserted city in the hills above Agra.

47

Margaret Drabble

FROM

The Millstone (1965)

Rosamund Stacey is in London studying for a postgraduate degree. She finds herself pregnant after a brief and unsatisfactory encounter. Unable to make up her mind about an abortion, she decides to have the baby. When Octavia is born Rosamund knows love for the first time and feels that the child's existence makes sense of her own life.

The midwife asked me if I would like to see the child. 'Please,' I said gratefully, and she went away and came back with my daughter wrapped up in a small grey bloodstained blanket, and with a ticket saying Stacey round her ankle. She put her in my arms and I sat there looking at her, and her great wide blue eyes looked at me with seeming recognition, and what I felt it is pointless to try to describe. Love, I suppose one might call it, and the first of my life.

I had expected so little, really. I never expect much. I had been told of the ugliness of newborn children, of their red and wrinkled faces, their waxy covering, their emaciated limbs, their hairy cheeks, their piercing cries. All I can say is that mine was beautiful and in my defence I must add that others said she was beautiful too. She was not red nor even wrinkled, but palely soft, each feature delicately reposed in its right place, and she was not bald but adorned with a thick, startling crop of black hair. One of the nurses fetched a brush and flattened it down and it covered her forehead, lying in a dense fringe that reached to her eyes. And her eyes, that seemed to see me and that looked into mine with deep gravity and charm, were a profound blue, the whites white with the gleam of alarming health. When they asked if they could have her back and put her back in her cradle for the night, I handed her over without reluctance, for the delight of holding her was too much for me. I felt as well as they that such pleasure should be regulated and rationed.

Adrienne Rich
(The Floating Poem, Unnumbered) (1978)

Whatever happens with us, your body
will haunt mine – tender, delicate
your lovemaking, like the half-curled frond
of the fiddlehead fern in forests
just washed by sun. Your traveled, generous thighs
between which my whole face has come and come –
the innocence and wisdom of the place my tongue has found there –
the live, insatiate dance of your nipples in my mouth –
your touch on me, firm, protective, searching
me out, your strong tongue and slender fingers
reaching where I had been waiting years for you
in my rose-wet cave – whatever happens, this is.[13]

---

[13] From 'Twenty-One Love Poems', published in *The Dream of a Common Language*, 1978.

DESIRE

In this section you will find many unruly women. When a woman feels, expresses and acts on the impulse of desire she becomes a whore, a slut, a tart, a harpy, a hussy, a nymphomaniac. Many of the writers who appear here have suffered such description: Sappho, Aphra Behn, Mary Wollstonecraft, Jean Rhys, Marilyn French. The women they write about – Salome, Mary Magdalene, Antoinette Rochester – are similarly accused. This is a bold and goodly company.

Here lust is urgent and frank. It knows the grasp of sexual desire, and it takes the most direct route to fulfilment. Sometimes this means seizing the opportunity of the casual meeting, as in Wanda Honn's short story and Anaïs Nin's episode. Sometimes it means concentration upon the moment without looking forward or back, as in French's *The Women's Room* and Rhys's *Wide Sargasso Sea*. Sometimes it means going out to find and ask for love, as in Carol Ann Duffy's poem and Jill Dawson's story. Sometimes it means the systematic removal of obstacles and resistance, as with Behn's importunate lover and Claudine's persistent wooing. Always it is selfish. Always it is unscrupulous. Often it is cruel.

When Nin's Louise has exhausted her lust she cries out with 'a hatred and a joy'. Desire in the raw makes this uncomfortable alliance. There is no civilisation, barely any humanity, in the coupling of Antonio and Louise. When Manley's Duke forces Charlot he brings the armoury of war to his assault. When Rochester takes Antoinette she 'dies' in his savagery. Salome's wicked desire is fuelled with hate, and Jill Dawson's tender lovemaking encompasses the sweet and the sharp. Lust is a primitive territory, untamed and barbaric.

There are no maps here. Only the shifting chart of the body. Sappho trembles and sweats as the 'delicate fire' overtakes her. 'Ephelia' reads the text of her self to find the evidence of her desire. Colette's Claudine fears that the open book of her face will betray her wanting. Mary

Wollstonecraft interprets the record of desire written on her own features, welcoming the 'live fire' of passion there. Only H.D.'s speaker, Simon the Pharisee, cannot, will not, decipher his mysterious obsession. Caught in the labyrinth of lust, his only thread is tangled in Mary's unveiled hair.

The oblique obscurity of Simon's vision contrasts with the clarity of frank speaking in these other texts. Cary's Salome is a 'custome-breaker' who begins 'to shew my Sexe the way to freedomes doore'. Wollstonecraft, and the women in Colette, Behn, Dawson, Honn, Duffy and the rest, know themselves. Admitting lust, confessing need, they break the custom of woman's silence and rend the assumption of woman's innocence. They know their desire. They also know how to get what they want.

Sappho

It Seems to Me that Man is Equal to the Gods
(c. mid C7th BC)

It seems to me that man is equal to the gods,
that is, whoever sits opposite you
and, drawing nearer, savours, as you speak,
the sweetness of your voice

and the thrill of your laugh, which have so stirred the heart
in my own breast, that whenever I catch
sight of you, even if for a moment,
then my voice deserts me

and my tongue is struck silent, a delicate fire
suddenly races underneath my skin,
my eyes see nothing, my ears whistle like
the whirling of a top

and sweat pours down me and a trembling creeps over
my whole body, I am greener than grass,

at such times, I seem to be no more than
a step away from death;

but all can be endured since even a pauper...

You've Come and You –
(c. mid C7th BC)

You've come and you –
oh, I was longing for you –
have cooled my heart
which was burning with desire[1]

Elizabeth Cary

FROM

The Tragedie of Mariam, Faire
Queene of Jewry (1613)

*Mariam is the chaste and loving wife of Herod, much despised by his
sister, Salome. Salome has two ambitions: one, to destroy the hated
Mariam; the other, to obtain a divorce from her husband Constabarus
in order to allow her to marry her lover Silleus.*

SALOME: Lives *Salome*, to get so base a stile
As foote, to the proud *Mariam Herods* spirit:
In happy time for her endured exile,
For did he live she should not misse her merit:
But he is dead: and though he were my Brother,
His death such store of Cinders cannot cast

[1] Both translations by Josephine Balmer, *Sappho: Poems and Fragments* (London,
1984), fragments 20 and 26. For the Greek, see *Poetarum Lesbiorum Fragmenta*, ed.
Edgar Lobel and Denys Page (Oxford, 1955), fragments 31 and 48.

My Coales of love to quench: for though they smother
The flames a while, yet will they out at last.

Had not my Fate bene too too contrary,
When I on *Constabarus* first did gaze,
Silleus had beene object to mine eye:
Whose lookes and personage must allyes amaze.
But now ill Fated *Salome*, thy tongue
To *Constabarus* by it selfe is tide:
And now except I doe the Ebrew wrong
I cannot be the faire *Arabian* Bride:

He loves, I love; what then can be the cause,
Keepes me for being the *Arabians* wife?
It is the principles of *Moses* lawes,
For *Constabarus* still remaines in life,
If he to me did beare as Earnest hate,
As I to him, for him there were an ease,
A separating bill might free his fate:
From such a yoke that did so much displease.
Why should such priviledge to man be given?
Or given to them, why bard from women then?
Are men then we in greater grace with Heaven?
Or cannot women hate as well as men?
Ile be the custome-breaker: and beginne
To shew my Sexe the way to freedomes doore,
And with an offring will I purge my sinne,
The lawe was made for none but who are poore.

'Ephelia'

Love's First Approach (1679)

Strephon[2] I saw, and started at the sight,
And interchangably look'd red and white;
I felt my Blood run swiftly to my heart,
And a chill Trembling seize each outward part:
My Breath grew short, my Pulse did quicker beat,
My Heart did heave, as it wou'd change its Seat:

---

[2] A common generic name for the rustic lover.

A faint cold Sweat o're all my Body spread,
A giddy Megrim[3] wheel'd about my head:
When for the reason of this change I sought,
I found my Eyes had all the mischief wrought;
For they my Soul to *Strephon* had betray'd
And my weak heart his willing Victim made:
The Traytors, conscious of the Treason
They had committed 'gainst my Reason,
Look'd down with such a bashful guilty Fear,
As made their Fault to every Eye appear.
Tho the first fatal Look too much had done,
The lawless wanderers wou'd still gaze on,
Kind Looks repeat, and Glances steal, till they
Had look'd my Liberty and Heart away:
Great Love, I yield; send no more Darts in vain,
I am already fond of my soft Chain;
Proud of my Fetters, so pleas'd with my state,
That I the very Thoughts of Freedom hate.
O Mighty Love! thy Art and Power joyn,
To make his Frozen breast as warm as mine;
But if thou try'st, and can'st not make him kind,
In Love such pleasant, real Sweets I find;
That though attended with Despair it be,
'Tis better still than a wild Liberty.[4]

Aphra Behn
The Willing Mistriss (1684)

Amyntas[5] led me to a Grove,
    Where all the Trees did shade us;
The Sun it self, though it had Strove,
    It could not have betray'd us:
The place secur'd from humane Eyes,
    No other fear allows,

[3] Headache.
[4] Published in *Female Poems on Several Occasions. Written by Ephelia* (London, 1679).
[5] A conventional soubriquet for the lover.

But when the Winds that gently rise,
Doe Kiss the yeilding Boughs.

Down there we satt upon the Moss,
And did begin to play
A Thousand Amorous Tricks, to pass
The heat of all the day.
A many Kisses he did give:
And I return'd the same
Which made me willing to receive
That which I dare not name.

His Charming Eyes no Aid requir'd
To tell their softning Tale;
On her that was already fir'd
'Twas Easy to prevaile.
He did but Kiss and Clasp me round,
Whilst those his thoughts Exprest:
And lay'd me gently on the Ground;
Ah who can guess the rest?[6]

Mary Delarivier Manley

FROM

The New Atalantis (1709)

*Charlot is the Duke's ward and his son's intended wife. The Duke,
however, succumbing to his passion, decides to seduce Charlot.*

The Duke had observed that Charlot had been, but with disgust, denied the
gay part of reading. It is natural for young people to choose the diverting
before the instructive. He sent for her into the gallery, where was a noble library
in all languages, a collection of the most valuable authors, with a mixture of the
most amorous. He told her that now her understanding was increased, with

---

[6] From *Poems on Several Occasions, with a Voyage to the Island of Love* (London,
1684).

her stature, he resolved to make her mistress of her own conduct; and as the first thing that he intended to oblige her in, that *Governante* who had hitherto had the care of her actions should be dismissed; because he had observed the severity of her temper had sometimes been displeasing to her. That she should henceforward have none above her that she should need to stand in awe of; and to confirm to her that good opinion that he seemed to have, he presented to her the key of that gallery, to improve her mind and seek her diversion among those authors he had formerly forbid her the use of.

Charlot made him a very low curtsey and, with a blushing grace, returned him thanks for the two favours he bestowed upon her. She assured him that no action of hers should make him repent the distinction; that her whole endeavour should be to walk in that path he had made familiar to her; and that virtue should ever be her only guide. Though this was not what the Duke wanted, it was nothing but what he expected. He observed formerly that she was a great lover of poetry, especially when it was forbid her. He took down an Ovid, and opening it just at the love of Myrra[7] for her father, conscious red overspread his face. He gave it her to read, she obeyed him with a visible delight. Nothing is more pleasing to young girls than in being first considered as women. Charlot saw the Duke entertained her with an air of consideration more than usual, passionate and respectful. This taught her to refuge in the native pride and cunning of her sex; she assumed an air more haughty, the leavings of a girl just beginning to believe herself capable of attaining that empire over mankind which they are all born and taught by instinct to expect.

She took the book and placed herself by the Duke. His eyes feasted themselves upon her face, thence wandered over her snowy bosom, and saw the young swelling breasts just beginning to distinguish themselves, and which were gently heaved at the impression of Myrra's sufferings made upon her heart. By this dangerous reading he pretended to show her that there were pleasures her sex were born for, and which she might consequently long to taste! Curiosity is an early and dangerous enemy to virtue. The young Charlot, who had by a noble inclination of gratitude a strong propension of affection for the Duke, whom she called and esteemed her papa, being a girl of wonderful reflection, and consequently application, wrought her imagination up to such a lively height at the father's anger after the possession of his ddaughter, which she judged highly unkind and unnatural, that she dropped her book, tears filled her eyes, sobs rose to oppress her, and she pulled out her handkerchief to cover the disorder.

The Duke, who was master of all mankind, could trace them in all the meanders of dissimulation and cunning, was not at a loss how to interpret the agitation of a girl who knew no hypocrisy; all was artless, the beautiful

---

[7] The mother of Adonis, Myrra conceived an unnatural passion for her own father.

product of innocence and nature. He drew her gently to him, drank her tears with his kisses, sucked her sighs, and gave her by that dangerous commerce (her soul before prepared to softness) new and unfelt desires. Her virtue was becalmed, or rather unapprehensive of him for an invader. He pressed her lips with his, the nimble beatings of his heart, apparently seen and felt through his open breast! the glowings! the trembling of his limbs! the glorious sparkles from his guilty eyes! his shortness of breath, and eminent disorder were all things new to her that had never seen, heard or read before of those powerful operations struck from the fire of the two meeting sex. Nor had she leisure to examine his disorders, possessed by greater of her own! Greater! because that modesty opposing nature forced a struggle of dissimulation. But the Duke's pursuing kisses overcame the very thoughts of anything; but that new and lazy poison stealing to her heart, and spreading swiftly and imperceptibly through all her veins, she closed her eyes with languishing delight! Delivered up the possession of her lips and breath to the amorous invader; returned his eager grasps and, in a word, gave her whole person into his arms in meltings full of delight!

The Duke, by that lovely ecstasy carried beyond himself, sunk over the expiring fair in raptures too powerful for description! calling her his admirable Charlot! his charming Angel! his adorable Goddess! But all was so far modest that he attempted not beyond her lips and breast, but cried that she should never be another's. The empire of his soul was hers; enchanted by inexplicable, irresistible magic! she had power beyond the gods themselves! Charlot, returned from that amiable disorder, was anew charmed at the Duke's words. Words that set her so far above what was mortal, the woman assumed in her, and she would have no notice taken of the transports she had shown. He saw and favoured her modesty, secure of that fatal sting he had fixed within her breast, that taste of delight, which powerful love and nature would call upon her to repeat. He owned he loved her; that he never could love any other; that 'twas impossible for him to live a day, an hour, without seeing her; that in her absence he had felt more than ever had been felt by mortal. He begged her to have pity on him, to return his love, or else he should be the most lost, undone thing alive. Charlot, amazed and charmed, felt all those dangerous perturbations of nature that arise from an amorous constitution. With pride and pleasure she saw herself necessary to the happiness of one that she had hitherto esteemed so much above her, ignorant of the power of love, that leveller of mankind; that blender of distinction and hearts. Her soft answer was that she was indeed reciprocally charmed, she knew not how; all he had said and done was wonderful and pleasing to her; and if he would still more please her (if there was a more) it should be never to be parted from her. The Duke had one of those violent passions where, to heighten it, resistance was not at all necessary; it had already reached the ultimate, it could not be more ardent; yet was he loth to rush upon the possession of the fair, lest the too early pretension might disgust her. He would steal himself into

her soul, he would make himself necessary to her quiet, as she was to his. . . .

After this tender, dangerous commerce, Charlot found everything insipid, nothing but the Duke's kisses could relish with her; all those conversations she had formerly delighted in were insupportable. He was obliged to return to court, and had recommended to her reading the most dangerous books of love, Ovid, Petrarch, Tibullus, those moving tragedies that so powerfully expose the force of love and corrupt the mind. He went even farther, and left her such as explained the nature, manner and raptures of enjoyment. Thus he infused poison into the ears of the lovely virgin. She easily (from those emotions she had found in herself) believed as highly of those delights as was imaginable; her waking thoughts, her golden slumber ran all of a bliss only imagined but never proved. She even forgot, as one that wakes from sleep and visions of the night, all those precepts of airy virtue which she found had nothing to do with nature. She longed again to renew those dangerous delights. The Duke was an age absent from her, she could only in imagination possess what she believed so pleasing. Her memory was prodigious, she was indefatigable in reading. The Duke had left orders she should not be controlled in anything. Whole nights were wasted by her in the gallery; she had too well informed herself of the speculative joys of love. There are books dangerous to the community of mankind; abominable for virgins and destructive to youth; such as explain the mysteries of nature, the congregated pleasures of Venus,[8] the full delights of mutual lovers, and which rather ought to pass the fire 8than the press. The Duke had laid in her way such as made no mention of Virtue or Hymen,[9] but only advanced native, generous and undissembled love. She was become so great a proficient that nothing of the theory was a stranger to her. . . . The season of the year was come that he must make the campaign with the King; he could not resolve to depart unblessed; Charlot still refused him that last proof of her love. He took a tender and passionate farewell. Charlot, drowned in tears, told him it was impossible she should support his absence; all the court would ridicule her melancholy. This was what he wanted; he bid her take care of that. A maid was but an ill figure that brought herself to be sport of laughters; but since her sorrow (so pleasing and glorious to him) was like to be visible, he advised her to pass some days at his villa, till the height of melancholy should be over, under the pretence of indisposition. He would take care that the Queen should be satisfied of the necessity of her absence; he advised her even to depart that hour. Since the King was already on his journey he must be gone that moment and endeavour to overtake him. He assured her he would write by every courier, and begged her not to admit of another lover, though he was sensible there were many (taking advantage of his absence, would endeavour to please her.) To all this she answered so as to disquiet his distrust and fears; her tears drowned her sighs, her words

8 The goddess of love.
9 The goddess of marriage.

were lost in sobs and groans! The Duke did not show less concern, but led her all trembling to put her in a coach that was to convey her to his villa; where he had often wished to have her, but she distrusted herself and would not go with him; nor had she ventured now, but that she thought he was to follow the King, who could not be without him.

Charlot no sooner arrived, but the weather being very hot, she ordered a bath to be prepared for her. Soon as she was refreshed with that, she threw herself down upon a bed with only one thin petticoat and a loose nightgown, the bosom of her gown and shift open; her nightclothes tied carelessly with a cherry-coloured ribbon which answered well to the yellow and silver stuff of her gown. She lay uncovered in a melancholy careless posture, her head resting upon one of her hands. The other held a handkerchief, that she employed to dry those tears that sometimes fell from her eyes; when raising herself a little at a gentle noise she heard from the opening of a door that answered to the bedside, she was quite astonished to see enter the amorous Duke. Her first emotions were all joy; but in a minute she recollected herself, thinking he was not come there for nothing. She was going to rise but he prevented her by flying to her arms where, as we may call it, he nailed her down to the bed with kisses. His love and resolution gave him a double vigour, he would not stay a moment to capitulate with her; whilst yet her surprise made her doubtful of his designs, he took advantage of her constitution to accomplish them; neither her prayers, tears, nor strugglings could prevent him, but in her arms he made himself a full amends for all those pains he had suffered for her.

Thus was Charlot undone! thus ruined by him that ought to have been her protector! It was very long before he could appease her; but so artful, so amorous, so submissive was his address, so violent his assurances, he told her that he must have died without the happiness. Charlot espoused his crime by sealing his forgiveness. He passed the whole night in her arms, pleased, transported and out of himself, whilst the ravished maid was not at all behindhand in ecstasies and guilty transports. He stayed a whole week with Charlot in a surfeit of love and joy! that week more inestimable than all the pleasures of his life before! whilst the court believed him with the King, posting to the army. He neglected Mars[10] to devote himself wholly to Venus; abstracted from all business, that happy week sublimed him almost to an immortal. Charlot was formed to give and take all those raptures necessary to accomplish the lover's happiness; none were ever more amorous! none were ever more happy!

[10] The god of war.

Mary Wollstonecraft
Letter to William Godwin (1796)

Mary Wollstonecraft and William Godwin became lovers late in 1796. When Mary found that she was pregnant with her second child, they married in March 1797. Mary Wollstonecraft died in September 1797 after giving birth to a daughter, Mary Shelley, in August.

If the felicity of last night has had the same effect on your health as on my countenance, you have no cause to lament your failure of resolution: for I have seldom seen so much live fire running about my features as this morning when recollections – very dear, called forth the blush of pleasure, as I adjusted my hair.

Colette
FROM
Claudine Married (1902)

Claudine, happily married to Renaud, has fallen in love with Rézi, a young woman who is also married. A teasing and perilous courtship is taking place. Arriving to visit Rézi, Claudine is told that she is ill in bed, but is shown up to her room.

She was as white as her *crêpe-de-Chine* dress, her eyes ringed with a mauve border that made them look blue. Slightly startled and moved, furthermore, by her grace and the look she gave me, I stood still:
'Rézi, are you really ill?'
'No; not now I see you.'

I gave a rude shrug. Then I was utterly taken aback. For, seeing my sarcastic smile, she was suddenly beside herself with rage.

'You can laugh? Get out of here, if you want to laugh!'

Knocked off my high horse by this sudden violence, I tried to get into the saddle:

'You surprise me, my dear. I thought you had such a sense of humour, with your taste for *games*, for rather elaborate *bits of teasing*.'

'You did? You believed what I said? It isn't true. I lied when I wrote to you, out of pure cowardice, so as to see you again, because I can't do without you, but...'

Her eagerness melted into incipient tears.

'...but it wasn't a joke, Claudine!'

She waited, fearfully, for what I would say and was frightened by my silence. She did not know that everything in me was fluttering in wild confusion, like a nest of agitated birds, and that I was flooded with joy. Joy at being loved and hearing myself told so, a miser's joy at a treasure lost and recovered, victorious pride to feel I was something more than an exciting toy. It was the triumphant downfall of my feminine decency. I realized that... But because she loved me, I could make her suffer still more.

'Dear Rézi...'

'Ah! Claudine!...'

She believed I was on the verge of yielding completely; she stood up, trembling all over, and held out her arms; her hair and her eyes glittered with the same pale fire... Alas! how the sight of anything I love, my friend's beauty, the soft shade of the Fresnois forests, Renaud's desire, always arouses in me the same craving to possess and embrace! Have I really only one mode of feeling?...

'Dear Rézi... am I to suppose, from the state you're in, that is the first time anyone has resisted you? When I look at you, I can so well understand that you must always have found women only too delighted and willing.'

Her arms, raised imploringly above the white dress that wound tightly about her, its train vanishing into the shadow like a mermaid's tail, dropped again. With her hands hanging limp, I saw her almost instantaneously recover her wits and turn angry. She said defiantly:

'The first time? Do you imagine that after eight years of living with that hollow brick, my husband, I haven't tried everything? That, to kindle any spark of love in me, I haven't searched for the sweetest, most beautiful thing in the world, a loving woman? Perhaps what you value more than anything else is the novelty, the clumsiness of a first... transgression. Oh, Claudine, there is something better, there is deliberately seeking and choosing.... I have chosen you,' she ended in a hurt voice, 'and you have only put up with me....'

A last grain of prudence stopped me from going closer to her; also, from where I was, I could admire her to the full. She was using every weapon of her charm – her grace, her voice – in the service of her rejected passion.

She had told me, truthfully; 'You are not the first,' because, in this case, truth struck home more shrewdly than a lie. Her frankness, I could swear, had been calculated, but she loved me!

I was dreaming of her, with her standing there before me, feasting my eyes on the sight of her. A movement of her neck conjured up the familiar Rézi, half-naked, at her dressing-table ... I gave a sudden shiver, it would be wise not to see her again like that...

Irritated and exhausted by my silence, she strained her eyes into the shadow, trying to make out mine.

'Rézi ...' (I spoke with a great effort) '...please ... let us give ourselves a rest today from all this and just wait for tomorrow to come...tomorrow that straightens out so many tangles! It isn't that you've made me angry, Rézi. I'd have come yesterday, and I'd have laughed or I'd have scolded, if I weren't so fond of you ....'

With that alert movement of an animal on the watch, she thrust out her chin, faintly cleft with a vertical dimple.

'...You must let me think, Rézi, without enveloping me so much, without casting such a net over me – a net of looks, gestures that come close without actually touching, persistent thoughts....You must come and sit over here near me, put your head on my knees and not say anything or move. Because, if you move, I shall go away....'

She sat down at my feet, laid her head on my lap with a sigh, and clasped her hands behind my waist. I could not stop my fingers from trembling as I ran them through her lovely hair, combing it into ringlets whose gleam was the only brightness left in the dark room. She did not stir. But her scent rose up from the nape of her neck, her burning cheeks warmed me and, against my knees, I could feel the shape of her breasts.... I was terrified lest she should move. For, had she seen my face and how profoundly disturbed I was ... [11]

Anaïs Nin

FROM

The Delta of Venus (1940–1)

The wife of one of the modern painters was a nymphomaniac. She was tubercular, I believe. She had a chalk-white face, burning black eyes deeply sunk in her face, with eyelids painted green. She had a voluptuous

[11]   Translated by Antonia White (London, 1960).

figure, which she covered very sleekly in black satin. Her waist was small in proportion to the rest of her body. Around her waist she wore a huge Greek silver belt, about six inches wide, studded with stones. This belt was fascinating. It was like the belt of a slave. One felt that deep down she *was* a slave – to her sexual hunger. One felt that all one had to do was to grip the belt and open it for her to fall into one's arms. It was very much like the chastity belt they showed in the Musée Cluny, which the crusaders were said to have put on their wives, a very wide silver belt with a hanging appendage that covered the sex and locked it up for the duration of their crusades. Someone told me the delightful story of a crusader who had put a chastity belt on his wife and left the key in care of his best friend in case of his death. He had barely ridden away a few miles when he saw his friend riding furiously after him, calling out: "You gave me the wrong key!"

'Such were the feelings that the belt of Louise inspired in everyone. Seeing her arrive at a café, her hungry eyes looking us over, searching for a response, an invitation to sit down, we knew she was out on a hunt for the day. Her husband could not help knowing about this. He was a pitiful figure, always looking for her, being told by his friends that she was at another café and then another, where he would go, which gave her time to steal off to a hotel room with someone. Then everyone would try to let her know where her husband was looking for her. Finally, in desperation, he began to beg his best friends to take her, so that at least she would not fall into strangers' hands.

'He had a fear of strangers, of South Americans in particular, and of Negroes and Cubans. He had heard remarks about their extraordinary sexual powers and felt that, if his wife fell into their hands, she would never return to him. Louise, however, after having slept with all his best friends, finally did meet one of the strangers.

'He was a Cuban, a tremendous brown man, extraordinarily handsome, with long, straight hair like a Hindu's and beautifully full, noble features. He would practically live at the Dome until he found a woman he wanted. And then they would disappear for two or three days, locked up in a hotel room, and not reappear until they were both satiated. He believed in making such a thorough feast of a woman that neither one wanted to see the other again. Only when this was over would he be seen sitting in the café again, conversing brilliantly. He was, in addition, a remarkable fresco painter.

'When he and Louise met, they immediately went off together. Antonio was powerfully fascinated by the whiteness of her skin, the abundance of her breasts, her slender waist, her long, straight, heavy blond hair. And she was fascinated by his head and powerful body, by his slowness and ease. Everything made him laugh. He gave one the feeling that the whole world was now shut out and only this sensual feast existed, that there would be no tomorrows, no meetings with anyone else – that there was only this room, this afternoon, this bed.

'When she stood by the big iron bed, waiting, he said, "Keep your belt on." And he began by slowly tearing her dress from around it. Calmly and with no

effort, he tore it into shreds as if it were made of paper. Louise was trembling at the strength of his hands. She stood naked now except for the heavy silver belt. He loosened her hair over her shoulders. And only then did he bend her back on the bed and kiss her interminably, his hands over her breasts. She felt the painful weight both of the silver belt and of his hands pressing so hard on her naked flesh. Her sexual hunger was rising like madness to her head, blinding her. It was so urgent that she could not wait. She could not even wait until he undressed. But Antonio ignored her movements of impatience. He not only continued to kiss her as if he were drinking her whole mouth, tongue, breath, into his big dark mouth, but his hands mauled her, pressed deeply into her flesh, leaving marks and pain everywhere. She was moist and trembling, opening her legs and trying to climb over him. She tried to open his pants.

"There is time," he said. "There is plenty of time. We are going to stay in this room for days. There is a lot of time for both of us."

Then he turned away and got undressed. He had a golden-brown body, a penis as smooth as the rest of his body, big, firm as a polished wood baton. She fell on him and took it into her mouth. His fingers went everywhere, into her anus, into her sex; his tongue, into her mouth, into her ears. He bit at her nipples, he kissed and bit her belly. She was trying to satisfy her hunger by rubbing against his leg, but he would not let her. He bent her as if she were made of rubber, twisted her into every position. With his two strong hands he took whatever part of her he was hungry for and brought it up to his mouth like a morsel of food, not caring how the rest of her body fell into space. Just so, he took her ass between his two hands, held it to his mouth, and bit and kissed her. She begged, "Take me, Antonio, take me, I can't wait!" He would not take her.

By this time the hunger in her womb was like a raging fire. She thought that it would drive her insane. Whatever she tried to do to bring herself to an orgasm, he defeated. If she even kissed him too long he would break away. As she moved, the big belt made a clinking sound, like the chain of a slave. She was now indeed the slave of this enormous brown man. He ruled like a king. Her pleasure was subordinated to his. She realised she could do nothing against his force and will. He demanded submission. Her desire died in her from sheer exhaustion. All the tautness left her body. She became as soft as cotton. Into this he delved with greater exultancy. His slave, his possession, a broken body, panting, malleable, growing softer under his fingers. His hands searched every nook of her body, leaving nothing untouched, kneading it, kneading it to suit his fancy, bending it to suit his mouth, his tongue, pressing it against his big shining white teeth, marking her as his.

For the first time, the hunger that had been on the surface of her skin like an irritation, retreated into a deeper part of her body. It retreated and accumulated, and it became a core of fire that waited to be exploded by his time and his rhythm. His touching was like a dance in which the two bodies turned and deformed themselves into new shapes, new arrangements, new designs. Now

they were cupped like twins, spoon-fashion, his penis against her ass, her breasts undulating like waves under his hands, painfully awake, aware, sensitive. Now he was crouching over her prone body like some great lion, as she placed her two fists under her ass to raise herself to his penis. He entered for the first time and filled her as none other had, touching the very depths of the womb.

'The honey was pouring from her. As he pushed, his penis made little sucking sounds. All the air was drawn from the womb, the way his penis filled it, and he swung in and out of the honey endlessly, touching the tip of the womb, but as soon as her breathing hastened, he would draw it out, all glistening, and take up another form of caress. He lay back on the bed, legs apart, his penis raised, and he made her sit upon it, swallow it up to the hilt, so that her pubic hair rubbed against his. As he held her, he made her dance circles around his penis. She would fall on him and rub her breasts against his chest, and seek his mouth, then straighten up again and resume her motions around the penis. Sometimes she raised herself a little so that she kept only the head of the penis in her sex, and she moved lightly, very lightly, just enough to keep it inside, touching the edges of her sex, which were red and swollen, and clasped the penis like a mouth. Then suddenly moving downwards, engulfing the whole penis, and gasping with the joy, she would fall over his body and seek his mouth again. His hands remained on her ass all the time, gripping her to force her movements so that she could not suddenly accelerate them and come.

'He took her off the bed, laid her on the floor, on her hands and knees, and said, "Move." She began to crawl about the room, her long blond hair half-covering her, her belt weighing her waist down. Then he knelt behind her and inserted his penis, his whole body over hers, also moving on its iron knees and long arms. After he had enjoyed her from behind, he slipped his head under her so that he could suckle at her luxuriant breasts, as if she were an animal, holding her in place with his hands and mouth. They were both panting and twisting, and only then did he lift her up, carry her to the bed, and put her legs around his shoulders. He took her violently and they shook and trembled as they came together. She fell away suddenly and sobbed hysterically. The orgasm had been so strong that she had thought she would go insane, with a hatred and a joy like nothing she had ever known. He was smiling, panting; they lay back and fell asleep.'[12]

---

[12] This extract is from 'Artists and Models'.

H. D.

FROM

The Flowering of the Rod (1946)

Jesus has been invited to dine at the house of Simon, one of the Pharisees. While he is there a 'woman of the city, who was a sinner' arrives bearing an alabaster flask of precious ointment.

She said, I have heard of you;
he bowed ironically and ironically murmured.

I have not had the pleasure,
his eyes now fixed on the half-open door;

she understood; this was his second rebuff
but deliberately, she shut the door;

she stood with her back against it;
planted there, she flung out her arms,

a further barrier,
and her scarf slipped to the floor;

her face was very pale,
her eyes darker and larger

than many whose luminous depth
had inspired some not-inconsiderable poets;

but eyes? he had known many women –
it was her hair – un-maidenly –

It was hardly decent of her to stand there,
unveiled in the house of a stranger.

But her voice was steady and her eyes were dry,
the room was small, hardly a room,

it was an alcove or a wide cupboard
with a closed door, a shaded window;

there was hardly any light from the window
but there seemed to be light somewhere,

as of moon-light on a lost river
or a sunken stream, seen in a dream

by a parched, dying man, lost in the desert . . .
or a mirage . . . it was her hair.

He who was unquestionably
master of caravans,

stooped to the floor;
he handed her her scarf;

it was unseemly that a woman
appear disordered, dishevelled;

it was unseemly that a woman
appear at all.

Anyhow, it is exactly written,
the house was filled with the odour of the ointment;

that was a little later and this was not such a small
    house
and was maybe already fragrant with boughs and
    wreaths,

for this was a banquet, a festival;
it was all very gay and there was laughter,

but Judas Iscariot turned down his mouth,
he muttered Extravagant under his breath,

for the nard though not potent,
had that subtle, indefinable essence

that lasts longer and costs more;
Judas whispered to his neighbour

and then they all began talking about the poor;
but Mary, seated on the floor,

like a child at a party, paid no attention;
she was busy; she was deftly un-weaving

the long, carefully-braided tresses
of her extraordinary hair.

But Simon the host thought,
we must draw the line somewhere;

he had seen something like this
in a heathen picture

or a carved stone-portal entrance
to a forbidden sea-temple;

they called the creature,
depicted like this,

seated on the sea-shore
or on a rock, a Siren,

a maid-of-the-sea, a mermaid;
some said, this mermaid sang

and that a Siren-song was fatal
and wrecks followed the wake of such hair;

she was not invited,
he bent to whisper

into the ear of his Guest,
I do not know her.

There was always a crowd hanging about outside
any door his Guest happened to enter;

he did not wish to make a scene,
he would call someone quietly to eject her;

Simon though over-wrought and excited,
had kept careful count of his guests;

things had gone excellently till now,
but this was embarrassing;

she was actually kissing His feet;
He does not understand;

they call him a Master,
but Simon questioned:

*this man if he were a prophet, would have known
who and what manner of woman this is.*[13]

13   See Luke 8 : 36–50.

Jean Rhys

FROM

Wide Sargasso Sea (1966)

In order to restore the family fortune Edward Fairfax Rochester has travelled to the West Indies to marry Antoinette Mason, an heiress. They are honeymooning in the mountains.

It was often raining when I woke during the night, a light capricious shower, dancing playful rain, or hushed, muted, growing louder, more persistent, more powerful, an inexorable sound. But always music, a music I had never heard before.

Then I would look at her for long minutes by candle-light, wonder why she seemed sad asleep, and curse the fever or the caution that had made me so blind, so feeble, so hesitating. I'd remember her effort to escape. (*No, I am sorry, I do not wish to marry you.*) Had she given way to that man Richard's[14] arguments, threats probably, I wouldn't trust him far, or to my half-serious blandishments and promises? In any case she had given way, but coldly, unwillingly, trying to protect herself with silence and a blank face. Poor weapons, and they had not served her well or lasted long. If I have forgotten caution, she has forgotten silence and coldness.

Shall I wake her up and listen to the things she says, whispers, in darkness. Not by day.

'I never wished to live before I knew you. I always thought it would be better if I died. Such a long time to wait before it's over.'

'And did you ever tell anyone this?'

'There was no one to tell, no one to listen. Oh you can't imagine Coulibri.'[15]

'But after Coulibri?'

'After Coulibri it was too late. I did not change.'

All day she'd be like any other girl, smile at herself in her looking-glass (*do you like this scent?*), try to teach me her songs, for they haunted me.

Adieu foulard, adieu madras, or *Ma belle ka di maman li*. My beautiful girl said to her mother (*No it is not like that. Now listen. It is this way*). She'd be silent, or angry for no reason, and chatter to Christophine[16] in

---

14 Antoinette's stepbrother.
15 The estate where she grew up.
16 Antoinette's black servant and confidante.

DESIRE

patois.
'Why do you hug and kiss Christophine?' I'd say.
'Why not?'
'*I* wouldn't hug and kiss them,' I'd say, 'I couldn't.'
At this she'd laugh for a long time and never tell me why she laughed.
But at night how different, even her voice was changed. Always this talk of death. (Is she trying to tell me that is the secret of this place? That there is no other way? She knows. She knows.)
'Why did you make me want to live? Why did you do that to me?'
'Because I wished it. Isn't that enough?'
'Yes, it is enough. But if one day you didn't wish it. What should I do then? Suppose you took this happiness away when I wasn't looking...'
'And lose my own? Who'd be so foolish?'
'I am not used to happiness,' she said. 'It makes me afraid.'
'Never be afraid. Or if you are tell no one.'
'I understand. But trying does not help me.'
'What would?' She did not answer that, then one night whispered, 'If I could die. Now, when I am happy. Would you do that? You wouldn't have to kill me. Say die and I will die. You don't believe me? Then try, try, say die and watch me die.'
'Die then! Die!' I watched her die many times. In my way, not in hers. In sunlight, in shadow, by moonlight, by candlelight. In the long afternoons when the house was empty. Only the sun was there to keep us company. We shut him out. And why not? Very soon she was as eager for what's called loving as I was – more lost and drowned afterwards.
She said, 'Here I can do as I like,' not I, and then I said it too. It seemed right in that lonely place. 'Here I can do as I like.'
We seldom met anyone when we left the house. If we did they'd greet us and go on their way.
I grew to like these mountain people, silent, reserved, never servile, never curious (or so I thought), not knowing that their quick sideways looks saw everything they wished to see.
It was at night that I felt danger and would try to forget it and push it away.
'You are safe,' I'd say. She'd liked that – to be told 'you are safe.' Or, I'd touch her face gently and touch tears. Tears – nothing! Words – less than nothing. As for the happiness I gave her, that was worse than nothing. I did not love her. I was thirsty for her, but that is not love. I felt very little tenderness for her, she was a stranger to me, a stranger who did not think or feel as I did.
One afternoon the sight of a dress which she'd left lying on her bedroom floor made me breathless and savage with desire. When I was exhausted I turned away from her and slept, still without a word or a caress. I woke and she was kissing me – soft light kisses. 'It is late,' she said and smiled. 'You must

70

let me cover you up – the land breeze can be cold.'
    'And you, aren't you cold?'
    'Oh I will be ready quickly. I'll wear the dress you like tonight.'
    'Yes, do wear it.'
    The floor was strewn with garments, hers and mine. She stepped over them carelessly as she walked to her clothes press. 'I was thinking, I'll have another made exactly like it,' she promised happily. 'Will you be pleased?'
    'Very pleased.'
    If she was a child she was not a stupid child but an obstinate one. She often questioned me about England and listened attentively to my answers, but I was certain that nothing I said made much difference. Her mind was already made up. Some romantic novel, a stray remark never forgotten, a sketch, a picture, a song, a waltz, some note of music, and her ideas were fixed. About England and about Europe. I could not change them and probably nothing would. Reality might disconcert her, bewilder her, hurt her, but it would not be reality. It would be only a mistake, a misfortune, a wrong path taken, her fixed ideas would never change.
    Nothing that I told her influenced her at all.
    Die then. Sleep. It is all that I can give you . . . wonder if she ever guessed how near she came to dying. In her way, not in mine. It was not a safe game to play – in that place. Desire, Hatred, Life, Death came very close in the darkness. Better not know how close. Better not think, never for a moment. Not close. The same. . . 'You are safe,' I'd say to her and to myself. 'Shut your eyes. Rest.'
    Then I'd listen to the rain, a sleepy tune that seemed as if it would go on for ever. . . Rain, for ever raining. Drown me in sleep. And soon.
    Next morning there would be very little sign of these showers. If some of the flowers were battered, the others smelt sweeter, the air was bluer and sparkling fresh. Only the clay path outside my window was muddy. Little shallow pools of water glinted in the hot sun, red earth does not dry quickly.

Marilyn French

FROM

The Women's Room (1978)

After a conventional and restrictive marriage, Mira is discovering new pleasures.

DESIRE

Mira got a little high that night, and so did Ben, and somehow – later she could not remember whose suggestion it was, or if there had been no suggestion at all, but simple single purpose – he ended up in her car, driving her to her apartment and when they arrived, he got out and saw her to the door and of course she asked him in for a nightcap and of course he came.

They were laughing as they climbed the steps, and they had their arms around each other. They were designing the perfect world, trying to outdo each other in silliness, and giggling to the point of tears at their own jokes. Mira fumbled with her key, Ben took it from her, dropped it, both of them giggling, picked it up and opened the door.

She poured them brandies. Ben following her to the kitchen, leaning over the counter and gazing at her as she prepared the drinks, talking, talking. He followed her out of the kitchen and right into the bathroom, until she turned with a little surprise and he caught himself, cried '*Oh!*' and laughed, and stepped out, but stood right beside the closed door talking to her through it while she peed. Then sat close beside her on the couch, talking, talking, laughing, smiling at her with shining eyes. And when he got up to get refills, she followed him into the kitchen and leaned across the counter gazing at him as he prepared the drinks, and he kept looking at her as he did it, and poured too much water in her glass. And they sat even closer this time, and there needed no forethought or calculation for the moment when they reached across and took each other's hands and it was only a few moments later that Ben was on her, leaning against her, his face searching in her face for something madly wanted that did not reside in faces, but searched, kept searching, and she too, in his. His body was lying on her now, his chest against her breasts, and the closeness of their bodies felt like completion. Her breasts were pressed flat under him: they felt soft and hard at once. Their faces stayed together mouths searching, probing, opening as if to devour, or rubbing softly together. Their cheeks too rubbed softly like the cheeks of tiny children just trying to feel another flesh, and hard, his beard, shaved though he was, harsh and hurtful on her cheek. He had her head in his hands, and he held it firmly, possessively, and gently, all at once, and he dipped his face into hers, searching for nourishment, hungry hungry. They rose together, like one body, and like one body walked into the bedroom, not separating even in the narrow hallway, just squeezing through together.

For Mira, Ben's lovemaking was the discovery of a new dimension. He loved her body. Her pleasure in this alone was so extreme that it felt like the discovery of a new ocean, mountain, continent. He loved it. He crowed over it as he helped her to undress, he kissed it and caressed it and exclaimed, and she was quieter, but adored his with her eyes as she helped him to undress, ran her hands over the smooth skin of his back, grabbed him from behind around the waist and kissed his back, the back of his neck, his shoulders. She was shy of his penis at first, but when he held her close and nestled against her, he pressed

his penis against her body, and her hand went out to it, held it, caressed it. Then he wrapped his legs around her, covered her, holding on to her tightly, and kissed her eyes, her cheeks, her hair. She pulled away from him gently and took his hands and kissed them, and he took hers and kissed the tips of her fingers.

She lay back again as he pressed against her, and he caressed her breasts. She felt that her body was floating out to sea on a warm gentle wave that had orders not to drown her, but she didn't even care if she drowned. Then, rather suddenly, he put his mouth to her breasts and nursed at them, and quickly entered her and quickly came, silently, with only an expelled breath, and a pang of self-pity hit her, her eyes filled with tears. No, no, not again, it couldn't be the same, it wasn't fair, was there really something wrong with her? He lay on top of her, holding her closely for a long time afterward, and she had time to swallow the tears and paste a smile on her face. She patted his back gently and reminded herself that she had at least had pleasure from it this time, and maybe that was a good sign. He had given her, if nothing else, more pleasure than she had ever had from her body before.

After a time, he leaned back and lay on his side close to her. They lighted cigarettes and sipped their drinks. He asked her about her girlhood: what kind of child had she been? She was surprised. Women ask such things, sometimes, but not men. She was delighted. She lay back and threw herself into it, talking as if it were happening there and then. Her voice changed and curled around its subject: she was five, she was twelve, she was fourteen. She hardly noticed at first that he had begun to caress her body again. It seemed simply natural that they would touch each other. He was gently rubbing her belly and sides, her shoulders. She put her cigarette out and caressed his shoulders. Then he was leaning over her, kissing her belly, his hands on her thighs, on the insides of her thighs. Desire rose up in her more fiercely than before. She caressed his hair, then his head moved down, and she tightened up, her eyes widened, he was kissing her genitals, licking them, she was horrified, but he kept stroking her belly, her leg, he kept doing it and when she tried to tighten her legs, he held them gently apart, and she lay back again and felt the warm wet pressure and her innards felt fluid and giving, all the way to her stomach. She tried to pull him up, but he would not permit it, he turned over, he kissed her back, her buttocks, he put his finger on her anus and rubbed it gently, and she was moaning and trying to turn over, and finally, she succeeded, and then he had her breast in his mouth and the hot shoots were climbing all the way to her throat. She wrapped her body around him, clutching him, no longer kissing or caressing, but only clinging now, trying to get him to come inside her, but he wouldn't. She surrendered her body to him, let him take control of it, and in an ecstasy of passivity let her body float out to the deepest part of the ocean. There was only body, only sensation: even the room had ceased to exist. He was rubbing her clitoris, gently, slowly, ritually, and she was making little gasps that she could hear from a distance. Then he took her breast in his mouth again and wrapped

his body around her and entered her. She came almost immediately and gave a sharp cry, but he kept going, and she came over and over again in a series of sharp pleasures that were the same as pain. Her face and body were wet, so were his, she felt, and still the pangs came, less now, and she clutched him to her, holding him as if she really might drown. The orgasms subsided, but still he thrust into her. Her legs were aching, and the thrust no longer felt like pleasure. Her muscles were weary, and she was unable to keep the motion going. He pulled out and turned her over and propped her on a pillow so that her ass was propped up, and entered her vagina from behind. His hand stroked her breast gently, he was humped over her like a dog. It was a totally different feeling, and as he thrust more and more sharply, she gave out little cries. Her clitoris was being triggered again, and it felt sharp and fierce and hot and as full of pain as pleasure and suddenly he came and thrust fiercely and gave off a series of loud cries that were nearly sobs, and stayed drooped over her like a flower, heaving, his wet face against her back.

When he pulled out, she turned over and reached up to him and pulled him down and held him. He put his arms around her and they lay together for a long time. His wet penis was against her leg, and she could feel semen trickling out of her onto the sheets. It began to feel cold, but neither of them moved. Then they moved a few inches and looked into each other's face. They stroked each other's faces, then began to laugh. They hugged each other hard, like friends rather than lovers, and sat up. Ben went into the bathroom and got some tissues and they dried themselves and the sheets. He went back and started water running in the tub. Mira was lying back against the pillow, smoking.

'Come on, woman, get up!' he ordered, and she looked at him startled, and he reached across and put his arms around her and lifted her from the bed, kissing her at the same time, and helped her to her feet, and they went together to the bathroom and both peed. The water was at bath level by then. Ben had put Mira's bath lotion in the water, and it was bubbly and smelled fresh, and they got in together and sat with bent knees intertwined, and gently threw water at each other and lay back enjoying the warmth and caressed each other beneath and above the water.

'I'm hungry,' she said.

'I'm famished,' he said.

Together, they pulled everything out of the refrigerator, and produced a feast of Jewish salami and feta cheese and hard-boiled eggs and tomatoes and black bread and sweet butter and half-sour pickles and big black Greek olives and raw Spanish onions and beer, and trotted all of it back to bed with them and sat there gorging themselves and talking and drinking and laughing and touching each other with tender fingertips. And finally they sat the platters and plates and beer cans on the floor and Ben nuzzled his face in her breast, but this time she pushed him down and got on top of him and, refusing to let him move, she kissed and caressed his body and slid her hands down his sides and along the insides of his thighs, held his balls gently, then slid down and took his penis in her mouth and he gasped with pleasure and

she moved her hands and head slowly up and down with it, feeling the vein throb, feeling it harden and melt little drops of semen, and wouldn't let him move until suddenly she raised her head and he looked startled and she got on top of him and set her own rhythms, rubbing her clitoris against him as she moved and she came, she felt like a goddess, triumphant, riding the winds, and she kept coming and he came too then, and she bent down her chest and clutched him, both of them moaning together, and ended, finally, exhausted.

They fell back on the rumpled sheets for a while, then Mira lighted a cigarette. Ben got up and smoothed the bedclothes out, and fluffed up the pillows, and got in beside her and pulled up the sheets and blankets and took a drag of her cigarette and put his arms behind his head and just lay there smiling.

It was five o'clock, and the sky above the houses was light, lightening, a pale streak of light blue. They were not tired, they said. They turned their heads toward each other, and just smiled, kept smiling. Ben took another drag of her cigarette, then she put it out. She reached out and switched off the lamp, and together they snuggled down in the sheets. They were still turned to each other, and they twisted their bodies together. They fell immediately asleep. When they awakened in the morning, they were still intertwined.

Carol Ann Duffy
Oppenheim's Cup and Saucer (1985)

She asked me to luncheon in fur. Far from
the loud laughter of men, our secret life stirred.

I remember her eyes, the slim rope of her spine.
This is your cup, she whispered, and this mine.

We drank the sweet hot liquid and talked dirty.
As she undressed me, her breasts were a mirror

and there were mirrors in the bed. She said Place
your legs around my neck, that's right. Yes.[17]

[17] From *Standing Female Nude* (London, 1985).

Wanda Honn

My Subway Lover (1987)

I got up in the morning looking forward to my new life. I wasn't exactly anxious to go to work, but I felt confident in a desire to put more into my vocation. I would try to be there more for the patients and really start exerting my knowledge and ability. I'd try harder to rekindle a friendship with Janey and start looking at all the women more platonically and with less lust. I would free myself from the confinements of my sexual desire.

As I walked to the subway, the air was crisp and clear. The sun was just coming up, slightly softening the barren, gray, winter environment of the city. I arrived at the platform with the other early morning rush hour people. I was always amazed that in New York morning rush hour seemed to start at 6 a.m. and last until almost noon. The platform was crowded as the train pulled up. I saw that it was going to be one of those days when I had to cram myself into the car. I squeezed through the throng and pushed my way to the area by the door that separates the cars. I leaned my back against the door for support.

As the car started moving I noticed, standing very close to me, a very beautiful woman. She was slightly shorter than I, with a soft, full face, shoulder-length curly brown hair, and a body that wouldn't quit. She had gorgeous large breasts that stood out firmly. Wow! Well, I can't help looking, I thought.

Soon the train stopped to let out a few and to take in even more. My friend got pushed in closer to me and was standing with her lovely bosom pushed up against my arm. I stiffened with embarrassment but also secretly felt delighted. The train moved on. I was immediately aware that the woman's breast rubbed up and down against me with the bouncing of the train. She smelled fresh from a morning shower and was wearing neat, clean clothes. Her hair radiated a flowery shampoo fragrance. I closed my eyes, felt her body moving against me, listened to the click-uh click-uh click-uh of the train. I was getting warm.

While absorbing these sensations, I noticed she had adjusted her position. Opening my eyes, I saw that what I felt was true. She was facing me squarely, our bodies shoved together, front to front. She looked at me and smiled slightly. My face must have reddened deeply, and I thought she sensed what I had been feeling.

Then I felt something on my outer thigh. She was touching me with her hand. Oh, glorious, wonderful life! I knew then that she probably did know my mind and had one like it. Subtly, I put my own hand over hers on my thigh and led it in towards my centre. She caught her breath, inhaled long

76

and deeply. Our two hands began to move up and down my zipper, dipping in between my legs. Still leaning against the door, I spread my legs a little more. We bounced with the movement of the train, and giggled. The noise of the train seemed to be getting louder. She pressed her body hard against mine and continued to rub my crotch. Her breasts squished into me, the train's movement causing them to rub and tease my own. My clit was titillated and extremely sensitive; I began to rock towards her, our bodies grinding together quietly. I felt my underpants getting wet.

The train came to another stop, tossing people about. The woman had been pushed away from me slightly. As everyone regained their balance, I spread my legs a little more, and she, amazingly, unzipped my pants and slipped her hand inside. With one movement, while pushing up against me again, she wiggled her fingers underneath the leg band of my underpants and we were flesh on flesh. She made a slight noise, exhaling air quickly, and I began to sweat and tingle all over. The train started up with a jolt, and she pressed her fingers hard against me. I jerked with the shot of pleasure that ran through me. The train was moving smoothly again, and she kept her fingers held against my clit, with the rest of her hand cupping my bush. As the train rocked us, her hand and body moved up and down, pressing and relaxing in rhythm. My pelvis was throbbing. I felt the rush coming on. Oh, please don't stop, I thought. I began to tremble. My knees got weak. I wanted to pull her to me tightly and jump on her hand. Water dripped from my armpits and brow. I struggled to stifle grunting noises that began to force their way out of my throat. My thrusting became more pronounced. I held on to the door of the car with my hands. The noise of the moving train seemed to pound in my skull.

Suddenly we screeched to a halt. At that moment, she pushed hard against me and moved her hand rapidly and with force against my saturated groin. A flash went through me, I shuddered all over, my legs and pelvis twitching. A hot sensation of mounting pleasure drained me. I clenched my teeth and groaned softly. Shivering, I caught myself from sliding to the floor.

As the train resumed its journey, she slowly removed her wet, shaking hand from me. Regaining my composure, I looked around us nonchalantly, trying to determine from people's faces whether they had noticed anything. Everyone seemed to be looking away or downward and gave no indication of interest in me or my friend. But I still worried that some of them might have seen it all. Oh well, I thought, I'll probably never see any of them again in my life; I hope. The cynical part of me said, yeah, one of them will probably end up being your new nursing supervisor or something.

Then I gazed into my friend's eyes. They were dancing as she smiled and blushed. I wanted to say something but I didn't know what. I was still trying to find words when the train stopped again. Oh, no, my subway lover was moving to get off. As she turned to leave, I grabbed her arm quickly, and said, 'Thank you.'

She turned her head, smiled fully, and said, 'Any time.'

I dropped my hand from her arm, and she rushed out of our rumbling crowded boudoir.[18]

Jill Dawson
Loving for Two (1990)

S he was cold in his pokey flat, and shivered. She wondered why she'd come; felt sure he would misunderstand her. He was in the kitchen, mixing up Jamaican dark rum and some pink syrup she didn't know the name of, singing Bob Marley songs to himself. 'And then Georgie would make the fire light; and love was burning through the night...'

Her heart turned over slowly.

'Well you can't live wit him in your pocket all your life,' he told her brutally. 'Everyting got to end sometime.' He stood, magnificently in the doorway, two chipped mugs in his hands, not tall but towering just the same. He put the mug on the floor at her feet.

'I shouldn't be drinking,' she said, her hand on her belly.

'One little sip ain't gonna hurt it. Real limes in that. I even salt the glass.' He raised his mug to her. She fixed her eyes on a spot in the middle of his t-shirt, his hot, flat stomach. She longed to lift up the t-shirt and plant a tiny kiss on it as if he were a little boy.

She sipped the rum and started to cry. When he touched her, the tightening in her belly told her that she had wanted this, expected this, had come for exactly this. He rubbed her shoulders, too roughly at first, then kissed the back of her neck, ruffled her hair, just as he had the first time. She could not tell if it was longing or sadness which made her breath catch. He stroked her back, fingers pressing through the shirt, his hair following his hands, the rough thick locks that brushed her coarsely, dragging every nerve to attention. He had not misunderstood, after all.

'Don't cry,' he whispered, and his voice was scented with rum, and limes. 'I put the fire on in me room.' At that she had to laugh. And at what he did next. Put his arms underneath her and lifted her, lifted the weight of her as if she was a baby, a leaf; one of his daughters, instead of the dead weight she felt she was.

He laid her gently on the bed, but that was too passive for her, she wanted him from behind, the animal way, the only way that was comfortable now. She undressed herself, and did not watch but knew he was removing jeans,

18 Published in *Rapture* (1987).

pulling his t-shirt over his head. The scent of him was enough, the memory of his sweet-sourness, the salt-taste of his sweat. She did not need to see his beauty, only feel his skin that covered her like hot satin sheets, and remember.

He clambered upon her; she rested the full weight of her belly in his spread fingers, and her breasts hung low, the tips stretched and darkened and aching with desire. Her body opened like a watermelon, then closed itself around him. He was sharp, sweet as a knife. His arms tightly around her middle, she pressed her buttocks into his stomach, while he moved with his familiar rhythm, reaching down for a moment to open her a little easier, purse her lips around him. He pushed and filled her, fingers working her hardened nipples, palms cupping her breasts, restoring her, enlivening her, until her crying stopped and the turmoil inside her took over; the pleasure so intense, she almost wanted to move away from it, but he was behind her, on top of her, inside her, the pleasure was rising, it was too great, her womb tightened and flattened, a cry flew from her like a bird, and bucking, she heaved her hips, jerking herself away from him, and came. Her cry drew him further, and hands around her breasts he held on, and was jerked and pulled towards his own orgasm, his breath in her ear, his spidery hair in hers, tangled.

Later, as she was leaving, she wanted to thank him, but had no words for it. Instead she asked him: 'Do you think it might damage the baby?' She was in the doorway; he helped her on with her leather jacket. 'A baby always makes room for its father,' he said, grinning.

And they laughed, because he wasn't its father.

FANTASY

E rotica happens in the head. It can also happen in the flesh, so that mind and body meet. But the erotic can never be restricted to the body alone; the imagination always plays a part.

Fantasy constructs images of desire and its expression which go on somewhere other than the present time and place. It does not confine itself to the known, the possible, or the practical, though it may choose to use all three. Anne Bradstreet's poem is written to her husband. She knows the effect of his warmth on her 'chilled limbs', and she looks at her offspring for the substantial and visible evidence of their union. The anonymous author of 'The Self-Examination' similarly looks into her self for the solid testimony of her passion, but moves from the facts of her bodily reaction to the promise of an imagined excitement aroused by her lover's reponse. Emily Dickinson, on the other hand, allows herself a vision which is far removed from any grounding in the real of here and now. Her vision remains fantastic.

Erotic fantasy does not need to be a fantasy for the self. Elizabeth Grymeston imagines a future for her son which includes erotic attraction both for him ('let her neither be so beautifull, as that every liking eye shall levell at her; nor yet so browne, as to bring thee to a loathed bed'), and for her prospective daughter-in-law ('seldome shalt thou see a woman out of hir owne love to pull a rose that is full blowen, deeming them alwaies sweetest at the first opening of the budde...').

The liberation of fantasy allows for the introduction of situations and worlds far removed from the everyday. Some of these are approached through traditional escape routes. Elizabeth Singer Rowe employs the romantic model of the Song of Solomon to create her erotic vision. Stevie Smith's 'I Rode With My Darling' is set in a fairytale world of abandoned

children alone in the dark wood. Edna O'Brien's Virginia Woolf succumbs to the seductive glamour of Vita's aristocratic style: her lineage, her inheritance, the ancestral home, fine wines, and exotic costume. Maureen Duffy's poem uses a fantasy blend of the romance garden with the hectic and overwrought world of the opera. Joan Crate's heroine visits a nightclub to indulge in the tawdry glitter of male striptease, all flashy costumes and bizarre stage props.

At first sight the excerpt from *The Mill on the Floss* may seem more everyday and less obviously erotic than even Anne Bradstreet's poem or Elizabeth Grymeston's letter. But this passage includes versions of many of the constituents for erotic fantasy. The 'Hill' toward which Maggie walks may be an 'insignificant rise', but it is still related to the glorious summits and ravines of the Italian scenery in Ann Radcliffe's gothic. Like Stevie Smith's 'dark wood', the Red Deeps is a place of vague sexual threat ('visions of robbers and fierce animals haunting every hollow'), and a summer pleasure garden. This is also a landscape of female sexuality, both in its shapes, in its name, and in the very nineteenth-century perception of the place as one to be approached with mingled loathing and liking. Maggie is about to enter into adult sexual life ('...one has a sense of uneasiness in looking at her – a sense of opposing elements, of which a fierce collision is imminent...there is a hushed expression...out of keeping with the resistant youth, which one expects to flash out in a sudden, passionate glance...like a damped fire leaping out again when all seemed safe'), but all erotic knowledge and power is displaced into the fantasy landscape around her.

Much erotic fantasy stays in the imagination. This means that the reader's part here is one of active engagement. In the case of *The Mill on the Floss* erotic suggestion passes directly from text to reader, bypassing Maggie herself. Joan Crate's scene is obviously about sex, but the reader has to build on titillation and promise. Edna O'Brien's text is more teasing still. We watch Vita telescope centuries, cross gender, mix seriousness and play; we see Virginia succumb to Vita's parody wooing; we hear Vita's narrative of seduction; we see her nakedness. And then no more. The curtain comes down. The fantasy is ours.

Elizabeth Grymeston

FROM

Miscelanae, Meditations, Memoratives (1604)

Elizabeth Grymeston's work is a tract addressed to her only son, Bernye, offering maternal advice on the whole of life's conduct, but revealing much of her own mind and attitudes in the process. The Miscelanae *is her only work; it was published in London in 1604 shortly after the death of the author.*

To her loving sonne Bernye Grymeston
My dearest sonne, there is nothing so strong as the force of love; there is no love so forcible as the love of an affectionate mother to hir naturall childe: there is no mother can either more affectionately shew hir nature, or more natually manifest hir affection, than in advising hir children out of hir owne experience. . . .

I have prayed for thee that thou mightest be fortunate in two houres of thy life time: In the houre of thy marriage, and at the houre of thy death. Marrie in thine owne ranke, and seeke especially in it thy contentment and preferment,[1] let her neither be so beautifull, as that every liking eye shall levell at her; nor yet so browne,[2] as to bring thee to a loathed bed. Deferre not thy marriage till thou commest to be saluted with a God speed you Sir, as a man going out of the world after fortie; neither yet to the time of God keepe you Sir, whilest thou art in thy best strength after thirtie; but marrie in the time of you are welcome Sir, when thou art comming into the world. For seldome shalt thou see a woman out of hir owne love to pull a rose that is full blowen, deeming them alwaies sweetest at the first opening of the budde. It was *Phaedra* her confession to Hippolitus, and it holdes for trueth with the most.[3]

---

[1] Preference.
[2] 'Browne' as the opposite of 'fair'.
[3] As an old man, Theseus married Phaedra who soon fell in love with Hippolytus, his son by the Amazon queen. Rebuffed by Hippolytus, Phaedra told Theseus that the boy had attempted her rape, and revenge and disaster followed.

Anne Bradstreet

A *Letter to her Husband, absent upon publick employment (1678)*

My head, my heart, mine Eyes, my life, nay more,[4]
My joy, my Magazine[5] of earthly store,
If two be one, as surely thou and I,
How stayest thou there, whilst I at *Ipswich*[6] lye?
So many steps, head from the heart to sever
If but a neck, soon should we be together:
I like the earth this season, mourn in black,
My sun is gone so far in's Zodiack,
Whom whilst I 'joy'd, nor storms, nor frosts I felt,
His warmth such frigid colds did cause to melt.
My chilled limbs now nummed lye forlorn:
Return, return sweet *Sol* from *Capricorn*,[7]
In this dead time, alas, what can I more
Then view those fruits which through thy heat I bore?
Which sweet contentment yield me for a space,
True living Pictures of their Fathers face.[8]
O strange effect! now thou art *Southward* gone,
I weary grow, the tedious day so long;
But when thou *Northward* to me shalt return,[9]
I wish my Sun may never set, but burn

---

[4] Bradstreet's husband Simon was a member of the General Court in Boston which was negotiating the unification of the colonies of New England.
[5] Storehouse, generally only used in relation to the storage of weapons and ammunition today.
[6] The Bradstreets had moved to Ipswich, about forty miles north of Boston in 1634 or 1635.
[7] The sun is in Capricorn in the winter (December–January). The conceit which describes the lover as the sun who retreats and returns with warmth is a common one in metaphysical poetry.
[8] Her children.
[9] A paradox, given that the south, in the northern hemisphere, should be the place to find long and warm days.

Within the Cancer[10] of my glowing breast,
The welcome house of him my dearest guest.
Where ever, ever stay, and go not thence,
Till natures sad decree shall call thee hence;
Flesh of thy flesh, bone of thy bone,
I here, thou there, yet both but one.[11]

Elizabeth Singer Rowe

Canticles 5:6 etc. (1695)

Oh! How his *Pointed Language*, like a Dart,
Sticks to the *softest Fibres* of my Heart,
Quite through my Soul the charming Accents slide,
That from his Life inspiring Portals glide;
And whilst I the inchanting sound admire,
My melting Vitals[12] in a Trance expire.
Oh Son of *Venus*,[13] Mourn thy baffled Arts,
For I defye the proudest of thy Darts:
Undazled now, *I* thy weak Taper View,
And find no fatal influence accrue;
Nor would *fond Child* thy feebler Lamp appear,
Should my bright *Sun* deign to approach more near;
Canst thou his Rival then pretend to prove?
Thou a false Idol, he the God of Love;
Lovely beyond Conception, he is all
Reason, or Fancy amiable call,
All that the most exerted thoughts can reach,
When sublimated to its utmost stretch.
Oh! altogether Charming, why in thee
Do the vain World no Form or Beauty see?
Why do they Idolize a dusty clod,
And yet refuse their Homage to a God?
Why from a *beautious* flowing Fountain turn,
For the Dead Puddle of a narrow *Urn?*
Oh Carnal Madness! sure we falsly call

---

[10] The sun is in Cancer in the summer (June–July).
[11] Published in *Several Poems* (1678).
[12] Vital organs.
[13] Cupid.

So dull a thing as Man is, rational;
Alas, my shining Love, what can there be
On Earth so splendid to *out-glitter thee?*
In whom the brightness of a God-head Shines,
With all its lovely and endearing Lines;
Thee with whose sight Mortallity once blest,
Would throw off its dark Veil to be possest;
Then altogether Lovely, why in thee
Do the vain World no Form or Beauty see.[14]

Anonymous, 'A Lady'
The Self-Examination (1773)

Why throbs my heart when he appears?
From whence this tender sigh?
Why are my eyes dissolved in tears,
When he's no longer nigh?

Where are my wonted pleasures fled?
Nor books nor lyre can please;
That lies untouched, and these unread:
All occupations tease.

One loved idea still employs
All hopes and all desires!
Walks are insipid, music's noise,
And conversation tires.

But when Philander[15] speaks, 'tis then
I all attention pay;
And fondly wish the power to pen
Whate'er he deigns to say!

O with what skill I strive to hide
The joy my bosom feels!

---

[14] Published in *Poems on Several Occasions. Written by Philomela* (London, 1696). 'Canticles 5:6' refers to the Song of Solomon 5:6: 'I opened to my beloved; but my beloved had withdrawn himself, and was gone: my soul failed when he spake: I sought him, but I could not find him; I called him, but he gave me no answer.'
[15] Philander is a conventional name for the lover used in the tradition of erotic and pastoral verse. His beloved is Phillis.

When he, oft seated by my side,
   To me his thoughts reveal.

Wit, sense, and genius then conspire
   Each faculty to seize!
And while I fondly thus admire,
   I lose the power to please.

A pause ensues, his eyes still speak,
   As waiting a reply:
My words in faltering accents break,
   Or on my lips they die.

Oh were Philander once to bear
   In all my woes a part;
And softly whisper in my ear
   The secret of his heart!

What pleasure through each sense would glide!
   What transport should I feel!
O say, my heart, thus sweetly tried,
   Couldst thou thy joys conceal?[16]

Emily Dickinson
Wild Nights – Wild Nights (c. 1861)

Wild Nights – Wild Nights!
Were I with thee
Wild Nights should be
Our luxury!

Futile – the Winds –
To a Heart in port –
Done with the Compass –
Done with the Chart!

[16] From *Original Poems, Translations and Imitations, From the French, etc. By a Lady* (London, 1773). The author may be Frances Villiers, Countess of Jersey (1753–1821), but there is some doubt about this; see *Eighteenth Century Women Poets*, ed. Roger Lonsdale (Oxford, 1989), p. 529.

Rowing in Eden –
Ah, the Sea!
Might I but moor – Tonight –
In Thee![17]

George Eliot

FROM

The Mill on the Floss (1862)

F *rom Book Fifth, Chapter 1, 'In the Red Deeps'. As a child Maggie Tulliver, the daughter of the miller, had been friendly with Philip Wakem, the son of the local lawyer and a companion at school of her brother Tom. The Tullivers have suffered a financial disaster which the miller blames on Wakem who now owns first interest in the mill. Maggie has been leading a quiet and restricted life of domestic self-sacrifice and, in obedience to her brother's dictate, has not seen Philip for some time.*

I t was far on in June now, and Maggie was inclined to lengthen the daily walk which was her one indulgence; but this day and the following she was so busy with work which must be finished that she never went beyond the gate, and satisfied her need of the open air by sitting out of doors. One of her frequent walks, when she was not obliged to go to St Ogg's,[18] was to a spot that lay beyond what was called the 'Hill' – an insignificant rise of ground crowned by trees, lying along the side of the road which ran by the gates of Dorlcote Mill. Insignificant I call it, because in height it was hardly more than a bank; but there may come moments when Nature makes a mere bank a means towards a fateful result, and that is why I ask you to imagine this high bank crowned with trees, making an uneven wall for some quarter of a mile along the left side of Dorlcote Mill and the pleasant fields behind it, bounded by the murmuring Ripple. Just where this line of bank sloped down again to

---

[17]   Written c. 1861, first published in 1891.
[18]   The local town.

FANTASY

the level a by-road turned off and led to the other side of the rise, where it was broken into very capricious hollows and mounds by the working of an exhausted stone-quarry, so long exhausted that both mounds and hollows were now clothed with brambles and trees, and here and there by a stretch of grass which a few sheep kept close-nibbled. In her childish days Maggie held this place, called the Red Deeps, in very great awe, and needed all her confidence in Tom's bravery to reconcile her to an excursion thither – visions of robbers and fierce animals haunting every hollow. But now it had the charm for her which any broken ground, any mimic rock and ravine, have for the eyes that rest habitually on the level – especially in summer, when she could sit on a grassy hollow under the shadow of a branching ash, stooping aslant from the steep above her, and listen to the hum of insects, like tiniest bells on the garment of Silence, or see the sunlight piercing the distant boughs, as if to chase and drive home the truant heavenly blue of the wild hyacinths. In this June time, too, the dog-roses were in their glory, and that was an additional reason why Maggie should direct her walk to the Red Deeps, rather than to any other spot, on the first day she was free to wander at her will – a pleasure she loved so well that sometimes, in her ardours of renunciation, she thought she ought to deny herself the frequent indulgence in it.

You may see her now, as she walks down the favourite turning, and enters the Deeps by a narrow path through a group of Scotch firs, her tall figure and old lavender gown visible through an hereditary black silk shawl of some wide-meshed net-like material; and now she is sure of being unseen, she takes off her bonnet and ties it over her arm. One would certainly suppose her to be farther on in life than her seventeenth year – perhaps because of the slow, resigned sadness of the glance, from which all search and unrest seem to have departed – perhaps because her broad-chested figure has the mould of early womanhood. Youth and health have withstood well the involuntary and voluntary hardships of her lot, and the nights in which she has lain on the hard floor for a penance have left no obvious trace; the eyes are liquid, the brown cheek is firm and rounded, the full lips are red. With her dark colouring and jet crown surmounting her tall figure, she seems to have a sort of kinship with the grand Scotch firs, at which she is looking up as if she loved them well. Yet one has a sense of uneasiness in looking at her – a sense of opposing elements, of which a fierce collision is imminent. Surely there is a hushed expression, such as one often sees in older faces under borderless caps, out of keeping with the resistant youth, which one expects to flash out in a sudden, passionate glance, that will dissipate all the quietude, like a damped fire leaping out again when all seemed safe.

But Maggie herself was not uneasy at this moment. She was calmly enjoying the fresh air while she looked up at the old fir-trees, and thought that those broken ends of branches were the records of past storms, which had only made the red stems soar higher. But while her eyes were still turned upward

88

she became conscious of a moving shadow cast by the evening sun on the grassy path before her, and looked down with a startled gesture to see Philip Wakem, who first raised his hat, and then, blushing deeply, came forward to her and put out his hand. Maggie, too, coloured with surprise, which soon gave way to pleasure. She put out her hand and looked down at the deformed figure before her with frank eyes, filled for the moment with nothing but the memory of her child's feelings – a memory that was always strong in her. She was the first to speak.

'You startled me,' she said, smiling faintly; 'I never meet anyone here. How came you to be walking here? Did you come to meet *me*?'

It was impossible not to perceive that Maggie felt herself a child again.

Stevie Smith
I Rode With My Darling (1950)

I rode with my darling in the dark wood at night
And suddenly there was an angel burning bright
Come with me or go far away he said
But do not stay alone in the dark wood at night.

My darling grew pale he was responsible
He said we should go back it was reasonable
But I wished to stay with the angel in the dark wood at night.

My darling said goodbye and rode off angrily
And suddenly I rode after him and came to a cornfield
Where had my darling gone and where was the angel now?
The wind bent the corn and drew it along the ground
And the corn said, Do not go alone in the dark wood.

Then the wind drew more strongly and black clouds covered the moon
And I rode into the dark wood at night.

There was a light burning in the trees but it was not the angel
And in the pale light stood a tall tower without windows
And a mean rain fell and the voice of the tower spoke,
Do not stay alone in the dark wood at night.

The walls of the pale tower were heavy, in a heavy mood
The great stones stood as if resisting without belief.

Oh how sad sighed the wind, how disconsolately,
Do not ride alone in the dark wood at night.

Loved I once my darling? I love him not now.
Had I a mother beloved? She lies far away.
A sister, a loving heart? My aunt a noble lady?
All all is silent in the dark wood at night.[19]

Maureen Duffy

Aria for Midsummer's Eve (1971)

Extol me her midsummer flesh,
Lay your praises over the wounds of absence,
Poultice of dew heavy leaves from the dream wood;
Wordspell solace.

All charms are hers. On this eve
Arias sing about her; there is wine
And strawberries by the water where queen
She leans and smiles.

Alone I wrench time and layer
Days and nights, sweet and sour, in my angel cake
Of loving since our clock has no hands,
Ours is ever,

And our occasions hang gauzing
Each other; this year last though absent I
Page beside you over the lawns, pin up
Froth of hedge lace

The white folds at your breast I traced,
Limning its silk swags' moondrawn swell as if
You lay pregnant with our high summer love,
Last night abed,

Span your belly with a warming hand
Yet double vision you driving home under
A night sieved with stars or late plucking for me
Dogrose kisses.[20]

[19] Published in *Harold's Leap* (1950).
[20] Published in *The Venus Touch* (1971).

Edna O'Brien

FROM

Virginia (1981)

*F*rom *Act II, scene 2. Edna O'Brien's play deals with the life of Virginia Woolf, often drawing on her writings to play across the facts of her life and the fictions of her creation.*

VIRGINIA: What I think of is arriving and seeing Vita[21] black and scarlet under a lamp.
Equanimity Mrs Woolf, practise equanimity.
I shall be cold, I shall be hostile, I shall be indifferent.
Mrs Nicolson.
[*She smiles*]
The Hon. Mrs Nicholson. Snob that I am, I trace your passions five hundred years back and they become romantic to me. I have a perfectly untrue but romantic vision of you in my mind, stamping out the hops in a great vat in Kent, stark naked . . . [*she laughs*] brown as a satyr and very beautiful. How long do you take to milk on your great estate and how do you cool it and do you churn and make butter. Facts Mrs Nicolson, facts.
Why am I talking to you. Simple I like to make you up. I assure you I have every need of illusion. . . .
Oh Mrs Nicolson, aren't you a card. Why didn't you come in, why run away.
My own garden in Tavistock Square. What a treat. I expect you're jealous.
[*To* LEONARD] Why don't you eat one. . .go on. Nibble a crocus.
[*To* VITA] You do, I suppose, disapprove of my dress, my apparel.
VITA: It's dreadful.
VIRGINIA: I was advised by the Editor of Vogue, a Mrs Todd, to wear this. It cost me four guineas and look at my gloves.
[*She is not wearing gloves.*]
VITA: Todd! So you whore after *her*.
VIRGINIA: Better whore after her than timidly copulate with the Editor of the Times Literary Supplement.

---

[21] Vita Sackville-West (Mrs Harold Nicolson). The hero/heroine of *Orlando* (1928) is drawn from Woolf's inspired perspective on, and love for, Vita.

VITA: So long as one goes the whole hog.

VIRGINIA: Oh. Mrs Nicolson...Do you cut up rough, like a baroness.

VITA: I would say not as rough as you. You see people, but you don't feel them...We, they, are all material to you.

VIRGINIA: In that case let's stick to literature, it's simpler. For instance one test of poetry is that without saying things, indeed saying the opposite, it conveys things. I read Crabbe and I think of fens, marshes, shingle, rivers...But there is nothing of the sort. There is how Lucy got engaged to Edward Shore.

VITA: You should wear shorter skirts and show off your shins.

VIRGINIA: They are not my best point.

VITA: Captious aren't you?

VIRGINIA: And you, what are you?

VITA: A woman – yes, but a million other things. A snob? Ancestors – proud of them. Greedy, luxurious, vicious, don't care a damn. Like lying in bed on fine linen listening to the pigeons.

VIRGINIA: Like giving pain.

VITA: Silver, victuals, wine, maids, footmen, spoilt perhaps.

VIRGINIA: You are so much in full sail, on the high tide.

VITA: When shall I take you there?

VIRGINIA: Where?

VITA: Home, to Long Barn.[22]

VIRGINIA: I shall see a table laid with jugs of chocolate and buns.

VITA: You shall sit beneath the arras, you shall eat game and there will be fireworks down by the frozen pond.

VIRGINA: [*marvelling*] Ottoline[23] took me motoring one night here in London and the effect was stupendous – St Paul's, Tower Bridge, moonlight, the river. Ottoline in full dress and paint, white and gaudy like a tombstone, all the hoppers and bargees coming home drunk. It was the Bank Holiday. Sometimes London can be very vivid. I was on the top of a bus going to Waterloo and there was an old beggar woman blind, in Kingsway, holding a mongrel in her arms and singing. There was a recklessness about her.[24]

VITA: Just say when.

VIRGINIA: [*to the audience*] I am not sure that I am not throwing myself overboard.

VITA: [*very sportingly*] What used we young fellows in the cockpit of the Marie Rose say about a woman who threw herself overboard. Ah, we had a word for her.

---

[22] The name for Vita's home in Kent.
[23] Ottoline Morell, a literary hostess. The Woolfs were frequent guests at her home in Garsington.
[24] An drawn image from Woolf's *Mrs Dalloway* (1925).

VIRGINIA: Ah, we must omit that word, it is disrespectful in the extreme.

VITA: Shall we say Tuesday?

VIRGINIA: I shall let Leonard decide that. [*To* LEONARD] I am growing old and want more mustard with my meat.

[VITA *and* VIRGINIA *come downstage.*]

I'm crack-brained . . . sometimes I am not Virginia at all.

VITA: And now?

VIRGINIA: Now I am a little drunk . . . this wine for instance, I see it as amber . . . and the beams are swaying and it's bliss, and I find you one of the nicest and most magnanimous of women.

VITA: Catch.

VIRGINIA: You say you esteem me. That's damn cold. Still, I accept it like the humble servant I am.

VIRGINIA: (V.O.)[25] She has found me, she has kissed me, all is shattered.

VITA: Good God, you are not going to give me chastity. The whole edifice of female government and wiliness is based on that foundation stone. Women are not chaste.

VIRGINIA: Do you know that from your husband?

VITA: I know it from my experience as a man.

VIRGINIA: Were you?

VITA: Yes.

[*Like a knight falls on one knee and speaks in a cavalier voice.*]

Falling on his knees, the Archduke Harry made the most passionate declaration of his suit. He told her that he had something like twenty million ducats in a strong box at his castle. He had more acres than any nobleman in England. The shooting was excellent. He could promise her a mixed bag of Ptarmigan and grouse such as no English moor or Scottish either could rival. True, the pheasants had suffered from the gape in his absence and the does had slipped their young.

VIRGINIA: [*in the same vein*] As he spoke enormous tears formed in his violet eyes.

VITA: [*unable to resist laughing*] But that don't count. Want to eat?

VIRGINIA: Can't eat.

VITA: A little of the fat, ma'am?

VIRGINIA: Not yet, ma'am.

VITA: Would you like to play Fly Loo?

VIRGINIA: What is it?

VITA: It's gambling. Great sums of money can be lost and if you lose you will have to marry me.

VIRGINIA: Show me.

VITA: I bet you . . . That a fly will land on this lump of sugar. Now you choose your lump.

---

[25] A stage instruction: 'voice over'.

93

[VIRGINIA *hesitates and then points to the one and then they both look around expecting flies.* VITA *snapes her fingers impatiently.*]

VITA: C'mon, flies, bluebottles, c'mon ... don't be so sluggish.

VIRGINIA: I expect they're asleep, it's winter.

VITA: We'll change that.

[VITA *lets out a whistle as she dashes from one corner to another to try and arouse them.*]

VIRGINIA: Life and a lover. It does not scan.

VITA: [*acting voice*] Dammit Madam, you are loveliness incarnate.

VIRGINIA: Trembled. Turned hot. Turned cold.

VITA: [*still acting voice*] For she smiled the involuntary smile which women smile when their own beauty seems not their own.
Confronts them all of a sudden in a glass. And then she listened and heard only the leaves blowing and the sparrows twittering and then she sighed, life and a lover, it does not scan.

VIRGINIA: Would you like to crack a man over the head and tell him he lies in his teeth.

VITA: A pox on them I say.

VIRGINIA: And then she turned on her heel with extraordinary rapidity, whipped her emeralds from her neck.

VITA: Stripped her satin from her back.

VIRIGINIA: Stood erect in her neat black silk knickerbockers and ... (*does it*) rang the bell.

[*The bell or gong is heard to ring throughout the house. No one answers it.*]

VITA: We are alone.

VIRGINIA: Let us go.

END OF SCENE TWO

Joan Crate

FROM

Breathing Water (1989)

*D*ione, Jewell and Randy are taking a holiday from the round of childcare and visiting a women's nightclub.

' **L**adies, I hear you, I hear you. Don't get too excited. The best is yet to come! And now, direct from Vancouver, just what you've been waiting for, Mr Nude Coast 1988, and Mr Beach Body 1989, the one, the only, the well-endowed and how, Michael Masters!'

A motor roars, and a leather-clad man rides a motorcycle onto the stage. The crowd screams as he twists a skilful figure eight, his leg stretched, his black boot snapping against the floor to keep the heavy bike from falling over. Again, the motor roars through the shrieks and the motorcycle charges down the ramp, the brakes squealing it to a sudden stop right beside Jewell. Triumphantly a well-muscled man steps from the bike, pulls out the kickstand and raises his arms to the crowd. Again the music starts. Elvis singing 'Hunka, hunka burning love,' Michael Masters struts in his fringed black leather jacket, shades, and light black leather pants that lovingly caress his muscular buttocks, his bulging penis. He grabs his glasses and tosses them carelessly over his shoulder. They slide over the hard-wood floor to the back of the stage. Something tightens in my stomach. His eyes are blue, too blue. 'Tinted contact lenses,' I mutter to Jewell and Randy, but Randy shakes her head, refusing to believe it.

His hair is blonde-streaked and as bountiful as the hair of the young women in the audience. He wears it brushed back at the front and sides, full and curly, but long and straight behind his ears.

'Permed,' I tell them.

'No,' Randy murmurs. She stares at him, at his tanned face, his male bulk. 'He can park his shoes under my bed any day.' Her lips stretch into an amused leer, but then begin to pull apart in amazement, and I look up to see Michael Masters strutting towards our table. One leather-gloved hand plucks Randy's hand, guides it to the heavy zipper at the top of the jacket. Joyfully she tugs, pulling it down to reveal a tight black t-shirt. He spins around the table, pulling the jacket off as he turns. He throws it and the zipper makes a scraping noise along the stage. Leather gloves kiss my neck, and I remain absolutely still. My eyes lock into his as he stares with his too-blue eyes. My God, it's him! It's the artist! He kisses me hard on the mouth as voices chorus around us. Up the arm of my chair his black leather leg slithers and his foot lands close to my fingers. 'Undo the zipper,' he hisses, and I notice the track at the ankle. I pull up and see a sliver of tanned skin, not milk white as I expected, and then it's gone and in front of me he spins, leather flapping free of one leg, the smell of leather stirring the air. Leaning closer he squats, capturing my eyes again in a vivid blue sea, his breath in my hair. 'Meet me after this set. My dressing room is the second one to the right of the ladies' can.' And he leaps back to the stage as 'Hunka hunka burnin' love' throbs to a finish. I drink my gin and tonic in one long swallow....

I walk to the back of the dark room, past the ladies washroom to the second door on the right. It's painted bright pink and has one large gold star at eye level. I knock. As the door swings open, I step into a long, narrow room, like a hallway that has been closed off at the ends. Right inside the doorway, leaning against

a wall is the motorcycle, and behind it a trunk bursting its gaudy contents: sparkling silver and gold lamé, white and red satin, strings of blue sequins, and black leather. All along the high walls are photographs of this man in a variety of skimpy bathing suits. Smiling, he twists into poses that reveal huge biceps and triceps, heavy thigh muscles, and knotted shoulders and chest.

Now, wearing the same tight black t-shirt and black leather pants he wore on the stage, he indicates the pictures with a tanned hand.'I'll give you one after, if you want. Autographed.' Then he steps towards me. 'Nice boobs.'

'I'm breastfeeding,' I tell him, quickly sheltering them with one arm.

'Kinky!' He winks one bright blue eye, and I wonder if I know him. I thought I did. I thought he was the artist, but now I'm not sure. I'd like to just ask him, but it may make him angry. His leather-gloved hands flex open and closed, open and closed.

'How did you get into this? Dancing?'

'It started as a side-line,' he answers tersely. Moving towards me, he places his hands on my waist and lifts me onto the black leather motorcycle seat. 'But if ya got it, ya might as well flaunt it! Now don't give me a hard time. Get it, hard time? Just take off those stupid shoes.'

I kick off my heels, and he reaches into the truck and retrieves a pair of black leather lace-up boots, much too big, shoves my feet inside and ties them from the top, fingers caressing my calves.

'Forty minutes till my next number,' he announces, glancing at a watch on the dressing table. 'I'm taking you for a ride.' He stoops to scoop the bright clothing back into the trunk, grabs the black leather jacket with fringes from the coat rack bolted to the side wall, and starts to steer the motorcycle down the narrow, pink room, past the glossy pictures of his sparkling smile, his body cut and defined by muscle like charts of beef at the butcher's.

At the end of the room the walls don't meet and I follow him and his machine through an opening to the left, to another door and outside to a small landing with a freight elevator. 'Kitchen's through here.' He points at the door behind us. I peer through the window and see a man in a suit pull a waitress in a black backless dress to him and kiss her.

Outside it's dark, and the streets are lit with neon and flashing computerized messages. I swing my leg over the motorcycle and grasp his waist. Eyes closed, I feel thunder break under me, then a surge of movement. We're flying! I stretch out my arms on the back of the motorcycle, try to grab the ribbons of light – red, green, pink, and blue – streaming by us. The wind slaps my face, tugs at my hair piled inside the helmet. When he turns the motorcycle, I lean with him, hold his thighs with my thighs. At the stop sign, my mouth finds the skin under the collar of his jacket, and I suck slowly like Warlock, like Dracula, a thin red stream that leaps into the light of Chinatown. Under the bridge, under our feet, the river is India ink and we roar past a couple of late night joggers, turn by old houses and brick apartments and leave the neon streamers lagging far behind. Ahead the street lights form a puzzle – match the

dots. Crow with her felt pens smearing pictures out of points, and we charge into them, our speed drawing light to light, making something out of all this space before it can catch up with us and be only lights again, strung along the highway between black smudges of nothing. Our bodies throb together and I hold him tight. There is no definition, no form, the wind in my eyes and everything melting. Faster, he races the motorcycle and we weave, skin prickly cold, between sluggish blurs of metal, move towards the sky. Then he slows, turns a corner, and we join up with the light-spotted street again, going back to where we came from.

Inside the narrow pink room, he tears off his jacket and shirt, unzips his trousers, then pushes me against a wall, kisses me hard, and unbuttons my blouse. His fingers squeeze my nipple, and milk shoots down towards them. 'No,' I tell him, but he won't stop. 'No, the milk's starting,' I mumble, trying to free my mouth from his. He slides his hands around my back, unhooks my bra, and his hand is back on my nipple, his finger and thumb stroking, then he lowers his mouth and sucks.

'Bastard!' As he raises his head, I squeeze the nipple between my fingers and squirt him in the eye with warm, blue milk. He smiles at me, milk dripping from his lower lid, and kisses me again, long and delicious.

'There,' he says drawing back, peeling off his pants, 'it goes. You're good for business.' I follow his eyes to his semi-erect penis and watch dumbly as he plucks a large silver ring from the shelf over the coat rack, and tries to fit it over the head. 'Shit! Too much. It won't go on.' He glances at the watch. 'Seven minutes! Throw me the silver shirt.' He points at the trunk. 'That's it. Now look for brown leather knee-high pants, full leg, and for chrissakes, cover your tits or it'll never go down.'

One hand pulling my blouse over my breasts, I forage through the trunk, find his breeches and throw them.

'Okay, now long silver socks and high brown boots. Should be to the right of the truck there.' I find the socks and toss them at him. As I reach for the boots, I look up at him. He yanks a brown patch over one eye, and pulls on a buccaneer's hat with a skull and crossbones painted in silver. Gingerly he fits the ring over his limp penis. 'Let's try this again, wench,' he mutters in a pirate's voice, shoving me against the wall. He squeezes my breasts together and buries his face between them, then pushes his hands over my ribs, down to the waistband of my skirt. He reaches into my panties, and presses his body against me. I can feel his penis rise.

'Good, very good.' He draws back and scrambles into his brown leather G-string, the leather breeches, his socks and boots, then hurriedly ties a silver sash around his waist. Just as he reaches for a long, curved sword from the shelf, a voice booms, 'And now ladies, prepare yourself for the fabulous, the entertaining, the award winning body of . . . Michaaaaeeeelll Maaaaaasters!'

He turns and tugs a photograph off the wall behind him. 'My address and number's on the back.' Then he snatches a pen from the shelf and scrawls

something before raising his sword and charging out the door.

I flip the picture over. The address and telephone number are from Vancouver. Before I slip it under the waistband of my skirt, I reach up and grab the second silver ring from the shelf, turn it round and round in my fingers. What a strange thing – I gather my hair up and pull it through – but how versatile.

TABOO

A taboo on the objects and performance of sexual love has no literal or absolute value. It is man's law, though often authorised by an attribution to God. As created ideas, constructed to regulate behaviour, they are directed at the mind and spirit. How powerful then is the craving of the flesh which breaks barriers, defies law.

Forbidden love, forbidden fruit; prohibition can be an aphrodisiac. Ford knew this when he showed the hot tension of Annabella's lust for her brother Giovanni in *'Tis Pity She's a Whore*; Laclos knew this when Valmont stormed Madame de Tourvel's stronghold of virtue in *Les Liaisons Dangereuses*. Little wonder that sexual taboos persist in their rigidity. To want to fuck so much that all regulation disappears into that need is a shocking anarchy.

But love is anarchic. It recognises no boundaries, it obeys no command. And desire is lawless. One focus sucks in all else, everything disappearing into its melting centre.

The oldest and most common taboo is sex outside marriage. Marriage polices the necessity of sexual congress for the continuance of the race. To go outside the law in the act of adultery is to invite chaos. The extracts here which deal with adultery, from Marie de France, Aphra Behn, Delarivier Manley and Kate Chopin, all centre on the transgression of women. Taboo in these cases is complicated by the fact that the subjects, as married women, are entitled to no independent life. They are goods for exchange between men. By acting on their desires they break both the written law of the marriage vow, and the unwritten law of their status as inanimate currency. In *Laüstic* the lady takes action to preserve her relation with her lover, but she becomes his possession as much as she was her husband's through her identification with the dead nightingale: '. . .the front of her tunic was bespattered with blood, just on her breast'. When the lover makes the nightingale's casket-tomb he also shuts the

lady and her illegal passion into a box.

In Aphra Behn's *Abdelazar* the scheming Queen Isabella breaks three laws with her 'confession'. Her story is one of adultery, rape and breaking the vow of chastity. She need not give physical details to 'tell the rest', for the encounter she describes already has enough steamy content in its illicit defiance. Homais, in Delarivier Manley's play, is unashamed in her surrender to desire. Homais knows about guilt. She also accepts it. Not for her the anxious 'cowardice' of Levan's consciousness of the barriers of incest and adultery.

Social conditioning is all that governs the taboos – and the miseries – of Kate Chopin's *The Awakening*. Edna Pontellier has come to terms with her impatient need. Her lover, on the other hand, is bound. He is bound by his belief in propriety and in a system which makes women the property of men. Only if Edna is 'given' to Robert by her husband can she belong to him. Denied love by the poverties of social expectation, Edna takes an equivocal control. She challenges the final taboo to find in suicide the erotic embrace which may free her into life.

Of the other taboos represented here not all are forbidden outside their place in history. In the fifteenth century Benedetta Carlini's desire appeared to be an act of corruption but it does not remain so. Her passion is indecent only in the eyes of the censuring viewer.

Historical context and cultural specificity also mean that some of these texts are innocent of any awareness of the potential for the taboo as an erotic catalyst. Carlini and her reporter are not consciously exploiting this aspect of her transgression. Neither is Dorothy Wordsworth, who was ignorant of the disturbingly erotic character of her romantic attachment to her brother. But some later reader of Dorothy's journal was not so innocent. In the manuscript of Dorothy's journal (now held in the Dove Cottage Museum at Grasmere) certain passages have been crossed out, apparently by a nineteenth-century reader, possibly a member of the family. Someone was sufficiently anxious about the implications of her record to cross out the reference to her illness during the days leading up to William's wedding and also the account of their private ring ceremony. That embarrassed reader saw a broken law, and attempted its repair.

Christina Rossetti's poem 'After Death' may not know the challenge to the taboo which it presents. But Rossetti is a very sophisticated poet, acutely aware of man's preference for the 'doll' woman which he can manipulate and use. As in the extract from Anaïs Nin's 'Pierre', a dead woman is just such an ideal instrument. When Rossetti writes 'He did not touch the shroud, or raise the fold/That hid my face, or take my

hand in his' the reader is forced to imagine all of these actions – and to acknowledge their suggestion. He did not do these things, but he could have done them, might have done them, might have longed to do them. Thus his illegitimate 'warmth' contrasts with the speaker's ironic cool.

The other extracts in this section are all consciously transgressive. Anaïs Nin is writing erotica and knows the value of the forbidden. Her writing deliberately investigates a shopping list of taboos. This is not an innocent exploration. In Nin's writing she relies upon the reader's knowledge of the illicit and the encounters she describes are erotic precisely because they permit the brief imagination of outlawed desire.

Sarah Murphy and Angela Carter also rely upon their readers' sophistication in the laws of the taboo. In 'The Bloody Chamber' Angela Carter described the meeting of innocence and knowledge, one naked, the other clothed, as 'the most pornographic of confrontations'. The conventions of pornography mean that the innocent is usually female, the wise exploiter, male. But in this extract from Carter's *Heroes and Villains* it is Marianne who knows, and who permits herself the excitement of the child's ignorant arousal. Sarah Murphy's speaker is also mature in sexual knowledge. She teases herself with imagining the unguarded surprise of the boy lover she pursues. Hers is a perverse and refined pleasure.

Murphy and Carter are both examining the anarchic extremes of desire. Mary Shelley takes on the grandest institutions of religious and social prohibition. The passage from *Frankenstein* was the first part of the novel to be written. Its insistent double focus on the body and on the workings of desire testify to the erotic pressures which produced the work. Frankenstein journeys from ardour to despair. He looks on beauty in fragments and corruption in the whole. He reaches for his lawful wife and takes the corpse of his mother in his arms.

Patterns across opposite poles are the price of transgression. To seize desire, strong and sweet, in the teeth of prohibition, is always to travel the perilous edge of the extreme.

Marie de France
Laüstic (c. second half of C12th)

*T*he Lais *of Marie de France are found in various manuscripts held in Paris and London. The stories seem to have been circulating the*

British courts in the 1170s and 1180s. They were first published in 1819;
see The Lais of Marie de France, *translated and with an introduction by*
Glyn S. Burgess and Keith Busby (London, 1986). The Lais are 'courtly'
in character (as opposed to epic or religious) because they address the
particular medieval code of behaviour known as 'courtesy'. The kind of
'courtly love' portrayed here is that where the lover admires and woos his
lady in a refined, but not necessarily platonic, manner. The highly formal
and stylised tone of the narratives does not succeed in diffusing altogether
the succinct sexual tension of the encounters described.

I shall relate an adventure to you from which the Bretons composed a lay. *Laüstic* is its name, I believe, and that is what the Bretons call it in their land. In French the title is *Rossignol*, and Nightingale is the correct English word.

In the region of St Malo was a famous town and two knights dwelt there, each with a fortified house. Because of the fine qualities of the two men the town acquired a good reputation. One of the knights had taken a wise, courtly and elegant wife who conducted herself, as custom dictated, with admirable propriety. The other knight was a young man who was well known amongst his peers for his prowess and great valour. He performed honourable deeds gladly and attended many tournaments, spending freely and giving generously whatever he had. He loved his neighbour's wife and so persistently did he request her love, so frequent were his entreaties and so many qualities did he possess that she loved him above all things, both for the good she had heard about him and because he lived close by. They loved each other prudently and well, concealing their love carefully to ensure that they were not seen, disturbed or suspected. This they could do because their dwellings were adjoining. Their houses, halls and keeps were close by each other and there was no barrier or division, apart from a high wall of dark-hued stone. When she stood at her bedroom window, the lady could talk to her beloved in the other house and he to her, and they could toss gifts to each other. There was scarcely anything to displease them and they were both very content except for the fact that they could not meet and take their pleasure with each other, for the lady was closely guarded when her husband was in the region. But they were so resourceful that day or night they managed to speak to each other and no one could prevent their coming to the window and seeing each other there. For a long time they loved each other, until one summer when the copses and meadows were green and the gardens in full bloom. On the flower-tops the birds sang joyfully and sweetly. If love is on anyone's mind, no wonder he turns his attention towards it. I shall tell you the truth about the knight. Both he and the lady made the greatest possible effort with their words and with their eyes. At night, when the moon was shining and her husband was asleep, she often rose from beside him and put on her mantle. Knowing her beloved would be doing the same, she would go and stand at the window and stay awake most of the night. They took delight

in seeing each other, since they were denied anything more. But so frequently did she stand there and so frequently leave her bed that her husband became angry and asked her repeatedly why she got up and where she went. 'Lord,' replied the lady, 'anyone who does not hear the song of the nightingale knows none of the joys of this world. This is why I come and stand here. So sweet is the song I hear by night that it brings me great pleasure. I take such delight in it and desire it so much that I can get no sleep at all.' When the lord heard what she said, he gave a spiteful, angry laugh and devised a plan to ensnare the nightingale. Every single servant in his household constructed some trap, net or snare and then arranged them throughout the garden. There was no hazel tree or chestnut tree on which they did not place a snare or bird-lime, until they had captured and retained it. When they had taken the nightingale, it was handed over, still alive, to the lord, who was overjoyed to hold it in his hands. He entered the lady's chamber. 'Lady,' he said, 'where are you? Come forward and speak to us. With bird-lime I have trapped the nightingale which has kept you awake so much. Now you can sleep in peace, for it will never awaken you again.' When the lady heard him she was grief-stricken and distressed. She asked her husband for the bird, but he killed it out of spite, breaking its neck wickedly with his two hands. He threw the body at the lady, so that the front of her tunic was bespattered with blood, just on her breast. Thereupon he left the chamber. The lady took the tiny corpse, wept profusely and cursed those who had betrayed the nightingale by constructing the traps and snares, for they had taken so much joy from her. 'Alas,' she said, 'misfortune is upon me. Never again can I get up at night or go to stand at the window where I used to see my beloved. I know one thing for certain. He will think I am faint-hearted, so I must take action. I shall send him the nightingale and let him know what has happened.' She wrapped the little bird in a piece of samite, embroidered in gold and covered in designs. She called one of her servants, entrusted him with her message and sent him to her beloved. He went to the knight, greeted him on behalf of his lady, related the whole message to him and presented him with the nightingale. When the messenger had finished speaking, the knight, who had listened attentively, was distressed by what had happened. But he was not uncourtly or tardy. He had a small vessel prepared, not of iron or steel, but of pure gold with fine stones, very precious and valuable. On it he carefully placed a lid and put the nightingale in it. Then he had the casket sealed and carried it with him at all times.

This adventure was related and could not long be concealed. The Bretons composed a lay about it which is called *Laüstic*.

Anonymous
(Benedetta Carlini)

FROM

Account of the Visit Made to the Theatine Nuns, Also Known as Holy Mary of Pescia (n.d., c. 1619)

*T*his undated account of a visit to the Theatine nuns is one of the documents in the State Archive at Florence *(Miscellanea Medicea 376, insert 28) which relate to the case of Benedetta Carlini who was subjected to fifteen ecclesiastical interrogations made between 27 May, 1619, and 26 July, 1620. It may be that this account was designed to be included in the preliminary set of findings for the trial of Carlini; see Appendix in* Immodest Acts: The Life of a Lesbian Nun in Renaissance Italy *by Judith C. Brown (Oxford, 1986), pp. 158–64.*

For two continuous years, two or three times a week, in the evening, after disrobing and going to bed waiting for her companion,[1] who serves her, to disrobe also, she would force her into the bed and kissing her as if she were a man she would stir on top of her so much that both of them corrupted themselves because she held her by force sometimes for one, sometimes for two, sometimes for three hours. And [she did these things] during the most solemn hours, especially in the mornings, at dawn. Pretending that she had some need, she would call her, and taking her by force she sinned with her as was said above. Benedetta, in order to have greater pleasure, put her face between the other's breasts and kissed them, and wanted always to be thus on her. And six or eight times, when the other nun did not want to sleep with her in order to avoid sin, Benedetta went to find her in her bed and, climbing on top, sinned with her by force. Also at that time, during the day, pretending to be sick and showing that she had some need, she grabbed her companion's hand by force, and putting it

[1] Bartolomea Crivelli.

under herself, she would have her put her finger in her genitals, and holding it there she stirred herself so much that she corrupted herself. And she would kiss her and also by force would put her own hand under her companion and her finger into her genitals and corrupted her. And when the latter would flee, she would do the same with her own hands. Many times she locked her companion in the study, and making her sit down in front of her, by force she put her hands under her and corrupted her; she wanted her companion to do the same to her, and while she was doing this she would kiss her. She always appeared to be in a trance while doing this. Her angel, Splenditello,[2] did these things, appearing as a boy of eight or nine years of age. This angel Splenditello through the mouth and hands of Benedetta, taught her companion to read and write, making her be near her on her knees and kissing her and putting her hands on her breasts. And the first time she made her learn all the letters without forgetting them; the second, to read the whole side of a page; the second day she made her take the small book of the Madonna and read the words; and Benedetta's two other angels listened to the lesson and saw the writing.

Aphra Behn

FROM

Abdelazar,
or The Moor's Revenge (1676)

*A*bdelazar *is on the point of seizing the throne of Spain, but first he has to eliminate Philip, the true heir, by calling his legitimacy into question. The Queen chooses to confess to infidelity, and names the Cardinal as Philip's father. She tells the Cardinal that she hopes that in this way she will first of all force a marriage to repair the avowed wrong, and secondly clear the way for his accession to the throne.*

ACT V, SCENE I. *A Presence-Chamber, with a Throne and Canopy*

Enter ABDELAZAR, CARDINAL, ALONZO, ORDONIO, RODERIGO, *and other Lords, one bearing the Crown, which is laid on the Table on a Cushion; the* QUEEN,·

---

[2] Splenditello was the name which Benedetta gave to the angel who appeared to her regularly.

LEONORA, *and Ladies. They all seat themselves, leaving the Throne and Chair of State empty.* ABDELAZAR *rises and bows,* RODERIGO *kneeling presents him with the Crown. . . .*

ABDELAZAR: Stay, Peers of Spain,
If young Prince Philip be King Philip's Son,
Then is he Heir to Philip, and his Crown;
But if a Bastard, then he is a Rebel,
And as a Traitor to the Crown shou'd bleed:
That dangerous popular Spirit must be laid.
Or Spain must languish under civil Swords:
And Portugal taking advantage of those Disorders.
Assisted by the Male-contents within,
If Philip live will bring Confusion home.
– Our Remedy for this is first to prove,
And then proclaim him Bastard.

ALONZO: That Project would be worth your Politicks [*Aside*]
– How shou'd we prove him Bastard?

ABDELAZAR: Her Majesty being lately urg'd by Conscience,
And much above her Honour prizing Spain,
Declar'd this Secret, but has not nam'd the Man;
If he be noble and a Spaniard born,
He shall repair her Fame by marrying her.

CARDINAL: No; Spaniard, or Moor, the daring Slave shall die.

QUEEN: Would I were cover'd with a Veil of Night, [*Weeps*]
That I might hide the Blushes on my Cheeks!
But when your Safety comes into Dispute,
My Honour, nor my life must come in competition.
– I'll therefore hide my Eyes, and blushing own,
That Philip's Father is i'th Presence now.

ALONZO: I'th' Presence! name him

QUEEN: The Cardinal – [*All rise in Amazement*]

CARDINAL: How's this, Madam!

ABDELAZAR: How! the Cardinal!

CARDINAL: I Philip's Father, Madam!

QUEEN: Dull Lover – is not this all done for thee?
Dost thou not fee a Kingdom and my self,
By this Confession, thrown into thy Arms?

CARDINAL: On Terms so infamous I must despise it.

QUEEN: Have I thrown by all my Sense of Modesty,
To render you the Master of my Bed,
To be refus'd – was there any other way? –

CARDINAL: I cannot yield; this Cruelty transcends
All you have ever done me – Heavens! what a Contest
Of Love and Honour swells my rising Heart!

QUEEN: By all my Love, if you refuse me now,
　　Now when I have remov'd all Difficulties,
　　I'll be reveng'd a thousand killing ways.
CARDINAL: Madam, I cannot own so false a thing,
　　My Conscience and Religion will not suffer me.
QUEEN: Away with all this Canting; Conscience, and Religion!
　　No, take advice from nothing but from Love.
CARDINAL: 'Tis certain I'm bewitch'd – she has a Spell
　　Hid in those charming Lips.
ALONZO: Prince Cardinal, what say you to this?
CARDINAL: I cannot bring it forth –
QUEEN: Do't, or thou'rt lost for ever.
CARDINAL: Death! What's a Woman's Power?
　　And yet I can resist it.
QUEEN: And dare you disobey me?
CARDINAL: Is't not enough I've given you up my Power.
　　Nay, and resign'd my Life into your Hands,
　　But you wou'd damn me too – I will not yield –
　　Oh now I find a very Hell within me:
　　How am I misguided by my Passion?
ALONZO: Sir, we attend your Answer.
QUEEN: 'Tis now near twenty Years, when newly married,
　　And 'tis the Custom here to marry young,
　　King Philip made a War in Barbary,
　　Won Tunis, conquer'd Fez, and hand to hand
　　Slew great Abdela, King of Fez, and Father
　　To this Barbarian Prince.
ABDELAZAR: I was but young, and yet I well remember
　　My Father's Wound – poor Barbary – but no more.
QUEEN: In absence of my King, I liv'd retir'd.
　　Shut up in my Apartment with my Women.
　　Suffering no Visits, but the Cardinal's.
　　To whom the King had left me as his Charge;
　　But he, unworthy of that Trust repos'd,
　　Soon turn'd his Business into Love.
CARDINAL: Heavens! how will this Story end? [Aside]
QUEEN: A Tale, alas! unpleasant to my Ear,
　　And for the which I banish'd him my Presence,
　　But oh the Power of Gold! he bribes my Women,
　　That they should tell me (as a Secret too)
　　The King (whose Wars were finish'd) would return
　　Without acquainting any with the time;
　　He being as jealous, as I was fair and young,
　　Meant to surprise me in the dead of Night:

This pass'd upon my Youth, which ne'er knew Art.
CARDINAL: Gods! is there any Hell but Woman's Falshood? [*Aside*]
QUEEN: The following Night I hasted to my Bed,
    To wait my expected Bliss – nor was it long
    Before his gentle Steps approach'd my Ears.
    Undress'd he came, and with vigorous haste
    Flew to my yielding Arms: I call'd him King,
    My dear lov'd Lord; and in return he breath'd
    Into my Bosom, in soft gentle Whispers,
    My Queen! my Angel! my lov'd Isabella!
    And at that Word – I need not tell the rest.
ALONZO: What's all this, Madam, to the Cardinal?
QUEEN: Ah, Sir, the Night too short for his Caresses,
    Made room for Day, Day that betray'd my Shame;
    For in my guilty Arms I found the Cardinal.
ALONZO: Madam, why did not you complain of this?
QUEEN: Alas, I was but young, and full of Fears;
    Bashful, and doubtful of a just Belief,
    Knowing King Philip's rash and jealous Temper;
    But from your Justice I expect Revenge.

Mary Delarivier Manley

FROM

The Royal Mischief (1696)

*H*omais, *young, passionate and unscrupulous, has been confined by her elderly and impotent husband the Prince of Libardian. She has fallen in love with her husband's nephew Levan Dadian and, assisted by her ex-lover Ismael, has engineered her first meeting with him with the explicit intention of seducing him.*

ACT III, SCENE I. *A room in the Castle of Phasia*

Enter HOMAIS, *alone.*
HOMAIS: He sleeps as sound as if he never were

To wake again. Now could one ask him what
Avails his prisons, spies, and jealousies?
Would he not say a woman's wit
Had made them fruitless all?
Strict silence fills the lodgings, the music's placed,
The banquet's ready, and I more so than all.
Will he not come? 'Tis a long parley.
Methinks on such a summons he should grow
Fond of a surrender. But hence, begone
These melancholy doubts that load my thoughts,
And turn them into fears. The phantoms
Cannot stand the day-break of my eyes, [*Looks in her glass*]
Ay, see, they fly before this lovely face.
My hopes glow in my cheeks and speak my joy,
My eyes take fire at their own lustre, and
All my charms receive addition from themselves,
Pleased at their own perfection.
    Enter ACMAT.[3]

ACMAT: The prince is coming, he follows hard
    Upon the scent, and soon the royal hunter
    Will press on to find your charms at bay.
    He seems disgusted at the Princess.
    You have a nobler game to play.
    Let him not find you vicious, and his throne
    And bed are surely yours forever.

HOMAIS: What? To conceal desire when every
    Atom of me trembles with it! I'll strip
    My passion naked of such guile, lay it
    Undressed and panting at his feet, then try
    If all his temper can resist it. [*Music flourish*]
    But hark! The sign the Prince is coming.
    My love distracts me. Where shall I run
    That I may gather strength to stem this tide
    Of joy? Should he now take my senses in
    Their hurry, the rage my passion gives would
    Make my fate more sudden than severest
    Disappointments. Coward heart, dar'st thou not
    Stand the enjoyment of thy own desires?
    Must I then grant thee time to reason with?
    Thy weakness be gone, and see thou do not
    Trifle moments more rich than all the
    Blooming years thou hast pass'd.

---

[3] A eunuch, and Homais's friend and confidant.

109

[She goes in. Song and music.]

> *Unguarded lies the wishing maid,*
> *Distrusting not to be betrayed,*
> *Ready to fall, with all her charms,*
> *A shining treasure to your arms.*
>
> *Who hears this story must believe,*
> *No swain can truer joy receive.*
> *Since to take love and give it too*
> *Is all that love for hearts can do.*

Enter LEVAN *and* ISMAEL.

LEVAN: Since I have entered this enchanted palace,
And trod the ground where Homais dwells,
Methinks I walk in clouds, and breath the air of love.
There's not a strain the music gave
But melted part of my resolves.
Where's the Protector?[4] My sinking virtue
Needs a prop. It staggers far, and much I
Doubt will ever re-collect again.

ISMAEL: No matter. Let the painted idol fall.
A tomb so rich as Homais' arms
Would make one fond of fate. Look back to ages
Past, and say 'What hero thought not love his
Richest purchase? That gave their sword the
Keenest edge, and sent them round the Universe
To hunt applause from the fair mouth of some
Exalted charmer.'

LEVAN: You speak of lawful loves. Were mine but such
I'd gladly lose the rank of kings, yet find
More joys than ever circled in a monarch's crown.
But incest shocks my nature, blisters my
Tongue, and carries venom in it. Avaunt,
Be gone, and do not crowd my thoughts, I'd tear
My reason from its centre ere that should
Make it giddy, divorce my body from
Its life rather than wallow in mud.
And yet the gathering cloud looks monstrous black;
Should it once burst, 'twould surely scatter fate.

ISMAEL: For shame, belie not thus our sex's courage!
Forgive me, Sir, I'm zealous for your joys.
I'll fetch the Princess' eyes, and try if they'll

---

4 The Prince of Libardian.

Not make you blush your cowardice away.
ISMAEL *leads* HOMAIS *in.*
LEVAN: By Heav'n, a greater miracle than Heav'n can show.
Not the bright empress of the sky
Can boast such majesty. No artist could
Define such beauty. See how the dazzling
Form gives on; she cuts the yielding air, and
Fills the space with glory. Respect should carry
Me to her, but admiration here has
Fixed my feet, unable to remove.
HOMAIS: Where shall I turn my guilty eyes?
Oh, I could call on mountains now to sink my shame,
Or hide me in the clefts of untried rocks,
Where roaring billows should outbeat remembrance.
Love, which gave courage till the trial came,
That led me on to this extravagance,
Proves much more coward than the heart he fills,
And like false friends in this extremity,
Thrusts me all naked on to meet a foe
Whose sight I have not courage to abide.
[*She leans on* ISMAEL, *and holds her handkerchief to her face*]
LEVAN: Permit me take this envious cloud away
That I may gaze on all the wonders there.
Oh, do not close those beauteous eyes, unless
Indeed you think there's nothing here deserves
Their shining.
HOMAIS: The light in yours eclipses mine.
See how they wink and cannot bear your lustre.
Oh, could I blush my shame away, then I
Would say your charms outgo my wishes
And I'm undone by too much excellence.
LEVAN: As strangers a salute is due. Were the
Protector here, he'd not refuse it. [*They kiss*]
'Tis ecstasy and more. What have I done?
Her heart beats at her lips, and mine flies up
To meet it. See the roses fade, her swimming
Eyes give lessening light, and now they dart no more.
She faints! By heav'n, I've caught the poison
Too, and grow unable to support her.
[*She sinks down in a chair, he falls at her feet.*]
ACMAT: (He's caught, as surely as we live.
Her eyes have truer magic than a philtre.
We'll not intrude into a monarch's secrets.
The god of love himself is painted blind,

111

To teach all other eyes they should be veiled
Upon his sacred mysteries.)
    [*He shuts the scene, screens and curtains are drawn to conceal the couple.*]

Dorothy Wordsworth

FROM

The Grasmere Journals (1802–3)

*D*orothy Wordsworth lived with her brother William for most of her life, keeping intermittent journals which document their life together. As Dorothy was especially interested in country matters and the changing face of the natural world, the journals are remarkable for their cool and evocative description. Extracts from the journals were first published in William Knight's* Life of Wordsworth *(1889). Dorothy also wrote some twenty poems, five of which were published in her lifetime, initially under William's name. These extracts are taken from* Journals of Dorothy Wordsworth, *ed. Mary Moorman (Oxford, 1971). For an account of Dorothy as a writer see Margaret Homans,* Women' Writers and Poetic Identity *(Princeton, N.J., 1980).*

Saturday, 14 February, 1802

I got tea when I reached home and read German till about 9 o'clock. Then Molly went away and I wrote to Coleridge. Went to bed at about 12 o'clock. I slept in Wm's bed, and I slept badly, for my thoughts were full of William.[5]

Monday, 15th February, 1802

I was starching small linen all the morning. It snowed a good deal and was terribly cold. After dinner it was fair, but I was obliged to run all the way to

---

[5] William is away visiting Mary Hutchinson to whom he is engaged.

the foot of the White Moss to get the least bit of warmth into me. I found a letter from C.[6] – he was much better – this was very satisfactory but his letter was not an answer to William's which I expected. A letter from Annette.[7] I got tea when I reached home and then set on to reading German. I wrote part of a letter to Coleridge, went late to bed and slept badly.

Tuesday, 16 February, 1802

A fine morning but I had persuaded myself not to expect William, I believe because I was afraid of being disappointed. I ironed all day. He came in just at Tea time, had only seen Mary H. for a couple of hours between Emont Bridge and Hartshorn tree. Mrs C.[8] better. He had had a difficult journey over Kirkstone, and came home by Threlkeld – his mouth and breath were very cold when he kissed me. We spent a sweet evening. He was better – had altered the pedlar.[9] We went to bed pretty soon and we slept better than we expected and had no bad dreams.

Saturday, 19th June, 1802

I sate up a while after William – he then called me down to him. (I was writing to Mary H.) I read Churchill's Rosciad. Returned again to my writing and did not go to bed till he called to me. The shutters were closed, but I heard the Birds singing. There was our own Thrush shouting with an impatient shout – so it sounded to me. The morning was still, the twittering of the little Birds was very gloomy. The owls had hooted a quarter of an hour before, now the cocks were crowing. It was near daylight, I put out my candle and went to bed. In a little time I thought I heard William snoring, so I composed myself to sleep – smiling at my sweet Brother.

Sunday, 20 June, 1802

He had slept better than I could have expected but he was far from well all day; we were in the orchard a great part of the morning. After tea we walked upon our own path for a long time. We talked sweetly together about the disposal of our riches. We lay upon the sloping Turf. Earth and sky were so lovely that they melted our very hearts. The sky to the north was of a chastened yet rich yellow fading into pale blue and streaked and scattered over with steady islands of purple melting away into shades of pink. It made my heart almost

6 Coleridge.
7 Annette Vallon, at one time William's mistress and the mother of his child.
8 Mrs Clarkson.
9 William's poem 'The Pedlar' was begun in the Spring of 1798, and revised early in 1802. It eventually formed part of *The Excursion*.

feel like a vision to me. We afterwards took our cloaks and sate in the orchard. Mr and Miss Simpson called. We told them of our expected good fortune. We were astonished and somewhat hurt to see how coldly Mr Simpson received it – Miss S. seemed very glad. We went into the house when they left us, and Wm went to bed. I sate up about an hour. He then called me to talk to him – he could not fall asleep.

Monday, 21 June, 1802

William was obliged to be in Bed late, he had slept so miserably. It was a very fine morning, but as we did not leave home till 12 o'clock, it was very hot. I parted from my Beloved[10] in the green lane above the Blacksmith's then went to dinner at Mr Simpson's. We walked afterwards in the garden.

October, 1802

Mary first met us in the avenue.[11] She looked so fat and well that we were made very happy by the sight of her. Then came Sara, and last of all Joanna. Tom was forking corn standing upon the corn cart.[12] We dressed ourselves immediately and got tea – the garden looked gay with asters and sweet peas. I looked at everything with tranquillity and happiness – was ill on Saturday and on Sunday and continued to be during most of the time of our stay.[13] . . . On Monday 4th October 1802, my Brother William was married to Mary Hutchinson. I slept a good deal of the night and rose fresh and well in the morning. At a little after 8 o'clock I saw them go down the avenue towards the Church. William had parted from me upstairs. I gave him the wedding ring – with how deep a blessing! I took it from my forefinger where I had worn it the whole of the night before – he slipped it again onto my finger and blessed me fervently.[14] When they were absent my dear little Sara prepared the breakfast. I kept myself as quiet as I could, but when I saw the two men[15] running up the walk, coming to tell us it was over, I could stand it no longer and threw myself on the bed where I lay it stillness, neither hearing or seeing any thing, till Sara came upstairs to me and said 'They are coming'. This forced me from the bed where I lay and I moved I knew not how straight forward, faster than my strength could carry me till I met my beloved William and fell upon his bosom.

10 William was going to Eusemere on business.
11 William and Dorothy travelled to the Hutchinsons for the forthcoming marriage.
12 Mary Hutchinson's sisters and brother.
13 This sentence is crossed out in the manuscript.
14 This sentence is crossed out in the manuscript.
15 Mary's brothers John and Tom who acted as witnesses to the marriage.

24 December, 1802, Christmas Eve

William is now sitting by me at half past 10 o'clock. I have been beside him ever since tea running the heel of a stocking, repeating some of his sonnets to him, listening to his own repeating, reading some of Milton's and the Allegro and Penseroso. It is a quiet keen frost. Mary is in the parlour below attending to the baking of cakes and Jenny Fletcher's pies. Sara is in bed in the toothache, and so we are – beloved William is turning over the leaves of Charlotte Smith's sonnets, but he keeps his hand to his poor chest pushing aside his breastplate. Mary is well and I am well. . .

Saturday, 9 January, 1803

Wm and I walked to Rydale – no letters. Still as mild as Spring, a beautiful moonlight evening and a quiet night but before morning the wind rose and it became dreadfully cold. We were not well on Sunday Mary and I.

Sunday, 9 January, 1803[16]

Mary lay long in bed, and did not walk. Wm and I walked in Brothers Wood. I was *astonished* with the beauty of the place, for I had never been there since my return home – never since before I went away in June!!

Mary Wollstonecraft Shelley

FROM

Frankenstein,
or The Modern Prometheus (1819)

V *ictor Frankenstein, an ambitious student of science, has left his family to study in Ingolstadt. His research leads him to attempt the creation*

---

[16] Dorothy made a mistake in writing the date. This entry was for Sunday, 10 January, 1803.

*of life, animating a monstrous being whom he has constructed out of
fragments from the charnel houses.*

I t was on a dreary night of November, that I beheld the accomplishment of
my toils. With an anxiety that almost amounted to agony, I collected the
instruments of life around me, that I might infuse a spark of being into the
lifeless thing that lay at my feet. It was already one in the morning; the rain
pattered dismally against the panes, and my candle was nearly burnt out, when,
by the glimmer of the half-extinguished light, I saw the dull yellow eye of the
creature open; it breathed hard, and a convulsive motion agitated its limbs.

How can I describe my emotions at this catastrophe, or how delineate the
wretch whom with such infinite pains and care I had endeavoured to form? His
limbs were in proportion, and I had selected his features as beautiful. Beautiful!
– Great God! His yellow skin scarcely covered the work of muscles and arteries
beneath; his hair was of a lustrous black, and flowing; his teeth of a pearly
whiteness; but these luxuriances only formed a more horrid contrast with his
watery eyes, that seemed almost of the same colour as the dun white sockets
in which they were set, his shrivelled complexion and straight black lips.

The different accidents of life are not so changeable as the feelings of
human nature. I had worked hard for nearly two years, for the sole purpose
of infusing life into an inanimate body. For this I had deprived myself of
rest and health. I had desired it with an ardour that far exceeded moderation; but now that I had finished, the beauty of the dream vanished, and
breathless horror and disgust filled my heart. Unable to endure the aspect
of the being I had created, I rushed out of the room, and continued a long
time traversing my bed-chamber, unable to compose my mind to sleep. At
length lassitude succeeded to the tumult I had before endured; and I threw
myself on the bed in my clothes, endeavouring to seek a few moments of
forgetfulness. But it was in vain: I slept, indeed, but I was disturbed by the
wildest dreams. I thought I saw Elizabeth,[17] in the bloom of health, walking
in the streets of Ingolstadt. Delighted and surprised, I embraced her; but
as I imprinted the first kiss on her lips, they became livid with the hue
of death; her features appeared to change, and I thought that I held the
corpse of my dead mother in my arms; a shroud enveloped her form, and
I saw the grave-worms crawling in the folds of the flannel. I started from
my sleep with horror; a cold dew covered my forehead, my teeth chattered,
and every limb became convulsed: when, by the dim and yellow light of the
moon, as it forced its way through the window shutters, I beheld the wretch
– the miserable monster whom I had created. He held up the curtain of the
bed; and his eyes, if eyes they may be called, were fixed on me. His jaws
opened, and he muttered some inarticulate sounds, while a grin wrinkled his
cheeks. He might have spoken, but I did not hear; one hand was stretched

[17] His adopted sister and fiancée.

out, seemingly to detain me, but I escaped, and rushed down stairs. I took refuge in the courtyard belonging to the house which I inhabited; where I remained during the rest of the night, walking up and down in the greatest agitation, listening attentively, catching and fearing each sound as if it were to announce the approach of the demoniacal corpse to which I had so miserably given life.

Christina Rossetti
After Death (1849)

The curtains were half drawn, the floor was swept
  And strewn with rushes, rosemary and may
  Lay thick upon the bed on which I lay,
Where through the lattice ivy-shadows crept.
He leaned above me, thinking that I slept
  And could not hear him; but I heard him say,
  'Poor child, poor child'; and as he turned away
Came a deep silence, and I knew he wept.
He did not touch the shroud, or raise the fold
  That hid my face, or take my hand in his,
  Or ruffle the smooth pillows for my head:
He did not love me living; but once dead
He pitied me; and very sweet it is
To know he still is warm though I am cold.

Kate Chopin
FROM
The Awakening (1899)

*E*dna Pontellier has decided to take her life into her own hands, in spite of social disapproval, and has left her husband and children. The man

that she loves has come to see her.

W hen she came back Robert was not examining the pictures and magazines as before; he sat off in the shadow, leaning his head back on the chair
as if in a reverie. Edna lingered a moment beside the table, arranging the books
there. Then she went across the room to where he sat. She bent over the arm
of his chair and called his name.

'Robert,' she said, 'are you asleep?'

'No,' he answered, looking up at her.

She leaned over and kissed him – a soft, cool, delicate kiss whose voluptuous
sting penetrated his whole being – then she moved away from him. He followed,
and took her in his arms, just holding her close to him. She put her hand up to
his face and pressed his cheek against her own. The action was full of love and
tenderness. He sought her lips again. Then he drew her down upon the sofa
beside him and held her hand in both of his.

'Now you know,' he said, 'now you know what I have been fighting against since
last summer at Grand Isle, what drove me away and drove me back again.'

'Why have you been fighting against it?' she asked. Her face glowed with
soft lights.

'Why? Because you were not free; you were Léonce Pontellier's wife. I couldn't
help loving you if you were ten times his wife, but so long as I went away from
you and kept away I could help telling you so.' She put her free hand up to his
shoulder, and then against his cheek, rubbing it softly. He kissed her again. His
face was warm and flushed.

'There in Mexico I was thinking of you all the time, and longing for you.'

'But not writing to me,' she interrupted.

'Something put into my head that you cared for me, and I lost my senses. I
forgot everything but a wild dream of your some way becoming my wife.'

'Your wife!'

'Religion, loyalty, everything would give way if only you cared.'

'Then you must have forgotten that I was Léonce Pontellier's wife.'

'Oh! I was demented, dreaming of wild, impossible things, recalling men who
had set their wives free, we have heard of such things.'

'Yes, we have heard of such things.'

'I came back full of vague, mad intentions. And when I got here – '

'When you got here you never came near me!' She was still caressing
his cheek.

'I realized what a cur I was to dream of such a thing, even if you had been
willing.'

She took his face between her hands and looked into it as if she would never
withdraw her eyes more. She kissed him on the forehead, the eyes, the cheeks,
and the lips.

'You have been a very, very foolish boy, wasting your time dreaming of

impossible things when you speak of Mr Pontellier setting me free! I am no longer one of Mr Pontellier's possessions to dispose of or not. I give myself where I choose. If he were to say, "Here, Robert, take her and be happy, she is yours", I should laugh at you both.'

His face grew a little white. 'What do you mean?' he asked.

There was a knock at the door. Old Celestine came in to say that Madame Ratignolle's servant had come around the back way with a message that Madame had been taken sick and begged Mrs Pontellier to go to her immediately.

'Yes, yes,' said Edna, rising. 'I promised. Tell her yes – to wait for me. I'll go back with her.'

'Let me walk over with you,' offered Robert.

'No,' she said, 'I will go with the servant.' She went into her room to put on her hat, and when she came in again she sat once more upon the sofa beside him. He had not stirred. She put her arms about his neck.

'Good-by, my sweet Robert. Tell me good-by.' He kissed her with a degree of passion which had not before entered into his caress, and strained her to him.

'I love you,' she whispered, 'only you, no one but you. It was you who awoke me last summer out of a life-long, stupid dream. Oh! you have made me so unhappy with your indifference. Oh! I have suffered, suffered! Now you are here we shall love each other, my Robert. We shall be everything to each other. Nothing else in the world is of any consequence. I must go to my friend; but you will wait for me? No matter how late; you will wait for me, Robert?'

'Don't go, don't go! Oh! Edna, stay with me,' he pleaded. 'Why should you go? Stay with me, stay with me.'

'I shall come back as soon as I can; I shall find you here.' She buried her face in his neck, and said good-by again. Her seductive voice, together with his great love for her, had enthralled his senses, had deprived him of every impulse but the longing to hold her and keep her.... [18]

She let herself in at the gate, but instead of entering she sat upon the step of the porch. The night was quiet and soothing. All the tearing emotion of the last few hours seemed to fall away from her like a sombre, uncomfortable garment, which she had but to loosen to be rid of. She went back to that hour before Adèle had sent for her; and her senses kindled afresh in thinking of Robert's words, the pressure of his arms, and the feeling of his lips upon her own. She could picture at that moment no greater bliss on earth than possession of the beloved one. His expression of love had already given him to her in part. When she thought that he was there at hand, waiting for her, she grew numb with the intoxication of expectancy. It was so late; he would be asleep perhaps. She would awaken him with a kiss. She hoped he would be asleep that she might arouse him with her caresses.

Still she remembered Adèle's voice whispering, 'Think of the children; think

[18] Edna is gone for some hours, and is reminded in the interval of her duty to her children.

of them.' She meant to think of them; that determination had driven into her soul like a death wound – but not tonight. Tomorrow would be time to think of everything.

Robert was not waiting for her in the little parlour. He was nowhere at hand. The house was empty. But he had scrawled on a piece of paper that lay in the lamplight:

'I love you. Good-by – because I love you.'

Edna grew faint when she read the words. She went and sat on the sofa. Then she stretched herself out there, never uttering a sound. She did not sleep. She did not go to bed. The lamp sputtered and went out. She was still awake in the morning, when Celestine unlocked the kitchen door and came in to light the fire. . . . [19]

The water of the Gulf stretched out before her, gleaming with the million lights of the sun. The voice of the sea is seductive, never ceasing, whispering, clamouring, murmuring, inviting the soul to wander in abysses of solitude. All along the white beach, up and down, there was no living thing in sight. A bird with a broken wing was beating the air above, reeling, fluttering, circling disabled down, down to the water.

Edna had found her old bathing suit still hanging, faded, upon its accustomed peg.

She put it on, leaving her clothing in the bath-house. But when she was there beside the sea, absolutely alone, she cast the unpleasant, pricking garments from her, and for the first time in her life she stood naked in the open air, at the mercy of the sun, the breeze that beat upon her, and the waves that invited her.

How strange and awful it seemed to stand naked under the sky! How delicious! She felt like some new-born creature, opening its eyes in a familiar world that it had never known.

The foamy wavelets curled up to her white feet, and coiled like serpents about her ankles. She walked out. The water was chill, but she walked on. The water was deep, but she lifted her white body and reached out with a long, sweeping stroke. The touch of the sea is sensuous, enfolding the body in its soft, close embrace.

She went on and on. She remembered the night she swam far out, and recalled the terror that seized her at the fear of being unable to regain the shore. She did not look back now, but went on and on, thinking of the bluegrass meadow that she had traversed when a little child, believing that it had no beginning and no end.

Her arms and legs were growing tired.

She thought of Léonce and the children. They were a part of her life. But they need not have thought that they could possess her, body and soul. How Mademoiselle Reisz would have laughed, perhaps sneered, if she knew! 'And you call yourself an artist! What pretensions, Madame! The artist must possess

[19] The next day Edna walks down to the beach.

the courageous soul that dares and defies.'
Exhaustion was pressing upon and overpowering her.
'Good-by – because, I love you.' He did not know; he did not understand.
He would never understand. Perhaps Doctor Mandelet would have understood
if she had seen him – but it was too late; the shore was far behind her, and her
strength was gone.

She looked into the distance, and the old terror flamed up for an instant, then
sank again. Edna heard her father's voice and her sister Margaret's. She heard
the barking of an old dog that was chained to the sycamore tree. The spurs of
the cavalry officer clanged as he walked across the porch. There was the hum
of bees, and the musky odour of pinks filled the air.

Anaïs Nin

FROM

The Delta of Venus (1940–1)

*W*hen *Henry Miller was offered a hundred dollars a month to write
erotic stories for a book collector, Anaïs Nin also took up the task.
Her stories were well received though she was directed to 'leave out the
poetry' and 'concentrate on sex'. She decided to publish her erotica in
1976 'because it shows the beginning efforts of a woman in a world that
had been the domain of men'. The extracts are taken from 'The Hungarian
Adventurer', 'Pierre' and 'The Basque and Bijou'.*

The Hungarian Adventurer

*B*ut after a few years he was off again. The habit was too strong; the habit of
freedom and change.

He travelled to Rome and took a suite at the Grand Hotel. The suite happened
to be next to that of the Spanish Ambassador, who was staying there with his
wife and two small daughters. The Baron charmed them, too. The Ambassador's
wife admired him. They became so friendly and he was so delightful with the
children, who did not know how to amuse themselves in this hotel, that soon
it became a habit of the two little girls, upon getting up in the morning, to go
and visit the Baron and awaken him with laughter and teasing, which they were
not permitted to lavish upon their more solemn father and mother.

ANAÏS NIN

So heated were the games, so great were the confusion of the battle and the abandon of the little girls at play, that very often his hand went everywhere he wanted it to go.

Pierre

W hen he was a youth, Pierre wandered off towards the quays very early one morning. He had been walking along the river for some time when he was arrested by the sight of a man trying to pull up a nude body from the river to the deck of one of the barges. The body was caught on the anchor chain. Pierre rushed to the man's help. Together they managed to get the body on the deck.

Then the man turned to Pierre and said, 'You wait while I get the police,' and he ran off. The sun was just beginning to rise, and it touched the naked body with a roseate glow. Pierre saw it was not only a woman, but a very beautiful woman. Her long hair clung to her shoulders and full, round breasts. Her smooth golden skin glistened. He had never seen a more beautiful body, washed clear by the water, with lovely soft contours exposed.

He watched her with fascination. The sun was drying her. He touched her. She was still warm and must have died but a short while before. He felt for her heart. It was not beating. Her breast seemed to cling to his hand.

He shivered, then leaned over and kissed her breast. It was elastic and soft under his lips, like a live breast. He felt a sudden violent sexual urge. He continued to kiss the woman. He parted her lips. As he did so, a little water came out from between them, which seemed to him like her very own saliva. He had the feeling that if he kissed her long enough she would come to life. The heat of his lips was passing into hers. He kissed her mouth, her nipples, her neck, her belly, and then his mouth descended to the wet curled pubic hair. It was like kissing her under water.

She lay stretched out, with her legs slightly parted, her arms straight along her sides. The sun was turning her skin to gold, and her wet hair looked like seaweed.

How he loved the way her body lay, exposed and defenseless. How he loved her closed eyes and slightly opened mouth. Her body had the taste of dew, of wet flowers, of wet leaves, of early morning grass. Her skin was like satin under his fingers. He loved her passivity and silence.

He felt himself burning, tense. Finally he fell on her, and as he began to penetrate her, water flowed from between her legs, as if he were making love to a naiad. His movements caused her body to undulate. He continued to thrust himself into her, expecting at any moment to feel her response, but her body merely moved in rhythm with his.

Now he was afraid the man and the police would arrive. He tried to hurry and satisfy himself, but he couldn't. He had never taken so long. The coolness and wetness of the womb, her passivity, his enjoyment so prolonged – yet he could not come.

123

He moved desperately, to rid himself of his torment, to inject his warm liquid into her cold body. Oh, how he wanted to come at this moment, while kissing her breasts, and he frantically urged his sex within her, but still he could not come. He would be found there by the man and the policeman, lying over the body of the dead woman.

Finally he lifted her body from the waist, bringing her up against his penis and pushing violently into her. Now he heard shouts all around, and at that moment he felt himself exploding inside of her. He withdrew, dropped the body, and ran away.

This woman haunted him for days. He could not take a shower without remembering the feel of the wet skin and seeing how she shone in the dawn. Never again would he see so beautiful a body. He could not hear rain without remembering how the water came out between her legs and out of her mouth, and how soft and smooth she was.

The Basque and Bijou

As she lay there a big dog appeared through the trees and came up to her. He began to sniff at her, with evident pleasure. Bijou screamed and struggled to raise herself. But the enormous dog had planted himself over her and was trying to insert his nose between her legs.

Then the Basque, a cruel expression in his eyes, made a signal to Elena's lover. Pierre understood. They held Bijou's arms and legs still and let the dog sniff his way to the place he wanted to smell. He began to lick the satin chemise with delight, in the very place a man would have liked to lick it.

The Basque unfastened her underwear and let the dog continue to lick her carefully and neatly. His tongue was rough, much rougher than a man's, and long and strong. He licked and licked with much vigour, and the three men were watching now.

Elena and Leila also felt as if they were being licked by the dog. They were restless. They all watched, wondering if Bijou was feeling any pleasure.

At first she was terrified and struggled violently. Then she grew weary of moving uselessly and hurting her wrists and ankles, held so strongly by the men. The dog was beautiful, with a big tousled head, a clean tongue.

The sun fell on Bijou's pubic hair, which looked like brocade. Her sex was glistening wet, but no one knew whether it was from the dog's tongue or her pleasure. When her resistance began to die down, the Basque got jealous, kicked off the dog and freed her.

Angela Carter

FROM

Heroes and Villains (1969)

Marianne is the daughter of a professor of history living in an em-battled city after a worldwide catastrophe. During a skirmish with the savages who live outside the city walls, Marianne has joined the barbarian Jewel who leads one of the lawless contingents. Now married to Jewel, Marianne is travelling with the tribe. Here she breaks away from the group to find that the half-witted child of Jewel's 'tutor', Dr Donally, usually chained up and regularly beaten, has followed her.

She sat on the bank and paddled her hand in the standing water. The setting sun beamed red darts through the brown stems of hazel and dyed the still stream with henna. The hazels were covered with nuts. She listened to the soft plop of water through her fingers. She was moist with sweat and had scarcely taken off her clothes for weeks, had slept, walked, ridden, attended a burial, killed a man/not-man and gone to a public execution of justice in the same shirt and trousers; it was a wonder she was not yet overwhelmed with lice, though she often trapped a flea. She put her burning cheek flat down against the cool face of the water and, when she raised her head, the half-witted boy was squatted on the bank beside her, as if they had made a secret assignation for this place but had forgotten to mention it to one another. Some trick of the amber light turned his bare shoulders a healthier colour than usual. He picked his nose with the finger that wore Jewel's ruby ring, if it were a real ruby and not glass. She saw the mark of his collar round his neck.

'Why does your father keep you chained up so much?' she asked him.

'He's afraid of me because I have better fits than he does,' said the boy. 'Watch me.'

He rolled his eyes, foamed at the mouth and threshed about on the grass so vigorously she was afraid he would hurt himself.

'Stop it,' she said firmly. He shuddered to a standstill and fixed her with white, astonished eyes. His foam-flecked tongue lolled over his pale, cracked, swollen lips.

'Of course, you're Jewel's woman, aren't you,' he said as though this explained everything.

'I'm his wife,' she said.

'Same thing.'

'No, it isn't. There's no choice in being a wife. It is entirely out of one's hands.'

He wagged his dirty brown head; he did not understand her.

'It's the same thing,' he insisted.

'No.'

''Tis.'

'No.'

''Tis! 'Tis! 'Tis!' Again he rolled over and over shouting ''Tis!' in a cracked, imperious voice until Marianne said firmly: 'You're making a fool of yourself.'

He started up, gazing at her with something like wonder because she stopped him.

'What do you mean?'

He was panting. The serpents on his breast writhed in and out and curled round the old bruises on his ribs.[20] He raised his hands and hid behind them, squinting through his fingers at her; his movements were sinuous but erratic, if he had known how to be graceful it would have been delightful to watch him. He rocked back and forth on his heels until, without the shadow of a warning, he jumped on her. He was weightless as a hollow-boned bird or an insect that carries its structure on its outside without a cargo within. She could have pushed him away maybe with one finger, even have thrown him into the stream had she wished to defend herself but she realized this was the first opportunity she had had to betray her husband and instantly she took advantage of it.

The gaunt, crazy, shameless child rolled her among the roots for a while as he probed underneath her clothes with fingers amazingly long and delicate but, it would seem, moved more by curiosity than desire and she wondered if he were too young to do it so she unbuttoned her shirt and rubbed his wet mouth against her breasts for him. The tips of her breasts were so tender she whined under her breath and he became very excited. He began to mutter incomprehensible snatches of his father's prayers and maxims and she roughly seized hold of him and crushed him inside her with her hand for she had not sufficient patience to rely on instinct. He made two or three huge thrusts and came with such a terrible cry it seemed the loss of his virginity caused him as much anguish or, at least, consternation as the loss of her own had done. He slid weakly out of her, shivering, but she retained him in her arms and kissed the tangles of his hair. She was unsatisfied but full of pleasure because she had done something irreparable, though she was not yet quite sure what it was. So they lay there for a while in the inexpressible stillness and sombre colours of evening. He touched her without sensible contact for his frail body gave out no warmth.

[20] The child's body is tattooed with serpents.

Sarah Murphy

FROM

Putting the Great Mother Together Again, or How the Cunt Lost its Tongue (1986)

*P*art *fiction, part theory, Murphy's protagonist considers the nature of the erotic. The extract is taken from* A Mazing Space: Writing Canadian Women Writing, *ed. Smaro Kamboureli and Shirley Neuman (Edmonton, 1986).*

Eros

— **E**ros – I think – Eros. Still there, moving through our world. And I get up quickly, startling my friend. – Back in a moment – I say and she nods, sure I have finally gone off, why didn't I do it before we sat down, I can hear the crack as my legs come apart, feel it too, to hunt the missing machine, and I hurry out after him, looking around, I know he must be here somewhere, a beginning for my quest: the Eros for our civilisation. But where has he gone, I know I saw him just a moment ago. And I stand and look around a moment, confused. Until I see a curly head, between two racks of blouses, the irregular Indian cottons and the regular polyesters, and I hurry off toward it, only to discover it belongs to an older black woman. – Excuse me – , I say, for coming upon her so quickly and so anxiously, before I go off again toward a short sandy head I see off toward the rows and rows of pantihose and tights becoming a little discouraged to discover it is a young woman with a punk haircut, – where's the net stuff – I hear her saying, and I turn to where there is a braid of black hair over by the cookies, tall and visible over the shelves, perfect I think a native Canadian Eros, only of course it is an especially tall South Asian immigrant, and I am not ready to ask yet, – are you by any chance related to our Great Mother Kunda? I am so sure I have seen him here that I must try once more, looking slowly around, hurrying quickly away, where, where, until I see another head of curly brown hair, a little tall, approaching the hotdog stand, that must be him, and hurry quickly over, yes, the shoulders are broad the hips slim, this must be it. Eros finally, I can ask him, what it is I need to know, and my hand reaches out just as I hear his voice whine – aw Mom, do I have to? – And my hand stops

suspended in mid-air. Only he must have felt its gesture somehow because he turns around. And I find myself looking up into the clear blue eyes and braced teeth of a 12-year-old hockey player.

A pretty 12-year-old hockey player if he would just keep his mouth closed. The kind who will be sitting around in those little change houses in four years complaining of how the girls try to seduce him, and who probably already leans over those anatomically specific pictures bought in the corner drugstores, the ones they will use for the Pervert, getting all hot breathed while he plays with his friends, their parts and not only hockey equipment, while gathered together in the backs of the wood shelters at the sides of unused summer rinks saying – so that's pussy. The kind I could have giggled over thirty years ago, never imagining him with more than his chest bare, complete with skates over the shoulder and a new Flames shirt his mother has picked out for him. Looking at me with his eyes and hands wide as I think what am I doing, what if I had grabbed him, what is this, me about to grab a young boy in the Bay basement, grabbed him *there* maybe – tell me about it – and his mother, paying for the hotdogs, what would she have said, am I just another pervert? Would there have been screams and accusations? So I smile and he smiles back, the hands going wider, a guilty expression coming over his face as he shows me they are empty, thank god, he thinks I'm a store detective maybe, accusing him of shoplifting, perfect I think and gather myself up to my full height which still isn't his, trying to look authoritative, what do I say now – you've stolen my sexual identity, my subjectivity, and I want it back – except that I can't blame him for something done so long ago, which leaves me with sneering, raising one part of my upper lip to say – sorry wrong person, you take care now – and to half smile, like I've got a secret, I know your secrets, which I think I do. More of his secrets than the shoplifted condom in the back pocket not for a 'chick' but for jerking off in his bedroom because I ask myself how I could have done it, gotten up to chase him when I need to go to the john, how I could have even taken it seriously, how the hell we got stuck with him anyway: with Eros, with an adolescent boy.

Because for all his nice young body I saw how he blushed. I saw the awkwardness in his hands I know how they breathe and come and their come embarrasses them even in dreams, how in other cultures other times they piss themselves the first night in whorehouses, the hours they spend in the john thinking of the girls they dare not approach, up off down, and clumsy. Beautiful and young and even good, and clumsy. In need of teaching and clumsy. How did I think, how could I have thought, that such a one as this would lead us out of this mess, that we could represent all our carnality in an inexperienced, searching, adolescent male. Until on my way back toward the bathroom I start to laugh, imagining him, not my hockey player Eros his first night in bed but the man who invented him, who borrowed Eros into our language, who one night decided that was the word to borrow – Eros yes, Eros – for *good* carnal love, for when it signified the edges of spirituality, for when it was divine, just soo-oo

divine, following in the path of the word 'erotic' that came into the language some 125 years before, directly from the French 'erotique' in 1651 the Oxford says, giving Eros as 1775, perfect, I think.

Imagining him vividly over his oak desk in his beautiful study behind leaded windows through which the moon shines, the Great Mother shining on him and all he can think of is adolescent boys. Which one of them was it I wonder. And who knows but the fact is I can't get rid of the image of a Benjamin Franklin type all dumpy in his silver buckled shoes and stockings tight to show the calves, though it must have been someone more like Pope – whatever is is right – , and only men *were* back then though women were allowed to kind of flutter around, and who else would you think of but the adolescent son of Aphrodite and Hermes, Venus and Mercury, I doubt even taking it back to when Eros was the son of the oldest of the Great Mothers the Great Mother night and had the strength of soul to guide men to Heaven, which is right enough I suppose, certainly that boy must need some kind of divinity to guide him to the difficult Heaven/haven of sexual discovery, a worthy task and probably necessary whispering to him the meaning of his mother's arms, but not exactly what the rest of us need and in any case that guy probably never even took it that far back but just correlated. Greeks were more 'in' in those neoclassical days than Romans, with Cupid who could only birth the word cupidity already become an insipid cherub. He probably just said: – well there's always Cupid, the god of love with his arrows, what's Greek for Cupid? Eros, okay Eros, we'll use Eros – , and here we are stuck with Eros through the years. Becoming the impulse toward bringing the world together in the sensual, the opposite of the puritanical, *Eros and Civilisation* and all the other wonderful tomes, and I am suddenly angry and not just for my Great Mother Porne, an aspect of Aphrodite who they made into a prostitute for having too many partners (*La Gran Puta* still a favourite Spanish curse and who knows in how many other languages) and named pornography after for writing about prostitutes, the dirty stinky cunty female side of sex, so that we still hate pornography and love eroticism and don't even know which word belongs to us, why we've accepted them.

But angry for all of us, angry for us now, angry even for the Pervert who after all bought it too, just a wee little bit exaggerated, you should at least have the good taste to wait for puberty, but who internalised into his cock all the values of a society which for so many hundreds of years has so profoundly hated the flesh, and feared in particular the female in the flesh, that for all we talk of it these days, the place it can least imagine sex is between consenting adults, especially if one of them happens to be a grown woman. Because sex is adolescent whether male or female, always adolescent, almost childish, so many of those airbrushed models, those perfect tens, no more than little boys with tits, preferably big tits but no longer and exclusively big tits, but let's make damn well sure about the lack of hips, about the narrow boyish hips and pert boyish ass, Eros trying on his mother's tits, no, not really his mother's tits, those tits have never completed any glandular mothering function, the virgin breast today more important than the

virgin vagina, a new purity through formula feeding pasted onto the body of an adolescent androgyne who can no longer even express the true hermaphrodite, Hermes and Aphrodite together, a functional whole, the Great Mother and her consort, the Great Mother and her penis, which attribute she takes to complete the cycle of time.

We get instead a store mannequin on whose broad chest and narrow hips penis or tits (but never cunt or even balls) can interchangeably be pasted, not a representation, but a reproduction that loses values or definition with each successive generation, each new stamping out of the coin, no matter how hard we exercise to keep his shape. Because who can possibly put any new energy (that energy always needed to renew symbol) toward making him last, to stop him from fading, into the woman in him, his other half, if even we are afraid of her, do specific exercises not to look like her, because who cares if your heart is sound and your body strong if it looks like a barrel shaped Central American peasant who's been through all the cycles and then some, a whole exercise class of daily tasks unto herself. Better an anorectic adolescent, even a pudgy prepubescent, and if we can't have the skin any more at least we can have the expressions, be eternally cute, like Doris Day was cute, or Linda Evans, beautiful and innocent and obviously pushing or pulling 50, still is; all sex kittens and never sex cats, the harmless cuteness not simply of the dependant but of the disembodied. An ethereal cheshire cat smile of a woman who even fading fast cannot grow or age or present any evidence of those dangerous cycles which make too evident the obvious for which the Great Mother was called Eve and thrown out of man's garden but whose voice still whispers through the pounding of the sexual workout: and one and two and three and four, and god and god and god and god and yes and yes and yes and yes (sex and death) and one and two and three and four fuck me fuck me fuck me fuck me (sex and birth) and one and two and three and four (sex and death) so good so good so good so good (sex and birth) and one and two and three and four (sex and death sex and death) YOU BITCH YOU BITCH YOU BITCH YOU WHORE (sex and control sex and technique sex and technology sex and violence). Sex. And the death of the other.

Alienation the only way out of the truth Eve tells us, the knowledge she gave us: that birth and death are inextricably connected, that sex connects them, that life is cyclic that the flesh sooner or later will rot, that yes, little Eros, just like Mommy Ishtar Aphrodite Arianrhod Kali Kore Coatlicue told you: sex is about making babies. Whether or not any one individual decides (as we finally can without giving up the workout) to have them or not, still the next generation is right there in all that spilled seed in all those wet cunts in all those babies small screaming mouths and shitty bums, the next generation and our death. And our continuance if we can let ourselves have it, the knowledge that tomorrow is of our making, poised on the edge of time and becoming. A place for the gods of maturity the adolescent too can worship instead of fear. Because it is that knowledge of standing on the edge, that return to the infancy of creation and

the creation of infancy that knows creation goes on, that is the profound centre in the middle of sex. In the middle of that little death, that little birth. From which we recoil and turn away in a rejection that may not simply cost us but this planet its life as we fail to look the future in the face and go back to pictures, images, reproductions, cruel or healthy, in the sexual exercise guide: and one and two and three and four, this is nothing nothing nothing nothing. Just a matter of friction.

DANGER

P leasure and pain are intimates. Both make the body achingly vulnerable. In love, as in suffering, there can be no holding back, no reserve, no secret places. Angela Carter's story makes the point: 'there is a striking resemblance between the act of love and the ministrations of a torturer'.

Torturer and victim, lover and beloved – if these are parallel, then a hierarchy in love is proposed. The connection between pleasure and pain is partly created by the assumption of a power-based relation. According to this formula there must be a 'top' and there must be a 'bottom'. In our culture, woman is always the 'bottom', man always the 'top'. She is the beloved, she is the victim; he is the lover, the wielder of power. Loving is something done to her; suffering is what she does.

The sado-masochistic patterns of heterosexual eroticism are pervasive and pernicious. It is difficult now to disentangle the true character of woman's acquiescence in the model of victim and torturer. Centuries of propaganda persuade some women that they are excited by surrender. Centuries of prohibition make it hard for other women to admit to, or act on, their desire for power.

The extracts in this section must be read with caution. The writer of the anonymous Greek love song is afraid; the speakers in Rossetti's poem and in Dickinson's are obscurely threatened with assault; Benedetta Carlini imagines herself tortured and beaten (and also married). But this should not suggest that the character of women's erotic life inevitably and 'naturally' includes fear, agreement to rape, or a wish to be beaten. What it does show is how convincingly and how persistently those elements have been forced into women's lives. So much so that, in the end, they do become an inextricable part of her sexual existence.

Acquiescence is dangerous. For Margaret Watson and Jean Lachlan, found guilty of witchcraft in 1645, it was fatal. The records of Watson's

132

confession reveal her assumption of passivity when she gives herself 'ower to Sathane and of thair soule and bodie totallie to his service'. By telling her story of sexual power ('...he appeired to the thryse, the first tyme lyke ane blak man and gripped the about the left pape and then had carnall deale withe the'), Watson became subject to another power – that of the state.

Death is the most extreme end of sexual complaisance. Loss of individuality is a slightly lower price. In Stevie Smith's poem the 'beautiful lady' is submerged in her fantasy lover. In Monique Wittig's text Ganymedea is ravished by the lightning power of Zeyna. In Charlotte Mew's story the authority of the church parallels the erotic power given over to men by women. Ella is on her honeymoon when she witnesses the sacrifice of the woman. The spectacle leaves her 'unstrung'; it leaves her brother exhilarated, admiring the dead woman's 'acquiescence in a rather splendid crime'.

Was the woman in Mew's story willing? Angela Carter's fairytale continues with the question of woman's complicity. When her heroine puts on the necklace of rubies she sees the reflection of a connoisseur's desire in her husband's eyes. She recognises her own 'potentiality for corruption'. When he, fully clothed, inspects her nakedness ('most pornographic of all confrontations') the heroine again sees herself with his eyes and, 'I was aghast to feel myself stirring'. At the end of the story she is rescued. But she must wear the mark of her shame, her complicity, her acquiescence, for the rest of her life.

'The Bloody Chamber' takes on the conventions of sado-masochism to deal with their implications with a feminist perspective. Two other texts here, though from widely different historical periods, suggest the possibility of a sexual role for woman which is not always that of victim.

In 'Les Deus Amanz' the princess begins by being exploited by her father; she 'had been a comfort to him ever since he had lost the queen. Many people reproached him for this...' In her relation with her lover the situation becomes more confused. She appears still to be the victim (she fasts, she is almost naked, she is to be carried), but in the course of the trial her power grows. The princess is literally on top. She remains strong and wise in recognising the limits of endurance. But her lover grows weak and foolishly insists on his own strength. Resisting the inference that he is not man enough, he will not drink the vitalising potion. In fact, the lover dies of an excess of virility.

Pat Califia's women have dispensed with men altogether. In 'The Calyx of Isis' the conventions of 'top' and 'bottom' are retained, but are

effectively subverted by being taken out of the thrall of heterosexuality. Power changes hands. The torturer is challenged. The pattern shatters.

Anonymous
Love Song (n.d. [BC])

Up, for mercy, and be going, –
　O will nothing rouse my dear?
These delays are my undoing;
　Up, or *he* will find us here.

What a mischief's in the making!
　Misery me, we're both undone!
See, the window, – dawn is breaking;
　Up, dear lover, and begone.[1]

Marie de France
Les Deus Amanz
(c. second half of C12th)

*T*he Lais of *Marie de France are found in various manuscripts held in Paris and London. The stories seem to have been circulating the British courts in the 1170s and 1180s. They were first published in 1819; see* The

---

[1] Translated by T. F. Higham, and taken from the *Oxford Book of Greek Verse in Translation*, ed. T. F. Higham and C. M. Bowra (Oxford, 1938).

Lais of Marie de France, *translated and with an introduction by Glyn S. Burgess annd Keith Busby (London, 1986).*

There once took place in Normandy a now celebrated adventure of two young people who loved each other and who both met their end because of love. The Bretons made a lay about them which was given the title *The Two Lovers*.

The truth is that in Neustria, which we call Normandy, there is a marvellously high mountain where the two young people lie. Near this mountain, on one side, a king, who was lord of the Pistrians, wisely and carefully had a city built which he named after the inhabitants and called Pitres. The name has survived to this day and there is still a town and houses there. We know the area well, for it is called the Valley of Pitres. The king had a beautiful daughter, a most courtly damsel who had been a comfort to him ever since he had lost the queen. Many people reproached him for thiss, and even his own people blamed him.[2] When he heard that people were talking thus, he was very sad and disturbed, and began to consider how he could prevent anyone seeking his daughter's hand. Far and near he had it proclaimed that whoever wanted to win his daughter ought to know one thing for certain: that it was decreed and destined that he should carry her in his arms, without resting, up the mountain outside the town. When the news was known and had spread throuughout the region, many made the atttempt, but without success. There weree some who made such an effort that they carried the girl halfway up the mountain, but could go no further and had to abandon the attempt. She remained unmarried for a long time, as no one wanted to seek her hand.

There was in the country a young man, noble and fair, the son of a count. He strove to perform well so as to be esteemed above all others and he frequented the king's court and often stayed there. He fell in love with the king's daughter and many times urged her to grant him her love and to love him truly. Because he was worthy and courtly, and because the king held him in high esteem, she granted him her love for which he humbly thanked her. They often spoke together and loved each other loyally, concealing their love as best they could so that no one would notice them. This suffering caused them much grief, but the young man considered it better to suffer these misfortunes than to make too much haste and thus fail. Love was a great affliction to him. Then once it happened that the young man, so wise, worthy and fair, came to his beloved and addressed his complaint to her, begging her in his anguish to elope with him, for he could no longer bear the pain. He knew full well that her father loved her so much that, if he asked for her, she would not be given to him unless he could carry her in his arms to the top of the mountain. The damsel answered him: 'Beloved, I know it is impossible for you to carry me, for you are not strong enough. But if I went away with you, my father would be sad and

---

[2] A curiously ambivalent formulation.

distressed and his life would be an endless torment. Truly, I love him so much
and hold him so dear that I would not wish to grieve him. You must decide
upon something else, for I will not hear of this. I have a relative in Salerno,
a rich woman with a large income, who has been there for more than thirty
years and who has practised the art of physic so much that she is well-versed
in medicines. She knows so much about herbs and roots that if you go to her,
taking with you a letter from me, and tell her your story, she will give thought
and consideration to the matter. She will give you such electuaries and such
potions as will revive you and increase your strength. When you come back
to this country, ask my father for me. He will consider you a child and tell
you about the agreement whereby he will give me to no one, however hard
he tries, unless he can carry me up the mountain in his arms without resting.'
The young man listened to the maiden's words and advice which brought him
great joy and he thanked his beloved, asking her for leave to depart.

He went back to his homeland and quickly equipped himself with rich clothes
and money, palfreys and pack-horses. Taking his most trusted men with him, the
young man went to stay at Salerno and speak with his beloved's aunt. He gave her
a letter from the girl and, when she had read it from start to finish, she retained
him with her until she knew all about him. She fortified him with medicines
and gave him a potion such that, however weary, afflicted, or burdened he might
be, it would refresh his whole body, even his veins and his bones, and restore
all his strength to him as soon as he had drunk it. Then he put the potion in
a vessel and took it back to his land.

On his return the young man, joyful and happy, did not stay long in his own
region. He went and asked the king for his daughter, saying that if he would
give her to him, he would take her and carry her up to the top of the mountain.
The king did not refuse him, and still considered it great folly as he was so
young, and as so many valiant, wise, and worthy men had made the attempt
unsuccessfully. He named the day, summoning his vassals, his friends, and all
those available to him, letting no one remain behind. People came from far
and wide because of the young girl and the young man who would attempt
to carry her up to the top of the mountain. The damsel made ready, fasting
and refraining from eating in order to lose weight, for she wished to help her
beloved. On the day everyone assembled, the young man, who had not forgotten
his potion, arrived first. The king led his daughter into the meadow towards the
Seine, where a great crowd gathered. She wore nothing but her shift, and the
young man took her in his arms. The little phial containing the potion (he well
knew that she had no wish to let him down) was given to her to carry, but I
fear it will be of little avail to him, because he knew no moderation. He set
off with her at a good pace and climbed the mountain half way. She brought
him such great happiness that he did not remember his potion, and when she
realized he was tiring, she said: 'My love, please drink. I know you are tiring,
so recover your strength.' The young man replied: 'Fair one, I feel my heart to
be strong. Providing I can still walk three paces, on no account shall I stop,

not even long enough to take a drink. These people would shout at us and deafen me with their noise, and they could easily distract me. I shall not stop here.' When he had climbed two thirds of the way, he nearly collapsed. The girl repeatedly begged him: 'My love, drink your potion.' Yet he would take no heed of her, and carried her onward in great pain. He reached the top, in such distress that he fell down and never rose again, for his heart left his body. The maiden saw her beloved and, thinking he had fainted, knelt down beside him and tried to make him drink. But he could not speak to her. Thus he died, just as I am telling you. She lamented him loudly and then threw away the vessel containing the potion, scattering its contents so that the mountain was well sprinkled with it, and the land and surrounding area much improved. Many good plants were found there which took root because of the potion.

Now I shall tell you about the girl: because she had lost her beloved, she was more distressed than ever before. She lay down beside him, took him in her arms and embraced him, kissing his eyes and his mouth repeatedly. Sorrow for him touched her heart and there this damsel died, who was so worthy, wise and fair. When the king and those who were waiting saw that they were not coming, they went after them and found them. The king fell to the ground in a swoon, and when he could speak, he lamented loudly, as did all the strangers. They left them there on the ground for three days, and then had a marble coffin brought and the two young people placed in it. On the advice of those present they buried them on top of the mountain and then departed.

Because of what happened to these two young people, the mountain is called The Mountain of the Two Lovers. The events took place just as I have told you, and the Bretons composed a lay about them.

Anonymous (Benedetta Carlini)

FROM

The First Investigation of Benedetta Carlini, 27 May 1619 and 8 July 1619

B *enedetta Carlini was investigated by the church authorities on several occasions in 1619 and 1620 because she was suspected of false*

137

accounts of visions and also of lesbian practices. These accounts of her visions are records made during the interrogation of 1619 and are among the documents in the State Archive at Florence (Miscellanea Medicea *376, insert 28). See Appendix in* Immodest Acts: The Life of a Lesbian Nun in Renaissance Italy *by Judith C. Brown (Oxford, 1986), pp. 141–9.*

On the twenty-seventh day of May, 1619

Benedetta confesses that on the second Friday of Lent of the year 1619, while in bed between two and three hours of the night[3] the thought came to her to suffer all the things suffered by Jesus Christ; and there appeared in front of her a crucified man as large as a good sized man, and he was alive and asked her if she were willing to suffer for his love because he was Jesus Christ; and she protested that if this were an illusion of the Devil she did not want to consent and would tell her Spiritual Father[4] and she made the sign of the cross. He assured her that he was God and that he wanted her to suffer for the duration of her life, that she should arrange herself in the form of a cross because he wanted to imprint his holy wounds in her body. When she did this, a flash burst forth from all of them, which she thought imprinted themselves in her hands. And on her head she saw many small rays that seemed to delineate her entire head and she felt great pains in it and in her hands. But afterwards a great contentment came into her heart. The large rays she saw were five, but those of the head were a great many more, but small ones; that she did not arrange her feet one on top of the other, but found them wounded and arranged without realising it; and she felt pain there. On Sundays they seem to be numb; on Mondays and Tuesdays she feels little or no pain; on all other days great pain; on Fridays more than any other days and on that day there is more bleeding, except for this morning as you have seen.

On the eighth day of July, 1619

To obey her Spiritual Father, she prayed to God that He send her travails instead of ecstasies and revelations, since it seemed to her that this would be safer against the deceits of the devil. And her prayer was heard, her bodily pains having started four years ago. But for almost the last two years they have been greater than in the first two since they come over her entire body, starting in the evening, and they last about six to eight hours in which there often appear young men armed with rough swords in hand to kill her. Other times they beat

[3] The hours for prayer, in this case, between 7 p.m. and 8 p.m..
[4] Her confessor.

her giving her great pain over her entire body. Another time there came one young man with a ring to tell her that he wanted her to be his bride and she answered him that she wanted to be the bride of Jesus. He wanted to put the ring on her finger by force, telling her companion to hold her hand. Other times they told her not to stay in this place, that she would become ill and that in the end she would not be certain of her salvation. And they said other things which she cannot remember. And this struggle, involving many temptations with these young men, lasted many times. [They told her] that she shouldn't persevere here but that she should leave, that this would be better for her. It seemed to her that she saw them infallibly, as she sees your Reverence. She seemed to recognise some, but she did not look at them except when she couldn't help it. And that they were from Pescia and she knew one from when he was small. She knew the one that wanted to marry her. They seemed handsome to her, but she didn't want to look at them. She hid from them and felt the pain of the beatings she received. It seemed to her that they pursued her with iron chains, sticks, and other objects, and swords in hand. She felt all bruised, but she did not see if she had bruises on her body. She never wanted that young man to touch her hand to put the ring on it. She was in bed when she saw them; and the pains that came from them were the worst she had, having them usually in the evening; and at first she didn't have them, but later they became worse. For two continuous winter nights they beat her, and they continued at other times, often in the summer. . . . She does not recall that they said anything to her, except for the one with the ring, but they spoke among themselves. Before the incident with the ring they beat her, and the one with the ring is always the first to beat her and is more presumptuous than the others and stronger at beating her. On the evening that he came to put the ring on her, he did not beat her at first, but came with much pretence and he spoke with the others; and it seemed that he wanted to do as she wished, that he would not alter her will; and because she did not want to consent, he turned to her enraged in order to beat her with all the others, he being the first. She does not recall that they said anything the first time she saw them, but it seemed to her they came with deceit and wanted to approach her with a certain deceitful look. And since she recognised that this is a trick of the Devil's, she turned the other way so as not to see them, and when they approached her, they came to her side even more enraged. She realised that they came to her side with a pleasing face and she turned so as not to see them, and she seemed to hear a voice that said she should not pay attention to them but should drive them away from her. And she saw them as a real presence not in her imagination. It seemed to her that they remained with her too long. The pains ceased gradually when they left. When she saw them appear, she would make the sign of the cross on her heart and it seemed to her that after doing this, they came nearer. . . . They seemed to be dressed in yellow-red gowns, and the one with the ring was dressed more neatly and handsomely than the others. And it seemed that he incited the others to beat her; without him it seemed they did nothing. It seemed to her that there

were four or five who beat her but all had companions; the former being the main ones but all beat her. And one time more of them came than ever, and she made the sign of the cross many times, and they could not come nearer, and they became more enraged and beat her harder than ever. Since they were two or three yards away, she did not know what they had in their hands, but although they started out handsome they turned ugly. And they beat her until the dawn bell, close to three or four hours of the night. She remained still and she seldom sent for another sister in order not to disturb anyone. At other times, the young men left enraged, but not as ugly as these last; this was in the winter. It seemed that they ceased to come before last Lent but she does not remember well. It seems that the last time they beat her and did not say anything. When they stopped coming, she felt little pain, and they stopped at Lent. She does not remember the day. And the pains stopped when the signs appeared, having at that time had few. And the worst pain was felt the evening that she received those signs, when she seemed to be beside herself. She does not remember having had either ecstasies or revelations during the pains.

Margaret Watson

Trial of Margaret Watson and Jean Lachlan, in the Parish of Carnwarth, for Witchcraft, by a Justiciary Court Held in Lanark (1644)

Excerpted from the account of the trial of Margaret Watson in The Register *of the Privy Council of Scotland, edited and abridged by P. Hume Brown, second series, vol. VIII, 1544–1660 (1908), pp. 146–51. Margaret Watson was found guilty and sentenced to death on 2 January, 1645.*

Followes the pointes of dittay gevin in and persweit be James Forrest, procuratour fiscall chosin and electit be the sadis justices, commissiouneres above writtin, against Margaret Watsoun and Jeane Lachland within the parochin of Carnewathe for witchecraft, consulteing with the devill, renunceing of ther baptisme and geving themselffes ower to Sathane and of thair soule and bodie totallie to his service, chairmeing be the devill his meanes, and quha themselffes ar possest be the devill and haveing of familiar spiriteis, and for practeising,

useing and frequenting with the devill and of his chairmes, airtes and pairtes of wichecraft respective and particularlie underwritten ilk ane of you for your awin pairtes as is heireefter dewydit, divers and severall tymes confest be yourselffes in presence of —,[5] be vertew of our soverane lordis commissioun gevin under his Hienes signet and subscriptiounes of ane number of his Majesteis Privie Counselloures, at Edinburgh, the sevint day of November, 1644. . . .

Thow being dilait be the saidis Helein Stewart and Katherein Schawe, tuo penitent wiches quha suffered deathe, as said is, quhairupone thow wes apprehendit as ane notorious wiche, thow hes (without any tortour or hard useage)[6] at Carnewathe the penult day of September, in presence of Sir John Daliel of Newtowne, knicht, Mr James Dowglas, minister at Carnewathe, William Inglis of Eastscheill, Mr Robert Alisowne and William Dowglas and of divers uthers, frielie confest as follows: – First, that thow was ane wiche and that malice and invy wes the caus and occasioun that thow enterit in covenant withe Sathan, and that he appeired to the thryse, the first tyme lyke ane blak man and gripped the about the left pape and then had carnall deale withe the, and thow decerned his nature to be cold, and that he come to the thrie severall tymes to thyne awin hous and promittit to give the ane mendes of suche as haid wrongit the, and particularlie of William Simpsone, father, quha, as thow alledgit, haid tane ane peace of land quhairof thow wes in possessioun. This thow art guyltie of lyke ane notorious wiche and this thow can not deny and art accused thairof. . . .

Thow hes confessed in presense of the saides persones, witnesses, that thow wes at diverse meitinges withe uther wiches in the devilleis companie, viz., at Niveinseat, heighe kirk of Lanark and in the kirk of Carnewathe (as the saids penitent wiches have declairit) and that all severall tymes in the night seasone at the wiche meitings thow and the rest of the wiches that wer withe the being ane great multitude did lift corpes of deceissit persones fra quhom ye tuik memberes, to accompleische thy devillische designes upone men and women, quhairby thow and they tuik severall lyffes, and at your meitings thow and the rest blasphamit Godis name and that ye usit to drink and daunce. Thir also thow art accused of, lyke ane notorious wiche, and this thow can not deny.

5 The names of the witnesses are not filled in in the original.
6 Torture and other 'hard usage' – sleep deprivation especially – was regularly used to extract confessions from suspected witches, but the practice was officially illegal in seventeenth-century Scotland.

Christina Rossetti
A Nightmare (1857)

This poem was left in manuscript at Rossetti's death and was published by her brother William Michael. He altered the manuscript reading of 'love' in the first line to 'friend'. He also changed 'rides' in the fifth line to 'hunts'.

I have a love in ghostland –
Early found, ah me how early lost! –
Blood-red seaweeds drip along that
    coastland
    By the strong sea wrenched
    and tost.

If I wake he rides me like a
    nightmare:
    I feel my hair stand up, my body
    creep:
Without light I see a blasting sight
    there,
    See a secret I must keep.

Emily Dickinson
He Fumbles at Your Soul (1862)

He fumbles at your Soul
As Players at the Keys
Before they drop full Music on –
He stuns you by degrees –
Prepares your brittle Nature
For the Ethereal Blow
By fainter Hammers – further heard –
Then nearer – Then so slow

Your Breath has time to straighten –
Your Brain – to bubble Cool –
Deals – One – imperial – Thunderbolt –
That scalps your naked Soul –

When Winds take Forests in their Paws –
The Universe – is still –

Charlotte Mew
A White Night (1903)

'The incident', said Cameron, 'is spoiled inevitably in the telling, by its merely accidental quality of melodrama, its sensational machinery, which to the view of anyone who didn't witness it, is apt to blur the finer outlines of the scene. The subtlety, or call it the significance, is missed, and unavoidably, as one attempts to put the thing before you, in a certain casual crudity, and inessential violence of fact. Make it a medieval matter – put it back some centuries – and the affair takes on its proper tone immediately, is tinctured with the sinister solemnity which actually enveloped it. But as it stands, a recollection, an experience, a picture, well, it doesn't reproduce; one must have the original if one is going to hang it on one's wall.'

In spite of which I took it down the night he told it and, thanks to a trick of accuracy, I believe you have the story as I heard it, almost word for word.

It was in the spring of 1876, a rainless spring, as I remember it, of white roads and brown crops and steely skies.

Sent out the year before on mining business, I had been then some eighteen months in Spain. My job was finished; I was leaving the Black Country, planning a vague look round, perhaps a little sport among the mountains, when a letter from my sister Ella laid the dust of doubtful schemes.

She was on a discursive honeymoon. They had come on from Florence to Madrid, and disappointed with the rank modernity of their last halt, wished to explore some of the least known towns of the interior: 'Something unique, untrodden, and uncivilised', she indicated modestly. Further, if I were free and amiable, and so on, they would join me anywhere in Andalusia. I was in fact to show them round.

I did 'my possible'; we roughed it pretty thoroughly, but the young person's passion for the strange bore her robustly through the risks and discomforts of those wilder districts which at best, perhaps, are hardly woman's ground.

King, on occasion nursed anxiety, and mourned his little luxuries; Ella accepted anything that befell, from dirt to danger, with a humorous composure dating back to nursery days – she had the instincts and the physique of a traveller, with a brilliancy of touch and a decision of attack on human instruments which told. She took our mule-drivers in hand with some success. Later, no doubt, their wretched beasts were made to smart for it, in the reaction from a lull in that habitual brutality which makes the animals of Spain a real blot upon the gay indifferentism of its people.

It pleased her to devise a lurid *Dies Irae* for these affable barbarians, a special process of reincarnation for the Spaniard generally, whereby the space of one dog's life at least should be ensured to him.

And on the day I'm coming to, a tedious, dislocating journey in a springless cart had brought her to the verge of quite unusual weariness, a weariness of spirit only, she protested, waving a hand toward our man who lashed and sang alternately, fetching at intervals a sunny smile for the poor lady's vain remonstrances before he lashed again.

The details of that day – our setting forth, our ride, and our arrival – all the minor episodes stand out with singular distinctness, forming a background in one's memory to the eventual, central scene.

We left our inn – a rough *posada* – about sunrise, and our road, washed to a track by winter rains, lay first through wide half-cultivated slopes, capped everywhere with orange trees and palm and olive patches, curiously bare of farms or villages, till one recalls the lawless state of those outlying regions and the absence of communication between them and town.

Abruptly, blotted in blue mist, vineyards and olives, with the groups of aloes marking off field boundaries, disappeared. We entered on a land of naked rock, peak after peak of it, cutting a jagged line against the clear intensity of the sky.

This passed again, with early afternoon our straight, white road grew feature-less, a dusty stretch, save far ahead the sun-tipped ridge of a sierra, and the silver ribbon of the river twisting among the barren hills. Toward the end we passed one of the wooden crosses set up on these roads to mark some spot of violence or disaster. These are the only signposts one encounters, and as we came up with it, our beasts were goaded for the last ascent.

Irregular grey walls came into view; we skirted them and turned in through a Roman gateway and across a bridge into a maze of narrow stone-pitched streets, spanned here and there by Moorish arches, and execrably rough to rattle over.

A strong illusion of the Orient, extreme antiquity and dreamlike stillness marked the place.

Crossing the grey arcaded Plaza, just beginning at that hour to be splashed with blots of gaudy colour moving to the tinkling of the mule-bells, we were soon upon the outskirts of the town – the most untouched, remote and, I believe, the most remarkable that we had dropped upon.

In its neglect and singularity, it made a claim to something like supremacy of charm. There was the quality of diffidence belonging to unrecognised abandoned personalities in that appeal.

That's how it's docketed in memory – a city with a claim, which, as it happened, I was not to weigh.

Our inn, a long, one-storeyed building with caged windows, most of them unglazed, had been an old palacio; its broken fortunes hadn't robbed it of its character, its air.

The spacious place was practically empty, and the shuttered rooms, stone-flagged and cool, after our shadeless ride, invited one to a prolonged siesta; but Ella wasn't friendly to a pause. Her buoyancy survived our meal. She seemed even to face the morrow's repetition of that indescribable experience with serenity. We found her in the small paved garden, sipping chocolate and airing Spanish with our host, a man of some distinction, possibly of broken fortunes too.

The conversation, delicately edged with compliment on his side, was on hers a little blunted by a limited vocabulary, and left us both presumably a margin for imagination.

Si, la Señora, he explained as we came up, knew absolutely nothing of fatigue, and the impetuosity of the *Señora*, this attractive eagerness to make acquaintance with it, did great honour to his much forgotten, much neglected town. He spoke of it with rather touching ardour, as a place unvisited, but *'digno de renombre illustre'*, worthy of high fame.

It has stood still, it was perhaps too stationary; innovation was repellent to the Spaniard, yet this conservatism, lack of enterprise, the virtue or the failing of his country – as we pleased – had its aesthetic value. Was there not, he would appeal to the *Señora*, *'una belleza de reposo'*, a beauty of quiescence, a dignity above prosperity? *'Muy bien.'* Let the *Señora* judge, you had it there!

We struck out from the town, perhaps insensibly toward the landmark of a Calvary, planted a mile or so beyond the walls, its three black shafts above the mass of roof and pinnacles, in sharp relief against the sky, against which suddenly a flock of vultures threw the first white cloud. With the descending sun, the clear persistence of the blue was losing permanence, a breeze sprang up and birds began to call.

The Spanish evening has unique effects and exquisite exhilarations: this one led us on some distance past the Calvary and the last group of scattered houses – many in complete decay – which straggle, thinning outwards from the city boundaries into the *campo*.

Standing alone, after a stretch of crumbling wall, a wretched little *venta*, like a stop to some meandering sentence, closed the broken line.

The place was windowless, but through the open door an oath or two – the common blend of sacrilege and vileness – with a smell of charcoal, frying oil-cakes and an odour of the stable, drifted out into the freshness of the evening air.

Immediately before us lay a dim expanse of treeless plain: behind, clear cut against a smokeless sky, the flat roof lines and towers of the city, seeming, as we looked back on them, less distant than in fact they were.

We took a road which finally confronted us with a huge block of buildings, an old church and convent, massed in the shadow of a hill and standing at the entrance to three cross-roads.

The convent, one of the few remaining in the south, not fallen into ruin, nor yet put, as far as one could judge, to worldly uses, was exceptionally large. We counted over thirty windows in a line upon the western side below the central tower with its pointed turret; the eastern wing, an evidently older part, was cut irregularly with a few square gratings.

The big, grey structure was impressive in its loneliness, its blank negation of the outside world, its stark expressionless detachment.

The church, of darker stone, was massive too; its only noticeable feature a small cloister with Romanesque arcades joining the nave on its south-western wall.

A group of peasant women coming out from vespers passed us and went chattering up the road, the last, an aged creature shuffling painfully some yards behind the rest still muttering her

Madre purisima,
Madre castisima,
Ruega por nosostros,

in a kind of automatic drone.

We looked in, as one does instinctively: the altar lights which hang like sickly stars in the profound obscurity of Spanish churches were being quickly blotted out.

We didn't enter then, but turned back to the convent gate, which stood half open, showing a side of the uncorniced cloisters, and a crowd of flowers, touched to an intensity of brilliance and fragrance by the twilight. Six or seven dogs, the sandy-coloured lurchers of the country, lean and wolfish-looking hounds, were sprawling round the gateway; save for this dejected crew, the place seemed resolutely lifeless; and this absence of a human note was just. One didn't want its solitude or silence touched, its really fine impersonality destroyed.

We hadn't meant – there wasn't light enough – to try the church again, but as we passed it, we turned into the small cloister. King, who had come to his last match, was seeking shelter from the breeze which had considerably freshened, and at the far end we came upon a little door, unlocked. I don't know why we tried it, but mechanically, as the conscientious tourist will, we drifted in and groped around. Only the vaguest outlines were discernible; the lancets of the lantern at the transept crossing, and a large rose window at the western end seemed, at a glance, the only means of light, and this was failing, leaving fast the fading panes.

One half-detected, almost guessed, the blind triforium, but the enormous width of the great building made immediate mark. The darkness, masking as it did distinctive features, emphasised the sense of space, which, like the spirit of a shrouded form, gained force, intensity, from its material disguise.

We stayed not more than a few minutes, but on reaching the small door again we found it fast; bolted or locked undoubtedly in the short interval. Of course we put our backs to it and made a pretty violent outcry, hoping the worthy sacristan was hanging round or somewhere within call. Of course he wasn't. We tried two other doors; both barred, and there was nothing left for it but noise. We shouted, I suppose for half an hour, intermittently, and King persisted hoarsely after I had given out.

The echo of the vast, dark, empty place caught our cries, seeming to hold them in suspension for a second in the void invisibility of roof and arches, then to fling them down in hollow repetition with an accent of unearthly mimicry which struck a little grimly on one's ear; and when we paused the silence seemed alert, expectant, ready to repel the first recurrence of unholy clamour. Finally, we gave it up; the hope of a release before the dawn, at earliest, was too forlorn. King, explosive and solicitous, was solemnly perturbed, but Ella faced the situation with an admirable tranquillity. Some chocolate and a muff would certainly, for her, she said, have made it more engaging, but poor dear men, the really tragic element resolved itself into – No matches, no cigar!

Unluckily we hadn't even this poor means of temporary light. Our steps and voices sounded loud, almost aggressive, as we groped about; the darkness then was shutting down and shortly it grew absolute. We camped eventually in one of the side chapels on the south side of the chancel, and kept a conversation going for a time, but gradually it dropped. The temperature, the fixed obscurity, and possibly a curious oppression in the spiritual atmosphere relaxed and forced it down.

The scent of incense clung about; a biting chillness crept up through the aisles; it got intensely cold. The stillness too became insistent; it was literally deathlike, rigid, exclusive, even awfully remote. It shut us out and held aloof; our passive presences, our mere vitality, seemed almost a disturbance of it; quiet as we were, we breathed, but it was breathless, and as time went on, one's impulse was to fight the sort of shapeless personality it presently assumed, to talk, to walk about and make a definite attack on it. Its influence on the others was presumably more soothing, obviously they weren't that way inclined.

Five or six hours must have passed. Nothing had marked them, and they hadn't seemed to move. The darkness seemed to thicken, in a way, to muddle thought and filter through into one's brain, and waiting, cramped and cold for it to lift, the soundlessness again impressed itself unpleasantly – it was intense, unnatural, acute.

And then it stirred.

The break in it was vague but positive; it might have been that, scarcely audible, the wind outside was rising, and yet not precisely that. I barely caught,

and couldn't localise the sound.

Ella and King were dozing, they had had some snatches of uncomfortable sleep; I, I suppose, was preternatural'y awake. I heard a key turn, and the swing back of a door, rapidly followed by a wave of voices breaking in. I put my hand out and touched King, and in a moment, both of them waked and started up.

I can't say how, but it at once occurred to us that quiet was our cue, that we were in for something singular.

The place was filling slowly with a chant, and then, emerging from the eastern end of the north aisle and travelling down just opposite, across the intervening dark, a line of light came into view, crossing the opening of the arches, cut by the massive piers, a moving, flickering line, advancing and advancing with the voices.

The outlines of the figures in the long procession weren't perceptible, the faces, palely lit and level with the tapers they were carrying, one rather felt than saw; but unmistakably the voices were men's voices, and the chant, the measured, reiterated cadences, prevailed over the wavering light.

Heavy and sombre as the stillness which it broke, vaguely akin to it, the chant swept in and gained upon the silence with a motion of the tide. It was a music neither of the senses, nor the spirit, but the mind, as set, as stately, almost as inanimate as the dark aisles through which it echoed; even, colourless and cold.

And then, quite suddenly, against its grave and passionless inflections something clashed, a piercing intermittent note, an awful discord, shrilling out and dying down and shrilling out again – a cry – a scream.

The chant went on; the light, from where we stood, was steadily retreating, and we ventured forward. Judging our whereabouts as best we could, we made towards the choir and stumbled up some steps, placing ourselves eventually behind one of the pillars of the apse. And from this point, the whole proceeding was apparent.

At the west end the line of light was turning; fifty or sixty monks (about – and at a venture) habited in brown and carrying tapers, walking two and two, were moving up the central aisle towards us, headed by three, one with the cross between two others bearing heavy silver candlesticks with tapers, larger than those carried by the rest.

Reaching the chancel steps, they paused; the three bearing the cross and candlesticks stood facing the altar, while those following diverged to right and left and lined the aisle. The first to take up this position were quite young, some almost boys; they were succeeded gradually by older men, those at the tail of the procession being obviously aged and infirm.

And then a figure, white and slight, erect – a woman's figure – struck a startling note at the far end of the brown line, a note as startling as the shrieks which jarred recurrently, were jarring still against the chant.

A pace or two behind her walked two priests in surplices, and after them another, vested in a cope. And on the whole impassive company her presence,

her disturbance, made no mark. For them, in fact, she wasn't there.

Neither was she aware of them. I doubt if to her consciousness, or mine, as she approached, grew definite, there was a creature in the place besides herself.

She moved and uttered her successive cries as if both sound and motion were entirely mechanical – more like a person in some trance of terror or of anguish than a voluntary rebel; her cries bespoke a physical revulsion into which her spirit didn't enter; they were not her own – they were outside herself; there was no discomposure in her carriage, nor, when we presently saw it, in her face. Both were distinguished by a certain exquisite hauteur, and this detachment of her personality from her distress impressed one curiously. She wasn't altogether real, she didn't altogether live, and yet her presence there was the supreme reality of the unreal scene, and lent to it, at least as I was viewing it, its only element of life.

She had, one understood, her part to play; she wasn't, for the moment, quite prepared; she played it later with superb effect.

As she came up with the three priests, the monks closed in and formed a semi-circle round them, while the priests advanced and placed themselves behind the monks who bore the cross and candlesticks, immediately below the chancel steps, facing the altar. They left her standing some few paces back, in the half-ring of sickly light shed by the tapers.

Now one saw her face. It was of striking beauty, but its age? One couldn't say. It had the tints, the purity of youth – it might have been extremely young, matured merely by the moment; but for a veil of fine repression which only years, it seemed, could possibly have woven. And it was itself – this face – a mask, one of the loveliest that spirit ever wore. It kept the spirit's counsel. Though what stirred it then, in that unique emergency, one saw – to what had stirred it, or might stir it gave no clue. It threw one back on vain conjecture.

Put the match of passion to it – would it burn? Touch it with grief and would it cloud, contract? With joy – and could it find, or had it ever found, a smile? Again, one couldn't say.

Only, as she stood there, erect and motionless, it showed the faintest flicker of distaste, disgust, as if she shrank from some repellent contact. She was clad, I think I said, from head to foot in a white linen garment; head and ears were covered too, the oval of the face alone was visible, and this was slightly flushed. Her screams were changing into little cries or moans, like those of a spent animal, from whom the momentary pressure of attack has been removed. They broke from her at intervals, unnoticed, unsuppressed, and now on silence, for the monks had ceased their chanting.

As they did so one realised the presence of these men, who, up to now, had scarcely taken shape as actualities, been more than an accompaniment – a drone. They shifted from a mass of voices to a row of pallid faces, each one lit by its own taper, hung upon the dark, or thrown abruptly, as it were, upon a screen; all different; all, at first distinct, but linked together by a subtle likeness, stamped with that dye which blurs the print of individuality – the signet of the cloister.

Taking them singly, though one did it roughly, rapidly enough, it wasn't difficult at starting to detect varieties of natural and spiritual equipment. There they were, spread out for sorting, nonentities and saints and devils, side by side, and what was queerer, animated by one purpose, governed by one law.

Some of the faces touched upon divinity; some fell below humanity; some were, of course, merely a blotch of book and bell, and all were set impassively toward the woman standing there.

And then one lost the sense of their diversity in their resemblance; the similarity persisted and persisted till the row of faces seemed to merge into one face – the face of nothing human – of a system, of a rule. It framed the woman's and one felt the force of it: she wasn't in the hands of men.

There was a pause filled only by her cries, a space of silence which they hardly broke; and then one of the monks stepped forward, slid into the chancel and began to light up the high altar. The little yellow tongues of flame struggled and started up, till first one line and then another starred the gloom.

Her glance had followed him; her eyes were fixed upon that point of darkness growing to a blaze. There was for her, in that illumination, some intense significance, and as she gazed intently on the patch of brilliance, her cries were suddenly arrested – quelled. The light had lifted something, given back to her an unimpaired identity. She was at last in full possession of herself. The flicker of distaste had passed and left her face to its inflexible, inscrutable repose.

She drew herself to her full height and turned towards the men behind her with an air of proud surrender, of magnificent disdain. I think she made some sign.

Another monk stepped out, extinguished and laid down his taper, and approached her.

I was prepared for something singular, for something passably bizarre, but not for what immediately occurred. He touched her eyes and closed them; then her mouth, and made a feint of closing that, while one of the two priests threw over his short surplice a black stole and started audibly with a *Sub venite*. The monks responded. Here and there I caught the words or sense of a reponse. The prayers for the most part were unintelligible: it was no doubt the usual office for the dead; and if it was, no finer satire for the work in hand could well have been devised. Loudly and unexpectedly above his unctuous monotone a bell clanged out three times. An *Ave* followed, after which two bells together, this time muffled, sounded out again three times. The priest proceeded with a *Miserere*, during which they rang the bells alternately, and there was something curiously suggestive and determinate about this part of the performance. The real action had, one felt, begun..

At the first stroke of the first bell her eyelids fluttered, but she kept them down; it wasn't until later at one point in the response, *'Non intres in judicium cum ancilla tua Domine'* she yielded to an impulse of her lips, permitted them the shadow of a smile. But for this slip she looked the thing of death they reckoned

to have made of her – detached herself, with an inspired touch, from all the living actors in the solemn farce, from all apparent apprehension of the scene. I, too, was quite incredibly outside it all.

I hadn't even asked myself precisely what was going to take place. Possibly I had caught the trick of her quiescence, acquiescence, annnd I went no further than she went; I waited – waited with her, as it were, to see it through. And I experienced a vague, almost resentful sense of interruption, incongruity, when King broke in to ask me what was up. He brought me back to Ella's presence, to the consciousness that this, so far as the spectators were concerned, was not a woman's comedy.

I made it briefly plain to them, as I knew something of the place and people, that any movement on our side would probably prove more rash, and turned again to what was going forward.

They were clumsily transforming the white figure. Two monks had robed her in a habit of their colour of her order, I suppose, and were now putting on the scapular and girdle. Finally they flung over her the long white-hooded cloak and awkwardly arranged the veil, leaving her face uncovered; then they joined her hands and placed between them a small cross.

This change of setting emphasised my first impression of her face; the mask was lovelier now and more complete.

Two voices started sonorously, '*Libera me, Domine*', the monks took up the chant, the whole assembly now began to move, the muffled bells to ring again at intervals, while the procession formed and filed into the choir. The monks proceeded to their stalls, the younger taking places in the rear. The two who had assisted at the robing led the passive figure to the centre of the chancel, where the three who bore the cross and candlesticks turned round and stood a short way off confronting her. Two others, carrying the censer and *bénitier*, stationed themselves immediately behind her with the priests and the officiant, who now, in a loud voice, began his recitations.

They seemed, with variations, to be going through it all again. I caught the '*Non intres in judicium*' and the '*Sub venite*' recurring with the force of a refrain. It was a long elaborate affair. The grave deliberation of its detail heightened its effect. Not to be tedious, I give it you in brief. It lasted altogether possibly two hours.

The priest assisting the officiant, lifting the border of his cope, attended him when he proceeded first to sprinkle, then to incense the presumably dead figure, with the crucifix confronting it, held almost like a challenge to its sightless face. They made the usual inclinations to the image as they passed it, and repeated the performance of the incensing and sprinkling with extreme formality at intervals, in all, I think, three times.

There was no break in the continuous drone proceeding from the choir; they kept it going; none of them looked up – or none at least of whom I had a view – when four young monks slid out, and, kneeling down in the clear space between her and the crucifix, dislodged a stone which must have previously

been loosened in the paving of the chancel, and disclosed a cavity, the depth of which I wasn't near enough to see.

For this I wasn't quite prepared, and yet I wasn't discomposed. I can't attempt to make it clear under what pressure I accepted this impossible *dénouement*, but I did accept it. More than that, I was exclusively absorbed in her reception of it. Though she couldn't, wouldn't see, she must have been aware of what was happening. But on the other hand, she was prepared, dispassionately ready, for the end.

All through the dragging length of the long offices, although she hadn't stirred or given any sign (except that one faint shadow of a smile) of consciousness, I felt the force of her intense vitality, the tension of its absolute impression. The life of those enclosing presences seemed to have passed into her presence, to be concentrated there. For to my view it was these men who held her in death's grip who didn't live, and she alone who was absorbently alive.

The candles, burning steadily on either side of the crucifix, the soft illumination of innumerable altar lights confronting her, intensified the darkness which above her and behind her – everywhere beyond the narrow confines of the feeble light in which she stood – prevailed.

This setting lent to her the aspect of an unsubstantial, almost supernatural figure, suddenly arrested in its passage through the dark.

She stood compliantly and absolutely still. If she had swayed, or given any hint of wavering, of an appeal to God or man, I must have answered magnetically. It was she who had the key to what I might have done but didn't do. Make what you will of it – we were inexplicably *en rapport*.

But failing failure I was backing her; it hadn't once occurred to me, without her sanction, to step in, to intervene; that I had anything to do with it beyond my recognition of her – of her part, her claim to play it as she pleased. And now it was – a thousand years too late!

They managed the illusion for themselves and me magnificently. She had come to be a thing of spirit only, not in any sort of clay. She was already in the world of shades; some power as sovereign and determinate as Death itself had lodged her there, past rescue or the profanation of recall.

King was in the act of springing forward; he had got out his revolver; meant, if possible, to shoot her before closing with the rest. It was the right and only workable idea. I held him back, using the first deterrent that occurred to me, reminding him of Ella, and the notion of her danger may have hovered on the outskirts of my mind. But it was not for her at all that I was consciously concerned. I was impelled to stand aside, to force him, too, to stand aside and see it through.

What followed, followed as such things occur in dreams; the senses seize, the mind, or what remains of it, accepts mechanically the natural or unnatural sequence of events.

I saw the grave surrounded by the priests and blessed; and then the woman and the grave repeatedly, alternately, incensed and sprinkled with deliberate

solemnity; and heard, as if from a great distance, the recitations of the prayers, and chanting of interminable psalms.

At the last moment, with their hands upon her, standing for a second still erect, before she was committed to the darkness, she unclosed her eyes, sent one swift glance towards the light, a glance which caught it, flashed it back, recaptured it and kept it for the lighting of her tomb. And then her face was covered with her veil.

The final act was the supreme illusion of the whole. I watched the lowering of the passive figure as if I had been witnessing the actual entombment of the dead.

The grave was sprinkled and incensed again, the stone replaced and fastened down. A long sequence of prayers said over it succeeded, at the end of which, the monks put out their tapers, only one or two remaining lit with those beside the Crucifix.

The priests and the officiant at length approached the altar, kneeling and prostrating there some minutes and repeating 'Pater Nosters', followed by the choir.

Finally in rising, the officiant pronounced alone and loudly 'Requiescat in pace'. The monks responded sonorously, 'Amen'.

The altar lights were one by one extinguished; at a sign, preceded by the cross, the vague, almost invisible procession formed and travelled down the aisle, reciting quietly the 'De Profundis' and guided now, by only, here and there, a solitary light. The quiet recitation, growing fainter, was a new and unfamiliar impression; I felt that I was missing something – what? I missed in fact, the chanting; then quite suddenly and certainly I missed – the scream. In place of it there was this 'De Profundis' and her silence. Out of her deep I realized it, dreamily, of course she would not call.

The door swung to; the church was dark and still again – immensely dark and still.

There was a pause, in which we didn't move or speak; in which I doubted for a second the reality of the incredibly remote, yet almost present scene, trying to reconstruct it in imagination, pit the dream against the fact, the fact against the dream.

'Good God!' said King at length, 'what are we going to do?'

His voice awoke me forcibly to something nearer daylight, to the human and inhuman elements in the remarkable affair, which hitherto had missed my mind; they struck against it now with a tremendous shock, and mentally I rubbed my eyes. I saw what King had all along been looking at, the sheer, unpicturesque barbarity. What *were* we going to do?

She breathed perhaps, perhaps she heard us – something of us – we were standing not more than a yard or so away; and if she did, she waited, that was the most poignant possibility, for our decision, our attack.

Ella was naturally unstrung: we left her crouching by the pillar; later I think she partially lost consciousness. It was as well – it left us free.

Striking, as nearly as we could, the centre of the altar, working from it, we made a guess at the position of the stone, and on our hands and knees felt blindly for some indication of its loosened edge. But everywhere the paving, to our touch, presented an unevenness of surface, and we picked at random, chiefly for the sake of doing something. In that intolerable darkness there was really nothing to be done but wait for dawn or listen for some guidance from below. For that we listened breathless and alert enough, but nothing stirred. The stillness had become again intense, acute, and now a grim significance attached to it.

The minutes, hours, dragged; time wasn't as it had been, stationary, but desperately, murderously slow.

Each moment of inaction counted – counted horribly, as we stood straining ears and eyes for any hint of sound, of light.

At length the darkness lifted, almost imperceptibly at first; the big rose window to the west became a scarcely visible grey blot; the massive piers detached themselves from the dense mass of shadow and stood out, immense and vague; the windows of the lantern just above us showed a ring of slowly lightening panes; and with the dawn, we found the spot and set to work.

The implements we improvised we soon discovered to be practically useless. We loosened, but we couldn't move the stone.

At intervals we stopped and put our ears to the thin crevices. King thought, and still believes, he heard some sound or movement; but I didn't. I was somehow sure, for that, it was too late.

For everything it was too late, and we returned reluctantly to a consideration of our own predicament; we had, if possible, to get away unseen. And this time luck was on our side. The sacristan, who came in early by the cloister door which we had entered by, without perceiving us, proceeded to the sacristy.

We made a rapid and effectual escape.

We sketched out and elaborated, on our way back to the town, the little scheme of explanation to be offered to our host, which was to cover an announcement of abrupt departure. He received it with polite credulity, profound regret. He ventured to believe that the *Señora* was unfortunately missing a unique experience – cities, like men, had elements of beauty, or of greatness which escape the crowd; but the *Señora* was not of the crowd, and he had hoped she would be able to remain.

Nothing, however, would induce her to remain for more than a few hours. We must push on without delay and put the night's occurrences before the nearest British Consul. She made no comments and admitted no fatigue, but on this point she was persistent to perversity. She carried it.

The Consul proved hospitable and amiable. He heard the story and was suitably impressed. It was a truly horrible experience – remarkably dramatic – yes. He added it – we saw him doing it – to his collection of strange tales.

The country was, he said, extremely rich in tragic anecdote; and men in his position earned their reputation for romance. But as to *doing* anything in this

case, as in others even more remarkable, why, there was absolutely nothing to be done!

The laws of Spain were theoretically admirable, but practically, well – the best that could be said of them was that they had their comic side.

And this was not a civil matter, where the wheels might often, certainly, be oiled. The wheel ecclesiastic was more intractable.

He asked if we were leaving Spain immediately. We said, 'Perhaps in a few days.' 'Take my advice,' said he, 'and make it a few hours.'

We did.

Ella would tell you that the horror of those hours hasn't ever altogether ceased to haunt her, that it visits her in dreams and poisons sleep.

She hasn't ever understood, or quite forgiven me my attitude of temporary detachment. She refuses to admit that, after all, what one is pleased to call reality is merely the intensity of one's illusion. My illusion was intense.

'Oh, for you,' she says, and with a touch of bitterness, 'it was a spectacle. The woman didn't really count.'

For me it was a spectacle, but more than that: it was an acquiescence in a rather splendid crime.

On looking back I see that, at the moment in my mind, the woman didn't really count. She saw herself she didn't. That's precisely what she made me see.

What counted chiefly with her, I suspect, was something infinitely greater to her vision than the terror of men's dreams.

She lies, one must remember, in the very centre of the sanctuary – has a place uniquely sacred to her order, the traditions of her kind. It was this honour, satisfying, as it did, some pride of spirit or of race, which bore her honourably through.

She had, one way or other, clogged the wheels of an inflexible machine. But for the speck of dust she knew herself to be, she was – oh horribly, I grant you – yet not lightly, not dishonourably, swept away.[7]

Stevie Smith
The River God (1950)

I may be smelly and I may be old,
Rough in my pebbles, reedy in my pools,
But where my fish float by I bless their swimming
And I like the people to bathe in me, especially women.

[7] Published in *Temple Bar*, CXXVII (May, 1903).

But I can drown the fools
Who bathe too close to the weir, contrary to rules.
And they take a long time drowning
As I throw them up now and then in a spirit of clowning.
Hi yih, yippity-yap, merrily I flow,
O I may be an old foul river but I have plenty of go.
Once there was a lady who was too bold
She bathed in me by the tall black cliff where the water runs cold,
So I brought her down here
To be my beautiful dear.
Oh will she stay with me will she stay
This beautiful lady, or will she go away?
She lies in my beautiful deep river bed with many a weed
To hold her, and many a waving reed.
Oh who would guess what a beautiful white face lies there
Waiting for me to smooth and wash away the fear
She looks at me with. Hi yih, do not let her
Go. There is no one on earth who does not forget her
Now. They say I am a foolish old smelly river
But they do not know of my wide original bed
Where the lady waits, with her golden sleepy head.
If she wishes to go I will not forgive her.

Monique Wittig

FROM

The Lesbian Body (1973)

A m I not Zeyna the all-powerful she who shakes her mane and grasps the lightnings in her hand?[8] see m/yself seated rigidly before abundantly laden tables refusing all the victuals the women offer m/e calling for the drinks of Ganymedea the absent.[9] At last you emerge hurriedly from the avenue of cherry-trees in the midst of the feast flushed breathless two amphorae supported on your

[8] 'Zeyna' is a feminine incarnation of Zeus, king of the gods in Greek mythology and the holder of the thunder and lightning.
[9] Ganymede the boy shepherd was ravished by Zeus in the form of an eagle. He was subsequently appointed as cup-bearer to the gods. Wittig makes her a girl.

straight hips eager to serve all the women who await you dry-throated, but it is by m/e that you first halt. I look at the trickle of sweat between your breasts and your lifted arms the curled damp tufts of your armpits lit by the sun, *I* grasp your straight unwaisted torso between m/y hands, you with a twist of the loins slipping from my clutch pouring a great quantity of wine into my cup. Your eyes are hidden by their lids, no blush comes to your cheeks when *I* ask you to sit beside m/e, your eyes do not see m/e, your ears do not hear m/e, the order of your gestures is undisturbed, then the fire of m/y lightnings expands in m/y breast ravaging m/y lungs m/y ribs m/y shoulderblades m/y breasts, m/y hands seizing them to thunder from the height of m/y anger, mute indifferent barely smiling you go and come soundlessly, you do not kiss the nape of m/y neck when you pass behind m/e. A growling rises in m/y throat, a rumbling develops in the cloudless sky, m/y lightnings shaken forth strike you in the belly the pubis so that you turn your face to the ground before m/e m/y so frightened one m/y so troubled one your eyes closed your hands over your ears, crying to m/e for mercy in such wise that ultimately I can lift you at arm's length to m/y mouth, that ultimately *I* can laugh in your ears, that ultimately I can turn you round and bite you in the hollow of your loins m/y goddess m/y so callipygous[10] one m/y adored.[11]

Angela Carter
The Bloody Chamber (1979)

A version of the tale of Bluebeard from a collection of revisionary fairytales of which this is the title story.

I remember how, that night, I lay awake in the wagon-lit in a tender, delicious ecstasy of excitement, my burning cheek pressed against the impeccable linen of the pillow and the pounding of my heart mimicking that of the great pistons ceaselessly thrusting the train that bore me through the night, away from Paris, away from girlhood, away from the white, enclosed quietude of my mother's apartment, into the unguessable country of marriage.

And I remember I tenderly imagined how, at this very moment, my mother would be moving slowly about the narrow bedroom I had left behind for ever,

[10] The Callipygian Venus is an antique statue especially famous for the beauty of her well-developed buttocks.
[11] First published in 1973 by Les Editions de Minuit. This extract is taken from the English translation by Peter Owen (1975).

DANGER

folding up and putting away all my little relics, the tumbled garments I would not need any more, the scores for which there had been no room in my trunks, the concert programmes I'd abandoned; she would linger over this torn ribbon and that faded photograph with all the half-joyous, half-sorrowful emotions of a woman on her daughter's wedding day. And, in the midst of my bridal triumph, I felt a pang of loss as if, when he put the gold band on my finger, I had, in some way, ceased to be her child in becoming his wife.

Are you sure, she'd said when they delivered the gigantic box that held the wedding dress he'd bought me, wrapped up in tissue paper and red ribbon like a Christmas gift of crystallized fruit. Are you sure you love him? There was a dress for her, too; black silk, with the dull, prismatic sheen of oil on water, finer than anything she'd worn since that adventurous girlhood in Indo-China, daughter of a rich tea planter. My eagle-featured, indomitable mother; what other student at the Conservatoire could boast that her mother had outfaced a junkful of Chinese pirates, nursed a village through a visitation of the plague, shot a man-eating tiger with her own hand and all before she was as old as I?

'Are you sure you love him?'

'I'm sure I want to marry him,' I said.

And would say no more. She sighed, as if it was with reluctance that she might at last banish the spectre of poverty from its habitual place at our meagre table. For my mother herself had gladly, scandalously, defiantly beggared herself for love; and, one fine day, her gallant soldier never returned from the wars, leaving his wife and child a legacy of tears that never quite dried, a cigar box full of medals and the antique service revolver that my mother, grown magnificently eccentric in hardship, kept always in her reticule, in case – how I teased her – she was surprised by footpads on her way home from the grocer's shop.

Now and then a starburst of lights splattered the drawn blinds as if the railway company had lit up all the stations through which we passed in celebration of the bride. My satin nightdress had just been shaken from its wrappings; it had slipped over my young girl's pointed breasts and shoulders, supple as a garment of heavy water, and now teasingly caressed me, egregious, insinuating, nudging between my thighs as I shifted restlessly in my narrow berth. His kiss, his kiss with tongue and teeth in it and a rasp of beard, had hinted to me, though with the same exquisite tact as this nightdress he'd given me, of the wedding night, which would be voluptuously deferred until we lay in his great ancestral bed in the sea-girt, pinnacled domain that lay, still, beyond the grasp of my imagination ... that magic place, the fairy castle whose walls were made of foam, that legendary habitation in which he had been born. To which, one day, I might bear an heir. Our destination, my destiny.

Above the syncopated roar of the train, I could hear his even, steady breathing. Only the communicating door kept me from my husband and it stood open. If I rose up on my elbow, I could see the dark, leonine shape of his head and my nostrils caught a whiff of the opulent male scent of leather and spices that always accompanied him and sometimes, during his courtship, had been the

only hint he gave me that he had come into my mother's sitting room, for, though he was a big man, he moved as softly as if all his shoes had soles of velvet, as if his footfall turned the carpet into snow.

He had loved to surprise me in my abstracted solitude at the piano. He would tell them not to announce him, then soundlessly open the door and softly creep up behind me with his bouquet of hot-house flowers or his box of marrons glacés, lay his offering upon the keys and clasp his hands over my eyes as I was lost in a Debussy prelude. But that perfume of spiced leather always betrayed him; after my first shock, I was forced always to mimic surprise, so that he would not be disappointed.

He was older than I. He was much older than I; there were streaks of pure silver in his dark mane. But his strange, heavy, almost waxen face was not lined by experience. Rather, experience seemed to have washed it perfectly smooth, like a stone on a beach whose fissures have been eroded by successive tides. And sometimes that face, in stillness when he listened to me playing, with the heavy eyelids folded over eyes that always disturbed me by their absolute absence of light, seemed to me like a mask, as if his real face, the face that truly reflected all the life he had led in the world before he met me, before, even, I was born, as though that face lay underneath this mask. Or else, elsewhere. As though he had laid by the face in which he had lived for so long in order to offer my youth a face unsigned by the years.

And, elsewhere, I might see him plain. Elsewhere. But, where?

In, perhaps, that castle to which the train now took us, that marvellous castle in which he had been born.

Even when he asked me to marry him, and I said: 'Yes,' still he did not lose that heavy, fleshy composure of his. I know it must seem a curious analogy, a man with a flower, but sometimes he seemed to me like a lily. Yes. A lily. Possessed of that strange, ominous calm of a sentient vegetable, like one of those cobra-headed, funereal lilies whose white sheaths are curled out of a flesh as thick and tensely yielding to the touch as vellum. When I said that I would marry him, not one muscle in his face stirred, but he let out a long, extinguished sigh. I thought: Oh! how he must want me! And it was as though the imponderable weight of his desire was a force I might not withstand, not by virtue of its violence but because of its very gravity.

He had the ring ready in a leather box lined with crimson velvet, a fire opal the size of a pigeon's egg set in a complicated circle of dark antique gold. My old nurse, who still lived with my mother and me, squinted at the ring askance: opals are bad luck, she said. But this opal had been his own mother's ring, and his grandmother's, and her mother's before that, given to an ancestor by Catherine de Medici . . . every bride that came to the castle wore it, time out of mind. And did he give it to his other wives and have it back from them? asked the old woman rudely; yet she was a snob. She hid her incredulous joy at my marital coup – her little Marquise – behind a façade of fault-finding. But, here, she touched me. I shrugged and turned my back pettishly on her. I did not want

to remember how he had loved other women before me, but the knowledge often teased me in the threadbare self-confidence of the small hours.

I was 17 and knew nothing of the world; my Marquis had been married before, more than once, and I remained a little bemused that, after those others, he should now have chosen me. Indeed, was he not still in mourning for his last wife? Tsk, tsk, went my old nurse. And even my mother had been reluctant to see her girl whisked off by a man so recently bereaved. A Romanian countess, a lady of high fashion. Dead just three short months before I met him, a boating accident, at his home, in Brittany. They never found her body but I rummaged through the back copies of the society magazines my old nanny kept in a trunk under her bed and tracked down her photograph. The sharp muzzle of a pretty, witty, naughty monkey; such potent and bizarre charm, of a dark, bright, wild yet worldly thing whose natural habitat must have been some luxurious interior decorator's jungle filled with potted palms and tame, squawking parakeets.

Before that? *Her* face is common property; everyone painted her but the Redon engraving I liked best, *The Evening Star Walking on the Rim of Night*. To see her skeletal, enigmatic grace, you would never think she had been a barmaid in a café in Montmartre until Puvis de Chavannes saw her and had her expose her flat breasts and elongated thighs to his brush. And yet it was the absinthe doomed her, or so they said.

The first of all his ladies? That sumptuous diva; I had heard her sing Isolde, precociously muscial child that I was, taken to the opera for a birthday treat. My first opera; I had heard her sing Isolde. With what white-hot passion had she burned from the stage! So that you could tell she would die young. We sat high up, halfway to heaven in the gods, yet she half-blinded me. And my father, still alive (oh, so long ago), took hold of my sticky little hand, to comfort me, in the last act, yet all I heard was the glory of her voice.

Married three times within my own brief lifetime to three different graces, now, as if to demonstrate the eclecticism of his taste, he had invited me to join this gallery of beautiful women, I, the poor widow's child with my mouse-coloured hair that still bore the kinks of the plaits from which it had so recently been freed, my bony hips, my nervous, pianist's fingers.

He was rich as Croesus. The night before our wedding – a simple affair, at the Mairie, because his countess was so recently gone – he took my mother and me, curious coincidence, to see *Tristan*. And, do you know, my heart swelled and ached so during the Liebestod that I thought I must truly love him. Yes. I did. On his arm, all eyes were upon me. The whispering crowd in the foyer parted like the Red Sea to let us through. My skin crisped at his touch.

How my circumstances had changed since the first time I heard those voluptuous chords that carry such a charge of deathly passion in them! Now, we sat in a loge, in red velvet armchairs, and a braided, betwigged flunkey brought us a silver bucket of iced champagne in the interval. The froth spilled over the rim of my glass and drenched my hands, I thought: My cup runneth

over. And I had on a Poiret dress. He had prevailed upon my reluctant mother to let him buy my trousseau; what would I have gone to him in, otherwise? Twice-darned underwear, faded gingham, serge skirts, hand-me-downs. So, for the opera, I wore a sinuous shift of white muslin tied with a silk string under the breasts. And everyone stared at me. And at his wedding gift.

His wedding gift, clasped round my throat. A choker of rubies, two inches wide, like an extraordinarily precious slit throat.

After the Terror, in the early days of the Directory, the aristos who'd escaped the guillotine had an ironic fad of tying a red ribbon round their necks at just the point where the blade would have sliced it through, a red ribbon like the memory of a wound. And his grandmother, taken with the notion, had her ribbon made up in rubies; such a gesture of luxurious defiance! That night at the opera comes back to me even now . . . the white dress; the frail child within it; and the flashing crimson jewels round her throat, bright as arterial blood.

I saw him watching me in the gilded mirrors with the assessing eye of a connoisseur inspecting horseflesh, or even of a housewife in the market, inspecting cuts on the slab. I'd never seen, or else had never acknowledged, that regard of his before, the sheer carnal avarice of it; and it was strangely magnified by the monocle lodged in his left eye. When I saw him look at me with lust, I dropped my eyes but, in glancing away from him, I caught sight of myself in the mirror. And I saw myself, suddenly, as he saw me, my pale face, the way the muscles in my neck stuck out like thin wire. I saw how much that cruel necklace became me. And, for the first time in my innocent and confined life, I sensed in myself a potentiality for corruption that took my breath away.

The next day, we were married.

The train slowed, shuddered to a halt. Lights; clank of metal; a voice declaring the name of an unknown, never-to-be visited station; silence of the night; the rhythm of his breathing, that I should sleep with, now, for the rest of my life. And I could not sleep. I stealthily sat up, raised the blind a little and huddled against the cold window that misted over with the warmth of my breathing, gazing out at the dark platform towards those rectangles of domestic lamplight that promised warmth, company, a supper of sausages hissing in a pan on the stove for the station master, his children tucked up in bed asleep in the brick house with the painted shutters . . . all the paraphernalia of the everyday world from which I, with my stunning marriage, had exiled myself.

Into marriage, into exile; I sensed it, I knew it – that, henceforth, I would always be lonely. Yet that was part of the already familiar weight of the fire opal that glimmered like a gypsy's magic ball, so that I could not take my eyes off it when I played the piano. This ring, the bloody bandage of rubies, the wardrobe of clothes from Poiret and Worth, his scent of Russian leather – all had conspired to seduce me so utterly that I could not say I felt one single twinge of regret for the world of tartines and maman that now receded from me as if drawn away on a string, like a child's toy, as the train began to throb again as if in delighted anticipation of the distance it would take me.

The first grey streamers of the dawn now flew in the sky and an eldritch half-light seeped into the railway carriage. I heard no change in his breathing but my heightened, excited senses told me he was awake and gazing at me. A huge man, an enormous man, and his eyes, dark and motionless as those eyes the ancient Egyptians painted upon their sarcophagi, fixed upon me. I felt a certain tension in the pit of my stomach, to be so watched, in such silence. A match struck. He was igniting a Romeo y Julieta fat as a baby's arm.

'Soon,' he said in his resonant voice that was like the tolling of a bell and I felt, all at once, a sharp premonition of dread that lasted only as long as the match flared and I could see his white, broad face as if it were hovering, disembodied, above the sheets, illuminated from below like a grotesque carnival head. Then the flame died, the cigar glowed and filled the compartment with a remembered fragrance that made me think of my father, how he would hug me in a warm fug of Havana, when I was a little girl, before he kissed me and left me and died.

As soon as my husband handed me down from the high step of the train, I smelled the amniotic salinity of the ocean. It was November; the trees, stunted by the Atlantic gales, were bare and the lonely halt was deserted but for his leather-gaitered chauffeur waiting meekly beside the sleek black car. It was cold; I drew my furs about me, a wrap of white and black, broad stripes of ermine and sable, with a collar from which my head rose like the calyx of a wildflower. (I swear to you, I had never been vain until I met him.) The bell clanged; the straining train leapt its leash and left us at that lonely wayside halt where only he and I had descended. Oh, the wonder of it; how all that might of iron and steam had paused only to suit his convenience. The richest man in France.

'Madame.'

The chauffeur eyed me; was he comparing me, invidiously, to the countess, the artist's model, the opera singer? I hid behind my furs as if they were a system of soft shields. My husband liked me to wear my opal over my kid glove, a showy, theatrical trick – but the moment the ironic chauffeur glimpsed its simmering flash he smiled, as though it was proof positive I was his master's wife. And we drove towards the widening dawn, that now streaked half the sky with a wintry bouquet of pink of roses, orange of tiger-lilies, as if my husband had ordered me a sky from a florist. The day broke around me like a cool dream.

Sea; sand; a sky that melts into the sea – a landscape of misty pastels with a look about it of being continuously on the point of melting. A landscape with all the deliquescent harmonies of Debussy, of the études I played for him, the reverie I'd been playing that afternoon in the salon of the princess where I'd first met him, among the teacups and the little cakes, I, the orphan, hired out of charity to give them their digestive of music.

And, ah! his castle. The faery solitude of the place; with its turrets of misty blue, its courtyard, its spiked gate, his castle that lay on the very bosom of the sea with seabirds mewing about its attics, the casements opening on to the

green and purple, evanescent departures of the ocean, cut off by the tide from land for half a day . . . that castle, at home neither on the land nor on the water, a mysterious, amphibious place, contravening the materiality of both earth and the waves, with the melancholy of a mermaiden who perches on her rock and waits, endlessly, for a lover who had drowned far away, long ago. That lovely, sad, sea-siren of a place!

The tide was low; at this hour, so early in the morning, the causeway rose up out of the sea. As the car turned on to the wet cobbles between the slow margins of water, he reached out for my hand that had his sultry, witchy ring on it, pressed my fingers, kissed my palm with extraordinary tenderness. His face was as still as ever I'd seen it, still as a pond iced thickly over, yet his lips, that always looked so strangely red and naked between the black fringes of his beard, now curved a little. He smiled; he welcomed his bride home.

No room, no corridor that did not rustle with the sound of the sea and all the ceilings, the walls on which his ancestors in the stern regalia of rank lined up with their dark eyes and white faces, were stippled with refracted light from the waves which were always in motion; that luminous, murmurous castle of which I was the châtclaine, I, the little music student whose mother had sold all her jewellery, even her wedding ring, to pay the fees at the Conservatoire.

First of all, there was the small ordeal of my initial interview with the housekeeper, who kept this extraordinary machine, this anchored, castellated ocean liner, in smooth running order no matter who stood on the bridge; how tenuous, I thought, might be my authority here! She had a bland, pale, impassive, dislikeable face beneath the impeccably starched white linen head-dress of the region. Her greeting, correct but lifeless, chilled me; daydreaming, I dared presume too much on my status . . . briefly wondered how I might install my old nurse, so much loved, however cosily incompetent, in her place. Ill-considered schemings! He told me this one had been his foster mother; was bound to his family in the utmost feudal complicity, 'as much part of the house as I am, my dear'. Now her thin lips offered me a proud little smile. She would be my ally as long as I was his. And with that, I must be content.

But, here, it would be easy to be content. In the turret suite he had given me for my very own, I could gaze out over the tumultuous Atlantic and imagine myself the Queen of the Sea. There was a Bechstein for me in the music room and, on the wall, another wedding present – an early Flemish primitive of Saint Cecilia at her celestial organ. In the prim charm of this saint, with her plump, sallow cheeks and crinkled brown hair, I saw myself as I could have wished to be. I warmed to a loving sensitivity I had not hitherto suspected in him. Then he led me up a delicate spiral staircase to my bedroom; before she discreetly vanished, the housekeeper set him chuckling with some, I dare say, lewd blessing for newlyweds in her native Breton. That I did not understand. That he, smiling, refused to interpret.

And there lay the grand, hereditary matrimonial bed, itself the size, almost, of my little room at home, with the gargoyles carved on its surfaces of ebony,

vermilion lacquer, gold leaf; and its white gauze curtains, billowing in the sea breeze. Our bed. And surrounded by so many mirrors! Mirrors on all the walls, in stately frames of contorted gold, that reflected more white lilies than I'd ever seen in my life before. He'd filled the room with them, to greet the bride, the young bride. The young bride, who had become that multitude of girls I saw in the mirrors, identical in their chic navy blue tailor-mades, for travelling, madame, or walking. A maid had dealt with the furs. Henceforth, a maid would deal with everything.

'See,' he said, gesturing towards those elegant girls. 'I have acquired a whole harem for myself!'

I found that I was trembling. My breath came thickly. I could not meet his eye and turned my head away, out of pride, out of shyness, and watched a dozen husbands approach me in a dozen mirrors and slowly, methodically, teasingly, unfasten the buttons of my jacket and slip it from my shoulders. Enough! No; more! Off comes the skirt; and, next, the blouse of apricot linen that cost more than the dress I had for first communion. The play of the waves outside in the cold sun glittered on his monocle; his movements seemed to me deliberately coarse, vulgar. The blood rushed to my face again, and stayed there.

And yet, you see, I guessed it might be so – that we should have a formal disrobing of the bride, a ritual from the brothel. Sheltered as my life had been, how could I have failed, even in the world of prim bohemia in which I lived, to have heard hints of *his* world?

He stripped me, gourmand that he was, as if he were stripping the leaves off an artichoke – but do not imagine much finesse about it; this artichoke was no particular treat for the diner nor was he yet in any greedy haste. He approached his familiar treat with a weary appetite. And when nothing but my scarlet, palpitating core remained, I saw, in the mirror, the living image of an etching by Rops from the collection he had shown me when our engagement permitted us to be alone together ... the child with her sticklike limbs, naked but for her button boots, her gloves, shielding her face with her hand as though her face were the last repository of her modesty; and the old, monocled lecher who examined her, limb by limb. He in his London tailoring; she, bare as a lamb chop. Most pornographic of all confrontations. And so my purchaser unwrapped his bargain. And, as at the opera, when I had first seen my flesh in his eyes, I was aghast to feel myself stirring.

At once he closed my legs like a book and I saw again the rare movement of his lips that meant he smiled.

Not yet. Later. Anticipation is the greater part of pleasure, my little love.

And I began to shudder, like a racehorse before a race, yet also with a kind of fear, for I felt both a strange, impersonal arousal at the thought of love and at the same time a repugnance I could not stifle for his white, heavy flesh that had too much in common with the armfuls of arum lilies that filled my bedroom in great glass jars, those undertakers' lilies with the heavy pollen that powders

your fingers as if you had dipped them in turmeric. The lilies I always associate with him; that are white. And stain you.

This scene from a voluptuary's life was now abruptly terminated. It turns out he has business to attend to; his estates, his companies – even on your honeymoon? Even then, said the red lips that kissed me before he left me alone with my bewildered senses – a wet, silken brush from his beard; a hint of the pointed tip of the tongue. Disgruntled, I wrapped a négligé of antique lace around me to sip the little breakfast of hot chocolate the maid brought me; after that, since it was second nature to me, there was nowhere to go but the music room and soon I settled down at my piano.

Yet only a series of subtle dischords flowed from beneath my fingers: out of tune ... only a little out of tune; but I'd been blessed with perfect pitch and could not bear to play any more. Sea breezes are bad for pianos; we shall need a resident piano-tuner on the premises if I'm to continue with my studies! I flung down the lid in a little fury of disappointment; what should I do now, how shall I pass the long, sea-lit hours until my husband beds me?

I shivered to think of *that*.

His library seemed the source of his habitual odour of Russian leather. Row upon row of calf-bound volumes, brown and olive, with gilt lettering on their spines, the octavo in brilliant scarlet morocco. A deep-buttoned leather sofa to recline on. A lectern, carved like a spread eagle, that held open upon it an edition of Huysmans's *Là-bas*, from some over-exquisite private press; it had been bound like a missal, in brass, with gems of coloured glass. The rugs on the floor, deep, pulsing blues of heaven and red of the heart's dearest blood, came from Isfahan and Bokhara; the dark panelling gleamed; there was the lulling music of the sea and a fire of apple logs. The flames flickered along the spines inside a glass-fronted case that held books still crisp and new. Eliphas Levy; the name meant nothing to me. I squinted at a title or two: *The Initiation, The Key of Mysteries, The Secret of Pandora's Box*, and yawned. Nothing, here, to detain a 17-year-old girl waiting for her first embrace. I should have liked, best of all, a novel in yellow paper; I wanted to curl up on the rug before the blazing fire, lose myself in a cheap novel, munch sticky liqueur chocolates. If I rang for them, a maid would bring me chocolates.

Nevertheless, I opened the doors of that bookcase idly to browse. And I think I knew, I knew by some tingling of the fingertips, even before I opened that slim volume with no title at all on the spine, what I should find inside it. When he showed me the Rops, newly bought, dearly prized, had he not hinted that he was a connoisseur of such things? Yet I had not bargained for this, the girl with tears hanging on her cheeks like stuck pearls, her cunt a split fig below the great globes of her buttocks on which the knotted tails of the cat were about to descend, while a man in a black mask fingered with his free hand his prick, that curved upwards like the scimitar he held. The picture had a caption: 'Reproof of curiosity'. My mother, with all the precision of her eccentricity, had told me what it was that lovers did; I was innocent but not naïve. *The Adventures of Eulalie*

at the Harem of the Grand Turk had been printed, according to the flyleaf, in Amsterdam in 1748, a rare collector's piece. Had some ancestor brought it back himself from that northern city? Or had my husband bought it for himself, from one of those dusty little bookshops on the Left Bank where an old man peers at you through spectacles an inch thick, daring you to inspect his wares . . . I turned the pages in the anticipation of fear; the print was rusty. Here was another steel engraving: 'Immolation of the wives of the Sultan'. I knew enough for what I saw in that book to make me gasp.

There was a pungent intensification of the odour of leather that suffused his library; his shadow fell across the massacre.

'My little nun has found the prayerbooks, has she?' he demanded, with a curious mixture of mockery and relish; then, seeing my painful, furious bewilderment, he laughed at me aloud, snatched the book from my hands and put it down on the sofa.

'Have the nasty pictures scared Baby? Baby mustn't play with grownups' toys until she's learned how to handle them, must she?'

Then he kissed me. And with, this time, no reticence. He kissed me and laid his hand imperatively upon my breast, beneath the sheath of ancient lace. I stumbled on the winding stair that led to the bedroom, to the carved, gilded bed on which he had been conceived. I stammered foolishly: We've not taken luncheon yet; and, besides, it is broad daylight. . .

All the better to see you.

He made me put on my choker, the family heirloom of one woman who had escaped the blade. With trembling fingers, I fastened the thing about my neck. It was cold as ice and chilled me. He twined my hair into a rope and lifted it off my shoulders so that he could the better kiss the downy furrows below my ears; that made me shudder. And he kissed those blazing rubies, too. He kissed them before he kissed my mouth. Rapt, he intoned: 'Of her apparel she retains/Only her sonorous jewellery.'

A dozen husbands impaled a dozen brides while the mewing gulls swung on invisible trapezes in the empty air outside.

I was brought to my senses by the insistent shrilling of the telephone. He lay beside me, felled like an oak, breathing stertorously, as if he had been fighting with me. In the course of that one-sided struggle, I had seen his deathly composure shatter like a porcelain vase flung against a wall; I had heard him shriek and blaspheme at the orgasm; I had bled. And perhaps I had seen his face without its mask; and perhaps I had not. Yet I had been infinitely dishevelled by the loss of my virginity.

I gathered myself together, reached into the cloisonné cupboard beside the bed that concealed the telephone and addressed the mouthpiece. His agent in New York. Urgent.

I shook him awake and rolled over on my side, cradling my spent body in my arms. His voice buzzed like a hive of distant bees. My husband. My

husband, who, with so much love, filled my bedroom with lilies until it looked like an embalming parlour. Those somnolent lilies, that wave their heavy heads, distributing their lush, insolent incense reminiscent of pampered flesh.

When he'd finished with the agent, he turned to me and stroked the ruby necklace that bit into my neck, but with such tenderness now, that I ceased flinching and he caressed my breasts. My dear one, my little love, my child, did it hurt her? He's so sorry for it, such impetuousness, he could not help himself; you see, he loves her so ... and this lover's recitative of his brought my tears in a flood. I clung to him as though only the one who had inflicted the pain could comfort me for suffering it. For a while, he murmured to me in a voice I'd never heard before, a voice like the soft consolations of the sea. But then he unwound the tendrils of my hair from the buttons of his smoking jacket, kissed my cheek briskly and told me the agent from New York had called with such urgent business that he must leave as soon as the tide was low enough. Leave the castle? Leave France! And would be away for at least six weeks.

'But it is our honeymoon!'

A deal, an enterprise of hazard and chance involving several millions, lay in the balance, he said. He drew away from me into that waxworks stillness of his; I was only a little girl, I did not understand. And, he said unspoken to my wounded vanity, I have had too many honeymoons to find them in the least pressing commitments. I know quite well that this child I've bought with a handful of coloured stones and the pelts of dead beasts won't run away. But, after he'd called his Paris agent to book a passage for the States next day – just one tiny call, my little one – we should have time for dinner together.

And I had to be content with that.

A Mexican dish of pheasant with hazelnuts and chocolates; salad; white, voluptuous cheese; a sorbet of muscat grapes and Asti spumante. A celebration of Krug exploded festively. And then acrid black coffee in precious little cups so fine it shadowed the birds with which they were painted. I had cointreau, he had cognac in the library, with the purple velvet curtains drawn against the night, where he took me to perch on his knee in a leather armchair beside the flickering log fire. He had made me change into that chaste little Poiret shift of white muslin; he seemed especially fond of it, my breasts showed through the flimsy stuff, he said, like little soft white doves that sleep, each one, with a pink eye open. But he would not let me take off my ruby choker, although I was growing very uncomfortable, nor fasten up my descending hair, the sign of a virginity so recently ruptured that still remained a wounded presence between us. He twined his fingers in my hair until I winced; I said, I remember, very little.

'The maid will have changed our sheets already,' he said. 'We do not hang the bloody sheets out of the window to prove to the whole of Brittany you are a virgin, not in these civilised times. But I should tell you it would have been the first time in all my married lives I could have shown my interested tenants such a flag.'

Then I realised, with a shock of surprise, how it must have been my innocence that captivated him – the silent music, he said, of my unknowingness, like *La Terrasse des audiences au clair de lune* played upon a piano with keys of ether. You must remember how ill at ease I was in that luxurious place, how unease had been my constant companion during the whole length of my courtship by this grave satyr who now gently martyrised my hair. To know that my naïvety gave him some pleasure made me take heart. Courage! I shall act the fine lady to the manner born one day, if only by virtue of default.

Then, slowly yet teasingly, as if he were giving a child a great, mysterious treat, he took out a bunch of keys from some interior hidey-hole in his jacket – key after key, a key, he said, for every lock in the house. Keys of all kinds – huge, ancient things of black iron; others slender, delicate, almost baroque; wafer-thin Yale keys for safes and boxes. And, during his absence, it was I who must take care of them all.

I eyed the heavy bunch with circumspection. Until that moment, I had not given a single thought to the practical aspects of marriage with a great house, great wealth, a great man, whose key ring was as crowded as that of a prison warder. Here were the clumsy and archaic keys for the dungeons, for dungeons we had in plenty although they had been converted to cellars for his wines; the dusty bottles inhabited in racks all those deep holes of pain in the rock on which the castle was built. These are the keys to the kitchens, this is the key to the picture gallery, a treasure house filled by five centuries of avid collectors – ah! he foresaw I would spend hours there.

He had amply indulged his taste for the Symbolists, he told me with a glint of greed. There was Moreau's great portrait of his first wife, the famous *Sacrificial Victim* with the imprint of the lacelike chains on her pellucid skin. Did I know the story of the painting of that picture? How, when she took off her clothes for him for the first time, she fresh from her bar in Montmartre, she had robed herself involuntarily in a blush that reddened her breasts, her shoulders, her arms, her whole body? He had thought of that story, of that dear girl, when first he had undressed me ... Ensor, the great Ensor, his monolithic canvas: *The Foolish Virgins*. Two or three late Gauguins, his special favourite the one of the tranced brown girl in the deserted house which was called: *Out of the Night We Come, Into the Night We Go*. And, besides the additions he had made himself, his marvellous inheritance of Watteaus, Poussins and a pair of very special Fragonards, commissioned for a licentious ancestor who, it was said, had posed for the master's brush himself with his own two daughters ... He broke off his catalogue of treasures abruptly.

Your thin white face, chérie; he said, as if he saw it for the first time. Your thin white face, with its promise of debauchery only a connoisseur could detect.

A log fell in the fire, instigating a shower of sparks; the opal on my finger spurted green flame. I felt as giddy as if I were on the edge of a precipice; I was afraid, not so much of him, of his monstrous presence, heavy as if he had been gifted at birth with more specific *gravity* than the rest of us, the presence

that, even when I thought myself most in love with him, always subtly oppressed me ... No. I was not afraid of him; but of myself. I seemed reborn in his unreflective eyes, reborn in unfamiliar shapes. I hardly recognised myself from his descriptions of me and yet, and yet – might there not be a grain of beastly truth in them? And, in the red firelight, I blushed again, unnoticed, to think he might have chosen me because, in my innocence, he sensed a rare talent for corruption.

Here is the key to the china cabinet – don't laugh, my darling; there's a king's ransom in Sèvres in that closet, and a queen's ransom in Limoges. And a key to the locked, barred room where five generations of plate were kept.

Keys, keys, keys. He would trust me with the keys to his office, although I was only a baby; and the keys to his safes, where he kept the jewels I should wear, he promised me, when we returned to Paris. Such jewels! Why, I would be able to change my earrings and necklaces three times a day, just as the Empress Josephine used to change her underwear. He doubted, he said, with that hollow, knocking sound that served him for a chuckle, I would be quite so interested in his share certificates although they, of course, were worth infinitely more.

Outside our firelit privacy, I could hear the sound of the tide drawing back from the pebbles of the foreshore; it was nearly time for him to leave me. One single key remained unaccounted for on the ring and he hesitated over it; for a moment, I thought he was going to unfasten it from its brothers, slip it back into his pocket and take it away with him.

'What is *that* key?' I demanded, for his chaffing had made me bold. 'The key to your heart? Give it me!'

He dangled the key tantalizingly above my head, out of reach of my straining fingers; those bare red lips of his cracked sidelong in a smile.

'Ah, no,' he said. 'Not the key to my heart. Rather, the key to my enfer.'

He left it on the ring, fastened the ring together, shook it musically, like a carillon. Then threw the keys in a jingling heap in my lap. I could feel the cold metal chilling my thighs through my thin muslin frock. He bent over me to drop a beard-masked kiss on my forehead.

'Every man must have one secret, even if only one, from his wife,' he said. 'Promise me this, my whey-faced piano-player; promise me you'll use all the keys on the ring except that last little one I showed you. Play with anything you find, jewels, silver plate; make toy boats of my share certificates, if it pleases you, and send them sailing off to America after me. All is yours, everywhere is open to you – except the lock that this single key fits. Yet all it is is the key to a little room at the foot of the west tower, behind the still-room, at the end of a dark little corridor full of horrid cobwebs that would get into your hair and frighten you if you ventured there. Oh, and you'd find it such a dull little room! But you must promise me, if you love me, to leave it well alone. It is only a private study, a hideaway, a "den", as the English say, where I can go, sometimes, on those infrequent yet inevitable occasions when the yoke of marriage seems to weigh too heavily on my shoulders. There I can go, you

understand, to savour the rare pleasure of imagining myself wifeless.'

There was a little thin starlight in the courtyard as, wrapped in my furs, I saw him to his car. His last words were, that he had telephoned the mainland and taken a piano-tuner on to the staff; this man would arrive to take up his duties the next day. He pressed me to his vicuña breast, once, and then drove away.

I had drowsed away that afternoon and now I could not sleep. I lay tossing and turning in his ancestral bed until another daybreak discoloured the dozen mirrors that were iridescent with the reflections of the sea. The perfume of the lilies weighed on my senses; when I thought that, henceforth, I would always share these sheets with a man whose skin, as theirs did, contained that toad-like, clammy hint of moisture, I felt a vague desolation that within me, now my female wound had healed, there had awoken a certain queasy craving like the cravings of pregnant women for the taste of coal or chalk or tainted food, for the renewal of his caresses. Had he not hinted to me, in his flesh as in his speech and looks, of the thousand, thousand baroque intersections of flesh upon flesh? I lay in our wide bed accompanied by a sleepless companion, my dark newborn curiosity.

I lay in bed alone. And I longed for him. And he disgusted me.

Were there jewels enough in all his safes to recompense me for this predicament? Did all that castle hold enough riches to recompense me for the company of the libertine with whom I must share it? And what, precisely, was the nature of my desirous dread for this mysterious being who, to show his mastery over me, had abandoned me on my wedding night?

Then I sat straight up in bed, under the sardonic masks of the gargoyles carved above me, riven by a wild surmise. Might he have left me, not for Wall Street but for an importunate mistress tucked away God knows where who knew how to pleasure him far better than a girl whose fingers had been exercised, hitherto, only by the practice of scales and arpeggios? And, slowly, soothed, I sank back on to the heaping pillows; I acknowledged that the jealous scare I'd just given myself was not unmixed with a little tincture of relief.

At last I drifted into slumber, as daylight filled the room and chased bad dreams away. But the last thing I remembered, before I slept, was the tall jar of lilies beside the bed, how the thick glass distorted their fat stems so they looked like arms, dismembered arms, drifting drowned in greenish water.

Coffee and croissants to console this bridal, solitary waking. Delicious. Honey, too, in a section of comb on a glass saucer. The maid squeezed the aromatic juice from an orange into a chilled goblet while I watched her as I lay in the lazy, midday bed of the rich. Yet nothing, this morning, gave me more than a fleeting pleasure except to hear that the piano-tuner had been at work already. When the maid told me that, I sprang out of bed and pulled on my old serge skirt and flannel blouse, costume of a student, in which I felt far

more at ease with myself than in any of my fine new clothes.

After my three hours of practice, I called the piano-tuner in, to thank him. He was blind, of course; but young, with a gentle mouth and grey eyes that fixed upon me although they could not see me. He was a blacksmith's son from the village across the causeway; a chorister in the church whom the good priest had taught a trade so that he could make a living. All most satisfactory. Yes. He thought he would be happy here. And if, he added shyly, he might sometimes be allowed to hear me play ... for, you see, he loved music. Yes. Of course, I said. Certainly. He seemed to know that I had smiled.

After I dismissed him, even though I'd woken so late, it was still barely time for my 'five o'clock'. The housekeeper, who, thoughtfully forewarned by my husband, had restrained herself from interrupting my music, now made me a solemn visitation with a lengthy menu for a late luncheon. When I told her I did not need it, she looked at me obliquely, along her nose. I understood at once that one of my principal functions as châtelaine was to provide work for the staff. But, all the same, I asserted myself and said I would wait until dinner-time, although I looked forward nervously to the solitary meal. Then I found I had to tell her what I would like to have prepared for me; my imagination, still that of a schoolgirl, ran riot. A fowl in cream – or should I anticipate Christmas with a varnished turkey? No; I have decided. Avocado and shrimp, lots of it, followed by no entrée at all. But surprise me for dessert with every ice-cream in the ice box. She noted all down but sniffed; I'd shocked her. Such tastes! Child that I was, I giggled when she left me.

But, now ... what shall I do, now?

I could have spent a happy hour unpacking the trunks that contained my trousseau but the maid had done that already, the dresses, the tailor-mades hung in the wardrobe in my dressing room, the hats on wooden heads to keep their shape, the shoes on wooden feet as if all these inanimate objects were imitating the appearance of life, to mock me. I did not like to linger in my overcrowded dressing room, nor in my lugubriously lily-scented bedroom. How shall I pass the time?

I shall take a bath in my own bathroom! And found the taps were little dolphins made of gold, with chips of turquoise for eyes. And there was a tank of goldfish, who swam in and out of moving fronds of weeds, as bored, I thought, as I was. How I wished he had not left me. How I wished it were possible to chat with, say, a maid; or, the piano-tuner ... but I knew already my new rank forbade overtures of friendship to the staff.

I had been hoping to defer the call as long as I could, so that I should have something to look forward to in the dead waste of time I foresaw before me, after my dinner was done with, but, at a quarter before seven, when darkness already surrounded the castle, I could contain myself no longer. I telephoned my mother. And astonished myself by bursting into tears when I heard her voice.

No, nothing was the matter. Mother, I have gold bath taps.

I said, gold bath taps!

No; I suppose that's nothing to cry about, Mother.

The line was bad, I could hardly make out her congratulations, her questions, her concern, but I was a little comforted when I put the receiver down.

Yet there still remained one whole hour to dinner and the whole unimaginable desert of the rest of the evening.

The bunch of keys lay, where he had left them, on the rug before the library fire which had warmed their metal so that they no longer felt cold to the touch but warm, almost, as my own skin. How careless I was; a maid, tending the logs, eyed me reproachfully as if I'd set a trap for her as I picked up the clinking bundle of keys, the keys to the interior doors of this lovely prison of which I was both the inmate and the mistress and had scarcely seen. When I remembered that, I felt the exhilaration of the explorer.

Lights! More lights!

At the touch of a switch, the dreaming library was brilliantly illuminated. I ran crazily about the castle, switching on every light I could find – I ordered the servants to light up all their quarters, too, so the castle would shine like a seaborne birthday cake lit with a thousand candles, one for every year of its life, and everybody on shore would wonder at it. When everything was lit as brightly as the café in the Gare du Nord, the significance of the possessions implied by that bunch of keys no longer intimidated me, for I was determined, now, to search through them all for evidence of my husband's true nature.

His office first, evidently.

A mahogany desk half a mile wide, with an impeccable blotter and a bank of telephones. I allowed myself the luxury of opening the safe that contained the jewellery and delved sufficiently among the leather boxes to find out how my marriage had given me access to a jinn's treasury – parures, bracelets, rings ... While I was thus surrounded by diamonds, a maid knocked on the door and entered before I spoke; a subtle discourtesy. I would speak to my husband about it. She eyed my serge skirt superciliously; did madame plan to dress for dinner?

She made a moue of disdain when I laughed to hear that, she was far more the lady than I. But, imagine – to dress up in one of my Poiret extravaganzas, with the jewelled turban and aigrette on my head, roped with pearl to the navel, to sit down all alone in the baronial dining hall at the head of that massive board at which King Mark was reputed to have fed his knights ... I grew calmer under the cold eye of her disapproval. I adopted the crisp inflections of an officer's daughter. No, I would not dress for dinner. Furthermore, I was not hungry enough for dinner itself. She must tell the housekeeper to cancel the dormitory feast I'd ordered. Could they leave me sandwiches and a flask of coffee in my music room? And would they all dismiss for the night?

Mais oui, madame.

I knew by her bereft intonation I had let them down again but I did not care; I was armed against them by the brilliance of his hoard. But I would

not find his heart amongst the glittering stones; as soon as she had gone, I began a systematic search of the drawers of his desk.

All was in order, so I found nothing. Not a random doodle on an old envelope, nor the faded photograph of a woman. Only the files of business correspondence, the bills from the home farms, the invoices from tailors, the billets-doux from international financiers. Nothing. And this absence of the evidence of his real life began to impress me strangely; there must, I thought, be a great deal to conceal if he takes such pains to hide it.

His office was a singularly impersonal room, facing inwards, on to the courtyard, as though he wanted to turn his back on the siren sea in order to keep a clear head while he bankrupted a small businessman in Amsterdam or – I noticed with a thrill of distaste – engaged in some business in Laos that must, from certain cryptic references to his amateur botanist's enthusiasm for rare poppies, be to do with opium. Was he not rich enough to do without crime? Or was the crime itself his profit? And yet I saw enough to appreciate his zeal for secrecy.

Now I had ransacked his desk, I must spend a cool-headed quarter of an hour putting every last letter back where I found it, and, as I covered the traces of my visit, by some chance, as I reached inside a little drawer that had stuck fast, I must have touched a hidden spring, for a secret drawer flew open within that drawer itself; and this secret drawer contained – at last! – a file marked: *Personal.*

I was alone, but for my reflection in the uncurtained window.

I had a brief notion that his heart, pressed flat as a flower, crimson and thin as tissue paper, lay in this file. It was a very thin one.

I could have wished, perhaps, I had not found that touching, ill-spelt note, on a paper napkin marked *La Coupole*, that began: 'My darling, I cannot wait for the moment when you may make me yours completely.' The diva had sent him a page of the score of *Tristan*, the Liebestod, with the single, cryptic word: 'Until . . .' scrawled across it. But the strangest of all these love letters was a postcard with a view of a village graveyard, among mountains, where some black-coated ghoul enthusiastically dug at a grave; this little scene, executed with the lurid exuberance of Grand Guignol, was captioned: 'Typical Transylvanian Scene – Midnight, All Hallows.' And, on the other side, the message: 'On the occasion of this marriage to the descendant of Dracula – always remember, "the supreme and unique pleasure of love is the certainty that one is doing evil". Toutes amitiés, C.'

A joke. A joke in the worst possible taste; for had he not been married to a Romanian countess? And then I remembered her pretty, witty face, and her name – Carmilla. My most recent predecessor in this castle had been, it would seem, the most sophisticated.

I put away the file, sobered. Nothing in my life of family love and music had prepared me for these grown-up games and yet these were clues to his self that showed me, at least, how much he had been loved, even if they did not

reveal any good reason for it. But I wanted to know still more; and, as I closed the office door and locked it, the means to discover more fell in my way.

Fell, indeed; and with the clatter of a dropped canteen of cutlery, for, as I turned the slick Yale lock, I contrived, somehow, to open up the key ring itself, so that all the keys tumbled loose on the floor. And the very first key I picked out of that pile was, as luck or ill fortune had it, the key to the room he had forbidden me, the room he would keep for his own so that he could go there when he wished to feel himself once more a bachelor.

I made my decision to explore it before I felt a faint resurgence of my ill-defined fear of his waxen stillness. Perhaps I half-imagined, then, that I might find his real self in his den, waiting there to see if indeed I had obeyed him; that he had sent a moving figure of himself to New York, the enigmatic, self-sustaining carapace of his public person, while the real man, whose face I had glimpsed in the storm of orgasm, occupied himself with pressing private business in the study at the foot of the west tower, behind the still-room. Yet, if that were so, it was imperative that I should find him, should know him; and I was too deluded by his apparent taste for me to think my disobedience might truly offend him.

I took the forbidden key from the heap and left the others lying there.

It was now very late and the castle was adrift, as far as it could go from the land, in the middle of the silent ocean where, at my orders, it floated like a garland of light. And all silent, all still, but for the murmuring of the waves.

I felt no fear, no intimation of dread. Now I walked as firmly as I had done in my mother's house.

Not a narrow, dusty little passage at all; why had he lied to me? But an ill-lit one, certainly; the electricity, for some reason did not extend here, so I retreated to the still-room and found a bundle of waxed tapers in a cupboard, stored there with matches to light the oak board at grand dinners. I put a match to my little taper and advanced with it in my hand, like a penitent, along the corridor hung with heavy, I think Venetian, tapestries. The flame picked out, here, the head of a man, there, the rich breast of a woman spilling through a rent in her dress – the Rape of the Sabines, perhaps? The naked swords and immolated horses suggested some grisly mythological subject. The corridor wound downwards; there was an almost imperceptible ramp to the thickly carpeted floor. The heavy hangings on the wall muffled my footsteps, even my breathing. For some reason, it grew very warm; the sweat sprang out in beads on my brow. I could no longer hear the sound of the sea.

A long, a winding corridor, as if I were in the viscera of the castle; and this corridor led to a door of worm-eaten oak, low, round-topped, barred with black iron.

And still I felt no fear, no raising of the hairs on the back of the neck, no prickling of the thumbs.

The key slid into the new lock as easily as a hot knife into butter.

No fear; but a hesitation, a holding of the spiritual breath.

If I had found some traces of his heart in a file marked: *Personal*, perhaps, here, in his subterranean privacy, I might find a little of his soul. It was the consciousness of the possibility of such a discovery, of its possible strangeness, that kept me for a moment motionless, before, in the foolhardiness of my already subtly tainted innocence, I turned the key and the door creaked slowly back.

'There is a striking resemblance between the act of love and the ministrations of a torturer,' opined my husband's favourite poet; I had learned something of the nature of that similarity on my marriage bed. And now my taper showed me the outlines of a rack. There was also a great wheel, like the ones I had seen in woodcuts of the martyrdoms of the saints, in my old nurse's little store of holy books. And – just one glimpse of it before my little flame caved in and I was left in absolute darkness – a metal figure, hinged at the side, which I knew to be spiked on the inside and to have the name: the Iron Maiden.

Absolute darkness. And, about me, the instruments of mutilation.

Until that moment, this spoiled child did not know she had inherited nerves and a will from the mother who had defied the yellow outlaws of Indo-China. My mother's spirit drove me on, into that dreadful place, in a cold ecstasy to know the very worst. I fumbled for the matches in my pocket; what a dim, lugubrious light they gave! And yet, enough, oh, more than enough, to see a room designed for desecration and some dark night of unimaginable lovers whose embraces were annihilation.

The walls of this stark torture chamber were the naked rock; they gleamed as if they were sweating with fright. At the four corners of the room were funerary urns, of great antiquity, Etruscan, perhaps, and, on three-legged ebony stands, the bowls of incense he had left burning which filled the room with a sacerdotal reek. Wheel, rack and Iron Maiden were, I saw, displayed as grandly as if they were items of statuary and I was almost consoled, then, and almost persuaded myself that I might have stumbled only upon a little museum of his perversity, that he had installed these monstrous items here only for contemplation.

Yet at the centre of the room lay a catafalque, a doomed, ominous bier of Renaissance workmanship, surrounded by long white candles and, at its foot, an armful of the same lilies with which he had filled my bedroom, stowed in a four-foot-high jar glazed with a sombre Chinese red. I scarcely dared examine this catafalque and its occupant more closely; yet I knew I must.

Each time I struck a match to light those candles round her bed, it seemed a garment of that innocence of mine for which he had lusted fell away from me.

The opera singer lay, quite naked, under a thin sheet of very rare and precious linen, such as the princes of Italy used to shroud those whom they had poisoned. I touched her, very gently, on the white breast; she was cool, he had embalmed her. On her throat I could see the blue imprint of his

175

strangler's fingers. The cool, sad flame of the candles flickered on her white, closed eyelids. The worst thing was, the dead lips smiled.

Beyond the catafalque, in the middle of the shadows, a white, nacreous glimmer; as my eyes accustomed themselves to the gathering darkness, I at last – oh, horrors! – made out a skull; yes, a skull, so utterly denuded, now, of flesh, that it scarcely seemed possible the stark bone had once been richly upholstered with life. And this skull was strung up by a system of unseen cords, so that it appeared to hang, disembodied, in the still, heavy air, and it had been crowned with a wreath of white roses, and a veil of lace, the final image of his bride.

Yet the skull was still so beautiful, had shaped with its sheer planes so imperiously the face that had once existed above it, that I recognised her the moment I saw her; face of the evening star walking on the rim of night. One false step, oh, my poor, dear girl, next in the fated sisterhood of his wives; one false step and into the abyss of the dark you stumbled.

And where was she, the latest dead, the Romanian countess who might have thought her blood would survive his depredations? I knew she must be here, in the place that had wound me through the castle towards it on a spool of inexorability. But, at first, I could see no sign of her. Then, for some reason – perhaps some change of atmosphere wrought by my presence – the metal shell of the Iron Maiden emitted a ghostly twang; my feverish imagination might have guessed its occupant was trying to clamber out, though, even in the midst of my rising hysteria, I knew she must be dead to find a home there.

With trembling fingers, I prised open the front of the upright coffin, with its sculpted face caught in a rictus of pain. Then, overcome, I dropped the key I still held in my other hand. It dropped into the forming pool of her blood.

She was pierced, not by one but by a hundred spikes, this child of the land of the vampires who seemed so newly dead, so full of blood . . . oh God! how recently had he become a widower? How long had he kept her in this obscene cell? Had it been all the time he had courted me, in the clear light of Paris?

I closed the lid of her coffin very gently and burst into a tumult of sobbing that contained both pity for his other victims and also a dreadful anguish to know I, too, was one of them.

The candles flared, as if in a draught from a door to elsewhere. The light caught the fire opal on my hand so that it flashed, once, with a baleful light, as if to tell me the eye of God – his eye – was upon me. My first thought, when I saw the ring for which I had sold myself to this fate, was, how to escape it.

I retained sufficient presence of mind to snuff out the candles round the bier with my fingers, to gather up my taper, to look around, although shuddering, to ensure I had left behind me no traces of my visit.

I retrieved the key from the pool of blood, wrapped it in my handkerchief to keep my hands clean, and fled the room, slamming the door behind me.

It crashed to with a juddering reverberation, like the door of hell.

I could not take refuge in my bedroom, for that retained the memory of his presence trapped in the fathomless silvering of his mirrors. My music room seemed the safest place, although I looked at the picture of Saint Cecilia with a faint dread; what had been the nature of her martyrdom? My mind was in a tumult; schemes for flight jostled with one another ... as soon as the tide receded from the causeway, I would make for the mainland – on foot, running, stumbling; I did not trust that leather-clad chauffeur, nor the well-behaved housekeeper, and I dared not take any of the pale, ghostly maids into my confidence, either, since they were his creatures, all. Once at the village, I would fling myself directly on the mercy of the gendarmerie.

But – could I trust them, either? His forefathers had ruled this coast for eight centuries, from this castle whose moat was the Atlantic. Might not the police, the advocates, even the judge, all be in his service, turning a common blind eye to his vices since he was milord whose word must be obeyed? Who, on this distant coast, would believe the white-faced girl from Paris who came running to them with a shuddering tale of blood, of fear, of the ogre murmuring in the shadows? Or, rather, they would immediately know it to be true. But were all honour-bound to let me carry it no further.

Assistance. My mother. I ran to the telephone; and the line, of course, was dead.

Dead as his wives.

A thick darkness, unlit by any star, still glazed the windows. Every lamp in my room burned, to keep the dark outside, yet it seemed still to encroach on me, to be present beside me but as if masked by my lights, the night like a permeable substance that could seep into my skin. I looked at the precious little clock made from hypocritically innocent flowers long ago, in Dresden; the hands had scarcely moved one single hour forward from when I first descended to that private slaughterhouse of his. Time was his servant, too; it would trap me, here, in a night that would last until he came back to me, like a black sun on a hopeless morning.

And yet the time might still be my friend; at that hour, that very hour, he set sail for New York.

To know that, in a few moments, my husband would have left France calmed my agitation a little. My reason told me I had nothing to fear; the tide that would take him away to the New World would let me out of the imprisonment of the castle. Surely I could easily evade the servants. Anybody can buy a ticket at a railway station. Yet I was still filled with unease. I opened the lid of the piano; perhaps I thought my own particular magic might help me, now, that I could create a pentacle out of music that would keep me from harm for, if my music had first ensnared him, then might it not also give me the power to free myself from him?

Mechanically, I began to play but my fingers were stiff and shaking. At first, I could manage nothing better than the exercises of Czerny but simply the act of

playing soothed me and, for solace, for the sake of the harmonious rationality of its sublime mathematics, I searched among his scores until I found *The Well-Tempered Clavier*. I set myself the therapeutic task of playing all Bach's equations, every one, and, I told myself, if I played them all through without a single mistake – then the morning would find me once more a virgin.

Crash of a dropped stick.

His silver-headed cane! What else? Sly, cunning, he had returned; he was waiting for me outside the door!

I rose to my feet; fear gave me strength. I flung back my head defiantly.

'Come in!' My voice astonished me by its firmness, its clarity.

The door slowly, nervously opened and I saw, not the massive, irredeemable bulk of my husband but the slight, stooping figure of the piano-tuner, and he looked far more terrified of me than my mother's daughter would have been of the Devil himself. In the torture chamber, it seemed to me that I would never laugh again; now, helplessly, laugh I did, with relief, and, after a moment's hesitation, the boy's face softened and he smiled a little, almost in shame. Though they were blind, his eyes were singularly sweet.

'Forgive me,' said Jean-Yves. 'I know I've given you grounds for dismissing me, that I should be crouching outside your door at midnight ... but I heard you walking about, up and down – I sleep in a room at the foot of the west tower – and some intuition told me you could not sleep and might, perhaps, pass the insomniac hours at your piano. And I could not resist that. Besides, I stumbled over these – '

And he displayed the ring of keys I'd dropped outside my husband's office door, the ring from which one key was missing. I took them from him, looked round for a place to stow them, fixed on the piano-stool as if to hide them would protect me. Still he stood smiling at me. How hard it was to make everyday conversation.

'It's perfect,' I said. 'The piano. Perfectly in tune.'

But he was full of the loquacity of embarrassment, as though I would only forgive him for his impudence if he explained the cause of it thoroughly.

'When I heard you play this afternoon, I thought I'd never heard such a touch. Such technique. A treat for me, to hear a virtuoso! So I crept up to your door now, humbly as a little dog might, madame, and put my ear to the keyhole and listened, and listened – until my stick fell to the floor through a momentary clumsiness of mine, and I was discovered.'

He had the most touchingly ingenuous smile.

'Perfectly in tune,' I repeated. To my surprise, now I had said it, I found I could not say anything else. I could only repeat: 'In tune ... perfect ... in tune,' over and over again. I saw a dawning surprise in his face. My head throbbed. To see him, in his lovely, blind humanity, seemed to hurt me very piercingly, somewhere inside my breast; his figure blurred, the room swayed about me. After the dreadful revelation of that bloody chamber, it was his tender look that made me faint.

When I recovered consciousness, I found I was lying in the piano-tuner's arms and he was tucking the satin cushion from the piano-stool under my head.

'You are in some great distress,' he said. 'No bride should suffer so much, so early in her marriage.'

His speech had the rhythms of the countryside, the rhythms of the tides.

'Any bride brought to this castle should come ready dressed in mourning, should bring a priest and a coffin with her,' I said.

'What's this?'

It was too late to keep silent; and if he, too, were one of my husband's creatures, then at least he had been kind to me. So I told him everything, the keys, the interdiction, my disobedience, the room, the rack, the skull, the corpses, the blood.

'I can scarcely believe it,' he said, wondering. 'The man ... so rich; so well-born.'

'Here's proof,' I said and tumbled the fatal key out of my handkerchief onto the silken rug.

'Oh God,' he said. 'I can smell the blood.'

He took my hand; he pressed his arms about me. Although he was scarcely more than a boy, I felt a great strength flow into me from his touch.

'We whisper all manner of strange tales up and down the coast,' he said. 'There was a Marquis, once, who used to hunt young girls on the mainland; he hunted them with dogs, as though they were foxes. My grandfather had it from his grandfather, how the Marquis pulled a head out of his saddle bag and showed it to the blacksmith while the man was shoeing his horse. "A fine specimen of the genus, brunette, eh, Guillaume?" And it was the head of the blacksmith's wife.'

But, in these more democratic times, my husband must travel as far as Paris to do his hunting in the salons. Jean-Yves knew the moment I shuddered.

'Oh, madame! I thought all these were old wives' tales, chattering of fools, spooks to scare bad children into good behaviour! Yet how could you know, a stranger, that the old name for this place is the Castle of Murder?'

How could I know indeed? Except that, in my heart, I'd always known its lord would be the death of me.

'Hark!' said my friend suddenly. 'The sea has changed key; it must be near morning, the tide is going down.'

He helped me up. I looked from the window, towards the mainland, along the causeway where the stoned gleamed wetly in the thin light of the end of the night and, with an almost unimaginable horror, a horror the intensity of which I cannot transmit to you, I saw, in the distance, still far away yet drawing moment by moment inexorably nearer, the twin headlamps of his great black car, gouging tunnels through the shifting mist.

My husband had indeed returned; this time, it was no fancy.

'The key!' said Jean-Yves. 'It must go back on the ring, with the others. As though nothing had happened.'

DANGER

But the key was still caked with wet blood and I ran to my bathroom and held it under the hot tap. Crimson water swirled down the basin but, as if the key itself were hurt, the bloody token stuck. The turquoise eyes of the dolphin taps winked at me derisively; they knew my husband had been too clever for me! I scrubbed the stain with my nail brush but still it would not budge. I thought how the car would be rolling silently towards the closed courtyard gate; the more I scrubbed the key, the more vivid grew the stain.

The bell in the gatehouse would jangle. The porter's drowsy son would push back the patchwork quilt, yawning, pull the shirt over his head, thrust his feet into his sabots ... slowly, slowly; open the door for your master as slowly as you can ...

And still the bloodstain mocked the fresh water that spilled from the mouth of the leering dolphin.

'You have no more time,' said Jean-Yves. 'He is here. I know it. I must stay with you.'

'You shall not!' I said. 'Go back to your room, now. Please.'

He hesitated. I put an edge of steel in my voice, for I knew I must meet my lord alone.

'Leave me!'

As soon as he had gone, I dealt with the keys and went to my bedroom. The causeway was empty; Jean-Yves was correct, my husband had already entered the castle. I pulled the curtains close, stripped off my clothes and pulled the bedcurtains round me as a pungent aroma of Russian leather assured me my husband was once again beside me.

'Dearest!'

With the most treacherous, lascivious tenderness, he kissed my eyes, and, mimicking the new bride newly awakened, I flung my arms around him, for on my seeming acquiescence depended my salvation.

'Da Silva of Rio outwitted me,' he said wryly. 'My New York agent telegraphed Le Havre and saved me a wasted journey. So we may resume our interrupted pleasures, my love.'

I did not believe one word of it. I knew I had behaved exactly according to his desires; had he not bought me so that I should do so? I had been tricked into my own betrayal to that illimitable darkness whose source I had been compelled to seek in his absence and, now that I had met that shadowed reality of his that came to life only in the presence of its own atrocities, I must pay the price of my new knowledge. The secret of Pandora's box; but he had given me the box, himself, knowing I must learn the secret. I had played a game in which every move was governed by a destiny as oppressive and omnipotent as himself, since that destiny was himself; and I had lost. Lost at that charade of innocence and vice in which he had engaged me. Lost, as the victim loses to the executioner.

His hand brushed my breast, beneath the sheet. I strained my nerves yet could not help but flinch from the intimate touch, for it made me think of

the piercing embrace of the Iron Maiden and of his lost lovers in the vault. When he saw my reluctance, his eyes veiled over and yet his appetite did not diminish. His tongue ran over red lips already wet. Silent, mysterious, he moved away from me to draw off his jacket. He took the gold watch from his waistcoat and laid it on the dressing table, like a good bourgeois; scooped out his rattling loose change and now – oh God! – makes a great play of patting his pockets officiously, puzzled lips pursed, searching for something that has been mislaid. Then turns to me with a ghastly, a triumphant smile.

'But of course! I gave the keys to you!'

'Your keys? Why, of course. Here, they're under the pillow; wait a moment – what – Ah! No . . . now, where can I have left them? I was whiling away the evening without you at the piano, I remember. Of course! The music room!'

Brusquely he flung my négligé of antique lace on the bed.

'Go and get them.'

'Now? This moment? Can't it wait until morning, my darling?'

I forced myself to be seductive. I saw myself, pale, pliant as a plant that begs to be trampled underfoot, a dozen vulnerable, appealing girls reflected in as many mirrors, and I saw how he almost failed to resist me. If he had come to me in bed, I would have strangled him, then.

But he half-snarled: 'No. It won't wait. Now.'

The unearthly light of dawn filled the room; had only one previous dawn broken upon me in that vile place? And there was nothing for it but to go and fetch the keys from the music stool and pray he would not examine them too closely, pray to God his eyes would fail him, that he might be struck blind.

When I came back into the bedroom carrying the bunch of keys that jangled at every step like a curious musical instrument, he was sitting on the bed in his immaculate shirtsleeves, his head sunk in his hands.

And it seemed to me he was in despair.

Strange. In spite of my fear of him, that made me whiter than my wrap, I felt there emanate from him, at that moment, a stench of absolute despair, rank and ghastly, as if the lilies that surrounded him had all at once begun to fester, or the Russian leather of his scent were reverting to the elements of flayed hide and excrement of which it was composed. The chthonic gravity of his presence exerted a tremendous pressure on the room, so that the blood pounded in my ears as if we had been precipitated to the bottom of the sea, beneath the waves that pounded against the shore.

I held my life in my hands amongst those keys and, in a moment, would place it between his well-manicured fingers. The evidence of that bloody chamber had showed me I could expect no mercy. Yet, when he raised his head and stared at me with his blind, shuttered eyes as though he did not recognise me, I felt a terrified pity for him, for this man who lived in such strange, secret places that, if I loved him enough to follow him, I should have to die.

The atrocious loneliness of that monster!

The monocle had fallen from his face. His curling mane was disordered, as if he had run his hands through it in his distraction. I saw how he had lost his impassivity and was now filled with suppressed excitement. The hand he stretched out for those counters in his game of love and death shook a little; the face that turned towards me contained a sombre delirium that seemed to me compounded of a ghastly, yes, shame but also of a terrible, guilty joy as he slowly ascertained how I had sinned.

The tell-tale stain had resolved itself into a mark the shape and brilliance of the heart on a playing card. He disengaged the key from the ring and looked at it for a while, solitary, brooding.

'It is the key that leads to the kingdom of the unimaginable,' he said. His voice was low and had in it the timbre of certain great cathedral organs that seem, when they are played, to be conversing with God.

I could not restrain a sob.

'Oh, my love, my little love who brought me a white gift of music,' he said, almost as if grieving. 'My little love, you'll never know how much I hate daylight!'

Then he sharply ordered: 'Kneel!'

I knelt before him and he pressed the key lightly to my forehead, held it there for a moment. I felt a faint tingling of the skin and, when I involuntarily glanced at myself in the mirror, I saw the heart-shaped stain had transferred itself to my forehead, to the space between the eyebrows, like the caste mark of a brahmin woman. Or the mark of Cain. And now the key gleamed as freshly as if it had just been cut. He clipped it back on the ring, emitting that same, heavy sigh as he had done when I said that I would marry him.

'My virgin of the arpeggios, prepare yourself for martyrdom.'

'What form shall it take?' I said.

'Decapitation,' he whispered, almost voluptuously. 'Go and bathe yourself; put on that white dress you wore to hear *Tristan* and the necklace that prefigures your end. And I shall take myself off to the armoury, my dear, to sharpen my great-grandfather's ceremonial sword.'

'The servants?'

'We shall have absolute privacy for our last rites; I have already dismissed them. If you look out of the window you can see them going to the mainland.'

It was now the full, pale light of morning; the weather was grey, indeterminate, the sea had an oily, sinister look, a gloomy day on which to die. Along the causeway I could see trouping every maid and scullion, every pot-boy and pan-scourer, valet, laundress and vassal who worked in that great house, most on foot, a few on bicycles. The faceless housekeeper trudged along with a great basket in which, I guessed, she'd stowed as much as she could ransack from the larder. The Marquis must have given the chauffeur leave to borrow the motor for the day, for it went last of all, at a stately pace, as though the procession were a cortège and the car already bore my coffin to the mainland for burial.

But I knew no good Breton earth would cover me, like a last, faithful lover; I had another fate.

'I have given them all a day's holiday, to celebrate our wedding,' he said. And smiled.

However hard I stared at the receding company, I could see no sign of Jean-Yves, our latest servant, hired but the preceding morning.

'Go, now. Bathe yourself; dress yourself. The lustratory ritual and the ceremonial robing; after that, the sacrifice. Wait in the music room until I telephone for you. No, my dear!' And he smiled, as I started, recalling the line was dead. 'One may call inside the castle just as much as one pleases; but, outside – never.'

I scrubbed my forehead with the nail brush as I had scrubbed the key but this red mark would not go away, either, no matter what I did, and I knew I should wear it until I died, though that would not be long. Then I went to my dressing room and put on that white muslin shift, costume of a victim of an auto-da-fé, he had bought me to listen to the Liebestod in. Twelve young women combed out twelve listless sheaves of brown hair in the mirrors; soon, there would be none. The mass of lilies that surrounded me exhaled, now, the odour of their withering. They looked like the trumpets of the angels of death.

On the dressing table, coiled like a snake about to strike, lay the ruby choker.

Already almost lifeless, cold at heart, I descended the spiral staircase to the music room but there I found I had not been abandoned.

'I can be of some comfort to you,' the boy said. 'Though not much use.'

We pushed the piano-stool in front of the open window so that, for as long as I could, I would be able to smell the ancient, reconciling smell of the sea that, in time, will cleanse everything, scour the old bones white, wash away all the stains. The last little chambermaid had trotted along the causeway long ago and now the tide, fated as I, came tumbling in, the crisp wavelets splashing on the old stones.

'You do not deserve this,' he said.

'Who can say what I deserve or no?' I said. 'I've done nothing; but that may be sufficient reason for condemning me.'

'You disobeyed him,' he said. 'That is sufficient reason for him to punish you.'

'I only did what he knew I would.'

'Like Eve,' he said.

The telephone rang a shrill imperative. Let it ring. But my lover lifted me up and set me on my feet; I knew I must answer it. The receiver felt heavy as earth.

'The courtyard. Immediately.'

My lover kissed me, he took my hand. He would come with me if I would lead him. Courage. When I thought of courage, I thought of my mother. Then I saw a muscle in my lover's face quiver.

'Hoofbeats!' he said.

I cast one last, desperate glance from the window and, like a miracle, I saw a horse and rider galloping at a vertiginous speed along the causeway, though the waves crashed, now, high as the horse's fetlocks. A rider, her black skirts tucked up around her waist so she could ride hard and fast, a crazy magnificent horsewoman in widow's weeds.

As the telephone rang again.

'Am I to wait all morning?'

Every moment, my mother drew nearer.

'She will be too late,' Jean-Yves said and yet he could not restrain a note of hope that, though it must be so, yet it might not be so.

The third, intransigent call.

'Shall I come up to heaven to fetch you down, Saint Cecilia? You wicked woman, do you wish me to compound my crimes by desecrating the marriage bed?'

So I must go to the courtyard where my husband waited in his London-tailored trousers and the shirt from Turnbull and Asser, beside the mounting block, with, in his hand, the sword which his great-grandfather had presented to the little corporal, in token of surrender to the Republic, before he shot himself. The heavy sword, unsheathed, grey as that November morning, sharp as childbirth, mortal.

When my husband saw my companion, he observed: 'Let the blind lead the blind, eh? But does even a youth as besotted as you are think she was truly blind to her own desires when she took my ring? Give it me back, whore.'

The fires in the opal had all died down. I gladly slipped it from my finger and, even in that dolorous place, my heart felt lighter for the lack of it. My husband took it lovingly and lodged it on the tip of his little finger; it would go no further.

'It will serve me a dozen more fiancées,' he said. 'To the block, woman. No – leave the boy; I shall deal with him later, utilizing a less exalted instrument than the one with which I do my wife the honour of her immolation, for do not fear that in death you will be divided.

Slowly, slowly, one foot before the other, I crossed the cobbles. The longer I dawdled over my execution, the more time it gave the avenging angel to descend. . .

'Don't loiter, girl! Do you think I shall lose appetite for the meal if you are so long about serving it? No; I shall grow hungrier, more ravenous with each moment, more cruel . . . Run to me, run! I have a place prepared for your exquisite corpse in my display of flesh!'

He raised the sword and cut bright segments from the air with it, but still I lingered although my hopes, so recently raised, now began to flag. If she is not here by now, her horse must have stumbled on the causeway, have plunged into the sea . . . One thing only made me glad; that my lover would not see me die.

My husband laid my branded forehead on the stone and, as he had done once before, twisted my hair into a rope and drew it away from my neck.

'Such a pretty neck,' he said with what seemed to be a genuine, retrospective tenderness. 'A neck like the stem of a young plant.'

I felt the silken bristle of his beard and the wet touch of his lips as he kissed my nape. And, once again, of my apparel I must retain only my gems; the sharp blade ripped my dress in two and it fell from me. A little green moss, growing in the crevices of the mounting block, would be the last thing I should see in all the world.

The whizz of that heavy sword.

And – a great battering and pounding at the gate, the jangling of the bell, the frenzied neighing of a horse! The unholy silence of the place shattered in an instant. The blade did *not* descend, the necklace did *not* sever, my head did *not* roll. For, for an instant, the beast wavered in his stroke, a sufficient split second of astonished indecision to let me spring upright and dart to the assistance of my lover as he struggled sightlessly with the great bolts that kept her out.

The Marquis stood transfixed, utterly dazed, at a loss. It must have been as if he had been watching his beloved *Tristan* for the twelfth, the thirteenth time and Tristan stirred, then leapt from his bier in the last act, announced in a jaunty aria interposed from Verdi that bygones were bygones, crying over spilt milk did nobody any good and, as for himself, he proposed to live happily ever after. The puppet master, open-mouthed, wide-eyed, impotent at the last, saw his dolls break free of their strings, abandon the rituals he had ordained for them since time began and start to live for themselves; the king, aghast, witnesses the revolt of his pawns.

You never saw such a wild thing as my mother, her hat seized by the winds and blown out to sea so that her hair was her white mane, her black lisle legs exposed to the thigh, her skirts tucked round her waist, one hand on the reins of the rearing horse while the other clasped my father's service revolver and, behind her, the breakers of the savage, indifferent sea, like the witnesses of a furious justice. And my husband stood stock-still, as if she had been Medusa, the sword still raised over his head as in those clockwork tableaux of Bluebeard that you see in glass cases at fairs.

And then it was as though a curious child pushed his centime into the slot and set all in motion. The heavy, bearded figure roared out aloud, braying with fury, and, wielding the honourable sword as if it were a matter of death or glory, charged us, all three.

On her eighteenth birthday, my mother had disposed of a man-eating tiger that had ravaged the villages in the hills north of Hanoi. Now, without a moment's hesitation, she raised my father's gun, took aim and put a single, irreproachable bullet through my husband's head.

We lead a quiet life, the three of us. I inherited, of course, enormous wealth but we have given most of it away to various charities. The castle is now a

school for the blind, though I pray that the children who live there are not haunted by any sad ghosts looking for, crying for, the husband who will never return to the bloody chamber, the contents of which are buried or burned, the door sealed.

I felt I had a right to retain sufficient funds to start a little music school here, on the outskirts of Paris, and we do well enough. Sometimes we can afford to go to the Opéra, though never to sit in a box, of course. We know we are the source of many whisperings and much gossip but the three of us know the truth of it and mere chatter can never harm us. I can only bless the – what shall I call it? – the *maternal telepathy* that sent my mother running headlong from the telephone to the station after I had called her, that night. I never heard you cry before, she said, by way of explanation. Not when you were happy. And who ever cried because of gold bath taps?

The night train, the one I had taken; she lay in her berth, sleepless as I had been. When she could not find a taxi at that lonely halt, she borrowed old Dobbin from a bemused farmer, for some internal urgency told her that she must reach me before the incoming tide sealed me away from her for ever. My poor old nurse, left scandalised at home – what? interrupt milord on his honeymoon? – she died soon after. She had taken so much secret pleasure in the fact that her little girl had become a marquise; and now here I was, scarcely a penny the richer, widowed at seventeen in the most dubious circumstances and busily engaged in setting up house with a piano-tuner. Poor thing, she passed away in a sorry state of disillusion! But I do believe my mother loves him as much as I do.

No paint nor powder, no matter how thick or white, can mask that red mark on my forehead; I am glad he cannot see it – not for fear of his revulsion, since I know he sees me clearly with his heart – but, because it spares my shame.

Pat Califia

FROM

The Calyx of Isis (1988)

*T*he Calyx of Isis is a lesbian nightclub specialising in supplying the *requisites for practitioners of sado-masochistic sex. Tyre, the 'madam',*

has arranged the enactment of a special union for Alex and her lover Roxanne.

❧

Tyre had pulled a slim blade, Damascus steel with a horn handle, from the sleeve of her jacket. She ran its edge up the back of Roxanne's legs. The girl stopped panting and immediately froze, obviously trained to mind the blade. 'I think I'm gonna wet my pants,' Kay said to Anne-Marie. 'This is too delicious.'

'I know just how you feel, dear. It's such a cleansing release. So good for the system.'

The knife travelled the inside of Roxanne's thighs. The girl had spread her feet as far apart as her manacles and chain permitted. When the tip of it probed her clit, she jumped a little, then steadied herself. Shoulders, neck, upper arm felt the fine scrape of Tyre's weapon. Then the blade disappeared between her slip and her skin, and its tip plunged up through the thin material. The silk made a grieving sound as it was cut, as if it knew it could not heal itself. Tyre let the elegant rags fall from Roxanne's body, and the girl shivered. Tiny goosebumps came out all over her. She smelled like pure sex. God, she was pretty.

Under the slip she wore a leather corset, cinched so tight that her waist was visibly compressed. Six short garters on each leg kept her stockings taut. Alex motioned everyone close, and all eight women held their hands above Roxanne, then simultaneously lowered them. She jumped when she felt herself handled by so many. The rude hands went everywhere. Obviously, much was going to be demanded from her. She shook beneath their hands, but her nipples got larger and as firm as cherries, and her pussy was already producing enough slippery stuff to pave the way for all of them to take her in turn. And, in fact, they did just that – hand after hand plunging as deep as it could go, turning slowly into her, then being withdrawn to give its neighbour a turn. She was being laid open to the pack, made equally the vessel of each of its members.

Alex took her head between her thighs and worked on the hood's laces. She let all the air out of the gag before peeling the thin kid off Roxanne's face and tweaking out the ear plugs. Tyre had unwound the rope from its cleat, and she slowly lowered her hands. Roxanne sank until she knelt in manacles at Alex's boots. Alex took the rubber band out of her hair and spread the long, curly mass out with both hands.

Roxanne had freckles and a turned-up, defiant nose. Her hazel eyes were clear and determined. She refused to look at anyone but Alex. The girl was no coward, but she was obviously relieved to find that her master was there. Tyre loved the look of her. She was the ultimate bar-femme, dressed up to play the whore for her butch. She might be a slave, but she was also tough. Try to separate her from Alex, and she'd go after you with a broken bottle. It wasn't, Tyre realised from the set of that grim little jaw, Roxanne who doubted the nature and the quality of their relationship. It was Alex – who was explaining

to Roxanne and all of them that she was giving them her 'flashy piece of trash' for the evening, to do with as they liked.

The pack stood in a small circle around the master and her property. Of course, Roxanne had an out. 'All you have to do,' Alex whispered, kneeling to plunge her hand between Roxanne's corset and her breasts, 'is tell me you don't belong to me, and you can walk.' She rubbed her nipples, producing a moan, and then stood, and moved right up to her. Roxanne knelt over her boot and wrapped her arms around Alex's thigh. She stared defiantly at the women behind Alex, and openly rubbed her pussy against the steel toe of Alex's engineering boot.

'Put rings in me now,' she said. Her voice was high and clear. 'I'm not going to change my mind. I belong to you and walking out wouldn't change that any more that it would make water run uphill. Beat me. Brand me. Let these bitches wear themselves out on me if it will entertain you. But I belong to you, Daddy.'

'Well, for now you belong to them,' Alex said, and the pack closed in as if on cue.[12]

---

[12] From *Macho Sluts* (1988).

FRUSTRATION

D esire which is frustrated begins, but does not necessarily end. Initiation and process are at the centre of these texts; consummation and arrival are relegated to second place. In terms of particular female desire there is some parallel with the special, and disreputable, skill of frottage where a woman rubs herself, perhaps to orgasm, while fully clothed. In terms of a literary model, frustration finds its analogue in those texts which exploit a rhetoric of denial and excess in an economy of repetition.

De Pizan's narratives are an example of this pattern. Each saint experiences and survives a variety of sexualised tortures. The process is repeated in another and yet another version, to culminate in triumphant exaggeration with Saint Ursula and her eleven thousand virgins. Queen Elizabeth's poem repeats her own refusals yet ends by contemplating a love which is refused to her. Elizabeth Thomas in her 'Triple League' seems three times to find the ideal beloved, but loses her again to be threatened with permanent unfulfilment. The lover of L.E.L.'s heroine appears with suddenness only to depart as promptly, leaving her with nothing but the mirror of literature as she makes a poem out of her experience of loss. Barrett Browning's nightingales sing Bianca's torturing frustration at the end of every stanza. Stein's anachronistically linked lovers make a harping fetish of the barriers to their union. Elizabeth Jennings repeats the swerves away from love in 'three movements'.

In these texts restraint or denial is signalled by the 'clothing' of the 'secret' or 'gift' which is denied to the importunate lover. De Pizan's martyrs withhold their submission; Rossetti's speaker teases her lover with the flaunting of her secret; the farmer's bride in Mew's poem retains her vulnerable virginity; Jennings's poem contemplates the mental and spiritual obstacles to bodily fulfilment; without her lover's permission, Hacker's persona is denied release; and the exposed beloved in

Califia's story allows herself to be sucked off while refusing to give out.

Inflaming pleasure and pain, frustrated desire includes torture along with a possibility of relief. This is why Sappho's fragment sets up an opposition between 'the sweetness of honey' and 'the sting of the bees'; why Califia's heroine knows jaw-breaking agony in the pursuit of pleasure; why Egerton complains of the torturing excesses of passion and prohibition.

The partners engaged in this mutual frottage often cannot distinguish between the torturer and the tortured. In Rossetti's 'Winter: My Secret', the poet uses the violent imagery of assault ('nipping', 'biting', 'buffetting', 'clipping') to describe the attack of the lover whom she resists. At the same time, she torments the lover with suggestion and refusal. In more extreme conditions, De Pizan's virgin martyrs persecute their torturers to fainting and death. Ardently desiring the acquiescence of the saints, relays of exhausted executioners fall victim to the insatiate and unremitting strength of the women.

Within this frame the processes of sexual arousal are emphasised over culmination. Frottage, irritation, and rubbing reiterate the advance and retreat of desire without focusing on an end. Orgasm is almost irrelevant. Even Califia's purposeful narrative concentrates upon process. And it acknowledges that priority with a conclusion which is actually a new invitation, a new beginning.

Sappho
I Want Neither (c. mid C7th BC)

[From our love]
I want neither
the sweetness of honey
nor the sting of the bees[1]

---

[1] Translation by Josephine Balmer, *Sappho: Poems and Fragments* (London, 1984), fragment 7. For the Greek, see *Poetarum Lesbiorum Fragmenta*, ed. Edgar Lobel and Denys Page (Oxford, 1955), fr. 146.

Christine de Pizan

FROM

The Book of the City of Ladies (1404–5)

*D*e Pizan wrote her allegory of a 'city' of famous ladies as a bastion against the judgement of famous men who declared that 'the behaviour of women is inclined to and full of every vice'. Guided by the three daughters of God – Reason, Justice and Rectitude – she visits the city, meeting heroines from myth and history, all of whom are celebrated for virtues of various kinds. Part III, from which this extract is taken, tells stories of the lives of the saints who make up the 'high roofs of the towers' and inhabit the 'great palaces and lofty mansions' of the city.

'We must not forget the blessed Martina, virgin. This blessed woman was born in Rome of noble parents and was extraordinarily beautiful. The emperor wanted to force her to become his wife and she refused, saying, "I am a Christian woman offered to the Living God who delights in a chaste body and pure body and to Him I sacrifice and commend myself."[2] Out of spite for her answer, the emperor ordered that she be brought to a temple and forced to worship the idols. She knelt down there, her eyes raised to Heaven and her hands clasped together, and made her prayer to God. Immediately the idols started to sway and fall down, and the temple was wrecked, and the priests serving these idols were killed. The devil residing in the largest idol cried out and proclaimed that Martina was God's servant. The tyrannical emperor delivered Martina to a cruel martyrdom, in order to avenge his gods, and God appeared to her and comforted her. She prayed for her torturers who were thereupon converted through her merits, and a great many spectators along with them. The emperor grew more obstinate than before because of this and had her tortured all the more with various cruel torments, whereupon her torturers cried out that they saw God and His saints standing before her, and they begged for mercy and were converted. As Martina interceded to God on their behalf, a light shone around them and a voice was heard from Heaven proclaiming, "Out of love for my beloved Martina, I will spare you." The prefect there shouted at them

---

[2] According to medieval belief, virginity in women brought them closer to the strength and status of men.

because they had been converted, "Fools, this enchantress Martina has deceived you!" Without the slightest fear they replied, "But the devil in you has deceived you, for you do not recognise your Creator." In a rage, the emperor ordered them to be hanged and their bodies broken, and they received their martyrdom joyfully praising God. Thereupon the emperor had Martina stripped nude, and her lily-white body dazzled the spectators because of its singular beauty. After the emperor who lusted after her had argued with her for a long time and realised she would not comply, he ordered that her body be slashed all over, and instead of blood, milk poured from her wounds, and she gave off a sweet scent. Raving all the more at her, the emperor ordered her body to be drawn and staked down and broken, but those who were martyring her became exhausted because God prevented her from dying too quickly so that the torturers and spectators would be moved to convert. They began to cry out, "Your Majesty, we can do no more, for the angels are beating us with chains." And fresh executioners arrived to torment her, but they died on the spot, and the confused emperor did not know what to do. He had her stretched out and set on fire with burning oil. She continued to praise God and a strong sweet odour issued from her mouth. When the tyrants were exhausted from torturing her, they threw her into a dark dungeon. . . .

The emperor raged all the more and ordered her stretched out and her flesh to be ripped off with iron hooks. She continued to worship God. When the emperor saw she was not dying, he ordered that she be thrown to the wild beasts. A large lion who had not eaten for three days approached her, bowed down, and lay down next to her as though he were a pet dog, and licked her wounds. And she blessed our Lord, saying, "God, may you be praised, who tame the cruelty of wild beasts with your virtue." The tyrant, angered by this, ordered the lion taken back to its pit, whereupon the lion arose in a rage, bounded up and killed Egalabalus, the emperor's cousin, which grieved the emperor greatly. He commanded her to be thrown into a large fire; as she stood joyfully in the flames, God sent a strong wind which extinguished the flames around her but burnt her torturers. Thereupon the emperor ordered her long and beautiful hair to be shaved off, for he claimed the power of her spells lay in her hair. And the virgin told him, "If you cut off the hair which, as the Apostle has said, is the ornament of women, God will take away your kingdom from you and will persecute you. You will wait for death in enormous pain." Then he commanded her to be shut up in a temple dedicated to his gods, and he himself sealed and nailed the door shut and affixed the door with his seal. He returned after three days and found the idols of his gods overturned and the virgin playing with the angels, healthy and whole. The emperor asked her what she had done with his gods and she replied, "The virtue of Jesus Christ has confounded them." Then he ordered her throat cut, whereupon a voice was heard from Heaven saying, "Martina, virgin, because you fought in My name, enter into My Kingdom with the saints and rejoice in eternity with Me." And in this way the blessed Martina died. The bishop of Rome, accompanied by

all the clergy, then came and buried her body honourably in a church. That same day, the emperor, who was named Alexander, was stricken with such a grievous affliction that he ate his own flesh.'

'There was another Saint Lucy, who came from the city of Syracuse. Once, while praying for her sick mother at the tomb of Saint Agatha, she beheld Saint Agatha in a vision, surrounded by angels and adorned with jewels, who said to her, "Lucy, my sister, virgin devoted to God, why do you ask me for something which you yourself can give to your mother? I tell you that, just as the city of Catania is protected by me, so too will the city of Syracuse receive your aid, for in your purity you have gathered together choice jewels for Jesus Christ." Lucy arose and after her mother's healing, she gave away all she owned for God and ended her life in martyrdom. Among her other tribulations, a judge threatened to have her imprisoned in an asylum for mad women and there, in spite of her husband, she would be raped. She replied, "The soul will never be sullied without the mind's consent. For if you rape me, my chastity will be doubled, as well as my victory." Just as they tried to take her there, she became so heavy that in spite of the oxen and other animals to which they hitched her, she could not be moved. They placed ropes around her feet to drag her away, but she remained as firm as a mountain. At her death she prophesied the future of the empire.'

'Justine, a holy virgin born in Antioch, very young and extraordinarily beautiful, overcame the Devil, who boasted during the invocation of a necromancer that he would succeed in making her do the will of a man who was completely taken with her love and who would not leave her in peace, for he thought the Devil could help where entreaties and promises were useless. But nothing helped, for the glorious Justine repeatedly chased away the Devil, who presented himself in various forms to tempt her, but she vanquished and conquered him, and with her preaching she converted the foolish man who lusted after her. The necromancer himself was also converted, a man named Cyprian, who had led an evil life and whom she changed into a good man. And many others were converted by the signs which our Lord showed forth in her. She departed this world in the end as a martyr.

'Similarly, the blessed virgin Eulalia, born in Spain, stole away at the age of 12 from her parents who held her shut in because she would not stop talking about Jesus Christ. She fled by night and went to a temple where she threw down the idols to the ground, and she cried out to the judges who persecuted the martyrs that they were deceived and that she wished to die in the Faith. So she was ranked among the soldiers of Jesus Christ and suffered many tortures. Many were converted by the signs which our Lord manifested through her.

'Another virgin saint, named Macra, was also harshly tortured because of her faith in God. Among the torments she suffered was having her breasts ripped off. Afterward, as she lay in prison, God sent His angel to her, who restored

her health, so that the prefect was completely stunned the following day. All the same he did not cease having her tortured with various torments. At last she gave up her spirit to God. Her body lies buried near the city of Reims.

'In like manner, the glorious virgin Saint Fida suffered martyrdom in her childhood and endured much torture. And our Lord finally crowned her in the view of the world when He sent His angel to bring her a crown of precious stones. God manifested many signs in her, through which many were converted.

'Similarly, the blessed virgin Marcianna saw a false idol being worshipped, whereupon she threw the idol to the ground and smashed it. For this deed she was brutally beaten and left for dead and then imprisoned where a treacherous priest thought he could rape her after nightfall. However, through divine grace, a high wall appeared between him and her so that he could not reach her. The following day all the people saw this wall and many were converted. She suffered horrible tortures but continued to preach in the name of Jesus Christ and finally she prayed that He take her soul to Himself to end her torment.

'Saint Eufemia likewise suffered many tortures for the name of Jesus. She was of very noble birth and had a singularly beautiful body. The prefect Priscus urged her to worship the idols and to renounce Jesus Christ. In answering, she put such a difficult question to him that he was unable to reply, and angered at having been beaten by a woman, he ordered her tortured with a variety of harsh torments. Even though her body was painfully broken, her mind constantly grew stronger and her answers were filled with the Holy Spirit. During her torture, God's angel descended and smashed the torture machine and tormented her persecutors. She came away from this completely whole and with a joyful countenance. The treacherous prefect ordered a fire lit in an oven, whose flame reached eleven cubits high, and he had her thrown in. She sang such melodious praises to God so loudly from within that all nearby could hear her. And when the fire had gone out, she came out safe and sound. The judge, angered all the more, had red-hot pincers brought in, to tear off her limbs, but her tormentors were too frightened to dare even to touch her, so that the tortures were interrupted, whereupon the false tyrant had four lions and two other ferocious wild beasts led in, but they approached her and bowed. And then the blessed virgin, longing to go to her God, prayed to Him, to take her, so that she died without a single beast having touched her. . . .

'Similarly in the time of the emperor Maximianus, the blessed virgin Barbara flourished in virtue. Because of her beauty, her father had her shut up in a tower.[3] She was inspired by faith in God, and because no one else could baptise her, she herself took water and baptised herself in the name of the Father, the Son, and the Holy Spirit. Her father sought a noble marriage for

---

[3] Many of de Pizan's stories in this section deal with virgins who were persecuted by their fathers. The arbitrary rule of earthly patriarchy is thus explicitly contrasted with the love of the heavenly father.

her, but she refused all offers for a long time. Finally she declared herself a Christian and dedicated her virginity to God. For this reason her father tried to kill her, but she was able to escape and flee. And when her father pursued her to put her to death, he finally found her through information provided by a shepherd, who immediately was turned to stone, both he and his animals. The father brought her before the prefect, who ordered her to be executed with excruciating tortures because she had disobeyed all his commands. And she said to him, "Coward, are you unable to see that tortures will not harm me?" Whereupon, flying into a rage, he commanded that her breasts be torn off, and in this state he had her led throughout the city. During the entire time she praised God, and because of her shame at having her virgin body seen naked, our Lord sent His angel who healed all of her wounds and covered her body with a white robe. After she had been led around enough, she was taken back to the prefect, who was beside himself with rage when he saw her completely healed and her face radiant like a star. He had her tortured again until her torturers were exhausted with tormenting her. She prayed to God to help all those who would entreat Him in her memory and who remembered her passion. And when she finished her prayer, a voice was heard, saying, "Come, beloved daughter, rest in your Father's kingdom and receive your crown, and all that you have asked for will be granted you." After she had climbed the mountain where she was to be beheaded, her criminal father cut off her head himself, and as he was coming down from the mountain, fire from heaven struck him down and reduced him to ashes.

The blessed virgin Dorothy likewise suffered martyrdom in Cappadocia. Because she did not want to take any man as her husband but spoke constantly of her husband Jesus Christ, the schoolmaster, named Theophilus, said to her mockingly as she was being led to be beheaded that when she was with her husband she could at least send him roses and apples from her husband's orchard. She said she would, and it happened that immediately following her martyrdom, a very beautiful child, around four years old, came to Theophilus and brought him a small basket filled with exquisitely beautiful roses and apples which had a marvellous aroma, and said that the virgin Dorothy had sent them to him. He was astonished, for this took place during the winter, in the month of February, whereupon he converted and subsequently suffered martyrdom for the name of Jesus Christ.

'If you want me to tell you about all the holy virgins who are in Heaven because of their constancy during martyrdom, it would require a long history, including Saint Cecilia, Saint Agnes, Saint Agatha, and countless others. If you want more examples, you need only look at the *Speculum historiale* of Vincent de Beauvais, and there you will find a great many. However, I will tell you about Saint Christine, both because she is your patron and because she is a virgin of great dignity. Let me tell you at greater length about her beautiful and pious life.'

'The blessed Saint Christine, virgin, was from the city of Tyre and was the

daughter of Urban, master of the knights. Her father shut her up in a tower because of her great beauty, and she had twelve maids with her. Her father also had a very beautiful chapel with idols built near Christine's chamber so that she could worship them. She, however, even as a 12-year-old child, had already been inspired by the faith of Jesus Christ and did not pay any attention to the idols, so that her maids were astonished and repeatedly urged her to sacrifice. Yet when she took the incense, as if to sacrifice to the idols, she knelt at a window facing east, looked up to Heaven, and offered her incense to the immortal God. She spent the greater part of the night at this window, watching the stars, and sighing, piously praying to God to help her against her enemies. The maids, clearly aware her heart was in Jesus Christ, would often kneel before her, their hands clasped together, begging her not to place her trust in a strange God but to worship her parents' gods, for if she were discovered they would all be killed. Christine would answer that the Devil was deceiving them by urging them to worship so many gods and that there was but one God. When her father at last realised that his daughter refused to worship his idols, he was terribly grieved and upbraided her a great deal. She replied that she would gladly worship the God of Heaven. He thought she meant Jupiter and he was overjoyed and wanted to kiss her, but she cried out, "Do not touch my mouth, for I wish to offer a pure offering to the celestial God." The father was even happy with this. She returned to her chamber and nailed the door shut, and then she knelt down and offered a holy prayer to God, weeping all the while. And the angel of the Lord descended and comforted her and brought her white bread and meat which she ate, for she had not tasted food for three days.... After he realised that he could not convince her with entreaties or threats, he had her sprawled completely nude and beaten so much that twelve men wearied at the task. And the father kept asking her what she thought and he said to her, "Daughter, natural affection wrings my heart terribly to torment you who are my own flesh, but the reverence I have for my gods forces me to do this because you scorn them." And the holy virgin replied, "Tyrant who should not be called my father but rather enemy of my happiness, you boldly torture the flesh which you engendered, for you can easily do this, but as for my soul created by my Father in Heaven, you have no power to touch it with the slightest temptation, for it is protected by my Saviour, Jesus Christ." The cruel father, all the more enraged, had a wheel brought in, which he had ordered built, and ordered that she be tied to it and a fire built below it, and then he had rivers of boiling oil poured over her body. The wheel turned and completely crushed her. But God, the Father of all mercies, took pity on His servant and dispatched His angel to wreck the torture machines and to extinguish the fire, delivering the virgin, healthy and whole, and killing more than a thousand treacherous spectators who had been watching her without pity and who blasphemed the name of God. And her father asked her, "Tell me who taught you these evil practices!" She replied, "Pitiless despot, have I not told you that my Father, Jesus Christ, taught me

this long-suffering as well as every right thing in the faith of the Living God? Because of this, I scorn your tortures and will repel all the Devil's assaults with God's strength!" Beaten and confounded, he ordered her thrown into a horrible, dark prison. While she was there, contemplating the extraordinary mysteries of God, three angels came to her in great radiance and brought her food and comforted her. Urban did not know what to do with her but could not stop devising new tortures for her. Finally, fed up completely and wishing to be free of her, he had a great stone tied around her neck and had her thrown into the sea. But as she was being thrown in, the angels took her, and she walked on the water with them. Then, raising her eyes to Heaven, Christine prayed to Jesus Christ, that it please Him for her to receive in this water the holy sacrament of baptism which she greatly desired to have; whereupon Jesus Christ descended in His own person with a large company of angels and baptised her and named her Christine, from His own name, and He crowned her and placed a shining star on her forehead and set her on dry land. That night Urban was tortured by the Devil and died. The blessed Christine, whom God wanted to receive through martyrdom (which she also desired), was led back to prison by these criminals. The new judge, named Dyon, knowing what had been done to her, summoned her to appear before him, and he lusted after her because of her beauty. When he saw that his alluring words were of no use, he had her tortured again. He ordered that a large cauldron be filled with oil and that a roaring fire be built beneath it, he had her thrown in, upside down, and four men used iron hooks to rotate her. And the holy virgin sang melodiously to God, mocking her torturers and threatening them with the pains of Hell. When this enraged criminal of a judge realised that nothing was of any avail, he ordered her to be hanged by her long golden hair in the square, in front of all. The women rushed up to her, and, wailing out of pity that such a young girl be so cruelly tortured, they cried out to the judge, saying, "Cruel felon, crueler than a savage beast, how could a man's heart conceive such monstrous cruelty against such a beautiful and tender maiden?" And all the women tried to mob him. The judge, who was afraid, said to her, "Christine, friend, do not let yourself be tortured anymore, but come with me and we will go worship the supreme God who has upheld you." He meant Jupiter, who was considered the supreme god, but she understood him in a completely different way and so she replied, "You have spoken well, so I consent." He had her taken down and brought up to the temple, and a large crowd followed them. Then he led her before the idols, thinking she would worship them, and she knelt down, looked up at Heaven, and prayed to God. Thereupon she stood up and, turning toward the idol, said, "I command you in the name of Jesus Christ, oh evil spirit residing in this idol, to come out." Whereupon the Devil immediately came out and made a loud and frightening din which scared all the spectators, who fell to the ground in fear. When the judge stood up again, he said, "Christine, you have moved our omnipotent god, and, out of pity for you, he came out to see his creature." This remark angered

FRUSTRATION

her, and she reproached him harshly for being too blind to recognise divine
virtue, so she prayed to God to overturn the idol and reduce it to dust, which
was done. And more than three thousand men were converted through the
words and signs of this virgin. The terrified judge exclaimed, "If the king finds
out what this Christine has done against our god, he will utterly destroy me."
Thereupon, full of anguish, he went out of his mind and died. A third judge,
named Julian, appeared, and he ordered that Christine be seized, boasting that
he would make her worship the idols. In spite of all the force he could apply,
he was unable physically to move her from the spot where she was standing,
so he ordered a large fire built around her. She remained in the fire for three
days, and from inside the flames was heard sweet melodies. Her tormentors
were terrified by the amazing signs they saw. When the fire had burned out,
she emerged fully healthy. The judge commanded that snakes be brought to
him and had two asps (with their deadly poisonous bite) and two adders
released upon her. But these snakes dropped down at her feet, their heads
bowed, and did not harm her at all. Two horrible vipers were let loose, and
they hung from her breasts and licked her. And Christine looked to Heaven
and said, "I give You thanks, Lord God, Jesus Christ, who have deigned to
grant through Your holy virtues that these horrible serpents would come to
know in me Your dignity." The obstinate Julian, seeing these wonders, yelled
at the snake-tender, "Have you too been enchanted by Christine, so that you
have no power to rouse the snakes against her?" Fearing the judge, he then
tried to provoke the snakes into biting her, but they rushed at him and
killed him. Since everyone was afraid of these serpents and no one dared
approach, Christine commanded them in God's name to return to their cages
without harming anyone, and they did so. She revived the dead man, who
immediately threw himself at her feet and was converted. The judge, blinded
by the Devil so that he was unable to perceive the divine mystery, said to
Christine, "You have sufficiently demonstrated your magic arts." Infuriated,
she replied, "If your eyes would see the virtues of God, you would believe
in them." Then in his rage he ordered her breasts ripped off, whereupon milk
rather than blood flowed out. And because she unceasingly pronounced the
name of Jesus Christ, he had her tongue cut out, but then she spoke even
better and more clearly than before of divine things and of the one blessed
God, thanking Him for the bounties which He had given to her. She prayed
that it please Him to receive her in His company and that the crown of her
martyrdom be finally granted to her. Then a voice was heard from Heaven,
saying, "Christine, pure and radiant, the heavens are opened to you and the
eternal kingdom waits, prepared for you, and the entire company of saints
blesses God for your sake, for you have upheld the name of Your Christ
from childhood on." And she glorified God, turning her eyes to Heaven.
The voice was heard saying, "Come, Christine, my most beloved and elect
daughter, receive the palm and everlasting crown and the reward for your
life spent suffering to confess My name." The treacherous Julian, who heard

this voice, castigated the executioners and said they had not cut Christine's tongue short enough and ordered them to cut it so short that she could not speak to her Christ, whereupon they ripped out her tongue and cut if off at the root. She spat this cut-off piece of her tongue into the tyrant's face, putting out one of his eyes. She then said to him, speaking as clearly as ever, "Tyrant, what does it profit you to have my tongue cut out so that it cannot bless God, when my soul will bless Him forever while yours languishes forever in eternal damnation? And because you did not heed my words, my tongue has blinded you, with good reason." She ended her martyrdom then, having already seen Jesus Christ sitting on the right hand of His Father, when two arrows were shot at her, one in her side and the other in her heart. One of her relatives whom she had converted buried her body and wrote out her glorious legend.'

O blessed Christine, worthy virgin favoured of God, most elect and glorious martyr, in the holiness with which God has made you worthy, pray for me, a sinner, named with your name, and be my kind and merciful guardian. Behold my joy at being able to make use of your holy legend and to include it in my writings, which I have recorded here at such length out of reverence for you. May this be ever pleasing to you! Pray for all women, for whom your holy life may serve as an example for ending their lives well. Amen.

'What else should I tell you, dear friend, in order to fill our City with such a company? May Saint Ursula come with her multitude of eleven thousand virgins, blessed martyrs for the name of Jesus Christ, all of them beheaded after they had been sent off to be married. They arrived in the land of unbelievers who tried to force them to renounce their faith in God: they chose to die rather than to renounce Jesus Christ their Saviour.'

Elizabeth Tudor, Queen of England
When I Was Fair and Young (c. 1590s)

When I was fair and young, then favour graced me;
Of many was I sought their mistress for to be,
But I did scorn them all, and answered them therefore:
'Go! go! go! seek some other where, importune me no more!'

How many weeping eyes, I made to pine with woe!
How many sighing hearts! I have no skill to show.

Yet I the prouder grew, and still this spake therefore:
'Go! go! go! seek some other where, importune me no more!'

Then spake fair Venus' son that proud victorious boy,[4]
Saying: 'You dainty dame for that you be so coy?
I will so pluck your plumes that you shall say no more:
"Go! go! go! seek some other where, importune me no more!"'

As soon as he had said, such change grew in my breast,
That neither night nor day, I could take any rest.
Then lo! I did repent that I had said before:
'Go! go! go! seek some other where, importune me no more.'[5]

Sarah Egerton
To One Who Said
I Must Not Love (1703)

Bid the fond mother spill her infant's blood,
The hungry epicure not think of food;
Bid the Antartic touch the Artic pole:
When these obey, I'll force love from my soul.
As light and heat compose the genial sun,
So love and I essentially are one:
Ere your advice, a thousand ways I tried
To ease the inherent pain, but 'twas denied,
Though I resolved, and grieved, and almost died.
Then I would needs dilate the mighty flame,
Play the coquette, hazard my dearest fame:
The modish remedy I tried in vain,
One thought of him contracts it all again.
Wearied at last, cursed Hymen's[6] aid I chose,

4 Cupid.
5 This poem is attributed to Elizabeth, though some critics doubt its authenticity; see *The Poems of Queen Elizabeth I*, ed. Leicester Bradner (Providence, R.I., 1964), p. 7. It may have been written during the time of Elizabeth's infatuation with the Earl of Essex, c. 1590–9.
6 The goddess of marriage. Seeking to find release from her passion by means of marriage to one, she only makes her love for the first a criminal offence.

But find the fettered soul has no repose.
Now I'm a double slave to love and vows:
As if my former sufferings were too small,
I've made the guiltless torture criminal.
Ere this, I gave a loose to fond desire,
Durst smile, be kind, look, languish and admire,
With wishing sighs fan the transporting fire.
But now these soft allays[7] are so like sin,
I'm forced to keep the mighty anguish in;
Check my too tender thoughts and rising sighs,
As well as eager arms and longing eyes.
My kindness[8] to his picture I refrain,
Nor now embrace the lifeless, lovely swain.
To press the charming shade, though through a glass,
Seems a Platonic[9] breach of Hymen's laws:
Thus nicely[10] fond, I only stand and gaze,
View the dear, conqucring form that forced my fate,
Till I become as motionless as that.
My sinking limbs deny their wonted aid:
Fainting, I lean against my frighted maid,
Whose cruel care restores my sense and pain,
For soon as I have life I love again,
And with the fated softness strive in vain.
Distorted Nature shakes at the control,
With strong convulsions rends my struggling soul;
Each vital string cracks with th' unequal strife,
Departing love racks like departing life;
Yet there the sorrow ceases with the breath,
But love each day renews th' torturing scene of death.[11]

---

[7] Goings forth, ventures.
[8] Strong feeling.
[9] The idea or imagination of infidelity. The notional breaking of her marriage vows is seen as almost as much of a sin as the actual performance.
[10] Discreetly, precisely contained.
[11] This poem may be autobiographical; before and after her second marriage, Sarah Egerton was apparently in love with Henry Pierce, a friend of her first husband. See *Eighteenth Century Women Poets*, ed. Roger Lonsdale (Oxford, 1989), p. 27.

Elizabeth Thomas

The Triple League to Mrs Susan Dove (1722)

Pensive *Eliza* lately sate,
Bewailing her unhappy Fate;
Careless her Dress, and wild her Air,
Her self an *Emblem* of Despair:
Upon her Hand, she lean'd her Head,
And sighing first, these Words she said:
Ye *Fates!* why am I thus perplex'd,
And why thus daily teaz'd and vex'd?
Each Hour, new Troubles you prepare,
And I am born but to despair.

The first dear Friendship I profest,
Center'd in noble *Celia's*[12] Breast!
Her Soul was great! her *Friendship* true!
Her *Conversation* always new:
But ravish'd hence, ah me! she's gone,
And left me here to mourn alone.

No not alone *Clemena*[13] said,
That fair! but ah forgetful Maid;
There still is one, will prove as true
As e'er bright *Celia* did to you;
See where *Clemena* does attend,
And willingly wou'd be your Friend
Why shou'd you then your Grief pursue,
She loves! and is related too.

Thus *Phoenix* like, she did disclose,
And out of Celia's Ashes rose:
Fair *Iris*[14] too bestow'd a Part
Of her majestick gen'rous Heart:

12   Celia Bew (d. 1697).
13   An unknown cousin.
14   Susan Dove.

'Twas then of all I wish'd possess'd,
Was poor *Eliza*, more than bless'd.

But this too happy was to last,
And much I fear my Joys are past;
To rural Shades, *Clemena's* gone,
And I no more am thought upon:
Unkindly thus she leaves her Friend,
And now will neither come nor send.

Direct me now, ye sacred Nine,[15]
Whilst here I for *Clemena* pine,
Will not dear *Iris* thus conclude,
Eliza's either false, or rude?
She paus'd –
When straight there shin'd a glorious Ray,
The gloomy Grott was bright as Day;
A fragrent Scent her Spirits cheer'd,
And whilst these *Omens* she rever'd,
Young *Cupids* came, and wanton'd there,
And gentle *Zephirs* fann'd the Air:
Room! Room! for her whom we adore!
A *Cupid* cry'd, and said no more:
But as she spoke there came along
Most beauteous Iris, fair and young;
So fine, so gay, so wond'rous Bright,
As was the first created Light:
Yet *she* both kind, and good appears,
And quite disperses all my Fears.

As when, in Dead of Night alone,
A poor Unhappy! makes his Moan,
Dismal Horror, silent Care,
Sighs, and Groans, and deep Despair,
Do this poor Mortal quite surround,
And's little Stock of Sense confound:
But if an Angel pity take,
And to's Relief a Tour doth make,
Soon as the heaven'ly Beams appear,
So soon is vanish'd all his Fear.

Such you, my *Lovely Angel*, came,
Expell'd my Doubts, and clear'd her Fame;
You did ev'n all a Friend cou'd do,
And for some Hours, you gave me you.

[15] The nine muses.

But say, sweet *Nymph*, can you forgive,
The *Slights* you did that Day receive?
If so: Pray send me in a Line,
That charming Iris still is mine.[16]

Letitia Elizabeth Landon
The Improvisatrice (1824)

The Improvisatrice *is a long narrative poem retailing the life, love and work of an Italian poet. Her special talent for spontaneous composition is based upon a fashion current in Italy in the late eighteenth century when a number of women performed publicly, improvising poetry on themes given by members of her audience. Madame de Staël's novel* Corinne, or Italy *(1806) offers the most influential fictional account of the woman poet and improvisatrice.*

I turned me from the crowd, and reached
A spot which seemed unsought by all –
An alcove filled with shrubs and flowers,
But lighted by the distant hall,
With one or two fair statues placed,
Like deities of the sweet shrine.
That human art should ever frame
Such shapes so utterly divine!
A deep sigh breathed, – I knew the tone;
My cheek blushed warm, my heart beat high; –
One moment more I too was known,
I shrank before LORENZO'S eye.
He leant beside a pedestal.
The glorious brow, of Parian stone,[17]

---

[16]   Susan Dove (b. before 1680), may be the daughter of Henry Dove, Archdeacon of Richmond. See *Kissing the Rod: An Anthology of Seventeenth-Century Women's Verse*, ed. Germaine Greer, Susan Hastings, Jeslyn Medoff, and Melinda Sansone (London, 1987), pp. 434–5.
[17]   Parian marble.

Of the Antinous,[18] by his side,
   Was not more noble than his own!
They were alike: he had the same
   Thick-clustering curls the Roman wore –
The fixed and melancholy eye –
   The smile which passed like lightning o'er
The curved lip. We did not speak,
But the heart breathed upon each cheek;
We looked round with those wandering looks,
   Which seek some object for their gaze,
As if each other's glance was like
   The too much light of morning's rays
I saw a youth beside me kneel;
I heard my name in music steal;
I felt my hand trembling in his; –
Another moment, and his kiss
Had burnt upon it; when, like thought,
   So swift it past, my hand was thrown
Away, as if in sudden pain.
   LORENZO like a dream had flown!
We did not meet again: – he seemed
   To shun each spot where I might be:
And, it was said, another claimed
   The heart – more than the world to me!

I loved him as young Genius loves,
   When its own wild and radiant heaven
Of starry thought burns with the light,
   The love, the life, by passion given.
I loved him, too, as woman loves –
   Reckless of sorrow, sin, or scorn:
Life had no evil destiny
   That, with him, I could not have borne!
I had been nurst in palaces;
   Yet earth had not a spot so drear,
That I should not have thought a home,
   In Paradise, had he been near!
How sweet it would have been to dwell,
Apart from all, in some green dell
Of sunny beauty, leaves and flowers;

---

[18] Antinous was the favourite of the Emperor Hadrian. The Antinous (so called) is an antique statue now in the Vatican Museum. In the nineteenth century it was considered the ideal of masculine beauty.

And nestling birds to sing the hours!
Our home, beneath some chesnut's shade,
But of the woven branches made:
Our vesper hymn,[19] the low, lone wail
The rose hears from the nightingale;
And waked at morning by the call
Of music from a waterfall.
But not alone in dreams like this,
Breathed in the very hope of bliss,
I loved: my love had been the same
In hushed despair, in open shame.
I would have rather been a slave,
   In tears, in bondage, by his side,
Than shared in all, if wanting him,
   This world had power to give beside!
My heart was withered, – and my heart
   Had ever been the world to me;
And love had been the first fond dream,
   Whose life was in reality.
I had sprung from my solitude
   Like a young bird upon the wing
To meet the arrow; so I met
   My poisoned shaft of suffering.
And as that bird, with drooping crest
And broken wing, will seek his nest,
But seek in vain; so vain I sought
My pleasant home of song and thought.
There was one spell upon my brain,
Upon my pencil, on my strain;
But one face to my colours came;
My chords replied but to one name –
LORENZO! – all seemed vowed to thee,
To passion, and to misery!
I had no interest in the things
   That once had been like life, or light;
No tale was pleasant to mine ear,
   No song was sweet, no picture bright.
I was wild with my great distress,
My lone, my utter hopelessness!
I would sit hours by the side
Of some clear rill, and mark it glide,
Bearing my tears along, till night

[19] Evening hymn.

Came with dark hours; and soft starlight
Watch o'er its shadowy beauty keeping,
   Till I grew calm: – then I would take
The lute, which had all day been sleeping
   Upon a cypress tree, and wake
The echoes of the midnight air
With words that love wrung from despair.

Song

FAREWELL! – we shall not meet again
   As we are parting now!
I must my beating heart restrain –
   Must veil my burning brow!
Oh, I must coldly learn to hide
   One thought, all else above –
Must call upon my woman's pride
   To hide my woman's love!
Check dreams I never may avow;
   Be free, be careless, cold as thou!
Oh! those are tears of bitterness,
   Wrung from the breaking heart,
When two, blest in their tenderness
   Must learn to live – apart!
But what are they to that long sigh,
   That cold and fixed despair,
That weight of wasting agony
   It must be mine to bear?
Methinks I should not thus repine,
If I had but one vow of thine.
I could forgive inconstancy
To be one moment loved by thee!
With me the hope of life is gone
   The sun of joy is set;
One wish my soul still dwells upon –
   The wish it could forget.
I would forget that look, that tone,
My heart hath all too dearly known.
But who could ever yet efface
From memory love's ensuring trace?
All may revolt, all may complain –
But who is there may break the chain?
Farewell! – I shall not be to thee
   More than a passing thought;

But every time and place will be
  With thy remembrance fraught!
Farewell! we have not often met –
  We may not meet again;
But on my heart the seal is set
  Love never sets in vain!
Fruitless as constancy may be,
No chance, no change, may turn from thee
One who has loved thee wildly, well –
But whose first love-vow breathed – farewell?

Christina Rossetti
Winter: My Secret (1857)

I tell my secret? No indeed, not I:
Perhaps some day, who knows?
But not to-day; it froze, and blows,
  and snows,
And you're too curious: fie!
You want to hear it? well:
Only, my secret's mine, and I won't
  tell.

Or, after all, perhaps there's none:
Suppose there is no secret after all,
But only just my fun.
To-day's a nipping day, a biting day;
In which one wants a shawl,
A veil, a cloak, and other wraps:
I cannot ope to every one who taps,
And let the draughts come whistling
  through my hall;
Come bounding and surrounding me,
Come buffeting, astounding me,
Nipping and clipping through my
  wraps and all.
I wear my mask for warmth: who
  ever shows
His nose to Russian snows
To be pecked àt by every wind that
  blows?

You would not peck? I thank you
  for good will,
Believe, but leave that truth untested
  still.

Spring's an expansive time: yet I
  don't trust
March with its peck of dust,
Nor April with its rainbow-crowned
  brief showers,
Nor even May, whose flowers
One frost may wither through the
  sunless hours.

Perhaps some languid summer day
When drowsy birds sing less and
  less,
And golden fruit is ripening to
  excess,
If there's not too much sun nor too
  much cloud,
And the warm wind is neither still
  nor loud,
Perhaps my secret I may say,
Or you may guess.

Elizabeth Barrett Browning
Bianca Among the Nightingales (1860)

W ritten in Italy some time after 1856, this poem employs the conventional opposition of north and south to contrast the passionate warmth of the Italian Bianca with the calculating beauty and icy
propriety of her English rival.

I

The cypress stood up like a church
  That night we felt our love would hold,
And saintly moonlight seemed to search

And wash the whole world clean gold;
The olives crystallised the vales'
  Broad slopes until the hills grew strong:
The fire-flies and the nightingales
  Throbbed each to either, flame and song,
The nightingales, the nightingales!

II

Upon the angle of its shade
  The cypress stood, self-balanced high;
Half up, half down, as double-made,
  Along the ground, against the sky;
And we, too! from such soul-height went
  Such leaps of blood, so blindly driven,
We scarce knew if our nature meant
  Most passionate earth or intense heaven.
The nightingales, the nightingales!

III

We paled with love, we shook with love,
  We kissed so close we could not vow;
Till Giulio whispered, 'Sweet, above
  God's Ever guaranties this Now.'
And through his words the nightingales
  Drove straight and full their long clear call,
Like arrows through heroic mails,
  And love was aweful in it all.
The nightingales, the nightingales!

IV

O cold white moonlight of the north,
  Refresh these pulses, quench this hell!
O coverture of death drawn forth
  Across this garden-chamber . . . well!
But what have nightingales to do
  In gloomy England, called the free . . .
(Yes, free to die in! . . .) when we two
  Are sundered, singing still to me?
And still they sing, the nightingales!

V

I think I hear him, how he cried
  'My own soul's life!' between their notes.
Each man has but one soul supplied,

And that's immortal. Though his throat's
On fire with passion now, to her
He can't say what to me he said!
And yet he moves her, they aver,
The nightingales sing through my head –
The nightingales, the nightingales!

VI

He says to her what moves her most.
He would not name his soul within
Her hearing, – rather pays her cost
With praises to her lips and chin.
Man has but one soul, 'tis ordained,
And each soul but one love, I add;
Yet souls are damned and love's profaned;
These nightingales will sing me mad!
The nightingales, the nightingales!

VII

I marvel how the birds can sing,
There's little difference, in their view,
Betwixt our Tuscan trees that spring
As vital flames into the blue,
And dull round blots of foliage meant,
Like saturated sponges here
To suck the fogs up. As content
Is he too in this land, 'tis clear.
And still they sing, the nightingales.

VIII

My native Florence! dear, foregone!
I see across the Alpine ridge[20]
How the last feast day of Saint John
Shot rockets from Carraia bridge.
The luminous city, tall with fire,
Trod deep down in that river of ours,
While many a boat with lamp and choir
Skimmed birdlike over glittering towers
I will not hear these nightingales.

---

[20] Bianca has followed Guilio to England.

IX

I seem to float, we seem to float
    Down Arno's stream[21] in festive guise;
A boat strikes flame into our boat,
    And up that lady seems to rise
As then she rose. The shock had flashed
    A vision on us! What a head,
What leaping eyeballs! – beauty dashed
    To splendour by a sudden dread.
And still they sing, the nightingales.

X

Too bold to sin, too weak to die;
    Such women are so. As for me,
I would we had drowned there, he and I,
    That moment, loving perfectly.
He had not caught her with her loosed
    Gold ringlets ... rarer in the south ...
Nor heard the 'Grazie tanto' bruised
    To sweetness by her English mouth.
And still they sing, the nightingales.

XI

She had not reached him at my heart
    With her fine tongue, as snakes indeed
Kill flies; nor had I, for my part,
    Yearned after, in my desperate need,
And followed him as he did her
    To coasts left bitter by the tide,
Whose very nightingales, elsewhere
    Delighting, torture and deride!
For still they sing, the nightingales.

XII

A worthless woman; mere cold clay
    As all false things are: but so fair,
She takes the breath of men away
    Who gaze upon her unaware.
I would not play her larcenous tricks
    To have her looks! She lied and stole,
And spat into my love's pure pyx[22]

---

[21] The river which runs through Florence.
[22] A sacred vessel, usually containing holy water.

212

The rank saliva of her soul.
And still they sing, the nightingales.

XIII

I would not for her white and pink,
   Though such he likes – her grace of limb,
Though such he has praised – nor yet, I think
   For life itself though spent with him,
Commit such sacrilege, affront
   God's nature which is love, intrude
'Twixt two affianced souls, and hunt
   Like spiders, in the altar's wood.
I cannot hear these nightingales.

XIV

If she chose sin, some gentler guise
   She might have sinned in, so it seems:
She might have pricked out both my eyes,
   And I still seen him in my dreams!
– Or drugged me in my soup or wine,
   Nor left me angry afterward:
To die here with his hand in mine,
   His breath upon me, were not hard.
(Our Lady hush these nightingales!)

XV

But set a springe²³ for him, 'mio ben,'
   My only good, my first last love!
Though Christ knows well what sin is, when
   He sees some things done they must move
Himself to wonder. Let her pass.
   I think of her by night and day.
Must I too join her ... out, alas! ...
   With Giulio, in each word I say?
And evermore the nightingales!

XXVI

Giulio, my Giulio! – sing they so,
   And you be silent? Do I speak,
And you not hear? An arm you throw
   Round someone, and I feel so weak?
– Oh, owl-like birds! They sing for spite,
   They sing for hate, they sing for doom.
They'll sing through death who sing through night,

---

²³ Trap.

They'll sing and stun me in the tomb –
The nightingales, the nightingales!

Charlotte Mew

The Farmer's Bride (1916)

Three Summers since I chose a maid,
Too young maybe – but more's to do
At harvest-time that bide and woo.
    When us was wed she turned afraid
Of love and me and all things human;
Like the shut of a winter's day.
Her smile went out, and 'twasn't a woman –
    More like a little frightened fay.[24]
    One night, in the Fall, she runned away.

'Out 'mong the sheep, her be,' they said,
'Should properly have been abed;
But sure enough she wasn't there
Lying awake with her wide brown stare.
So over seven-acre field and up-along across the down
We chased her, flying like a hare
Before our lanterns. To Church-Town
    All in a shiver and a scare
We caught her, fetched her home at last
    And turned the key upon her, fast.

She does the work about the house
As well as most, but like a mouse:
    Happy enough to chat and play
    With birds and rabbits and such as they,
    So long as men-folk keep away.
'Not near, not near!' her eyes beseech
When one of us comes within reach.
    The women say that beasts in stall
    Look round like children at her call.
    I've hardly heard her speak at all.

Shy as a leveret, swift as he,
Straight and slight as a young larch tree,

---

[24] Fairy.

Sweet as the first wild violets, she,
To her wild self. But what to me?

The short days shorten and the oaks are brown,
    The blue smoke rises to the low grey sky,
One leaf in the still air falls slowly down,
    A magpie's spotted feathers lie
On the black earth spread white with rime,[25]
The berries redden up to Christmas-time.
    What's Christmas-time without there be
    Some other in the house than we![26]

    She sleeps up in the attic there
    Alone, poor maid. 'Tis but a stair
Betwixt us. Oh! my God! the down,
The soft young down of her, the brown,
The brown of her – her eyes, her hair, her hair!

Gertrude Stein

FROM

The Mother of Us All (1946)

*T*his extract is taken from Act II of the opera libretto which Stein
wrote for the American composer Virgil Thomson. It focuses on the
life of the nineteenth-century American feminist Susan B. Anthony, but
anachronistically mingles figures from nineteenth- and twentieth-century
history (and some from Stein's private life) in its dramatic landscape. The
opera was first performed at Columbia University in May 1947. It was
recorded in 1977.

JOHN ADAMS:[27] Dear Miss Constance Fletcher, it is a great pleasure that I kneel
    at your feet, but I am Adams, I kneel at the feet of none, not any one,
    dear Miss Constance Fletcher dear dear Miss Constance Fletcher I kneel
    at your feet, you would have ruined my father if I had had one but I have

[25] Frost.
[26] That is, children.
[27] John Adams (sixth president of the United States), in 1825.

had one and you had ruined him, dear Miss Constance Fletcher if I had not been an Adams I would have kneeled at your feet.

CONSTANCE FLETCHER:[28] And kissed my hand.

J. ADAMS: [*shuddering*] And kissed your hand.

CONSTANCE FLETCHER: What a pity, no not what a pity it is better so, but what a pity what a pity it is what a pity.

J. ADAMS: Do not pity me kind beautiful lovely Miss Constance Fletcher do not pity me, no do not pity me, I am an Adams and not pitiable.

CONSTANCE FLETCHER: Dear dear me if he had not been an Adams he would have kneeled at my feet and he would have kissed my hand. Do you mean that you would have kissed my hand or my hands, dear Mr Adams.

J. ADAMS: I mean that I would have first kneeled at your feet and then I would have kissed one of your hands and then I would still kneeling have kissed both of your hands, if I had not been an Adams.

CONSTANCE FLETCHER: Dear me Mr Adams dear me.

ALL THE CHARACTERS: If he had not been an Adams he would have kneeled at her feet and he would have kissed one of her hands, and then still kneeling he would have kissed both of her hands still kneeling if he had not been an Adams.

Elizabeth Jennings
Love in Three Movements (1985)

Comings
In moonlight or in sunlight, the immediate
Heat of summer laying on the leaves
Hot hands. A little breeze, a wisp of breath
Cools the purpose of the heyday noon.

Goings
In winter or in autumn when nostalgia
Cancels the present, stops the clocks, endures
In our imaginations of a better,
A standing-still world, stable universe.

---

[28] Constance Fletcher (a contemporary of Stein's), in 1905–10. Throughout the opera, Adams and Fletcher conduct an intermittent flirtation which includes an argument about the theory and character of marriage.

Retreats
As bonfire smoke hides figures in the streets.

The spirit's urgency –
How it will exercise our passions, put
Power not ours on our blunt purposes.
The spirit moves inquiring fingers, lips
Touching, pressing, then the mind asks questions,
Gives an order. How our spirits threaten
The bodies' movements they intend to sweeten.

Marilyn Hacker

FROM

Love, Death and the Changing of the Seasons (1987)

Sometimes, when you're asleep, I want to do
it to myself while I'm watching you. It
would be easy, two fingers along my clit,
back, in, back out. Your skin's heat comes into
me, adjacent. Through the mussed chrysanthemum
petals, your big child's sleep-face, closed around
its openness, gives me your mouth to ground
on, but only with my eyes. I could come
like that, but I don't – take you against your will,
it seems like, and I wouldn't; rather wait
adrowse in sunlight with this morning heat
condensing, a soft cloud above my groin
gently diffusing brightness there, until
you wake up, and you bring it down like rain.

Pat Califia

FROM

A Dash of Vanilla[29] *(1988)*

You're lucky you're handsome and I'm in love. Otherwise, I wouldn't bother.

It's very difficult to get you off. I'm complaining, but there's also a part of me that likes it. Most women are difficult to get off, and in the past, I've dealt with that by encouraging them to masturbate while I suck on their tits or fuck them or talk dirty to them. I'm glad you resist that, saving masturbation for the times when we're too tired or too sick to come any other way, and need some quick and easy stimulation and release before we can fall asleep. I'm glad you insist that I get you off, insist that I keep trying and work harder to get better at it. When your climax finally does come, it's precious to me because I've put so much sweat and effort into getting you there. I sometimes think it's better than the quick, helpless orgasms I have when you've been fucking me for only five minutes, because I always want more, I always need to come again and again. The one you have leaves you drained. You seem completely satisfied. You're able to stop. I'm not.

Making love to you doesn't start out feeling difficult. The summers here are very hot, so you take your clothes off as soon as you walk into the bedroom, and then you lounge around and read your mail. Your legs just naturally seem to come to rest with your knees bent and far apart. I never know if you are deliberately exposing your cunt to me, how much of your behaviour is exhibitionistic or provocative, and how much of it is just an attempt to get comfortable in the heat, or unselfconsciousness about your own nudity. It's probably the latter. You are always surprised when I tell you how powerfully your body attracts me. You do not believe you are beautiful. . . . When I look at the dark, fuzzy curls of your pubic triangle (some of your pubic hair wanders up your belly and down the inside of your thighs), the rose colour of your crinkled sex-lips and clit, it seems easy and natural to roll over onto my belly between your legs and start licking you.

You always taste good, even if you go for days without showering. In fact, I love you better when you are pungent. It drives me crazy, licking and licking, because the more I lick, the wetter your cunt gets and the stronger the flavour is.

---

[29] 'Vanilla': polite and straightforward sexual expression – as opposed to the ruder excesses of sado-masochism.

I can't lick it away. I imagine you will produce more and more fluid until I could actually gulp it down, swallow it by the mouthful, like water or semen.

You always respond quickly to that first lick, with a groan that says, 'Oh, God, yes, she's doing that, I need it, will she do it more?' This encourages me, and I begin to think about pleasing you, making you come, instead of just pleasing myself by filling my mouth with the texture and musky taste of your cunt. . . . You like it when I flick my tongue quickly against the hard bud, hummingbird-quick, but I can't keep this up for very long, so I'm reluctant to start it. Now, in the beginning, before I've committed myself to a clear pattern of stimulation, I feel like I can tease you a little without frustrating you, so I slip further down to run my tongue around the inside of your vagina, as far in as I can get, and sometimes tip your ass up and your legs back over your head so I can eat your ass, too.

You've told me to stay in one place and do the same thing until you come. You've also told me that you sometimes need to move around to put my tongue in just the right place. So I never know when I should let my mouth follow your hips, or when I should hold my head still and let your hips drift past my face until you settle into a more effective rhythm and location. You never seem to be able to tell me what's going on while it's happening, so I have to guess, and half of the time I'm right and half of the time I'm wrong.

You also confuse me because if you are really turned on, you hold absolutely still, for fear that I'll move off the right spot. But when you get close to coming, you move a lot, fast enough and hard enough to hurt me if I'm not quick enough to follow you. But in the beginning, if you move, it's usually a sign that you're frustrated and want it to feel better and are starting to worry that it's not going to work. I do the best I can to tell the difference, but there's always a point when I'm eating you where I lose touch with you completely and lose all my self-confidence, too. I think, 'I'm so clumsy and inadequate, I'll never be able to make her come. I'll bet I never really made any of my lovers come. They were all faking it.' . . .

By now, you are usually holding still, not making any noise at all, barely breathing, and my neck is starting to hurt and my hands are tingling. Perversely, just as I abandon my ego, I get very turned on to the idea of servicing you, of having you use my mouth for hours, and I start humping the bed and coming, about once every five to eight minutes. I come even if I hold my legs apart and try desperately not to, because it disrupts my rhythm and embarrasses me. Sometimes you catch fire from the noises I make and the grovelling motions I'm making with my hips, and you make a little sex music with me, saying, 'Oh, yeah, baby, go ahead, come, come now!' or simply moan and thrust yourself against my mouth. But I get progressively more depressed and full of despair anyway, because nothing seems to be happening or changing or getting better with your body and its physical response, and I want to make you come, I don't want this to be for my benefit, you allowing me to suck you – even though you don't get off on it – simply because I get off on it.

FRUSTRATION

I start making questioning noises, asking you with whimpers and moans or outright words if you want me to continue.

You usually respond, 'God, yes!' But sometimes you tell me, 'No, you can stop now,' and I'm crushed, even if I know you are just trying to be kind, reluctant to wear me out when there's no hope that it's going to work. And I can understand that, because there are times when I'm not going to come, no matter what somebody does for me or to me. But I know I have failed you, failed to give you bliss and relief, and I will never be good for anything.

I hate this feeling. . . .

My neck really hurts. I'm having trouble holding my head up. Sweat is running down my forehead and I can't wipe it off, so it runs into my eyes and stings. My hands are completely numb, and so are my forearms, all the way up to the elbow. I can't tell if I am still gripping your labia or not. I can only tell by the shape of your clit in my mouth just how far back I'm still managing to keep them. I am angry with you because you are taking so long, angry because you leave me alone down here, with no idea what is going on with you, if you are enjoying it or not, no indication of how close you are, how much longer it's going to take. I want to shout, 'Are you ever going to come?' I desperately need some help, and I begin to whisper, 'please, please,' sometimes loud enough for you to hear me. Any kind of groan or sigh you make is of life-or-death importance to me now and keeps me going for a few more minutes. But I feel as if I am hanging from a cliff face by my skinned and bleeding palms, and I know I cannot hold on to the bare rock for much longer. . . .

Still I work on and on, mechanically, softly, like the Colorado River carving the Grand Canyon one eon at a time, like a bird flying across the ocean that can't stop no matter how tired she is because there is no place to land. Save me, give it to me, help me, seize my head between your thighs and drown me! Come, come!

Sometimes, not all the time, at a time I am never able to predict and for reasons I still do not understand, you promise me a miracle. You begin to talk to me. After your long silence, it feels very odd, being talked to. I pay close attention to what you have to say. It must be important if you can't keep quiet any more.

'Oh, lover,' you say, 'I'm going to come. Can you feel it? Lover!'

Now I am moving fast and sloppy, but it doesn't matter, you will come now no matter what I do, and anyway we are finally in sync, finally in this together . . . shove my fingers into you, past your locked thighs, just as you begin to come. After the shouting, you lie very still, like someone who has fainted. I am still terribly excited. As soon as your thighs relax a little, I push my hand between them, put my fingers up to feel how wet you are, and slide them in. You always say, 'No. No, lover, don't.'

And I say, 'Why? Why not? I want it. You can't stop me. Give it to me.' Then I fuck you. You don't like it, but it makes you come anyway, you can't help it, you jerk and throb around my hand and lock me between your thighs once

more, and come until you're screaming obscenities at me, it feels so good to you. If I can, I fuck you yet again, and this time you really protest. It's too much, you're too tired, you're sore. But I am adamant. I've worked so hard to get you to this place, thrown open to me, responding with these free and easy, quick and intense orgasms, that I have to use your pussy as often as you will let me take it. It's what I want myself, for you to pin me down and fuck me, but coming has left you too enervated to struggle with me, so I fuck you instead and like it just as much as coming myself. Besides, this is the only time you can come when I fuck you, right after you've been eaten into an orgasm. You love to get fucked and will take literally hours of it, but never give in and come completely around me, come until you are satisfied. . . .

Yes, it's difficult to make you come. You are difficult in other ways, too. You expect me to do things for you that I think people should do for themselves. I try anyway, and in return you hurt my feelings by complaining that I don't take good enough care of you. My desire for you is desperate, as if making you respond in bed could make up for all the things that go wrong elsewhere and give me back what I lose when you make a contemptuous remark about something I love or tell a story that is supposed to prove you will always be better than me at everything I care about doing well. I take it because I love you. But making love to you barely salvages my self-esteem, and keeps me addicted to you. Anybody could do this for you.

I will know I don't love you any more, that the anger has outweighed the lust, when I stop myself from taking that first puppy-lick, ice-cream-cone-lick, you-are-the-most-desirable-woman-in-the-world-lick that leads to two hours of being muzzled by your cunt, my tongue chasing itself around your clit, aching to have your wet and coming cunt plastered across my nose and mouth, my neck in the scissors of your thighs, hurting for those few seconds when I don't need to breathe or think or remember my name or my pride.

It's so difficult to make you come that only three of your lovers have been able to do it. Did any of them have the stamina to eat you twice in one night? How would you like to come again?[30]

---

30   From *Macho Sluts* (1988).

VOYEURISM

Looking is for men only. Whether it's David observing Bathsheba's bath, Peeping Tom spying on Godiva, 'What the Butler Saw', or the calendar in the local garage, this fact remains. Only men look – and what they look at is women.

Women have eyes too. And sight is often the beginning of the erotic adventure. Attraction begins when the lover sees a pleasing sight; it is fuelled by gazing on that face, that form, and inflamed by the return of the gaze as the beloved looks back upon the lover.

One reason why women have been denied the privilege of looking is that romantic convention insists that a woman is passive in love. She must always be the object of the male gaze. She can never be the subject who sees and desires. If she allows herself that active role, it is only too clear that she is breaking the rules. Salome and Mae West looked; but they weren't nice girls.

Voyeurism goes beyond looking and desiring. It suggests the character of what is being looked at. It suggests the effect produced on the viewer. If looking itself is forbidden to women, how much more illicit is looking on.

So what happens when women write about opening their eyes and seeing and feeling? Quite often they can only do this by writing about men. In the two extracts from Aphra Behn the conventions of voyeurism are retained. Lady Fulbank and Sylvia are passive, while their men dispose of them to other men, arranging pictures which they then look on with excitement, if not with unalloyed pleasure. Sir Cautious despatches Gayman to his wife's bed to pay his gambling debt; Philander marries Sylvia to Brilliard to secure his own possession of her. In neither case is the woman allowed a choice. She becomes a property to be exploited in the sexual competition between men. Sir Cautious sees in his mind's eye (as does the audience) the passionate commerce which is taking place

in the bedchamber. But his voyeuristic excitement concentrates upon Gayman's part in that performance. Brilliard pictures Sylvia in Philander's arms and he is aroused by the image of another man's pleasure. Sylvia is a mere accessory.

In Elizabeth Gaskell's *Cousin Phillis* the same passivity is reserved for Phillis. Her image is used by one man for his pleasure and the other is aroused by the spectacle. This story was published in the 1860s, so a proper distance is preserved. But Holdsworth's direct admiration for Phillis is disturbing to Paul, and it is Holdsworth's notice that first makes him look at her. Even more disturbing is the invasion which takes place when Holdsworth writes in Phillis's books. The erotic nature of his act – and of Paul's reaction – is clear ('I was not sure if he was not taking a liberty: it did not quite please me, and yet I did not know why').

In Lucy Snowe we have a heroine who looks, indeed she frankly stares. Lucy's rude gaze is given a polite explanation (she had realised that she had met Dr John before), but no amount of tardy excuses can diffuse the erotic pressure aroused in Lucy by the sight of this man. When Lucy is forced to witness the happy union of Dr John and Paulina her feelings are as acute, though made more painful and compelling by her position as voyeur.

The other extracts in this section allow women to do the looking. They also allow them that perverse and delicate pleasure which comes with seeing and not touching. Delarivier Manley hears her lover's passion for another women and craves that expression for herself. Dorothy Parker's Mrs Lanier appropriates Gwennie's sexual life to put it into her own self-portrait. Mrs Lanier may be unaware of her substitute erotic life but the narrative is wickedly knowing. By contrast, Elizabeth Jolley's Hester recognises her joy in Kathy's vibrant life. Feeding on that vision, she borrows Kathy's physicality to give her own body its second-hand pleasure.

Marguerite Duras's heroine wants everything, first- and second-hand. In defiance of all convention and pattern she knows her own pleasure and greedily doubles it in the mirror of another self. She looks, she desires, and she acts.

Aphra Behn

FROM

Love Letters Between a Nobleman and His Sister (1684–7)

P hilander, married to Myrtilla, has fallen in love with Sylvia, Myrtilla's sister. Finding that his passion is reciprocated, the couple run away together. Upon being threatened with discovery and prosecution, Philander suggests that, for form's sake only, Sylvia marry his servant, Brilliard.

W e'll see how our lovers fared; who being lodged all on one stair-case (that is, *Philander, Sylvia*, and *Brilliard*) it was not hard for the lover to steal into the longing arms of the expecting *Sylvia*; no fatigues of tedious journeys, and little voyages, had abated her fondness, or his vigour; the night was like the first, all joy! All transport! *Brilliard* lay so near as to be a witness to all their sighs of love, and little soft murmurs, who now began from a servant to be permitted as an humble companion; since he had had the honour of being married to *Sylvia*, though yet he durst not lift his eyes or thoughts that way; yet it might be perceived he was melancholy and sullen whenever he saw their dalliances; nor could he know the joys his lord nightly stole, without an impatience, which, if but minded or known, perhaps had cost him his life. He began, from the thoughts she was his wife, to fancy fine enjoyment, to fancy authority which he durst not assume, and often wished his lord would grow cold, as possessing lovers do, that then he might advance his hope, when he should even abandon or slight her: he could not see her kissed without blushing with resentment; but if he has assisted to undress him for her bed, he was ready to die with anger, and would grow sick, and leave the office to himself: he could not see her naked charms, her arms stretched out to receive a lover, with impatient joy, without madness; to see her clasp him fast, when he threw himself into her soft, white bosom, and smother him with kisses: no, he could not bear it now, and almost lost his respect when he beheld it, and grew saucy unperceived. And it was in vain that he looked back upon the reward he had to stand for that necessary cypher a husband. In vain he considered the reasons why, and the occasion wherefore; he now seeks precedents of usurped dominion, and thinks she is his wife, and has forgot that he is her creature, and *Philander's* vassal. These thoughts disturbed him all the night, and a certain jealousy, or rather

APHRA BEHN

curiosity to listen to every motion of the lovers, while they were employed after a different manner.

FROM

The Lucky Chance (1686)

The elderly Sir Cautious is gambling with Gayman and Sir Feeble. Gayman is in love with Sir Cautious's wife, Lady Fulbank, and has devised a plot to win her with her husband's consent.

From ACT IV, SCENE I

[*They all go to play at the table, leaving* SIR CAUTIOUS, SIR FEEBLE *and* GAYMAN.]

SIR CAUTIOUS: Hum, must it all go? (A rare sum, if a man were but sure the Devil would stand neuter now.) Sir, I wish I had anything but ready money to stake: three hundred pounds, a fine sum!

GAYMAN: You have moveables Sir, goods, commodities.

SIR CAUTIOUS: That's all one, Sir. That's money's worth, Sir, but if I had anything that were worth nothing.

GAYMAN: You would venture it. I thank you Sir. I would your lady were worth nothing.

SIR CAUTIOUS: Why so, Sir?

GAYMAN: Then I would set all 'gainst that nothing.

SIR CAUTIOUS: What, set it against my wife?

GAYMAN: Wife, Sir! Ay, your wife.

SIR CAUTIOUS: Hum my wife against three hundred pounds! What, all my wife, Sir!

GAYMAN: All your wife! Why Sir, some part of her would serve my turn.

SIR CAUTIOUS: Hum – my wife. (Why, if I should lose, he could not have the impudence to take her.)

GAYMAN: Well, I find you are not for the bargain, and so I put up.

SIR CAUTIOUS: Hold, Sir, why so hasty? My wife? No, put up your money, Sir. What, lose my wife for three hundred pounds!

GAYMAN: Lose her, Sir! Why, she shall be never the worse for my wearing, Sir! (The old covetous rogue is considering on't I think.) What say you to a night? I set it to a night. There's none need know it, Sir.

SIR CAUTIOUS: Hum – a night! Three hundred pounds for a night! (Why, what a lavish whoremaker's this? We take money to marry our wives but very seldom part with 'em, and by the bargain get money.) For a night, say you? (Gad, if I should take the rogue at his word 'twould be a pure jest.)

SIR FEEBLE: Are you not mad, brother?

225

ii0lSIR CAUTIOUS: No, but I'm wise, and that's as good. Let me consider.

SIR FEEBLE: What, whether you shall be a cuckold or not?

SIR CAUTIOUS: Or lose three hundred pounds – consider that. A cuckold! Why 'tis a word, an empty sound; 'tis breath, 'tis air, 'tis nothing. But three hundred pounds, Lord, what will not three hundred pounds do? You may chance to be a cuckold for nothing, Sir.

SIR FEEBLE: It may be so, but she shall do't discreetly then.

SIR CAUTIOUS: Under favour, you're an ass, brother. This is the discreetest way of doing it, I take it.

SIR FEEBLE: But would a wise man expose his wife?

SIR CAUTIOUS: Why, Cato was a wiser man than I, and he lent his wife to a young fellow they call Hortensius, as story says, and can a wise man have a better precedent than Cato?

SIR FEEBLE: I say Cato was an ass, Sir, for obliging any young rogue of 'em all.

SIR CAUTIOUS: But I am of Cato's mind. Well, a single night, you say.

GAYMAN: A single night: to have, to hold, possess and so forth at discretion.

SIR CAUTIOUS: A night. I shall have her safe and sound i'th'morning?

SIR FEEBLE: Safe, no doubt on't, but how sound?

GAYMAN: And for non-performance you shall pay me three hundred pounds. I'll forfeit as much if I tell –

SIR CAUTIOUS: Tell? Why, make your three hundred pounds six hundred, and let it be put into the *Gazette* if you will, man. But is't a bargain?

GAYMAN: Done. Sir Feeble shall be witness, and there stands my hat.

> GAYMAN *puts down his hat of money and each of them takes a box and dice, and kneel on the stage. The others come and watch.*

SIR CAUTIOUS: He that comes first to one and thirty wins.

> *They throw and count.*

LADY FULBANK: What are you playing for?

SIR FEEBLE: Nothing, nothing, but a trial of skill between an old man and a young – and your Ladyship is to be Judge.

LADY FULBANK: I shall be partial, Sir.

SIR CAUTIOUS: Six and five's eleven. [*Throws, and pulls the hat towards him*]

GAYMAN: Quatre, trois. Pox of the dice.

SIR CAUTIOUS: Two fives – one and twenty. [*Sets up, pulls the hat nearer*]

GAYMAN: Now, luck – doublets of sixes – nineteen.

SIR CAUTIOUS: Five and four – thirty. [*Draws the hat to him*]

SIR FEEBLE: Now if he wins it, I'll swear he has a fly indeed. 'Tis impossible without doublets of sixes.

GAYMAN: Now Fortune smile, and for the future frown. [*Throws*]

SIR CAUTIOUS: Hum, two sixes. [*He rises and looks dolefully around*]

LADY FULBANK: How now? What's the matter you look so like an ass, what have you lost?

SIR CAUTIOUS: A bauble, a bauble! 'Tis not for what I've lost, but because I have not won.

SIR FEEBLE: You look very simple, Sir, what think you of Cato now?
SIR CAUTIOUS: A wise man may have his failings.
LADY FULBANK: What has my husband lost?
SIR CAUTIOUS: Only a small parcel of ware that lay dead upon my hands, sweetheart.
GAYMAN: But I shall improve 'em, Madam, I'll warrant you.
LADY FULBANK: Well, since 'tis no worse, bring in your fine dancer, Cousin, you say you brought to entertain your mistress with.
BEARJEST[1] *goes out.*
GAYMAN: Sir, you'll take care to see me paid tonight?
SIR CAUTIOUS: Well, Sir, but my Lady, you must know, Sir, has the common frailties of her sex, and will refuse what she even longs for if persuaded by me.
GAYMAN: 'Tis not in my bargain to solicit her, Sir. You are to procure her, or three hundred pounds, Sir, choose you whether.
SIR CAUTIOUS: Procure her! With all my soul, Sir. Alas, you mistake my honest meaning, I scorn to be so unjust as not to see you abed together; and then agree as well as you can, I have done my part. In order to this, Sir, get but yourself conveyed in a chest to my house with a direction upon it for me, and for the rest –
GAYMAN: I understand you.
SIR FEEBLE: Ralph, get supper ready.
Enter BEARJEST *with dancers. All go out but* SIR CAUTIOUS.
SIR CAUTIOUS: Well, I must break my mind, if possible, to my Lady, but if she should be refractory now, and make me pay three hundred pounds...?
Why, sure, she won't have so little grace. Three hundred pounds saved is three hundred pounds got, by our account. Could all
Who of this City-Privilege are free,
Hope to be paid for cuckoldom like me,
Th'unthriving merchant, whom grey hair adorns,
Before all ventures would ensure his horns,
For thus, while he but lets spare rooms to hire,
His wife's cracked credit keeps his own entire....

ACT V, SCENE IV. Lady Fulbank's Ante-Chamber

She is discovered at her glass with SIR CAUTIOUS, *undressed.*
LADY FULBANK: But why tonight? Indeed you're wondrous kind, methinks.
SIR CAUTIOUS: Why, I don't know, a wedding is a sort of an alarm to love, it calls up every man's courage.
LADY FULBANK: Ay, but will it come when 'tis called?
SIR CAUTIOUS: (I doubt you'll find it, to my grief.) But I think 'tis all one to

[1] The servant.

thee, thou care'st not for my compliment, no, thou'dst rather have a young fellow.

LADY FULBANK: I am not used to flatter much. If forty years were taken from your age 'twould render you something more agreeable to my bed, I must confess.

SIR CAUTIOUS: Ay, ay, no doubt on't.

LADY FULBANK: Yet you may take my word without an oath; were you as old as Time and I were young and gay as April flowers, which all are fond to gather, my beauties all should wither in the shade, e'er I'd be worn in a dishonest bosom.

SIR CAUTIOUS: Ay, but you're wondrous free methinks, sometimes, which gives shrewd suspicions.

LADY FULBANK: What, because I cannot simper, look demure, and justify my honour when none questions it? Cry 'fie', and 'out upon the naughty women', because they please themselves, and so would I?

SIR CAUTIOUS: How, would what, cuckold me?

LADY FULBANK: Yes, if it pleased me better than virtue, Sir. But I'll not change my freedom and my humour, to purchase the dull fame of being honest.

SIR CAUTIOUS: Ay, but the world, the world.

LADY FULBANK: I value not the censures of the crowd.

SIR CAUTIOUS: But I am old.

LADY FULBANK: That's your fault, not mine.

SIR CAUTIOUS: But being so, if I should be good-natured and give thee leave to love discreetly –

LADY FULBANK: I'd do't without your leave, Sir.

SIR CAUTIOUS: Do't? What, cuckold me!

LADY FULBANK: No, love discreetly, Sir, love as I ought, love honestly.

SIR CAUTIOUS: What, in love with anybody but your own husband?

LADY FULBANK: Yes.

SIR CAUTIOUS: Yes, quoth'a! Is that your loving as you ought?

LADY FULBANK: We cannot help our inclinations, Sir, no more than time or light from coming on. But I can keep my virtue, Sir, entire.

SIR CAUTIOUS: What, I'll warrant, this is your first love, Gayman?

LADY FULBANK: I'll not deny that truth, though even to you.

SIR CAUTIOUS: Why, in consideration of my age, and your youth, I'd bear a conscience provided you do things wisely.

LADY FULBANK: Do what thing, Sir?

SIR CAUTIOUS: You know what I mean. . .

LADY FULBANK: Hah – I hope you would not be a cuckold, Sir.

SIR CAUTIOUS: Why, truly in a civil way, or so.

LADY FULBANK: There is but one way, Sir, to make me hate you, and that would be tame suffering.

SIR CAUTIOUS: (Nay, and she be thereabouts there's no discovering.)

LADY FULBANK: But leave this fond discourse, and if you must, let us to bed.

SIR CAUTIOUS: Ay, ay, I did but try your virtue, mun, dost think I was in earnest?
Enter SERVANT.
SERVANT: Sir, here's a chest directed to your Worship.
SIR CAUTIOUS: (Hum, 'tis Wasteall. Now does my heart fail me.) A chest, say you...to me...so late. I'll warrant it comes from Sir Nicholas Smuggle, some prohibited goods that he has stolen the custom of and cheated his Majesty. Well, he's an honest man, bring it in.
Exit SERVANT.
LADY FULBANK: What, into my apartment, Sir, a nasty chest?
SIR CAUTIOUS: By all means, for if the searchers come, they'll never be so uncivil to ransack thy lodgings, and we are bound in Christian charity to do for one another. Some rich commodities, I am sure, and some fine nic-nac will fall to thy share, I'll warrant thee. (Pox on him for a young rogue, how punctual he is!)
SERVANTS *re-enter with the chest.*
Go my dear, go to bed. I'll send Sir Nicholas a receipt for the chest, and be with thee presently.
SIR CAUTIOUS, SERVANTS *and* LADY FULBANK *leave.*
GAYMAN *peeps out of the chest, and looks round him, wondering.*
GAYMAN: Hah, where am I? By Heaven, my last night's vision! 'Tis that enchanted room, and yonder's the alcove! Sure 'twas indeed some witch, who, knowing of my infidelity, has by enchantment brought me hither. 'Tis so, I am betrayed. [*He pauses.*] Hah! Or was it Julia that last night gave me that lone opportunity? But hark, I hear someone coming. [*He shuts himself in.*]
Enter SIR CAUTIOUS
SIR CAUTIOUS: [*lifting up the chest-lid*]: So, you are come, I see. [*He goes and locks the door.*]
GAYMAN: (Hah – he here! Nay then, I was deceived, and it was Julia that last night gave me the dear assignation.)
SIR CAUTIOUS *peeps into the main bedchamber.*
LADY FULBANK: [*within*] Come, Sir Cautious, I shall fall asleep and then you'll waken me.
SIR CAUTIOUS: Ay, my dear, I'm coming. She's in bed. I'll go put out the candle and then . . .
GAYMAN: Ay, I'll warrant you for my part.
SIR CAUTIOUS: Ay, but you may over-act your part, and spoil all. But, Sir, I hope you'll use a Christian conscience in this business.
GAYMAN: Oh doubt not, Sir, but I shall do you reason.
SIR CAUTIOUS: Ay, Sir, but. . .
GAYMAN: Good Sir, no more cautions; you, unlike a fair gamester, will rook me out of half my night. I am impatient.
SIR CAUTIOUS: Good Lord, are you so hasty? If I please, you shan't go at all.
GAYMAN: With all my soul, Sir. Pay me three hundred pounds, Sir.
SIR CAUTIOUS: Lord, Sir, you mistake my candid meaning still. I am content to

be a cuckold, Sir, but I would have things done decently, d'ye mind me?
GAYMAN: As decently as a cuckold can be made, Sir. But no more disputes,
I pray, Sir.
SIR CAUTIOUS: I'm gone! I'm gone! But hark ye, Sir, you'll rise before day?
SIR CAUTIOUS goes out, then returns.
GAYMAN: Yet again!
SIR CAUTIOUS: I vanish, Sir, but hark ye, you'll not speak a word, but let her
think 'tis I.
GAYMAN: Begone, I say, Sir.
SIR CAUTIOUS runs out.
I am convinced last night I was with Julia.
O sot, insensible and dull!
Enter softly to the main bedchamber SIR CAUTIOUS.
SIR CAUTIOUS: So, the candle's out. Give me your hand.
He leads GAYMAN softly in....

From ACT V, SCENE VIII. Scene Changes to the Ante-Chamber

Enter SIR CAUTIOUS.
SIR CAUTIOUS: Now cannot I sleep, but am as restless as a merchant in stormy
weather, that has ventured all his wealth in one bottom. Woman is a leaky
vessel: if she should like the young rogue now, and they should come to
a right understanding, why then I am a Wittal, that's all, and shall be put
in print at Snowhill with my effigies o'th'top, like the sign of Cuckold's
Haven. Hum, they're damnable silent. Pray Heaven he has not murdered
her, and robbed her. Hum, hark, what's that? A noise! He has broke his
covenant with me, and shall forfeit the money. How loud they are! Ay, ay,
the plot's discovered, what shall I do? Why, the Devil is not in her, sure,
to be refractory now, and peevish. If she be, I must pay my money yet,
and that would be a damned thing. Sure, they're coming out. I'll retire
and hear how 'tis with them.
He retires.
*Enter LADY FULBANK undressed, GAYMAN half undressed upon his knees
following her, holding her gown.*
LADY FULBANK: Oh! You unkind! What have you made me do? Unhand me, false
deceiver, let me loose!
SIR CAUTIOUS: [*peeping*] Made her do? So, so, 'tis done. I'm glad of that.
GAYMAN: Can you be angry, Julia, because I only seized my right of love.
LADY FULBANK: And must my honour be the price of it? Could nothing but
my fame reward your passion? What, make me a base prostitute, a foul
adult'ress? Oh, be gone, be gone, dear robber of my quiet.
SIR CAUTIOUS: (Oh fearful!)
GAYMAN: Oh! Calm your rage, and hear me. If you are so,
You are an innocent adult'ress.

It was the feeble husband you enjoyed
In cold imagination, and no more.
Shyly you turned away, faintly resigned.
SIR CAUTIOUS: (Hum, did she so?)
GAYMAN: Till excess of love betrayed the cheat.
SIR CAUTIOUS: (Ay, ay, that was my fear.)
LADY FULBANK: Away, be gone. I'll never see you more.
GAYMAN: You may as well forbid the Sun to shine.
Not see you more! Heavens! I before adored you,
But now I rave! And with my impatient love,
A thousand mad and wild desires are burning!
I have discovered now new worlds of charms,
And can no longer tamely love and suffer.
SIR CAUTIOUS: (So, I have brought an old house upon my head, Entailed
cuckoldom upon myself.)
LADY FULBANK: I'll hear no more. Sir Cautious! Where's my husband? Why have
you left my honour thus unguarded?
SIR CAUTIOUS: (Ay, ay, she's well enough pleased, I fear, for all.)
GAYMAN: Base as he is, 'twas he exposed this treasure, like silly Indians bartered
thee for trifles.
SIR CAUTIOUS: (Oh treacherous villain!)
LADY FULBANK: Hah, my husband do this?
GAYMAN: He, by love, he was the kind procurer,
Contrived the means, and brought me to thy bed.
LADY FULBANK: My husband! My wise husband!
What fondness in my conduct had he seen,
To take so shameful and so base revenge?
GAYMAN: None. 'Twas filthy avarice seduced him to't.
LADY FULBANK: If he could be so barbarous to expose me, Could you, who loved
me, be so cruel too?
GAYMAN: What, to possess thee when the bliss was offered?
Possess thee too without a crime to thee?
Charge not my soul with so remiss a flame,
So dull a sense of virtue to refuse it.
LADY FULBANK: I am convinced the fault was all my husband's. [*Kneels*]
And here I vow, by all things just and sacred.
To separate forever from his bed.
SIR CAUTIOUS: (Oh, I am not able to endure it.)
Hold, oh hold, my dear.
He kneels as she rises.
LADY FULBANK: Stand off! I do abhor thee. . . .

Mary Delarivier Manley
Song (1714)

A ccording to the autobiographical Adventures of Rivella (1714) this song was composed when Manley, in the midst of an affair with Sir Thomas Skipwith (manager of the Drury Lane Theatre where some of her plays were produced), discovered a letter from one Mrs Pym, a rival for Skipwith's love. The competition between the two women and Manley's composition delighted the vain Skipwith, who had the poem set to music and reputedly sang it wherever he could find a listener, earning himself the nickname of 'Dangerous Swain'.

Ah Dangerous Swain, tell me no more,
Thy Happy Nymph you Worship and Adore;
When thy fill'd Eyes are sparkling at her Name,
I raving wish that mine had caus'd the Flame.

If by your fire to her you can impart
Diffusive heat to warm another's heart:
Ah dangerous Swain, what wou'd the ruine be,
Shou'd you but once persuade you burn for me.

Charlotte Brontë

FROM

Villette (1853)

L ucy Snowe has travelled to Brussels to teach in a girls' boarding school. Always feeling herself to be a 'looker-on' at life, when Lucy meets Dr John, an Englishman who attends the infant daughters of Madame, she observes him at a distance and nurtures her secret passion.

It was not perhaps my business to observe the mystery of his bearing, or search out its origin or aim; but, placed as I was, I could hardly help it. He laid himself open to my observation, according to my presence in the room just that

degree of notice and consequence a person of my exterior habitually expects; that is to say, about what is given to unobtrusive articles of furniture, chairs of ordinary joiner's work, and carpets of no striking pattern. Often, while waiting for Madame, he would muse, smile, watch, or listen like a man who thinks himself alone. I, meantime, was free to puzzle over his countenance and movements, and wonder what could be the meaning of that peculiar interest and attachment – all mixed up with doubt and strangeness, and inexplicably ruled by some presiding spell which wedded him to this demi-convent, secluded in the built-up core of a capital. He, I believe, never remembered that I had eyes in my head, much less a brain behind them.

Nor would he ever have found this out, but that one day, while he sat in the sunshine and I was observing the colouring of his hair, whiskers, and complexion – the whole being of such a tone as a strong light brings out with somewhat perilous force (indeed I recollect I was driven to compare his beamy head in my thoughts to that of the 'golden image' which Nebuchadnezzar,[2] the king, had set up), an idea new, sudden, and startling, riveted my attention with an overmastering strength and power of attraction.[3] I know not to this day how I looked at him: the force of surprise, and also of conviction, made me forget myself; and I only recovered wonted consciousness when I saw that his notice was arrested, and that it had caught my movement in a clear little oval mirror fixed in the side of the window recess – by the aid of which reflector Madame often secretly spied persons walking in the garden below. Though of so gay and sanguine a temperament, he was not without a certain nervous sensitiveness which made him ill at ease under a direct, inquiring gaze. On surprising me thus, he turned and said, in a tone which, though courteous, had just so much dryness in it as to mark a shade of annoyance, as well as to give to what was said the character of rebuke –

'Mademoiselle does not spare me: I am not vain enough to fancy that it is my merits which attract her attention; it must then be some defect. Dare I ask – what?'

I was confounded, as the reader may suppose, yet not with an irrecoverable confusion; being conscious that it was from no emotion of incautious admiration, nor yet in a spirit of unjustifiable inquisitiveness, that I had incurred this reproof. I might have cleared myself on the spot, but would not. I did not speak. I was not in the habit of speaking to him. Suffering him, then, to think what he chose and accuse me of what he would, I resumed some work I had dropped, and kept my head bent over it during the remainder of his stay. There is a perverse mood of the mind which is rather soothed than irritated by misconstruction; and in quarters where we can never be rightly known, we take pleasure,

---

[2] King of Babylon; see David 4 : 29–33.
[3] Lucy realises that she had been acquainted with Dr. John years ago in England though knowing him by a different name. Reticent even with her reader, she does not reveal this information until much later in her story.

I think, in being consummately ignored. What honest man, on being casually taken for a housebreaker, does not feel rather tickled than vexed at the mistake?[4]

Some time later Lucy, having rigidly suppressed all feeling for Dr John, has buried his treasured letters in the garden of the school where a nun was once said to have been walled up alive in punishment for the breaking of her vow of chastity. Dr John is now engaged to Paulina, and Lucy is her confidante.

'Child as I was,' remarked Paulina, 'I wondered how I dared be so venturous. To me he seems now all sacred, his locks are inaccessible, and Lucy, I feel a sort of fear when I look at his firm, marble chin, at his straight Greek features. Women are called beautiful, Lucy; he is not like a woman, therefore I suppose he is not beautiful, but what is he then? Do other people see him with my eyes? Do *you* admire him?'

'I'll tell you what I do, Paulina,' was once my answer to her many questions, '*I never see him*. I looked at him twice or thrice about a year ago, before he recognized me, and then I shut my eyes; and if he were to cross their balls twelve times between each day's sunset and sunrise, except from memory, I should hardly know what shape had gone by.'

'Lucy, what do you mean?' said she, under her breath.

'I mean that I value vision, and dread being struck stone blind.' It was best to answer her strongly at once, and to silence for ever the tender, passionate confidences which left her lips sweet honey, and sometimes dropped in my ear – molten lead. To me she commented no more on her lover's beauty.[5]

Elizabeth Gaskell

FROM

Cousin Phillis (1863–4)

*H*oldsworth, Paul's admired colleague and mentor, has been seri-ously ill. Paul suggests that Holdsworth should spend a period of

---

4   From Chapter 10.
5   From Chapter 37.

convalescence in the country where his aunt lives with her husband and daughter Phillis, Paul's childhood friend.

The morrow was blue and sunny, and beautiful; the very perfection of an early summer's day. Mr Holdsworth was all impatience to be off into the country; morning had brought back his freshness and strength, and consequent eagerness to be doing. I was afraid we were going to my cousin's farm rather too early, before they would expect us; but what could I do with such a restless vehement man as Holdsworth was that morning? We came down upon the Hope Farm before the dew was off the grass on the shady side of the lane; the great house-dog was loose, basking in the sun, near the closed side door. I was surprised at this door being shut, for all summer long it was open from morning to night; but it was only on latch. I opened it, Rover watching me with half-suspicious, half-trustful eyes. The room was empty.

'I don't know where they can be,' said I. 'But come in and sit down while I go and look for them. You must be tired.'

'Not I. This sweet balmy air is like a thousand tonics. Besides, this room is hot, and smells of those pungent wood-ashes. What are we to do?'

'Go round to the kitchen. Betty will tell us where they are.'

So we went round into the farmyard, Rover accompanying us out of a grave sense of duty. Betty was washing out her milk-pans in the cold bubbling spring-water that constantly trickled in and out of a stone trough. In such weather as this most of her kitchen-work was done out of doors.

'Eh, dear!' said she, 'the minister and missus is away at Hornby! They ne'er thought of your coming so betimes! The missus had some errands to do, and she thought as she'd walk with the minister and be back by dinner-time.'

'Did not they expect us to dinner?' said I.

'Well, they did, and they did not, as I may say. Missus said to me the cold lamb would do well enough if you did not come; and if you did I was to put on a chicken and some bacon to boil; and I'll go do it now, for it is hard to boil bacon enough.'

'And is Phillis gone, too?' Mr Holdsworth was making friends with Rover.

'No! She's just somewhere about. I reckon you'll find her in the kitchen-garden, getting peas.'

'Let us go there,' said Holdsworth, suddenly leaving off his play with the dog.

So I led the way into the kitchen-garden. It was in the first promise of a summer profuse in vegetables and fruits. Perhaps it was not so much cared for as other parts of the property; but it was more attended to than most kitchen-gardens belonging to farm-houses. There were borders of flowers along each side of the gravel walks; and there was an old sheltering wall on the north side covered with tolerably choice fruit-trees; there was a slope down to the fish-pond at the end, where there were great strawberry-beds; and raspberry-bushes and rose-bushes grew wherever there was a space; it seemed

a chance which had been planted. Long rows of peas stretched at right angles from the main walk, and I saw Phillis stooping down among them, before she saw us. As soon as she heard our cranching steps on the gravel, she stood up, and shading her eyes from the sun, recognized us. She was quite still for a moment, and then came slowly towards us, blushing a little from evident shyness. I had never seen Phillis shy before.

'This is Mr Holdsworth, Phillis,' said I, as soon as I had shaken hands with her. She glanced up at him, and then looked down, more flushed than ever at his grand formality of taking his hat off and bowing; such manners had never been seen at Hope Farm before.

'Father and mother are out. They will be so sorry; you did not write, Paul, as you said you would.'

'It was my fault,' said Holdsworth, understanding what she meant as well as if she had put it more fully into words. 'I have not yet given up all the privileges of an invalid; one of which is indecision. Last night, when your cousin asked me at what time we were to start, I really could not make up my mind.'

Phillis seemed as if she could not make up her mind as to what to do with us. I tried to help her, –

'Have you finished getting peas?' taking hold of the half-filled basket she was unconsciously holding in her hand; 'or may we stay and help you?'

'If you would. But perhaps it will tire you, sir?' added she, speaking now to Holdsworth.

'Not a bit,' said he. 'It will carry me back twenty years in my life, when I used to gather peas in my grandfather's garden. I suppose I may eat a few as I go along?'

'Certainly, sir. But if you went to the strawberry-beds you would find some strawberries ripe, and Paul can show you where they are.'

'I am afraid you distrust me. I can assure you I know the exact fulness at which peas should be gathered. I take great care not to pluck them when they are unripe. I will not be turned off, as unfit for my work.'

This was a style of half-joking talk that Phillis was not accustomed to. She looked for a moment as if she would have liked to defend herself from the playful charge of distrust made against her, but she ended by not saying a word. We all plucked our peas in busy silence for the next five minutes. Then Holdsworth lifted himself up from between the rows, and said, a little wearily, –

'I am afraid I must strike work. I am not as strong as I fancied myself.'

Phillis was full of penitence immediately. He did, indeed, look pale; and she blamed herself for having allowed him to help her.

'It was very thoughtless of me. I did not know – I thought, perhaps, you really liked it. I ought to have offered you something to eat, sir! Oh, Paul, we have gathered quite enough; how stupid I was to forget that Mr Holdsworth had been ill!' And in a blushing hurry she led the way towards the house. We went in, and she moved a heavy cushioned chair forwards, into which Holdsworth

was only too glad to sink. Then with deft and quiet speed she brought in a little tray, wine, water, cake, home-made bread, and newly-churned butter. She stood by in some anxiety till, after bite and sup, the colour returned to Mr Holdsworth's face, and he would fain have made us some laughing apologies for the fright he had given us. But then Phillis drew back from her innocent show of care and interest, and relapsed into the cold shyness habitual to her when she was first thrown into the company of strangers. She brought out the last week's county paper (which Mr Holdsworth had read five days ago), and then quietly withdrew; and then he subsided into languor, leaning back and shutting his eyes as if he would go to sleep. I stole into the kitchen after Phillis; but she had made the round of the corner of the house outside, and I found her sitting on the horse-mount, with her basket of peas, and a basin into which she was shelling them. Rover lay at her feet, snapping now and then at the flies. I went to her, and tried to help her, but somehow the sweet crisp young peas found their way more frequently into my mouth than into the basket, while we talked together in a low tone, fearful of being overheard through the open casements of the house-place in which Holdsworth was resting.

'Don't you think him handsome?' asked I.

'Perhaps – yes – I have hardly looked at him,' she replied. 'But is not he very like a foreigner?'

'Yes, he cuts his hair foreign fashion,' said I.

'I like an Englishman to look like an Englishman.'

'I don't think he thinks about it. He says he began that way when he was in Italy, because everybody wore it so, and it is natural to keep it on in England.'

'Not if he began it in Italy because everybody there wore it so. Everybody here wears it differently.'

I was a little offended with Phillis's logical fault-finding with my friend; and I determined to change the subject.

'When is your mother coming home?'

'I should think she might come any time now; but she had to go and see Mrs Morton, who was ill, and she might be kept, and not be home till dinner. Don't you think you ought to go and see how Mr Holdsworth is going on, Paul? He may be faint again.'

I went at her bidding; but there was no need for it. Mr Holdsworth was up, standing by the window, his hands in his pockets; he had evidently been watching us. He turned away as I entered.

'So that is the girl I found your good father planning for your wife, Paul, that evening when I interrupted you! Are you of the same coy mind still? It did not look like it a minute ago.'

'Phillis and I understand each other,' I replied, sturdily. 'We are like brother and sister. She would not have me as a husband if there was not another man in the world; and it would take a deal to make me think of her – as my father wishes' (somehow I did not like to say 'as a wife'), 'but we love each other dearly.'

'Well, I am rather surprised at it – not at your loving each other in a brother-and-sister kind of way – but at your finding it so impossible to fall in love with such a beautiful woman.'

Woman! beautiful woman! I had thought of Phillis as a comely but awkward girl; and I could not banish the pinafore from my mind's eye when I tried to picture her to myself. Now I turned, as Mr Holdsworth had done, to look at her again out of the window: she had just finished her task, and was standing up, her back to us, holding the basket, and the basin in it, high in air, out of Rover's reach, who was giving vent to his delight at the probability of a change of place by glad leaps and barks, and snatches at what he imagined to be a withheld prize. At length she grew tired of their mutual play, and with a feint of striking him, and a 'Down, Rover! do hush!' she looked towards the window where we were standing, as if to reassure herself that no one had been disturbed by the noise, and seeing us, she coloured all over, and hurried away, with Rover still curving in sinuous lines about her as she walked.

'I should like to have sketched her,' said Mr Holdsworth, as he turned away. He went back to his chair, and rested in silence for a minute or two. Then he was up again.

'I would give a good deal for a book,' he said. 'It would keep me quiet.' He began to look round; there were a few volumes at one end of the shovel-board.

'Fifth volume of Matthew Henry's *Commentary*, said he, reading their titles aloud. '*Housewife's complete Manual*; *Berridge on Prayer*; *L'Inferno* – Dante!' in great surprise. 'Why, who reads this?'

'I told you Phillis read it. Don't you remember? She knows Latin and Greek, too.'

'To be sure! I remember! But somehow I never put two and two together. That quiet girl, full of household work, is the wonderful scholar, then, that put you to rout with her questions when you first began to come here. To be sure, "Cousin Phillis!" What's here: a paper with the hard, obsolete words written out. I wonder what sort of a dictionary she has got. Baretti won't tell her all these words. Stay! I have got a pencil here. I'll write down the most accepted meanings, and save her a little trouble.'

So he took her book and the paper back to the little round table, and employed himself in writing explanations and definitions of the words which had troubled her. I was not sure if he was not taking a liberty: it did not quite please me, and yet I did not know why.

Dorothy Parker

The Custard Heart (1939)

No living eye, of human being or caged wild beast or dear, domestic animal, had beheld Mrs Lanier when she was not being wistful. She was dedicated to wistfulness, as lesser artists to words and paint and marble. Mrs Lanier was not of the lesser; she was of the true. Surely the eternal example of the true artist is Dickens's actor who blacked himself all over to play Othello. It is safe to assume that Mrs Lanier was wistful in her bathroom, and slumbered soft in wistfulness through the dark and secret night.

If nothing should happen to the portrait of her by Sir James Weir, there she will stand, wistful for the ages. He has shown her at her full length, all in yellows, the delicately heaped curls, the slender, arched feet like elegant bananas, the shining stretch of the evening gown; Mrs Lanier habitually wore white in the evening, but white is the devil's own hue to paint, and could a man be expected to spend his entire six weeks in the States on the execution of a single commission? Wistfulness rests, immortal, in the eyes dark with sad hope, in the pleading mouth, the droop of the little head on the sweet long neck, bowed as if in submission to the three ropes of Lanier pearls. It is true that, when the portrait was exhibited, one critic expressed in print his puzzlement as to what a woman who owned such pearls had to be wistful about; but that was doubtless because he had sold his saffron-coloured soul for a few pennies to the proprietor of a rival gallery. Certainly, no man could touch Sir James on pearls. Each one is as distinct, as individual as is each little soldier's face in a Meissonier battle scene.

For a time, with the sitter's obligation to resemble the portrait, Mrs Lanier wore yellow of evenings. She had gowns of velvet like poured country cream and satin with the lacquer of buttercups and chiffon that spiralled about her like golden smoke. She wore them, and listened in shy surprise to the resulting comparisons to daffodils, and butterflies in the sunshine, and such; but she knew.

'It just isn't me,' she sighed at last, and returned to her lily draperies. Picasso had his blue period, and Mrs Lanier her yellow one. They both knew when to stop.

In the afternoons, Mrs Lanier wore black, thin and fragrant, with the great pearls weeping on her breast. What her attire was by morning, only Gwennie, the maid who brought her breakfast tray, could know; but it must, of course, have been exquisite. Mr Lanier – certainly there was a Mr Lanier; he had even been seen – stole past her door on his way out to his office, and the servants glided and murmured, so that Mrs Lanier might be spared as long as possible from the bright new cruelty of the day. Only when the littler, kinder hours had

succeeded noon could she bring herself to come forth and face the recurrent sorrows of living.

There was duty to be done, almost daily, and Mrs Lanier made herself brave for it. She must go in her town car to select new clothes and to have fitted to her perfection those she had ordered before. Such garments as hers did not just occur; like great poetry, they required labour. But she shrank from leaving the shelter of her house, for everywhere without were the unlovely and the sad, to assail her eyes and her heart. Often she stood shrinking for several minutes by the baroque mirror in her hall before she could manage to hold her head high and brave, and go on.

There is no safety for the tender, no matter how straight their route, how innocent their destination. Sometimes, even in front of Mrs Lanier's dressmaker's or her furrier's or her lingère's or her milliner's, there would be a file of thin girls and small, shabby men, who held placards in their cold hands and paced up and down and up and down with slow, measured steps. Their faces would be blue and rough from the wind, and blank with the monotony of their treadmill. They looked so little and poor and strained that Mrs Lanier's hands would fly to her heart in pity. Her eyes would be luminous with sympathy and her sweet lips would part as if on a whisper of cheer, as she passed through the draggled line into the shop.

Often there would be pencil-sellers in her path, a half of a creature set upon a sort of roller-skate thrusting himself along the pavement by his hands, or a blind man shuffling after his wavering cane. Mrs Lanier must stop and sway, her eyes closed, one hand about her throat to support her lovely, stricken head. Then you could actually see her force herself, could see the effort ripple her body, as she opened her eyes and gave these miserable ones, the blind and the seeing alike, a smile of such tenderness, such sorrowful understanding, that it was like the exquisite sad odour of hyacinths on the air. Sometimes, if the man was not too horrible, she could even reach in her purse for a coin and, holding it as lightly as if she had plucked it from a silvery stem, extend her slim arm and drop it in his cup. If he was young and new at his life, he would offer her pencils for the worth of her money; but Mrs Lanier wanted no returns. In gentlest delicacy she would slip away, leaving him with mean wares intact, not a worker for his livelihood like a million others, but signal and set apart, rare in the fragrance of charity.

So it was, when Mrs Lanier went out. Everywhere she saw them, the ragged, the wretched, the desperate, and to each she gave her look that spoke with no words.

'Courage,' it said. 'And you – oh, wish me courage, too!'

Frequently, by the time she returned to her house, Mrs Lanier would be limp as a freesia. Her maid Gwennie would have to beseech her to lie down, to gain the strength to change her gown for a filmier one and descend to her drawing-room, her eyes darkly mournful, but her exquisite breasts pointed high.

In her drawing-room, there was sanctuary. Here her heart might heal from the blows of the world, and be whole for its own sorrow. It was a room suspended above life, a place of tender fabrics and pale flowers, with never a paper or a book to report the harrowing or describe it. Below the great sheet of its window swung the river, and the stately scows went by laden with strange stuff in rich tapestry colours; there was no necessity to belong to the sort who must explain that it was garbage. An island with a happy name lay opposite, and on it stood a row of prim, tight buildings, naïve as a painting by Rousseau. Sometimes there could be seen on the island the brisk figures of nurses and internes, sporting in the lanes. Possibly there were figures considerably less brisk beyond the barred windows of the buildings, but that was not to wondered about in the presence of Mrs Lanier. All those who came to her drawing-room came in one cause: to shield her heart from hurt.

Here in her drawing-room, in the lovely blue of the late day, Mrs Lanier sat upon opalescent taffeta and was wistful. And here to her drawing-room, the young men came and tried to help her bear her life.

There was a pattern to the visits of the young men. They would come in groups of three or four or six, for a while; and then there would be one of them who would stay a little after the rest had gone, who presently would come a little earlier than the others. Then there would be days when Mrs Lanier would cease to be at home to the other young men, and that one young man would be alone with her in the lovely blue. And then Mrs Lanier would be no longer be at home to that one young man, and Gwennie would have to tell him and tell him, over the telephone, that Mrs Lanier was out, that Mrs Lanier was ill, that Mrs Lanier could not be disturbed. The groups of young men would come again; that one young man would not be with them. But there would be, among them, a new young man; who presently would stay a little later and come a little earlier, who eventually would plead with Gwennie over the telephone.

Gwennie – her widowed mother had named her Gwendola, and then, as if realising that no other dream would ever come true, had died – was little and compact and unnoticeable. She had been raised on an upstate farm by an uncle and aunt hard as the soil they fought for their lives. After their deaths, she had no relatives anywhere. She came to New York, because she had heard stories of jobs; her arrival was at the time when Mrs Lanier's cook needed a kitchen-maid. So in her own house, Mrs Lanier had found her treasure.

Gwennie's hard little farm-girl's fingers could set invisible stitches, could employ a flatiron as if it were a wand, could be as summer breezes in the robing of Mrs Lanier and the tending of her hair. She was as busy as the day was long; and her days frequently extended from daybreak to daybreak. She was never tired, she had no grievance, she was cheerful without being expressive about it. There was nothing in her presence or the sight of her to touch the heart and thus cause discomfort.

Mrs Lanier would often say that she didn't know what she would do without

her little Gwennie; if her little Gwennie should ever leave her, she said, she just couldn't go on. She looked so lorn and fragile as she said it that one scowled upon Gwennie for the potentialities of death or marriage that the girl carried within her. Yet there was no pressing cause for worry, for Gwennie was strong as a pony and had no beau. She had made no friends at all, and seemed not to observe the omission. Her life was for Mrs Lanier; like all others who were permitted close, Gwennie sought to do what she could to save Mrs Lanier from pain.

They could all assist in shutting out reminders of the sadness abroad in the world, but Mrs Lanier's private sorrow was a more difficult matter. There dwelt a yearning so deep, so secret in her heart that it would often be days before she could speak of it, in the twilight, to a new young man.

'If I only had a little baby,' she would sigh, 'a little, little baby, I think I could be almost happy.' And she would fold her delicate arms, and lightly, slowly rock them, as if they cradled that little, little one of her dear dreams. Then, the denied madonna, she was at her most wistful, and the young man would have lived or died for her, as she bade him.

Mrs Lanier never mentioned why her wish was unfulfilled; the young man would know her to be too sweet to place blame, too proud to tell. But, so close to her in the pale light, he would understand, and his blood would swirl with fury that such clods as Mr Lanier remained unkilled. He would beseech Mrs Lanier, first in halting murmurs, then in rushes of hot words, to let him take her away from the hell of her life and try to make her almost happy. It would be after this that Mrs Lanier would be out to the young man, would be ill, would be incapable of being disturbed.

Gwennie did not enter the drawing-room when there was only one young man there; but when the groups returned she served unobtrusively, drawing a curtain or fetching a fresh glass. All the Lanier servants were unobtrusive, light of step and correctly indistinct of feature. When there must be changes made in the staff, Gwennie and the housekeeper arranged the replacements and did not speak of the matter to Mrs Lanier, lest she should be stricken by desertions or saddened by tales of woe. Always the new servants resembled the old, alike in that they were unnoticeable. That is, until Kane, the new chauffeur, came.

The old chauffeur had been replaced because he had been the old chauffeur too long. It weighs cruelly heavy on the tender heart when a familiar face grows lined and dry, when familiar shoulders seem daily to droop lower, a familiar nape is hollow between cords. The old chauffeur saw and heard and functioned with no difference; but it was too much for Mrs Lanier to see what was befalling him. With pain in her voice, she had told Gwennie that she should could stand the sight of him no longer. So the old chauffeur had gone, and Kane had come.

Kane was young, and there was nothing depressing about his straight shoulders and his firm, full neck to one sitting behind them in the town car. He stood, a fine triangle in his fitted uniform, holding the door of the

car open for Mrs Lanier and bowed his head as she passed. But when he was not at work, his head was held high and slightly cocked, and there was a little cocked smile on his red mouth.

Often, in the cold weather when Kane waited for her in the car, Mrs Lanier would humanely bid Gwennie to tell him to come in and wait in the servants' sitting-room. Gwennie brought him coffee and looked at him. Twice she did not hear Mrs Lanier's enamelled electric bell.

Gwennie began to observe her evenings off; she had disregarded them and stayed to minister to Mrs Lanier. There was one night when Mrs Lanier had floated late to her room, after a theatre and a long conversation, done in murmurs, in the drawing-room. And Gwennie had not been waiting, to take off the white gown, and put away the pearls, and brush the bright hair that curled like the petals of forsythia. Gwennie had not yet returned to the house from her holiday. Mrs Lanier had had to arouse a parlour-maid and obtain unsatisfactory aid from her.

Gwennie had wept, next morning, at the pathos of Mrs Lanier's eyes; but tears were too distressing for Mrs Lanier to see, and the girl stopped them. Mrs Lanier delicately patted her arm, and there had been nothing more of the matter, save that Mrs Lanier's eyes were darker and wider for this new hurt.

Kane became a positive comfort to Mrs Lanier. After the sorry sights of the streets, it was good to see Kane standing by the car, solid and straight and young, with nothing in the world the trouble with him. Mrs Lanier came to smile upon him almost gratefully, yet wistfully, too, as if she would seek of him the secret of not being sad.

And then, one day, Kane did not appear at his appointed time. The car, which should have been waiting to convey Mrs Lanier to her dressmaker's, was still in the garage, and Kane had not appeared there all day. Mrs Lanier told Gwennie immediately to telephone the place where he roomed and find out what this meant. The girl had cried out at her, cried out that she had called and called and called, and he was not there and no one there knew where he was. The crying out must have been due to Gwennie's loss of head in her distress at this disruption of Mrs Lanier's day; or perhaps it was the effect on her voice of an appalling cold she seemed to have contracted, for her eyes were heavy and red and her face pale and swollen.

There was no more of Kane. He had had his wages paid him on the day before he disappeared, and that was the last of him. There was never a word and not another sight of him. At first, Mrs Lanier could scarcely bring herself to believe that such betrayal could exist. Her heart, soft and sweet as a perfectly made *crème renversée*, quivered in her breast, and in her eyes lay the far light of suffering.

'Oh, how could he do this to me?' she asked piteously of Gwennie. 'How could he do this to poor me?'

There was no discussion of the defection of Kane; it was too painful a subject. If a caller heedlessly asked whatever had become of that nice-looking chauffeur,

Mrs Lanier would lay her hand over her closed lids and slowly wince. The caller would be suicidal that he had thus unconsciously added to her sorrows, and would strive his consecrated best to comfort her.

Gwennie's cold lasted for an extraordinarily long time. The weeks went by, and still, every morning, her eyes were red and her face white and puffed. Mrs Lanier often had to look away from her when she brought the breakfast tray.

She tended Mrs Lanier as carefully as ever; she gave no attention to her holidays, but stayed to do further service. She had always been quiet, and she became all but silent, and that was additionally soothing. She worked without stopping and seemed to thrive, for, save for the effects of the curious cold, she looked round and healthy.

'See,' Mrs Lanier said in tender raillery, as the girl attended the group in the drawing-room 'see how fat my little Gwennie's getting! Isn't that cute?'

The weeks went on, and the pattern of the young men shifted again. There came the day when Mrs Lanier was not at home to a group; when a new young man was to come and be alone with her, for his first time, in the drawing-room. Mrs Lanier sat before her mirror and lightly touched her throat with perfume, while Gwennie heaped the golden curls.

The exquisite face Mrs Lanier saw in the mirror drew her closer attention, and she put down the perfume and leaned towards it. She dropped her head a little to the side and watched it closely; she saw the wistful eyes grow yet more wistful, the lips curve to a pleading smile. She folded her arms close to her sweet breast and slowly rocked them, as if they cradled a dream-child. She watched the mirrored arms sway gently, caused them to sway a little slower.

'If I only had a little baby,' she sighed. She shook her head. Delicately she cleared her throat, and sighed again on a slightly lower note. 'If I only had a little, little baby, I think I could be almost happy.'

There was a clatter from behind her, and she turned, amazed. Gwennie had dropped the hair-brush to the floor and stood swaying, with her face in her hands.

'Gwennie!' said Mrs Lanier, 'Gwennie!'

The girl took her hands from her face, and it was as if she stood under a green light.

'I'm sorry,' she panted. 'Sorry. Please excuse me. I'm – oh, I'm going to be sick!'

She ran from the room so violently that the floor shook.

Mrs Lanier sat looking after Gwennie, her hands at her wounded heart. Slowly she turned back to her mirror, and what she saw there arrested her; the artist knows the masterpiece. Here was the perfection of her career, the sublimation of wistfulness; it was that look of grieved bewilderment that did it. Carefully she kept it upon her face as she rose from the mirror and, with her lovely hands still shielding her heart, went down to the new young man.

Marguerite Duras

FROM

The Lover (1984)

A *t a distance of many years,* The Lover *retails the memory of a consuming affair between the 15-year-old protagonist and her sophisticated Chinese lover. Hélène Lagonelle is one of her school friends.*

I come back to Hélène Lagonelle. She's lying on a bench, crying because she thinks I'm going to leave. I sit on the bench. I'm worn out by the beauty of Hélène Lagonelle's body lying against mine. Her body is sublime, naked under the dress, within arm's reach. Her breasts are such as I've never seen. I've never touched them. She's immodest, Hélène Lagonelle, she doesn't realize, she walks around the dormitories without any clothes on. The most beautiful of all the things given by God is this body of Hélène Lagonelle's, peerless, the balance between her figure and the way the body bears the breasts, outside itself, as if they were separate. Nothing could be more extraordinary than the outer roundness of these breasts proffered to the hands, this outwardness held out toward them. Even the body of my younger brother, like that of a little coolie, is as nothing beside this splendour. The shapes of men's bodies are miserly, internalised. Nor do they get spoiled like those of such girls as Hélène Lagonelle, which never last, a summer or so perhaps, that's all. She comes from the high plateaus of Da Lat. Her father works for the post office. She came quite recently, right in the middle of the school year. She's frightened, she comes up and sits beside you and stays there without speaking, crying sometimes. She has the pink-and-brown complexion of the mountains, you can always recognize it here where all the other children are pale green with anaemia and the torrid heat. Hélène Lagonelle doesn't go to high school. She's not capable of it, Hélène L. She can't learn, can't remember things. She goes to the primary classes at the boarding school, but it's no use. She weeps up against me, and I stroke her hair, her hands, tell her I'm going to stay here with her. She doesn't know she's very beautiful, Hélène Lagonelle. Her parents don't know what to do with her, they want to marry her off as soon as possible. She could have all the financés she likes, Hélène Lagonelle, but she doesn't like, she doesn't want to get married, she wants to go back to

her mother. She, Hélène L. Hélène Lagonelle. In the end she'll do what her mother wants. She's much more beautiful than I am, the girl in the clown's hat and lamé shoes, infinitely more marriageable, she can be married off, set up in matrimony, you can frighten her, explain it to her, what frightens her and what she doesn't understand, tell her to stay where she is, wait.

Hélène Lagonelle is 17, seventeen, yet she still doesn't know what I know. It's as if I guessed she never will.

Hélène Lagonelle's body is heavy, innocent still, her skin's as soft as that of certain fruits, you almost can't grasp her, she's almost illusory, it's too much. She makes you want to kill her, she conjures up a marvellous dream of putting her to death with your own hands. Those flour-white shapes, she bears them unknowingly, and offers them for hands to knead, for lips to eat, without holding them back, without any knowledge of them and without any knowledge of their fabulous power. I'd like to eat Hélène Lagonelle's breasts as he eats mine in the room in the Chinese town where I go every night to increase my knowledge of God. I'd like to devour and be devoured by those flour-white breasts of hers.

I am worn out with desire for Hélène Lagonelle.

I am worn out with desire.

I want to take Hélène Lagonelle with me to where every evening, my eyes shut, I have imparted to me the pleasure that makes you cry out. I'd like to give Hélène Lagonelle to the man who does that to me, so he may do it in turn to her. I want it to happen in my presence, I want her to do it as I wish, I want her to give herself where I give myself. It's via Hélène Lagonelle's body, through it, that the ultimate pleasure would pass from him to me.

A pleasure unto death.[6]

---

[6]   Published in 1984 by Les Editions de Minuit. Translated by Barbara Bray (1985).

Elizabeth Jolley

FROM

The Well (1986)

*H*ester Harper, middle-aged and lame, lives alone in the bush with her aged father. On impulse, she decides to take Kathy, a girl from the local orphanage to live with her. One night, succumbing to Kathy's pleas, she takes the girl to a party at the hotel in town so that Kathy can practise her dancing and dream of a partnership with John Travolta.

'You know, there's something I have been wanting to say to you for some time,' Mrs Borden, still serious, dropped her voice. 'I hope you will understand. . .'

'Yes?' Hester moved uneasily on the uncomfortable sofa. She leaned forward, inclining her head with a stiff movement. In the tremendous noise it was hard to hear. 'Well yes,' Mrs Borden echoed Miss Harper's way of speaking, 'wc don't, that is Mr Borden and I don't think, that is, we think that it is not right to keep Katherine, a young woman like Katherine shut away. I mean, she must think of men, a man? Sometimes?' The hat brim dipped forward deeply and then came up again and Hester had Rosalie Borden's bright inquisitive eyes directly opposite her own. 'You must realise,' her voice changed to a teasing note, 'that not every woman wishes to remain single.' The two women glanced quickly, Hester's glance following Mrs Borden's at the room full of couples and intending couples. As Hester made no reply Mrs Borden rushed on. 'I don't want to seem interfering,' she said, 'but it does seem that Katherine is intelligent. She could be a teacher, primary of course, or had you thought of nursing as a career?' She paused and then continued, 'Or if not a career, she must surely be thinking of wedding bells? This might sound old fashioned,' Mrs Borden laughed, 'but then she is what I call an old-fashioned girl. She is very pretty in a pale sort of way, she should be . . . ' Mrs Borden, seeing the cold tight expression on Hester's face, changed the subject. 'Perhaps,' she said, 'we should go and watch the dancing. Shall we?'

'Oh yes, of course,' Hester, wishing to be independent of Rosalie Borden's plump kindly arm, struggled to her feet. 'I must watch the dancing,' she said with a grudging little smile as if offering a kindness when she knew privately that it gave her infinite secret pleasure to watch Kathy abandon herself to her

own energy. Whenever she watched Kathy dancing, Hester, though outwardly showing no signs, moved in a wonderful freedom within herself. Her tiniest, most obscure muscles all took part. Unseen, her heart beat faster. She breathed more rapidly. In the privacy beneath her strict clothing she knew she was capable of an inner excitement which belonged only to her. It was a solitary experience but she did not mind this, being simply grateful for it. The music, the beat and the rhythm of the dancing filled her with a glow of satisfaction and a realisation of deep happiness. She felt as if she had been singing and dancing, moving in time with the music and with other people. She felt as if her hair was loose and as if her clothes were bright and light and as if they moved too, easily with her own rhythm. She felt free of bitterness, jealousy and longing. She was free from anxiety; who minded now, at this moment, about drought or about floods. She forgot she was lame and had always to depend upon a stick.

'I don't suppose you care for all this modern stuff.' Mrs Borden's voice, close to Hester, broke in upon the sweetest consolation.

CONSUMPTION

The gourmet reads the menu and savours promise. The lover lingers on the beauties of the loved one and tastes delight. The recitations of the dinner table resemble the lists of the heart.

Food and sex go together. Texts as far apart as the Song of Solomon and Wilde's *De Profundis* confirm this. Each is a love letter. Both speak not of love, but of food: 'I am come into my garden, my sister, my spouse; I have gathered my myrrh with my spice; I have eaten my honeycomb with my honey; I have drunk my wine with my milk; eat, O friends; drink, yea, drink abundantly, O beloved'; 'I have still got to pay my debts. The Savoy dinners – the clear turtle soup, the lucious ortolans wrapped in their crinkled Sicilian vine-leaves, the heavy amber-coloured, indeed almost amber-scented Champagne – Dagonet 1880, I think, was your favourite wine? – all still have to be paid for. The suppers at Willis's the special *cuvée* of Perrier-Jouet reserved always for us...'.

The earliest sensation of physical pleasure that we know is the ha,d sweet nipple taken into the mouth. The lover's mouth rediscovers that delight, tasting the scent of the beloved body, the taut, aching hardness, the yielding, swollen softness.

For women, it is not just the baby's experience which is recapitulated in the processes of sexual love. Much of women's sexual experience has been denied them. It has been named as prohibited behaviour or improper activity. The process is reversed with breastfeeding, but the results are the same. Like pregnancy, suckling has been sanitised and rendered asexual. It has been made into something done for the health of the child, something to be endured as an inconvenience, hidden as an embarrassment. But to see the nursing mother with her contented child – she opulent, the child relaxed – is to perceive one of the treasures of women's sexual pleasure. As with the acts of love, this performance can be slow, lazy and rounded; or it can be vibrant, sharp and climactic. Alicia Ostriker's poem shows the first; Naomi Mitchison's passage, the second.

To speak of one thing and mean another is commonplace in the texts of love. To displace the pleasure of sex into the pleasure of food is peculiarly appropriate. It still focuses on the hungry clamour of the body. It also entails a literary propriety, in that the existence of the text itself precludes the presence of the food or the sex. You cannot (or without some difficulty) talk, write or read while eating or having sex.

Three of these extracts tease out the resemblances between the consumption of food and the consumption of sex. Anaïs Nin's characters recall their early sexual knowledge, acquired with the flavour of ginger and the scent of the wardrobe. Julia Lee's cheeky song puns on spinach and sex. Christina Rossetti's *Goblin Market* crosses the fruit metaphor with the dangers of illicit knowledge: 'She thought of Jeanie in her grave,/Who should have been a bride./But who for joys brides hope to have/Fell sick and died . . .'.

When Lizzie cures her sister by offering the juices on her body to Laura's eager mouth, Rossetti sets up a coded prototype for the erotic poetry of lesbian love. Wittig and Fallon associate fruitfulness, nourishment, pungency and fulfilment with a positive image of the female body. The literal suggestion behind this textual surface yields the erotic. Your mouth on her other mouth; hers on yours. Kissing lips, speaking together.

This is the positive side of erotic consumption. In colloquial language we are familiar with the edible woman, but these are not comfortable associations. Woman is a tart, a cherry, a dish, crumpet, honey, sugar. She is consumable and she disappears.

The dissolution of the individual woman in the processes of love takes in Angela of Foligno's meditations. There she plays on the notion of transubstantiation when she craves a draught of Christ's blood. She assists in her own erosion when she refuses to eat. Mary Stuart surrenders her selfhood to be washed away in her lover. And 'Eliza' blends sexual compliance with religious 'death' as she succumbs to the dart of God's love.

The language of love and the language of food employ the same ideas and phrases: 'I'm hungry for you'. Nicole Brossard's *French Kiss* uniquely attempts to blend text and sex. Camomille's mouth consumes just as we consume her text. Literature and love meet in the mouth: 'Again, Camomile, your mouth, that's good, you get me off!'

Blessed Angela of Foligno

FROM

Liber de Vere Fidelium Experientia (c. 1290–6)

The Book of the Experience of the Truly Faithful is the record of a vision of God's love which Angela experienced while making a pilgrimage to Assisi to the shrine of St Francis. She dictated the work to her confessor Fra Arnaldo. Addressed to a religious audience, the book was widely circulated and highly influential. It recounts the steps or stages which lead to her union with Christ, beginning with the recognition of sin and culminating in the account of her vision.

17. Fourteenth. While I was in prayer, keeping vigil, Christ showed himself to me on the cross with such clarity – that is, that he gave me greater knowledge of him. And then he called me and said I should put my mouth to the wound in his side.[1] And it seemed to me that I saw and drank his blood flowing freshly from his side. And I was given to understand that by this he would cleanse me. And at this I began to feel great joy, although when I thought about the passion I felt sadness. And I prayed the Lord that he would cause me to shed all my blood for his love, just as he had done for me. And I so disposed myself on account of his love that I wished that all my limbs might suffer a death unlike his passion, that is, a more vile death. And I was meditating and desiring that if I could find someone to kill me, in some way that it would be lawful to kill me, on account of his faith or his love, that I would beg him to do this favour for me, that is, that since Christ was crucified on the wood of the cross he should crucify me in a low place, or in some unsavoury place or with a loathsome weapon. And I could not think of a death as vile as I desired, and I grieved deeply that I could not find a vile death that would in no way be like those of the saints, for I was totally unworthy.

18. The fifteenth. I fixed my attention on St John and on the Mother of God, meditating on their grief and praying them to obtain this grace for me,

[1] The wound made by a Roman soldier's spear in order to check that Jesus was dead and could be removed from the cross.

that is, that I might always feel the pain of the passion, or at least their pain. And they came to me, and for this purpose. Thus one time St John gave me so much [of his pain] that it was the greatest suffering I have ever felt. And I was given to understand that St John endured so much pain at the passion and death of Christ and at the pain of the Mother of Christ, that I thought then, and still think, that he was more than a martyr.

From this there was then given to me the desire of disposing of everything with so much will that although I was much attacked so that I would not do this, and I was often tempted by these remarks, and although it was forbidden to me by the friars and by you, and by all from whom it was appropriate for me to ask advice, nevertheless I could in no way hold back, either for the good or for the evil they might do to me. And if I had not been able to give to the poor otherwise, I would give away all my goods completely, for it did not seem to me that I could hold anything back for myself without great sin. Nevertheless my soul was still feeling bitter sorrow for my sins, and I didn't know if what I was doing pleased God. So I cried out in the most sorrowful weeping, saying, 'Lord, if I am damned, still I'm going to do this penance and I will give everything away and serve you.' And up to that point I was feeling bitter sorrow for my sins and I did not yet feel divine sweetness. I was transformed from that state in the following way . . .

21. The eighteenth. Afterwards I had feelings of God, and I felt such delight in prayer that I didn't remember to eat. And I wished that it were not necessary to eat, so that I might remain in prayer. But intermixed with this was a certain temptation, that is, that I shouldn't eat, or if I ate, that I would only eat a very small amount – but I recognised this as a temptation. And in my heart the fire of love was so great that I wasn't tired by genuflexions[2] nor by any other penitential act. Still later I came to so much greater a fire of love that I screamed if I heard anyone talking about God. Even if someone had stood over me with an axe ready to kill me, I could not have prevented myself. This happened to me for the first time when I sold a piece of land so that I could give to the poor. It was the best land that I had. And before I used to make fun of Petrucchio, but afterwards I could not. Moreover, when people said to me that I was demonically possessed so that I couldn't stop myself, I was very ashamed, and I too said the same, that I was ill and possessed, and I could not satisfy those who were maligning me. And when I saw depicted the passion of Christ, I could hardly endure it, but fever took me and I fell ill. So my companion hid from me pictures of the Passion or tried to hide them.

22. The nineteenth. But during this period of screaming, after that illumination which I miraculously received during the *pater noster*,[3] the first great consolation of the sweetness of God I sensed in this way, that is, as I was one time inspired and drawn to meditating on the delight there is in the contemplation of the

2 Ritual kneeling.
3 The prayer, 'Our father which art in heaven . . .'

divinity and humanity of Christ. And this was the greatest consolation I had experienced, in so much as for the major part of that day I stood on my feet in the cell where I was accustomed to praying, overwhelmed and alone. And my heart was in that delectation. After this I fell down and lost all speech. And my companion then came to me and thought that I was dying or might be dead. But it irritated me that she disturbed me in that greatest consolation.[4]

Mary Stuart, Queen of Scotland

FROM

Sonnets to Bothwell (1567?)

These twelve sonnets were among the papers found in the famous silver casket which contained letters cited at Mary Stuart's first trial. There is some doubt about the attribution to Mary, but it is generally accepted that they are authentic. The first collected edition of her poems was Poems of Mary Queen of Scots, *ed. Julian Sharman (London, 1873).*

IX

Pour luy aussi ie iete mainte larme

For him what countless tears I must have shed:
First, when he made himself my body's lord
Before he had my heart: and afterward
When I became distraught because he bled
So copiously that almost life went out:
And at that sight fear seized my heart and head
Both for the love I bore him and the dread
Of losing my sole rampart and redoubt.
For him I turned my honour to disgrace,
Though honour is our one sure joy and pride:

[4] Translated by Elizabeth Petroff (1985). This extract is taken from *Medieval Women's Visionary Literature*, ed. Elizabeth Alvilda Petroff (Oxford, 1986), p. 257 and p. 259.

For him bade Conscience find a humbler place
Chilled my most-trusted friends, and set aside
Every consideration! . . . What would I do?
Make a love-compact, Love of my heart, with you![5]

'Eliza'

The Dart (1652)

Shoot from above
Thou God of Love,[6]
And with heavn's dart
Wound my blest heart.

Descend sweet life,
And end this strife:
Earth would me stay,
But I'le away.

I'le dye for love
Of thee above,
Then should I bee
Made one with thee.

And let be sed
Eliza's dead,
And of love dy'd,
That love defi'd.

By a bright beam, shot from above,
She did ascend to her great Love,
And was content of love to dye,
Shot with a dart of Heavens bright eye.[7]

---

[5] Written in French. This translation, by Cliffard Bax, is taken from *Letters and Poems of Mary, Queen of Scots, supposed author*, ed. Clifford Bax (New York, 1947).
[6] Cupid, shooting his arrows.
[7] From *Eliza's Babes: or the Virgins-Offering. Being Divine Poems, and Meditations. Written by a Lady, who only desires to advance the glory of God, and not her own* (London, 1652).

Christina Rossetti
Goblin Market (1859)

*F*irst published in Goblin Market and Other Poems *(1862), this adult fairytale has been described by Isobel Armstrong as a poem 'so subversive it can only be given to children'. When William Michael produced a list of 'Leading Themes or Key-notes of Feeling' for the 1904 edition of his sister's works, he listed 'Goblin Market' under the heading of 'Love of Animals' ...*

Morning and evening
Maids heard the goblins cry:
'Come buy our orchard fruits,
Come buy, come buy:
Apples and quinces,
Lemons and oranges,
Plump unpecked cherries,
Melons and raspberries,
Bloom-down-cheeked peaches,
Swart-headed mulberries,
Wild free-born cranberries,
Crab-apples, dewberries,
Pine-apples, blackberries,
Apricots, strawberries; –
All ripe together
In summer weather, –
Morns that pass by,
Fair eves that fly;
Come buy, come buy:
Our grapes fresh from the vine,
Pomegranates full and fine,
Dates and sharp bullaces,
Rare pears and greengages,
Damsons and bilberries,
Taste them and try:
Currants and gooseberries,
Bright-fire-like barberries,
Figs to fill your mouth,
Citrons from the South,
Sweet to tongue and sound to eye;
Come buy, come buy.'

255

Evening by evening
Among the brookside rushes,
Laura bowed her head to hear,
Lizzie veiled her blushes:
Crouching close together
In the cooling weather,
With clasping arms and cautioning
   lips,
With tingling cheeks and finger tips.
'Lie close,' Laura said,
Pricking up her golden head:
'We must not look at goblin men,
We must not buy their fruits:
Who knows upon what soil they fed
Their hungry thirsty roots?'
'Come buy,' call the goblins
Hobbling down the glen.
'Oh,' cried Lizzie, 'Laura, Laura,
You should not peep at goblin men.'
Lizzie covered up her eyes,
Covered close lest they should look;
Laura reared her glossy head,
And whispered like the restless brook:
'Look, Lizzie, look, Lizzie,
Down the glen tramp little men.
One hauls a basket,
One bears a plate,
One lugs a golden dish
Of many pounds' weight.
How fair the vine must grow
Whose grapes are so luscious
How warm the wind must blow
Through those fruit bushes.'

'No,' said Lizzie: 'No, no, no;
Their offers should not charm us,
Their evil gifts would harm us.'
She thrust a dimpled finger
In each ear, shut eyes and ran:
Curious Laura chose to linger
Wondering at each merchant man.
One had a cat's face,
One whisked a tail,
One tramped at a rat's pace,
One crawled like a snail,

One like a wombat prowled obtuse
   and furry,
One like a ratel tumbled hurry skurry.
She heard a voice like voice of doves
Cooing all together:
They sounded kind and full of loves
In the pleasant weather.

Laura stretched her gleaming neck
Like a rush-imbedded swan,
Like a lily from the beck,
Like a moonlit poplar branch,
Like a vessel at the launch
When its last restraint is gone.

Backwards up the mossy glen
Turned and trooped the goblin men,
With their shrill repeated cry,
'Come buy, come buy.'
When they reached where Laura was
They stood stock still upon the moss,
Leering at each other,
Brother with queer brother;
Signalling each other,
Brother with sly brother.
One set his basket down,
One reared his plate;
One began to weave a crown
Of tendrils, leaves, and rough nuts
   brown
(Men sell not such in any town);
One heaved the golden weight
Of dish and fruit to offer her:
'Come buy, come buy,' was still
   their cry.
Laura stared but did not stir,
Longed but had no money.
The whisk-tailed merchant bade her
   taste
In tones as smooth as honey,
The cat-faced purr'd,
The rat-paced spoke a word
Of welcome, and the snail-paced
   even was heard;
One parrot-voiced and jolly

Cried 'Pretty Goblin' still for 'Pretty
    Polly';
One whistled like a bird.

But sweet-tooth Laura spoke in
    haste:
'Good Folk, I have no coin;
To take were to purloin:
I have no copper in my purse,
I have no silver either,
And all my gold is on the furze
That shakes in windy weather
Above the rusty heather.'
'You have much gold upon your
    head,'
They answered all together:
'Buy from us with a golden curl.'
She clipped a precious golden lock,
She dropped a tear more rare than
    pearl,
Then sucked their fruit globes fair
    or red.
Sweeter than honey from the rock,
Stronger than man-rejoicing wine,
Clearer than water flowed that juice;
She never tasted such before,
How should it cloy with length of
    use?
She sucked and sucked and sucked
    the more
Fruits which that unknown orchard
    bore;
She sucked until her lips were sore;
Then flung the emptied rinds away
But gathered up one kernel stone,
And knew not was it night or day
As she turned home alone.

Lizzie met her at the gate
Full of wise upbraidings:
'Dear, you should not stay so late,
Twilight is not good for maidens;
Should not loiter in the glen
In the haunts of the goblin men.
Do you not remember Jeanie,

How she met them in the moonlight,
Took their gifts both choice and
   many,
Ate their fruits and wore their
   flowers
Plucked from bowers
Where summer ripens at all hours?
But ever in the noonlight
she pined and pined away;
Sought them by night and day,
Found them no more, but dwindled
   and grew grey;
Then fell with the first snow,
While to this day no grass will grow
Where she lies low:
I planted daisies there a year ago
That never blow.
You should not loiter so.'
'Nay, hush,' said Laura:
'Nay, hush, my sister:
I ate and ate my fill,
Yet my mouth waters still:
To-morrow night I will
Buy more;' and kissed her.
'Have done with sorrow;
I'll bring you plums to-morrow
Fresh on their mother twigs,
Cherries worth getting;
You cannot think what figs
My teeth have met in,
What melons icy-cold
Piled on a dish of gold
Too huge for me to hold,
What peaches with a velvet nap,
Pellucid grapes without one seed:
Odorous indeed must be the mead
Whereon they grow, and pure the
   wave they drink
With lilies at the brink,
And sugar-sweet their sap.'

Golden head by golden head,
Like two pigeons in one nest
Folded in each other's wings,

They lay down in their curtained
    bed:
Like two blossoms on one stem,
Like two flakes of new-fall'n snow,
Like two wands of ivory
Tipped with gold for awful kings.
Moon and stars gazed in at them,
Wind sang to them lullaby,
Lumbering owls forebore to fly,
Not a bat flapped to and fro
Round their nest:
Cheek to cheek and breast to breast
Locked together in one nest.

Early in the morning
When the first cock crowed his
    warning,
Neat like bees, as sweet and busy,
Laura rose with Lizzie:
Fetched in honey, milked the cows,
Aired and set to rights the house,
Kneaded cakes of whitest wheat,
Cakes for dainty mouths to eat,
Next churned butter, whipped up
    cream,
Fed their poultry, sat and sewed;
Talked as modest maidens should:
Lizzie with an open heart,
Laura in an absent dream,
One content, one sick in part;
One warbling for the mere bright
    day's delight,
One longing for the night.

At length slow evening came:
They went with pitchers to the
    reedy brook;
Lizzie most placid in her look,
Laura most like a leaping flame.
They drew the gurgling water from
    its deep.
Lizzie plucked purple and rich
    golden flags,
Then turning homeward said: 'The
    sunset flushes

Those furthest loftiest crags;
Come, Laura, not another maiden
   lags.
No wilful squirrel wags,
The beasts and birds are fast asleep.'
But Laura loitered still among the
   rushes,
And said the bank was steep.

And said the hour was early still,
The dew not fall'n, the wind not
   chill;
Listening ever, but not catching
The customary cry,
'Come buy, come buy,'
With its iterated jingle
Of sugar-baited words:
Not for all her watching
Once discerning even one goblin
Racing, whisking, tumbling, hobbling –
Let alone the herds
That used to tramp along the glen,
In groups or single,
Of brisk fruit-merchant men.

Till Lizzie urged, 'O Laura, come;
I hear the fruit-call, but I dare not
   look:
You should not loiter longer at this
   brook:
Come with me home.
The stars rise, the moon bends her
   arc,
Each glow-worm winks her spark,
Let us get home before the night
   grows dark:
For clouds may gather
Though this is summer weather,
Put out the lights and drench us
   through;
Then if we lost our way what should
   we do?'

Laura turned cold as stone
To find her sister heard that cry
    alone,
That goblin cry,
'Come buy our fruits, come buy.'
Must she then buy no more such
    dainty fruit?
Must she no more such succous
    pasture find,
Gone deaf and blind?
Her tree of life drooped from the
    root:
She said not one word in her heart's
    sore ache:
But peering thro' the dimness,
    nought discerning,
Trudged home, her pitcher dripping
    all the way;
So crept to bed, and lay
Silent till Lizzie slept;
Then sat up in a passionate yearning,
And gnashed her teeth for baulked
    desire, and wept
As if her heart would break.

Day after day, night after night,
Laura kept watch in vain
In sullen silence of exceeding pain.
She never caught again the goblin
    cry,
'Come buy, come buy;' –
She never spied the goblin men
Hawking their fruits along the glen:
But when the noon waxed bright
Her hair grew thin and grey;
She dwindled, as the fair full moon
    doth turn
To swift decay and burn
Her fire away.

One day remembering her kernel-stone
She set it by a wall that faced the
    south;
Dewed it with tears, hoped for a
    root,

Watched for a waxing shoot,
But there came none.
It never saw the sun,
It never felt the trickling moisture
   run:
While with sunk eyes and faded
   mouth
She dreamed of melons, as a
   traveller sees
False waves in desert drouth
With shade of leaf-crowned trees,
And burns the thirstier in the sandful
   breeze.

She no more swept the house,
Tended the fowls or cows,
Fetched honey, kneaded cakes of
   wheat,
Brought water from the brook:
But sat down listless in the chimney-nook
And would not eat.

Tender Lizzie could not bear
To watch her sister's cankerous care,
Yet not to share.
She night and morning
Caught the goblins' cry:
'Come buy our orchard fruits,
Come buy, come buy:' –
Beside the brook, along the glen,
She heard the tramp of goblin men,
The voice and stir
Poor Laura could not hear;
Longed to buy fruit to comfort her,
But feared to pay too dear.
She thought of Jeanie in her grave,
Who should have been a bride.
But who for joys brides hope to have
Fell sick and died
In her gay prime,
In earliest winter time,
With the first glazing rime,
With the first snow-fall of crisp
   winter time.

Till Laura dwindling
Seemed knocking at Death's door.
Then Lizzie weighed no more
Better and worse;
But put a silver penny in her purse,
Kissed Laura, crossed the heath
   with clumps of furze
At twilight, halted by the brook:
And for the first time in her life
Began to listen and look.

Laughed every goblin
When they spied her peeping:
Came towards her hobbling,
Flying, running, leaping,
Puffing and blowing,
Chuckling, clapping, crowing,
Clucking and gobbling,
Mopping and mowing,
Full of airs and graces,
Pulling wry faces,
Demure grimaces,
Cat-like and rat-like,
Ratel- and wombat-like,
Snail-paced in a hurry,
Parrot-voiced and whistler,
Helter skelter, hurry skurry,
Chattering like magpies,
Fluttering like pigeons,
Gliding like fishes, –
Hugged her and kissed her:
Squeezed and caressed her:
Stretched up their dishes,
Panniers, and plates:
'Look at our apples
Russet and dun,
Bob at our cherries,
Bite at our peaches,
Citrons and dates,
Grapes for the asking,
Pears red with basking
Out in the sun,
Plums on their twigs;
Pluck them and suck them, –
Pomegranates, figs.'

'Good folk,' said Lizzie,
Mindful of Jeanie:
'Give me much and many:'
Held out her apron,
Tossed them her penny.
'Nay, take a seat with us,
Honour and eat with us,'
They answered grinning:
'Our feast is but beginning.
Night yet is early,
Warm and dew-pearly,
Wakeful and starry:
Such fruits as these
No man can carry;
Half their bloom would fly,
Half their dew would dry,
Half their flavour would pass by.
Sit down and feast with us,
Be welcome guest with us,
Cheer you and rest with us.' –
'Thank you,' said Lizzie: 'But one
    waits
At home alone for me:
So without further parleying,
If you will not sell me any
Of your fruits though much and many,
Give me back my silver penny
I tossed you for a fee.' –
They began to scratch their pates,
No longer wagging, purring,
But visibly demurring,
Grunting and snarling.
One called her proud,
Cross-grained, uncivil;
Their tones waxed loud,
Their looks were evil,
Lashing their tails
They trod and hustled her,
Elbowed and jostled her,
Clawed with their nails,
Barking, mewing, hissing, mocking,
Tore her gown and soiled her
    stocking,

Twitched her hair out by the roots,
Stamped upon her tender feet,
Held her hands and squeezed their
    fruits
Against her mouth to make her eat.

White and golden Lizzie stood,
Like a lily in a flood, –
Like a rock of blue-veined stone
Lashed by tides obstreperously, –
Like a beacon left alone
In a hoary roaring sea,
Sending up a golden fire, –
Like a fruit-crowned orange-tree
White with blossoms honey-sweet
Sore beset by wasp and bee, –
Like a royal virgin town
Topped with gilded dome and spire
Close beleaguered by a fleet
Mad to tug her standard down.

One may lead a horse to water,
Twenty cannot make him drink.
Though the goblins cuffed and caught
    her,
Coaxed and fought her,
Bullied and besought her,
Scratched her, pinched her black as
    ink,
Kicked and knocked her,
Mauled and mocked her,
Lizzie uttered not a word;
Would not open lip from lip
Lest they should cram a mouthful in:
But laughed in heart to feel the drip
Of juice that syruped all her face,
And lodged in dimples of her chin,
And streaked her neck which quaked
    like curd.
At last the evil people,
Worn out by her resistance,
Flung back her penny, kicked their
    fruit
Along whichever road they took,
Not leaving root or stone or shoot;

Some writhed into the ground,
Some dived into the brook
With ring and ripple,
Some scudded on the gale without a
   sound,
Some vanished in the distance.

In a smart, ache, tingle,
Lizzie went her way;
Knew not was it night or day;
Sprang up the bank, tore thro' the
   furze,
Threaded copse and dingle,
And heard her penny jingle
Bouncing in her purse, –
Its bounce was music to her ear.
She ran and ran
As if she feared some goblin man
Dogged her with gibe or curse
Or something worse:
But not one goblin skurried after,
Nor was she pricked by fear;
The kind heart made her windy-paced
That urged her home quite out of
   breath with haste
And inward laughter.

She cried, 'Laura,' up the garden,
'Did you miss me?
Come and kiss me.
Never mind my bruises,
Hug me, kiss me, suck my juices
Squeezed from goblin fruits for you,
Goblin pulp and goblin dew.
Eat me, drink me, love me;
Laura, make much of me;
For your sake I have braved the glen
And had to do with goblin merchant
   men.'

Laura started from her chair,
Flung her arms up in the air,
Clutched her hair:
'Lizzie, Lizzie, have you tasted

Nor my sake the fruit forbidden?
Must your light like mine be hidden,
Your young life like mine be wasted,
Undone in mine undoing,
And ruined in my ruin,
Thirsty, cankered, goblin-ridden?' –
She clung about her sister,
Kissed and kissed and kissed her:
Tears once again
Refreshed her shrunken eyes,
Dropping like rain
After long sultry drouth;
Shaking with anguish fear, and pain,
She kissed and kissed her with a
    hungry mouth.

Her lips began to scorch,
That juice was wormwood to her
    tongue,
She loathed the feast:
Writhing as one possessed she leaped
    and sung,
Rent all her robe, and wrung
Her hands in lamentable haste,
And beat her breast.
Her locks streamed like the torch
Borne by a racer at full speed,
Or like the mane of horses in their
    flight,
Or like an eagle when she stems the
    light
Straight toward the sun,
Or like a caged thing freed,
Or like a flying flag when armies run.

Swift fire spread through her veins,
    knocked at her heart,
Met the fire smouldering there
And overbore its lesser flame;
She gorged on bitterness without a
    name:
Ah fool, to choose such part
Of soul-consuming care!
Sense failed in the mortal strife:
Like the watch-tower of a town

Which an earthquake shatters down,
Like a lightning-stricken mast,
Like a wind-uprooted tree
Spun about,
Like a foam-topped waterspout
Cast down headlong in the sea,
She fell at last;
Pleasure past and anguish past,
Is it death or is it life?

Life out of death.
That night long Lizzie watched by
    her,
Counted her pulse's flagging stir,
Felt for her breath,
Held water to her lips, and cooled
    her face
With tears and fanning leaves.
But when the first birds chirped
    about their eaves,
And early reapers plodded to the
    place
Of golden sheaves,
And dew-wet grass
Bowed in the morning winds so brisk
    to pass,
And new buds with new day
Opened of cup-like lilies on the
    stream,
Laura awoke as from a dream,
Laughed in the innocent old way,
Hugged Lizzie but not twice or
    thrice;
Her gleaming locks showed not one
    thread of grey,
Her breath was sweet as May,
And light danced in her eyes.

Days, weeks, months, years
Afterwards, when both were wives
With children of their own;
Their mother-hearts beset with fears,
Their lives bound up in tender lives;
Laura would call the little ones
And tell them of her early prime,

Those pleasant days long gone
Of not-returning time:
Would talk about the haunted glen,
The wicked quaint fruit-merchant
    men,
Their fruits like honey to the throat
But poison in the blood
(Men sell not such in any town):
Would tell them how her sister
    stood
In deadly peril to do her good,
And win the fiery antidote:
Then joining hands to little hands
Would bid them cling together, –
'For there is no friend like a sister
In calm or stormy weather;
To cheer one on the tedious way,
To fetch one if one goes astray,
To lift one if one totters down,
To strengthen whilst one stands.'

Naomi Mitchison

FROM

The Corn King and the Spring Queen (1931)

By and by he began to give little panting, eager cries of desire for food and the warmth and the tenderness that went with it. Erif's breasts answered to the noise with a pleasant hardening, a faint ache waiting to be assuaged. Their tips turned upward and outward, and the centre of the nipple itself grew velvet soft and tender and prepared for the softness of the baby. She unpinned her dress and picked him up and snuggled down over him on to a heap of cushions. He moved his blind, silly mouth from side to side eagerly. For a moment she teased him, withholding herself; then, as she felt the milk in her springing towards him, she let him

settle, thrusting her breast deep into the hollow of his mouth, that seized on her with a rhythmic throb of acceptance, deep sucking of lips and tongue and cheeks. Cheated, her other breast let its milk drip in large bluish-white drops on to his legs, then softened and sagged and waited. For a time he was all mouth, then his free arm began to waver and clutch, sometimes her face, sometimes a finger, sometimes grabbing the breast with violent, untender little soft claws. She laughed and caught his eye, and the sucking lips began to curve upward in spite of themselves. He let go suddenly to laugh, and her breast, released, spurted milk over his face.[8]

Anaïs Nin

FROM

The Delta of Venus (1940–1)

Everyone was laughing at her story. 'I think,' said Brown, 'that when we are children we are much more inclined to be fetishists of one kind or another. I remember hiding inside of my mother's closet and feeling ecstasy at smelling her clothes and feeling them. Even today I cannot resist a woman who is wearing a veil or tulle or feathers, because it awakens the strange feelings I had in that closet.'

As he said this I remembered how I hid in the closet of a young man when I was only 13, for the same reason. He was 25 and he treated me like a little girl. I was in love with him. Sitting next to him in a car in which he took all of us for long rides, I was ecstatic just feeling his leg alongside mine. At night I would get into bed and, after turning out the light, take out a can of condensed milk in which I had punctured a little hole. I would sit in the dark sucking at the sweet milk with a voluptuous feeling all over my body that I could not explain. I thought then that being in love and sucking at the sweet milk were related. Much later I remembered this when I tasted sperm for the first time.

Mollie remembered that at the same age she liked to eat ginger while she smelled camphor balls. The ginger made her body feel warm and languid

---

[8] Mitchison wrote this description in around 1925 when she was nursing her own child.

and the camphor balls made her a little dizzy. She would get herself in a sort of drugged state this way, lying there for hours.[9]

Julia Lee

The Spinach Song, or I Didn't Like it the First Time (c. 1949)

L ike so many women singing the blues in the 1920s, 30s and 40s, Julia Lee wrote provocative and daring songs which, far from bewailing her lovelorn lot, announced the independence and strength of women.

Spinach has vitamins A, B and D,
But spinach never appealed to me
But one day while having dinner
With a guy, I decided
To give it a try.

I didn't like it the first time
It was so new to me.
I didn't like it the first time
I was so young you see.
I used to run away from the stuff
But now somehow I can't get enough,
I didn't like it the first time
But O how it grew on me.

I didn't like it the first time
I had it on a date.
Although the first was the worst time,
Right now I think it's great.

---

9   This extract is taken from the story 'Artists and Models'.

Somehow its always hitting the spot,
Especially when they bring it in hot.
I didn't like it the first time
But O how it grew on me.

I didn't like it the first time
I thought it was so strange.
I wasn't getting much younger,
So I just made the change.
No longer is the stuff on the shelf,
'Cause I make a pig of myself.
I didn't like it the first time
But O how it grew on me.

I didn't like it the first time
When I was just sixteen.
I didn't like it the first time,
Guess I was mighty green.
But I've stocked up, 'cause I've gotten wise,
I've got enough for two dozen guys.
I didn't like it the first time
But O how it grew on me.

I didn't like it the first time,
But O how it grew on me.

Monique Wittig

FROM

The Lesbian Body (1973)

O*n the islands of the Amazons, the domains of women,* The Lesbian
Body *makes a fiction which realises the female body, reciting a
lesbian text 'in a context of total rupture with masculine culture'
(Wittig's 'Author's Note').*

W e descend directly legs together thighs together arms entwined m/y hands
touching your shoulders m/y shoulders held by your hands breast

273

against breast open mouth against open mouth, we descend slowly. The sand swirls round our ankles, suddenly it surrounds our calves. It's from then on that the descent is slowed down. At the moment your knees are reached you throw back your head, *I* see your teeth, you smile, later you look at m/e you speak to m/e without interruption. Now the sand presses on the thighs. *I* shiver with gooseflesh, *I* feel your skin stirring, your nails dig into m/y shoulders, you look at m/e, you do not stop looking at m/e, the shape of your cheeks is changed by the greatest concern. The engulfment continues steadily, the touch of the sand is soft against m/y legs. You begin to sigh. When *I* am sucked down to m/y thighs *I* start to cry out, in a few moments *I* shall be unable to touch you, m/y hands on your shoulders your neck will be unable to reach your vulva, anguish grips m/e, the tiniest grain of sand between your belly and m/ine can separate us once for all. But you fierce joyful eyes shining hold m/e against you, you press m/y back with your large hands, *I* begin to throb in m/y eyelids, *I* throb in m/y brain, *I* throb in m/y thorax, *I* throb in m/y belly, *I* throb in m/y clitoris while you speak faster and faster clasping m/e *I* clasping you clasping each other with a marvellous strength, the sand is round our waists, at a given moment your skin splits from throat to pubis, m/ine in turn from below upwards, *I* spill m/yself into you, you mingle with m/e m/y mouth fastened on your mouth your neck squeezed by m/y arms, *I* feel our intestines uncoiling gliding among themselves, the sky darkens suddenly, it contains orange gleams, the outflow of the mingled blood is not perceptible, the most severe shuddering affects you affects m/e both together, collapsing you cry out, *I* love you m/y dying one, your emergent head is for m/e most adorable and most fatal, the sand touches your cheeks, m/y mouth is filled.[10]

Alicia Ostriker
Greedy Baby (1980)

Greedy baby
sucking the sweet tit
your tongue tugging the nipple tickles your mama
your round eyes open appear to possess understanding
when you suckle I am slowly moved
in my sensitive groove
you in your mouth are alive, I in my womb

[10] Published in 1973. This translation is by Peter Owen (1975).

a book lies in my lap I pretend to read
I turn some pages, when satiated
a moment you stop sucking
to smile up with your toothless milky mouth
I smile down, and my breast leaks
it hurts, return
your lashes close, your mouth again clamps on
you are attentive as a business man
your fisted fingers open relaxing and
all rooms are rooms for suckling in
all woods are woods for suckling in
all boulevards for suckling
sit down anywhere, all rivers
are rivers for suckling by –
I have read that in all wars, when a city is taken,
women are raped, and babies stabbed in their little bellies
and hoisted up to the sky on bayonets –
Accept women; accept the love of women; accept loving women.
There I saw her at her window
early morning, white nightgown
when I looked out of my window
early morning, white nightgown.[11]

Nicole Brossard

FROM

French Kiss,
or A Pang's Progress (1986)

Just Once

In which the text slows down in Camomille's mouth, salivating letters and words of love the better to ... suck on fragments of fiction. With all the energy of irrigations and convergences. Membranes that meet and meet some more till the last contractions, to exhaustion. The ulimate dilation.

[11] From *The Mother/Child Papers* (1980).

CONSUMPTION

Ecstatic perfusion in Camomille's mouth. An exile throughout the long lingual journey over those plausible surfaces and mucous membranes connecting in her mouth. As if in a muffled world filled with liquid symptoms, concentric desires, capsules within to be opened and discovered, little scaly pink fish of that 'miraculous catch' whose stirring and harmonious lilt we feel in the merest reflex. Lick at those walls. Prolong the desires with the telling, the narration of a long uninterrupted kiss. How hard it is to articulate or devise compromise. The kiss, a ball of fire. Life's serum restored with undulant and penetrating movement, a reliving of the taste and smell of birth for a tongue consumed in dance beneath Camomille's palatal dome, Camomille whom I love with all my power of intervention. A wish: to abolish walls between mouths. Mm-mmm the taste of it.

Luckily keeps flowing in the text and on my tongue, erotic substitutes, and luckily that tipsy feeling in the dark, inside beside a cheek so just enjoy, rejoice in the juice, turn and return to that first excitement. What is excitement? Encouragement to do what you feel like doing when seen by someone else / the reader in company with Lucy, Georges or Alexandre, or Elle; being used to spinning out one's dreams by muddling one's own reflection in the mirror so marvellously that paradoxes come to life and whatever the cost force a retake of the sentences, the caresses that started the excitement (what did we say it was?), stimulated spine and breasts dandled in a hand, a phallus emerged invitation to oblivion, to the feel of rhythmic shudder, loins more titillating than some corny happy-ever-after tale, pelvic basins the pornographic mudholes of one's imagination. Narrator fem. / masc. Pelvic basins liquid base. Stop and ruminate a moment near the pond, the basin in Lafontaine Park with its little boats going just fast enough to the music of the band on a Sunday made for sunning in a park with sunning playing fountains. The water basin changes shape to triangle or rectangle. Like imagining Versailles made avant-garde. But how old and worn the film, how grotesque, like some faded foreign boulevardier ... then, as if from one exploration to the next, a long hop to Chambly Basin, immersion there in unmuddied waters fed by springs, our origins, a running brook of words rippling-aroused tracing a thigh-line like a hand, retracing the story line the better to write it down. From that point on it's ink and blotter and quill by power of suggestion. Confusion springs.

Again, Camomille, your mouth, that's good, you get me off!

When the text lets Lucy move, we'll make her arms stir just barely round him / her, her partner, for Lucy's seductiveness is bounded only by the italics in a sentence and italics become her like any pleasurable and prettifying artifice, disguising her almost. So seeing them together we, in the guise of narrator, end up flitting deliciously from one image of them half naked to the next as

in some threatening text, brandishing blackmail photos before pale frightened eyes, above a man undone, struck dumb, – a movie *Caligari* lurking round the background. And those corridors. Tongues slipping through. Chew in ardour and get chewed. Reptiles about to shed a too tight skin. Mimes of fiction in the tender realm of Camomille's mouth and mine, I reaching for the limit of how / where to pass beyond and leave you to whatever, Camomille, or persuade you to cross with Lucy to pleasure's realms, with Georges to pleasure's realms.

The moment of the kiss comes at the moment traffic sounds cross St Denis Street from one side to the other, on the heels of pedestrians, getting stuck between the wheels of buses, caught like a sound in an ear in a baseball glove. Traffic / circulation in the heartbeat's private mutterings. *Lakes* had taken shape in Camomille's eyes I recall – though her lids were closed – hunting and fishing lakes in spring at dawn when the mists don't rise, don't rise even for eyes asleep and gently moving, shadowy reflections of signs left over from the night before, and spun of dreams, sufferings, self-completion when the body's smitten with lovely images, in fluid mood.

Camomille, it's good inside your mouth. You (I) send me bats completely bats . . .

Each mouth leaves its colour its copy on the other. Each endures the other like a wintry cold, lips trapped in ice. Exceeds its bounds, a circus of two, two educated animals alone occupying sweetly all the surfaces of desire. The tongue's like a cutting word, a flicking whip, Camomille, arch your tongue – the way you do your back – a whip that flicks until it bites your tender flesh. My sanity's a hemisphere.

Words get confused
so hotly used
phonemes
celebration

The language of the birds speaks for itself

and what follows flows saliva lips scars spoken aloud over which to linger a long expectant moment, to dream as it were or to make mirrors talk back to us, ambiguously and resonating on our eardrums. The city, the fragile clink of glasses raised then put down on tables. The curious lapping sound of tongues before they find each other in the dark spaces over Adam's apples that bob as if in warning. Mouths touch and salivate beyond control, venture blindly toward each other. Toward the dark. Each to lose itself inside the other's geography. Camomille regains her breath, the other's breath, its difference marking her deeper than the fingernail she's digging into Georges's arm. An assault by a ramifying thing irradiating all its surface, edpidermis – her desire.

Her tongue folds, unfolds, folds again, sucks at the other tongue, triggers, lubricious and circumstantial metamorphosis under the palate's / palace dome – under the verandah, pull down your pants, I won't tell (gustatory memory: popsicles, pink jujubes, popcorn, licorice, tootsie rolls, rock chocolate, peanuts) – like a deposed queen, her tongue yields to the other weakly with tenderness, disengages, drifts, a multiform body sought. On a wave of vagueness.

A detail on vagueness: Camomille agrees to make mirrors and shadows and incongruous details talk. Nuclear love. Brings a lump to my throat. Almost makes me think I'll always love you. Time to catch anoth-other breath.

This morning everything was wet. Sometimes I think I'm sinking inside you. Downtime for Camomille.[12]

Mary Fallon

FROM

Working Hot (1989)

*L*oving each other, loving women, Toto, Freda Peach, One Iota and *Kinky Trinkets inhabit a world on the fringes of the everyday in the cities of Australia.*

bereft stranded beached
image
a woman with her legs apart masturbating furiously
under floodlights in an empty stadium
image
a swamp being drained
image
you deliberately sopping up gravy with chunks of bread
image
you treading determinedly and mechanically
on an old Singer sewing machine
the needle stabbing in and out of the material under

---

[12]   Translation by Patricia Claxton (1986).

your keen eye
image
the mystery as tight as a pearl milked from me

realising you're just lazy
'you're just lazy Freda just a fucking lazy lover'
'yes I know – it's true – I am'
Toto masturbates
a voyeur rubs her breasts and belly

saying to herself
'it means too much
divest it
it means too much
divest it
it means too much
divest it'

oh I am bereft stranded beached
your body is sometimes
such a honeycomb
then
such a Canberra rock

I am suddenly
breaking
my
teeth
and
fall back
off you
humiliated

'we desire to be desired' says that bitch
Freda Peach 'chew me'
no stamina no straight answers
she whispered hoarsely 'chew me'

the oyster eaters
and
in my mouth full
my imagination and
imagining full of
a flesh flower

a fat marzipan rose
an intricate radish rose

a sex salad
a lucky muff diver
what a lucky licker
muff diver dyke
sportswoman chewer
glutton to some
you say
'you'll never have enough'
or
'you'd come at anything'

to be full of you
is to be full of myself
like a fat shadow

you fall asleep like a kid with a bellyful
apple cores and passionfruit skins
composting at the bottom of the bed

at the bottom of the bed
is where your head was

I found a tongue twister
engorged in the tuft of your muff
I stuffed

OK now you try it

CONSUMMATION

She smiles in her sleep. She cries out as she . comes, arching and swearing. She sways, langorous, melting, her mouth red, open ... 'oh sweetheart'. Consummation.

Completing, arriving, perfecting, finishing – the consummations in this section include all of these. Framing those smaller arrivals and departures are the larger ones of birth and death. Beatrijs of Nazareth is being created anew; Elizabeth Barrett Browning's Aurora Leigh drowns in a rebirth; Margaret Drabble knows the complete death of the old self in the feel of a new life.

Here is completion, rounded and whole, sufficient. The lovers in these extracts are content with only their selves. Katherine Philips abandons the 'dull world' for her 'sacred union'. Anne Batten Cristall pursues her lover through the seasons but finds her at home: 'Mutual we glow, and kindling love/ Draws every wish to me'. Kathy Acker's Scott and Marcia, though living on the street, are enclosed in their private world; like Winterson's lovers they know 'no separation'. Tsvetayeva's speaker is closer to her lover than the woman who carried him in her womb: 'when she forgot/ all things in motionless triumph/ only to carry you:/ she did not hold you closer'.

The orgasm in the extract from *Mrs Dalloway* swells and splits with healing rapture. Relief, release, expansion, and fullness come with consummation. Beatrijs of Nazareth, Barrett Browning, Aspen and Mary Dorcey all exploit the idea of the flood which gushes and nourishes. Images of softness, warmth, colour and sweetness coax the reader toward fulfilment. Beatrijs experiences 'an overflowing fullness of great delight'; Kathy Acker's lovers are 'wet and dark', vulnerable and safe; Hacker's woman-manly lover blazes in life-giving 'red-gold flames'.

Consummation also explains. Knowledge is here, and power. Both

are given as treasures to be held and retained, icons of communion and understanding. Woolf speaks of the 'illumination', the 'revelation' of the moment. Sally's kiss – 'the most exquisite moment of [Clarissa's] whole life' – is a precious gift: 'And she felt that she had been given a present, wrapped up, and told just to keep it, not to look at it – a diamond, something infinitely precious, wrapped up ...' Katherine Philips hoards the secret jewel: 'Thy heart locks up my secrets richly set,/And my brest is thy private cabinet'. Winterson's princess gloats over a coil of hair, the sacred relic of something valuable, found and lost.

The treasure is the self revealed; it is the treasure of the heart. These abandoned lovers are exposed and open in ecstasy. They know their difference, but postpone that recognition in the transport of union. In love consummated there is a self, and no self. There are two, but there is only one. Acker's lovers have arrived at the blurring of individuality, 'out of control and not knowing it'. Their surrender means that they know themselves intensely, yet lose themselves entirely: 'You think you are the other person. You begin to forget what you feel.' Absorbed into each other, these lovers lose themselves. They are twins. Nothing else is true. Nothing else is.

'Listen to this flesh.
It is far truer than poems'.

Beatrijs of Nazareth

FROM

There are Seven Manners of Loving (c. 1230–68)

'The Seven Manners of Loving' may have been part of an autobiography written by Beatrijs after she became prioress at the Convent of Nazareth. It is a mystic text written in the vernacular, and not in

Latin, which suggests that it was intended for a secular as well as a religious audience.

In the fourth manner of loving, it is our Lord's custom to give sometimes great joy, sometimes great woe; and let us now speak of this.

Sometimes it happens that love is sweetly awakened in the soul and joyfully arises and stirs itself in the heart without any help from human acts. And then the heart is so tenderly touched in love, so powerfully assailed, so wholly encompassed and so lovingly embraced in love that the soul is altogether conquered by love. Then it feels a great closeness to God and a spiritual brightness and a wonderful richness and a noble freedom and a great compulsion of violent love, and an overflowing fullness of great delight. And then the soul feels that all its senses and its will have become love, that it has sunk down so deeply and been engulfed so completely in love, that it has itself entirely become love. Love's beauty has adorned the soul, love's power has consumed it, love's sweetness has submerged it, love's righteousness has engulfed it, love's excellence has embraced it, love's purity has enhanced it, love's exaltedness has drawn it up and enclosed it, so that the soul must be nothing else but love and do nothing else.

When the soul feels itself to be thus filled full of riches and in such fullness of heart, the spirit sinks away down into love, the body seems to pass away, the heart to melt, every faculty to fail; and the soul is so utterly conquered by love that often it cannot support itself, often the limbs and the senses lose their powers. And just as a vessel filled up to the brim will run over and spill if it is touched, so at times the soul is so touched and overpowered by this great fullness of the heart that in spite of itself it spills and overflows.

In the fifth manner, it also sometimes happens that love is powerfully strengthened in the soul and rises violently up, with great tumult and force, as if it would break the heart with its assault and drag the soul out of itself in the exercise and the delight of love. And then the soul is drawn in the longing to love to fulfill the great and pure deeds of love and the desires implanted by love's many promptings. Or sometimes the soul longs to rest in the sweet embrace of love, in that desirable state of richness and satisfaction which comes from the possession of love, so that the heart and all the senses long and seek eagerly and long wholly for this. When the soul is in this state, it is so strong in spirit, so open in heart to receive all things, so stronger in bodily power to do all things, more able to accomplish its works, achieving so much, that it seems to the soul itself that there is nothing which it cannot do and perform, even though in the body it were to remain idle. At the same time the soul feels itself so greatly stirred from within, such an utter dependence upon love, such an impatient desire for love and the countless sorrows of a deep dissatisfaction. And sometimes when the soul experiences love that brings it woe without it ever knowing why, or it may be because it

CONSUMMATION

is so stirred to long for love, or because it is filled with dissatisfaction that it cannot know love's full delight.

And at times love becomes so boundless and so overflowing in the soul, when it itself is so mightily and violently moved in the heart, that it seems to the soul that the heart is wounded again and again, and that these wounds increase every day in bitter pain and in fresh intensity. It seems to the soul that the veins are bursting, the blood spilling, the marrow withering, the bones softening, the heart burning, the throat parching, so that the body in its every part feels this inward heat, and this is the fever of love. Sometimes the soul feels that the whole body is transfixed, and it is as if every sense would fail; and like a devouring fire, seizing upon everything and consuming everything which it can master, love seems to be working violently in the soul, relentless, uncontrollable, drawing everything into it and devouring it.

All this torments and afflicts the soul, and the heart grows sick and the powers dwindle; yet it is so that the soul is fed and love is fostered and the spirit is subjected to love.

For love is exalted so high above the soul's comprehension, above all that the soul can do or suffer, that even though at such times it may long to break the bond that unites it to love, that cannot harm love's singleness; and the soul is so fettered with the bond of love, so conquered by the boundlessness of love, that it cannot rule itself by reason, cannot reason through understanding, cannot spare itself this weariness, cannot hold fast to human wisdom.

For the more there is given from above to the soul, the more is demanded of it: the more is revealed to the soul, the more it is filled with longing to come close to the light of that truth, that purity, that excellence and that delight which are love's attributes. Always the soul will be driven and goaded on, never will it be satisfied and at rest. For what most afflicts and torments the soul is that which most heals and assuages it; what gives the soul its deepest wounds brings to it best relief.[1]

Katherine Philips
L'Amitie. To Mrs Mary Awbrey (1664)

Soule of my soule! my Joy, my crown, my friend!
A name which all the rest doth comprehend;
How happy are we now, whose souls are grown,

[1] Translated by Eric Colledge (1965). This extract is taken from *Medieval Women's Visionary Literature*, ed. Elizabeth Alvilda Petroff (Oxford, 1986), p. 202.

By an incomparable mixture, One:
Whose well acquainted minds are now as neare
As Love, or vows, or secrets can endeare.
I have no thought but what's to thee reveal'd,
Nor thou desire that is from me conceal'd.
Thy heart locks up my secrets richly set,
And my brest is thy private cabinet.
Thou shedst no teare but what my moisture lent,
And if I sigh, it is thy breath is spent.
United thus, what horrour can appeare
Worthy our sorrow, anger, or our feare?
Let the dull world alone to talk and fight,
And with their vast ambitions nature fright;
Let them despise so inocent a flame,
While Envy, pride, and faction play their game:
But we by Love sublim'd so high shall rise,
To pitty Kings, and Conquerours despise,
Since we that sacred union have engrost,
Which they and all the sullen world have lost.[2]

Anne Batten Cristall
Song (1795)

Through springtime walks, with flowers perfumed,
    I chased a wild capricious fair,
Where hyacinths and jonquils bloomed,
    Chanting gay sonnets through the air:
Hid amid a briary dell,
    Or 'neath a hawthorn tree,
Her sweet enchantments led me on,
    And still deluded me.

While summer's splendent glory smiles,
    My ardent love in vain essayed;
I strove to win her heart by wiles,

[2] First published in an unauthorised edition of 1664. In an autograph manuscript in the National Library of Wales (MS 775) the poem is dated '6t Aprill 1651'. Mary Aubrey (1631–1700) was a schoolfriend of the poet.

But still a thousand pranks she played;
Sill o'er each sun-burnt furzy hill,
  Wild, playful, gay and free,
She laughed and scorned, I chased her still,
  And still she bantered me.

When autumn waves her golden ears,
  And wafts o'er fruits her pregnant breath,
The sprightly lark its pinions rears,
  I chased her o'er the daisied heath;
Sweet harebells trembled in the vale,
  And all around was glee;
Still, wanton as the timid hart,
  She swiftly flew from me.

Now winter lights its cheerful fire,
  While jests with frolic mirth resound,
And draws the wandering beauty nigher,
  'Tis now too cold to rove around:
The Christmas game, the playful dance,
  Incline her heart to glee;
Mutual we glow, and kindling love
  Draws every wish to me.[3]

Elizabeth Barrett Browning

FROM

Aurora Leigh (1857)

*T*he daughter of an Englishman and his Italian wife, Aurora Leigh *is a successful poet who has settled in her native Florence after making her career in England. She is living with Marian who was once engaged to Aurora's cousin Romney and whom she found in Paris, destitute and the mother of a baby son, born as the result of rape. Ten years ago Aurora had refused to marry Romney when he*

---

[3] Published in *The Gentleman's Magazine* (1795). The poem is an address to the muse.

expressed some scorn for her calling as a poet. Since then she has
gradually come to realise that she does indeed love her cousin. One
night Romney arrives unexpectedly at Aurora's villa in Florence.

Book VIII

The heavens were making room to hold the night,
The sevenfold heavens unfolding all their gates
To let the stars out slowly (prophesied
In close-approaching advent, not discerned),
While still the cue-owls from the cypresses
Of the Poggio[4] called and counted every pulse
Of the skyey palpitation. Gradually
The purple and transparent shadows slow
Had filled up the whole valley to the brim,
And flooded all the city, which you saw
As some drowned city in some enchanted sea,
Cut off from nature, – drawing you who gaze,
With passionate desire, to leap and plunge,
And find a sea-king with a voice of waves,
And treacherous soft eyes, and slippery locks
You cannot kiss but you shall bring away
Their salt upon your lips. The duomo-bell[5]
Strikes ten, as if it struck ten fathoms down,
So deep; and fifty churches answer it
The same, with fifty various instances.
Some gaslights tremble along squares and streets
The Pitti's[6] palace-front is drawn in fire:
And, past the quays, Maria Novella's Place,
In which the mystic obelisks[7] stand up
Triangular, pyramidal, each based
On a single trine of brazen tortoises,
To guard that fair church, Buonarroti's Bride,[8]
That stares out from her large blind dial-eyes,
Her quadrant and armillary dials, black
With rhythms of many suns and moons, in vain

[4] An avenue leading to the Villa Poggio outside Florence.
[5] The cathedral in Florence, Santa Maria del Fiore.
[6] The Palazzo Pitti, residence of the Grand Duke of Tuscany.
[7] In the square in front of the church of Santa Maria Novella are two obelisks which mark the extent of a race which took place regularly on the feast day of St John.
[8] Santa Maria Novella was so admired by Michelangelo that he used to call it his 'bride'.

Enquiry for so rich a soul as his, –
Methinks I have plunged, I see it all so clear . . .
And, oh my heart, . . . the sea-king!

In my ears
The sound of waters. There he stood, my king!

I felt him, rather than beheld him. Up
I rose, as if he were my king indeed,
And then sate down, in trouble at myself,
And struggling for my woman's empery.

After a lengthy conversation and many misunderstandings, Romney reveals that he has lost his sight in a fire which destroyed his ancestral home. Aurora declares her love for him and they are finally united.

Book IX

But oh, the night! oh, bitter-sweet! oh, sweet!
O dark, O moon and stars, O ecstasy
Of darkness! O great mystery of love, –
In which absorbed, loss, anguish, treason's self
Enlarges rapture, – as a pebble dropt
In some full wine-cup, over-brims the wine!
While we to sate together, leaned that night
So close, my very garments crept and thrilled
With strange electric life; and both my cheeks
Grew red, then pale, with touches from my hair
In which his breath was; while the golden moon
Was hung before our faces as the badge
Of some sublime inherited despair,
Since ever to be seen by only one, –
A voice said, low and rapid as a sigh,
Yet breaking, I felt conscious, from a smile, –
'Thank God, who made me blind, to make me see!
Shine on, Aurora, dearest light of souls,
Which rule'st for evermore both day and night!
I am happy.'
I flung closer to his breast,
As sword that, after battle, flings to sheathe;
And, in that hurtle of united souls,
The mystic motions which in common moods
Are shut beyond our sense, broke in on us,
And, as we sate, we felt the old earth spin,

And all the starry turbulence of worlds
Swing round us in their audient circles, till
If that same golden moon were overhead
Or if beneath our feet, we did not know.

Marina Tsvetayeva

FROM

The Poem of the End (1924)

*T*his long poem cycle in fourteen sections records the circumstances
of a passionate love affair which took place in Prague while the
poet was living in long exile from Russia and which came to an end
in December 1923. This extract is section 8 of the poem.

Last   bridge   I won't
give up or take out my hand
this is the last bridge
the last bridging between

water   and firm land: ·
and I am saving these
coins for death
for Charon, the price of Lethe[9]

this   shadow money
from my dark hand I press
soundlessly into
the shadowy darkness of his

shadow money it is
no gleam and tinkle in it
coins for shadows:
the dead have enough poppies

---

[9]   In Greek mythology Charon is the boatman who ferries the dead across the
river Lethe to Hades. Lethe is also the metaphorical name for forgetfulness.

CONSUMMATION

This bridge

Lovers for the most
part are without hope: passion
also is just
a bridge, a means of connection

It's warm: to nestle
close at your ribs, to move in
a visionary pause
towards nothing, beside nothing

no   arms no   legs
now, only the bone of my
side is alive where
it presses directly against you

life in that side
only, ear and echo is it: there
I stick like white to
egg yolk, or an eskimo to his fur

adhesive, pressing
joined to you: Siamese
twins are no nearer.
The woman you call mother

when she forgot
all things in motionless triumph
only to carry you:
she did not hold you closer.

Understand: we have
grown into one as we slept and
now I can't jump
because I can't let go your hand.

and I won't be torn off
as I press close to you: this
bridge is no husband
but a lover: a just slipping past

our support: for the
river is fed with bodies!
I bite in like a tick
you must tear out my roots to be rid of me

like ivy   like a tick
inhuman   godless

to throw me away like a thing,
where there is

no thing I ever prized
in this empty world of things.
Say this is only dream,
night still and afterwards morning

an express   to Rome?
Granada? I won't know myself
as I push off
the Himalayas of bedclothes.

But this dark is deep:
now I warm you with my blood, listen
to this flesh.
It is far truer than poems.

If you are warm, who
will you go to tomorrow for that?
This is delirium,
please say this bridge cannot

end
      as it ends.

– Here then? His gesture could
be made by a child, or a god.
– And so? – I am biting in!
For a little more time. The last of it.[10]

Virginia Woolf

FROM

Mrs Dalloway (1925)

*C larissa is the wife of Richard Dalloway, a Member of Parliament.
On this morning she is preparing for a party which she is giving*

[10]   From *Selected Poems of Marina Tsvetayeva*, translated by Elaine Feinstein (London, 1986). Feinstein worked from a literal translation by Angela Livingstone.

tonight and where the Prime Minister is expected.

Like a nun withdrawing, or a child exploring a tower, she went, upstairs, paused at the window, came to the bathroom. There was the green linoleum and a tap dripping. There was an emptiness about the heart of life; an attic room. Women must put off their rich apparel. At mid-day they must disrobe. She pierced the pincushion and laid her feathered yellow hat on the bed. The sheets were clean, tight stretched in a broad white band from side to side. Narrower and narrower would her bed be. The candle was half burnt down and she had read deep in Baron Marbot's *Memoirs*. She had read late at night of the retreat from Moscow. For the House sat so long that Richard insisted, after her illness, that she must sleep undisturbed. And really she preferred to read of the retreat from Moscow. He knew it. So the room was an attic; the bed narrow; and lying there reading, for she slept badly, she could not dispel a virginity preserved through childbirth which clung to her like a sheet. Lovely in girlhood, suddenly there came a moment – for example on the river beneath the woods at Clieveden – when, through some contraction of this cold spirit, she had failed him. And then at Constantinople, and again and again. She could see what she lacked. It was not beauty; it was not mind. It was something central which permeated; something warm which broke up surfaces and rippled the cold contact of man and woman, or of women together. For *that* she could dimly perceive. She resented it, had a scruple picked up Heaven knows where, or, as she felt, sent by Nature (who is invariably wise); yet she could not resist sometimes yielding to the charm of a woman, not a girl, of a woman confessing, as to her they often did, some scrape, some folly. And whether it was pity, or their beauty, or that she was older, or some accident – like a faint scent, or a violin next door (so strange is the power of sounds at certain moments), she did undoubtedly then feel what men felt. Only for a moment; but it was enough. It was a sudden revelation, a tinge like a blush which one tried to check and then, as it spread, one yielded to its expansion, and rushed to the farthest verge and there quivered and felt the world come closer, swollen with some astonishing significance, some pressure of rapture, which split its thin skin and gushed and poured with an extraordinary alleviation over the cracks and sores. Then, for that moment, she had seen an illumination; a match burning in a crocus; an inner meaning almost expressed. But the close withdrew; the hard softened. It was over – the moment. Against such moments (with women too) there contrasted (as she laid her hat down) the bed and Baron Marbot and the candle half-burnt. Lying awake, the floor creaked; the lit house was suddenly darkened, and if she raised her head she could just hear the click of the handle released as gently as possible by Richard, who slipped upstairs in his socks and then, as often as not, dropped his hot-water bottle and swore! How she laughed!

But this question of love (she thought, putting her coat away), this falling in love with women. Take Sally Seton,[11] her relation in the old days with Sally Seton. Had not that, after all, been love?

She sat on the floor – that was her first impression of Sally – she sat on the floor with her arms round her knees, smoking a cigarette. Where could it have been? The Mannings'? The Kinloch-Jones's? At some party (where she could not be certain), for she had a distinct recollection of saying to the man she was with, 'Who is *that?*' And he had told her, and said that Sally's parents did not get on (how that shocked her – that one's parents should quarrel!). But all that evening she could not take her eyes off Sally. It was an extraordinary beauty of the kind she most admired, dark, large-eyed, with that quality which, since she hadn't got it herself, she always envied – a sort of abandonment, as if she could say anything, do anything; a quality much commoner in foreigners than in Englishwomen. Sally always said she had French blood in her veins, an ancestor had been with Marie Antoinette, had his head cut off, left a ruby ring. Perhaps that summer she came to stay at Bourton, walking in quite unexpectedly without a penny in her pocket, one night after dinner, and upsetting poor Aunt Helena to such an extent that she never forgave her. There had been some awful quarrel at home. She literally hadn't a penny that night when she came to them – had pawned a brooch to come down. She had rushed off in a passion. They sat up till all hours of the night talking. Sally it was who made her feel, for the first time, how sheltered the life at Bourton was. She knew nothing about sex – nothing about social problems. She had once seen an old man who had dropped dead in a field – she had seen cows just after their calves were born. But Aunt Helena never liked discussion of anything (when Sally gave her William Morris, it had to be wrapped in brown paper). There they sat, hour after hour, talking in her bedroom at the top of the house, talking about life, how they were to reform the world. They meant to found a society to abolish private property, and actually had a letter written, though not sent out. The ideas were Sally's, of course – but very soon she was just as excited – read Plato in bed before breakfast; read Morris; read Shelley by the hour.

Sally's power was amazing, her gift, her personality. There was her way with flowers, for instance. At Bourton they always had stiff little vases all the way down the table. Sally went out, picked hollyhocks, dahlias – all sorts of flowers that had never been seen together – cut their heads off, and made them swim on the top of water in bowls. The effect was extraordinary – coming in to dinner in the sunset. (Of course Aunt Helena thought it wicked to treat flowers like that.) Then she forgot her sponge, and ran along the passage naked. That grim old housemaid, Ellen Atkins, went about grumbling – 'Suppose any of

[11] The friend of her youth. Sally, now married to a Northern industrialist and the mother of five boys, will also attend Clarissa's party.

the gentlemen had seen?' Indeed she did shock people. She was untidy, Papa said.

The strange thing, on looking back, was the purity, the integrity, of her feeling for Sally. It was not like one's feeling for a man. It was completely disinterested, and besides, it had a quality which could only exist between women, between women just grown up. It was protective, on her side; sprang from a sense of being in league together, a presentiment of something that was bound to part them (they spoke of marriage always as a catastrophe), which led to this chivalry, this protective feeling which was much more on her side than Sally's. For in those days she was completely reckless; did the most idiotic things out of bravado; bicycled round the parapet on the terrace; smoked cigars. Absurd, she was – very absurd. But the charm was overpowering, to her at least, so that she could remember standing in her bedroom at the top of the house holding the hot-water can in her hands and saying aloud, 'She is beneath this roof ... She is beneath this roof!'

No, the words meant absolutely nothing to her now. She could not even get an echo of her old emotion. But she could remember going cold with excitement and doing her hair in a kind of ecstasy (now the old feeling began to come back to her, as she took out her hairpins, laid them on the dressing-table, began to do her hair), with the rooks flaunting up and down in the pink evening light, and dressing, and going downstairs, and feeling as she crossed the hall 'if it were now to die 'twere now to be most happy.' That was her feeling – Othello's feeling, and she felt it, she was convinced, as strongly as Shakespeare meant Othello to feel it, all because she was coming down to dinner in a white frock to meet Sally Seton!

She was wearing pink gauze – was that possible? She *seemed*, anyhow, all light, glowing, like some bird or air ball that has flown in, attached itself for a moment to a bramble. But nothing is so strange when one is in love (and what was this except being in love?) as the complete indifference of other people. Aunt Helena just wandered off after dinner; Papa read the paper. Peter Walsh might have been there, and old Miss Cummings; Joseph Breitkopf certainly was, for he came every summer, poor old man, for weeks and weeks, and pretended to read German with her, but really played the piano and sang Brahms without any voice.

All this was only a background for Sally. She stood by the fireplace talking, in that beautiful voice which made everything she said sound like a caress, to Papa, who had begun to be attracted rather against his will (he never got over lending her one of his books and finding it soaked on the terrace), when suddenly she said, 'What a shame to sit indoors!' and they all went out on to the terrace and walked up and down. Peter Walsh and Joseph Breitkopf went on about Wagner. She and Sally fell a little behind. Then came the most exquisite moment of her whole life passing a stone urn with flowers in it. Sally stopped; picked a flower; kissed her on the lips. The whole world might have turned upside down! The others disappeared; there she was alone with Sally. And she felt that she had been given a present, wrapped up,

and told just to keep it, not to look at it – a diamond, something infinitely precious, wrapped up, which, as they walked (up and down, up and down), she uncovered, or the radiance burnt through, the revelation, the religious feeling! – when old Joseph and Peter faced them:

'Star-gazing?' said Peter.

It was like running one's face against a granite wall in the darkness! It was shocking; it was horrible!

Margaret Drabble
The Pleasure of Children (1974)

Being pregnant was horrible. I worried myself ill about eating and drinking the wrong things, and fainted in telephone kiosks. I didn't feel much sense of communion with the unborn, though I know others do. Labour wasn't much fun either, until the last stages. But the last stages were spectacular. Ah, what an incomparable thrill. All that heaving, the amazing damp slippery wetness and hotness, the confused sight of dark grey ropes of cord, the blood, the baby's cry. The sheer pleasure of the feeling of a born baby on one's thighs is like nothing on earth.

Kathy Acker

FROM

The Adult Life of Toulouse Lautrec by Henri Toulouse Lautrec (1975)

Scott and Marcia are two young lovers who are living together on the street.

CONSUMMATION

B eing wet and dark with someone.
Being touched and being able to know the person will touch you again.
Being in a cave you don't want to leave and don't have to leave. Being in a place in which you're able to be open and stupid and boring.

You're open and wet and your edges are rough and hurt. You remember that you've always been this: totally vulnerable. You don't want to forget who you are. Being with someone has made you remember that you're totally vulnerable.

Marcia and Scott now always felt these ways. Being out of control and not knowing it. Being in total danger and believing that you're safer than you've ever been in your life, you're inside and so you can open yourself and make yourself raw to the other person.

Suddenly seeing something you've never seen before. You're willing to compromise yourself for this person. Forget what you've just thought. You don't have any more thoughts of yourself. You want to know everything about the other person:

What was your childhood like?

What do you like to do the most?

Have you ever fucked any weirdos?

When did you start being an adult?

You think you are the other person. You begin to forget what you feel.

Scott and Marcia now were living on the street cause they didn't have any money. Caught between the devil and the deep blue sea: The other person's frightened of you. He's scared if he lets you into his wetness and heat, you'll disrupt everything. You want him wet and hot so badly, you act so heavy, he gets more scared, you put him out of your head. You want nothing to do with him. Finally you can think one thought which isn't about him. The second you see him again and his hand barely grazes your hand, your heart flops over, you almost faint, you feel like you're turning inside out. When he holds you, you forget the room exists. You can't act like he's the most casual fuck in the world. You can't tell him you're madly in love with him cause then he'll never see you again. You're screwed.

Marcia and Scott didn't even notice they didn't have any money. You're a man. You're not going to take anything from anyone cause you're a man. When you see her your mouth dries up and your eyes can't leave her face. You want her so much you can't handle it. You flee. You tell her you don't want her warmth. You tell her to go fuck herself. You can't let her go because you and she are, at one point, one. The more she wants you, the crazier you get. You have to let her go and you want to sink into her body.

You tell her you're in love with other women. When you wake up in the morning, holding her warm sleeping body in the curve of your body, you tell her you want to fall in love with someone.

Marcia and Scott hardly had enough money to eat and they were sleeping on the street. They'd lie on top of one blue blanket and place newspapers

over their huddling bodies. Being at ease and in paradise. Every person you see looks proud and interesting. Every person you meet gives you information you want to hear. Every object in the store windows looks beautiful and yet doesn't drive you crazy with desire. Doesn't torment you with the knowledge of how poor you are. Every new street, every alleyway you see is a new stage of the voodoo ritual you're part of: A series of rooms. In each room a new magic event which changes you takes place. You're fascinated and scared. One room contains swamps and alligators and floating moss and voodoo doctors. In another room your sex is cut open and you become a third weird sex. You feel freaked. In another room, a little table covered with a white cloth, serves as an altar upon which offerings are placed, and a candle burns on the dirt floor as its base, where the vevers are drawn. For the greater part of the time, Ogoun, and then Ghede mount the houngenikon. You place your hand on the heads of lions and wolves whom you're now equal to and who stand next to you. You find yourself outside: in a green grassy world, outside the wooden building.

Marcia and Scott knew that if the cops ever noticed they were people and not pieces of garbage strewn on the street, the cops would beat them up and put them in jail. The cops would forcibly separate them. Being so happy that you forget everything. You don't know whether you love or don't love. Forget you ever felt anything. Forget you can feel anything. You sleep cause you have to sleep and you piss in the streets. You're learning to know everything a new way.[12]

Aspen

for lyser (1977)

gravely i burn the dancing candle
and taste the flames   let me
drink your wet smooth body
my slow, lazy, discovering love
emerges

[12] This extract is taken from the beginning of Chapter 6, 'The Future'. 'The Adult Life of Toulouse Lautrec' was published with 'Kathy Goes to Haiti' and 'Florida' under the collective title of *Young Lust* (London, 1989).

the waves uncurl
along for your breast
cheek on cheek, lips feel
lips, our skin, your hair my hair
our legs entwine enfold
can you feel the surge, the
swarm, this mad joy swallow us whole
fall sinking through
we flow needing
pressing
skin on skin, breast on breast
careful, gently fingers stroke
me inside me
nursing her womb tongues entwine
belly rises, we go under
immerse, emerge
fold your chin on my neck
hands in my hair
your seaweed excitement
dripping puddles on my legs
i rise carefully   let me
breathe your ocean   flow
into me into you   feel
the soft colourful sea bed   let me
breathe your ocean   rise
on your waves   feel
the swell   let me
breathe your ocean   taste
your flood.[13]

Mary Dorcey
Sea Change (1983)

Your thighs your belly –
their sweep and strength –
your breasts so sudden;

[13] From *One Foot on the Mountain: An Anthology of British Feminist Poetry*, ed. Lilian Mohin (London, 1979).

nipples budding in my hands,
the sheen of your back
under my palms
your flanks smooth as flame.

Your skin – that inner skin
like silk,
your mouth deepening
full as an orchid
honey on my tongue.

The dizzy lurch and sway –
seaflowers under water;
changing skins with every touch
and then and again, that voice
– your voice, breaking over me,
opening earth with its call
and rocking the moon in her tide.[14]

Marilyn Hacker

FROM

Love, Death and the Changing of the Seasons (1987)

Your face blazing above me like a sun-deity,
framed in red-gold flames, gynandre[15]
in the travail of pleasure, urgent, tender
terrible – my epithalamion[16]
circles that luminous intaglio[17]
– and you under me as I take you there,
and you opening me in your mouth where
the waves inevitably overflow

[14] From *Kindling* (London, 1983).
[15] Woman-manly.
[16] Marriage poem.
[17] A precious gem or stone bearing a cut out design.

restraint. No, no, that isn't the whole thing
(also you drive like cop shows, and you sing
gravel and gold, are street-smart, book-smart
laugh from your gut) but it is (a soothing
poultice applied to my afflicted part)
the central nervous system and the heart.

Jeanette Winterson

FROM

Sexing the Cherry (1989)

*Jordan is a wanderer travelling the maps of the interior. In the course
of his journeys he meets eleven of the twelve dancing princesses. This
is the story told by the seventh princess.*

I never wanted anyone but her. I wanted to run my finger from the cleft
in her chin down the slope of her breasts and across the level plains
of her stomach to where I knew she would be wet. I wanted to turn her
over and ski the flats of my hands down the slope of her back. I wanted
to pioneer the secret passage of her arse.

When she lay down I massaged her feet with mint oil and cut her toenails
with silver scissors. I coiled her hair into living snakes and polished her teeth
with my saliva.

I pierced her ears and filled them with diamonds. I dropped belladònna
into her eyes.

When she was sick I wiped her fever with my own towels and when she
cried I kept her tears in a Ming vase.

There was no separation between us. We rose in the morning and slept
at night as twins do. We had four arms and four legs, and in the afternoons,
when we read in the cool orchard, we did so sitting back to back.

I liked to feel the snake of her spine.

We kissed often, our mouths filling up with tongue and teeth and spit and
blood where I bit her lower lip, and with my hands I held her against my
hip bone.

We made love often, especially in the afternoons with the blinds half pulled
and the cold flag floor against our bodies.

For eighteen years we lived alone in a windy castle and saw no one but each other. Then someone found us and then it was too late.

The man I had married was a woman. They came to burn her. I killed her with a single blow to the head before they reached the gates, and fled that place, and am come here now.

I still have a coil of her hair.

LOVING SELF

L oving another starts with the loving self. If loving is giving – and it
is – then that gift of the self has to be valuable, beautiful, graciously
surrendered.

But how can you make a present of something which has been
devalued and degraded? Cixous and Irigaray argue that women have
been alienated from their bodies by a cultural process which, while
it exploits and uses women's bodies as a currency of exchange, simultaneously downgrades their intrinsic value. For centuries the female
body has been described by men as disgusting, obscurely threatening,
something to be loathed and feared.

In history (as now for some) women themselves came to accept this
evaluation. How not to do so when the persuasions are so consistent,
so authoritative? How not to do so when women have been denied all
practical means of resistance (education, status, money, authority, time),
and when those who did resist were persecuted as whores, witches,
scolds? The power of the process is written into the language. Feminist
linguists regularly point out the appalling misogyny which underlies the
use of the word 'cunt' as the most obscene of insults. Women have been
'driven from' their bodies, driven from their erotic life, so that they can
no longer 'give' but are 'taken'.

In defiance, Hélène Cixous proclaims a new agenda. Woman, she
says, must know and speak herself, her body, in all its infinite desires.
Her speaking out spreads a new freedom for herself and for others:
'Airborne swimmer, in flight, she does not cling to herself; she is
dispersable, prodigious, stunning, desirous and capable of others, of
the other woman that she will be, of the other woman she isn't, of
him, of you.'

All of the texts in this section are exhortations. They imagine a place
where woman's desire can be expressed and can be lived. Sometimes
that place is conjured in the context of larger political action. Emma

302

Goldman advocates the destruction of the inhibiting institution of marriage. But her anarchist hymn to the freedoms of love contains a message to women which is more subversive still. Institutions are changed by individuals. And the individual woman who recognises her body's power, re-inscribes her selfhood and contributes to the rhetoric of women's strength.

Between women, the rhetoric of strength shows itself in the sharing of love, admiration and support. Sappho affirms her continuing devotion to women and evokes the blessing of sleep with the 'tender companion'; the nine maidens worshipping Demeter look with admiration on each other and on their selves; Anne Finch's Ardelia holds up a mirror of love and friendship to Ephelia; Emily Dickinson writes her homage to Elizabeth Barrett Browning and casts herself as the older woman's lover and 'bridegroom'.

Loving and respecting each other, these women love and respect their own selves. Ida Cox's raunchy song is no joke: she will not take less than she needs; she knows her claims, takes herself seriously, insists on the rightness of her 'requirements'.

The extracts from Adrienne Rich, Penelope Shuttle and Anne Hooper also, in their different ways, plead for the respect which should be awarded all the aspects of woman's sexual life. Rich insists that women take back the ancient powers connected to their life-giving role in motherhood; Shuttle's tender poem celebrates the body of woman as new life unfurls within her; Hooper's menstruation diary emphasises knowledge of the body through all its pleasuring rhythms.

Where love is, there is no place for shame. Cixous explains the enforced burden of guilt and secrecy too often attached (for women) to self loving whether acted, written or spoken. But Luce Irigaray boldly reclaims wanking for women. She gleefully points out woman's special independence in self-stimulation. Woman 'touches herself' without mediation. Her 'two lips' constantly embrace. This most secret erotic knowledge is a public proclamation in Cixous's text and Irigaray's, as it is in Marilyn Hacker's poem 'Self'. Rosalind Belben's 'Mary' discovers that she (and her toothbrush) is her best lover. Tee Corinne's 'Woman Who Loves Sex' loves sex, loves desire, loves herself. There is no shame where love is.

Female sexuality is rehabilitated in these texts. It is given back its variety, its beauty, its pride, its infinite possibilities. Woman and her desires have been reduced long enough. She is more than a 'vagina', more than a 'sheath' for the male member, more than a 'waste' on the margins of the masculine erotic. She is diffuse, versatile, varied, spread wide.

'Woman has sex organs just about everywhere. She experiences pleasure almost everywhere ... the geography of her pleasure is much more diversified, more multiple in its differences, more complex, more subtle, than is imagined ...'

The women writing here make their bodies speak. They write out their desire. They claim their original rights; to their own bodies, to their own selves, to their own voices. 'The old single-grooved mother tongue' is made to speak a language other than the language of men. She finds new expressions, new phrases, new tones. She finds new ways for women to speak very old truths about themselves.

'Pleasure connects
those parts, nerves whose duty is delight:
a self-containted utopian
dialogue on the beautiful: quintessentially human'.

Sappho
Beautiful Women (c. mid C7th BC)

Beautiful women,
my feelings for you
will never falter

May You Sleep (c. mid C7th BC)

May you sleep on the breast
of your tender companion[1]

---

[1] Both translations by Josephine Balmer, *Sappho: Poems and Fragments* (London, 1984), fragments 11 and 12. For the Greek, see *Poetarum Lesbiorum Fragmenta*, ed. Edgar Lobel and Denys Page (Oxford, 1955), fragments 41 and 126.

Anonymous
Maidens' Song (c. C4th BC)

Nine[2] are we who enter each maiden votaress
Come to great Demeter[3] in a pretty dress;
A pretty dress, a necklet of clean-cut ivory
Gleaming like the star-shine, beautiful to see.[4]

Anne Finch, Countess of Winchilsea
Friendship, Between Ardelia and Ephelia (1713)

EPHELIA: What Friendship is, Ardelia, show.
ARDELIA: 'Tis to love as I love you.
EPHELIA: This account, so short (though kind)
    Suits not my enquiring mind.
    Therefore farther now repeat:
    What is Friendship when complete?
ARDELIA: 'Tis to share all joy and grief;
    'Tis to lend all due relief
    From the tongue, the heart, the hand,
    'Tis to mortgage house and land;
    For a friend be sold a slave;
    'Tis to die upon a grave
    If a friend do therein lie.
EPHELIA: This indeed, though carried high;
    This, though more than e'er was done

---

[2] Possibly an allusion to the Nine Muses, the daughters of Zeus and Mnemosyne and the presiding deities of the arts and sciences.
[3] In Greek legend Demeter is the corn goddess, overseeing the fertility of the earth.
[4] Translated by T. F. Higham. From *The Oxford Book of Greek Verse in Translation* ed. T. F. Higham and C. M. Bowra (Oxford, 1938).

Underneath the rolling sun,
This has all been said before.
Can Ardelia say no more?
ARDELIA: Words indeed no more can show:
But 'tis to love as I love you.[5]

Emily Dickinson
Her – 'Last Poems' – (1862)

This poem was written in response to the publication of Elizabeth Barrett Browning's Last Poems *(1862). Dickinson was an admirer of Barrett Browning's work, particularly* Aurora Leigh, *and many allusions to and quotations from her poetry are to be found in Dickinson's verse.*

Her – 'last Poems' –
Poets – ended –
Silver – perished – with her Tongue –
Not on Record – bubbled other,
Flute – or Woman –
So divine –
Not unto its Summer – Morning
Robin – uttered Half the Tune –
Gushed too free for the Adoring
From the Anglo-Florentine –[6]
Late – the Praise –
'Tis dull – conferring
On the Head too High to Crown –
Diadem – or Ducal Showing –
Be its Grave – sufficient sign –
Nought – that We – No Poet's Kinsman –
Suffocate – with easy woe –
What, and if, Ourself a Bridegroom –
Put Her down – in Italy?

---

[5] Published in *Miscellany Poems on Several Occasions Written by a Lady* (London, 1713). Ardelia was Anne Finch's name for herself.
[6] Barrett Browning settled in Florence in 1847.

Emma Goldman

FROM

Marriage and Love (1911)

This essay was first published in Anarchism and Other Essays *(1911). Goldman argues that the institution of marriage is corrupt, that it is especially pernicious for women, and is rather the destroyer than the protector of love.*

L ove, the strongest and deepest element in all life, the harbinger of hope, of joy, of ecstasy; love, the defier of all laws, of all conventions; love, the freest, the most powerful moulder of human destiny; how can such an all-compelling force be synonymous with that poor little State· and Church-begotten weed, marriage?

Free love? As if love is anything but free! Man has bought brains, but all the millions in the world have failed to buy love. Man has subdued bodies, but all the power on earth has been unable to subdue love. Man has conquered whole nations, but all his armies could not conquer love. Man has chained and fettered the spirit, but he has been utterly helpless before love. High on a throne, with all the splendour and·pomp his gold can command, man is yet poor and desolate, if love passes him by. And if it stays, the poorest hovel is radiant with warmth, with life and colour. Thus love has the magic power to make of a beggar a king. Yes, love is free; it can dwell in no other atmosphere. In freedom it gives itself unreservedly, abundantly, completely. All the laws on the statutes, all the courts in the universe, cannot tear it from the soil, once love has taken root. If, however, the soil is sterile, how can marriage make it bear fruit? It is like the last desperate struggle of fleeting life against death.

Love needs no protection; it is its own protection. So long as love begets life no child is deserted, or hungry, or famished for the want of affection. I know this to be true. I know women who became mothers in freedom by the men they loved. Few children in wedlock enjoy the care, the protection, the devotion free motherhood is capable of bestowing....

In our present pygmy state love is indeed a stranger to most people. Misunderstood and shunned, it rarely takes root; or if it does, it soon withers and dies. Its delicate fibre can not endure the stress and strain of the daily grind. Its soul is too complex to adjust itself to the slimy woof of our social

fabric. It weeps and moans and suffers with those who have need of it, yet lack the capacity to rise to love's summit.

Some day, some day men and women will rise, they will reach the mountain peak, they will meet big and strong and free, ready to receive, to partake, and to bask in the golden rays of love. What fancy, what imagination, what poetic genius can foresee even approximately the potentialities of such a force in the life of men and women. If the world is ever to give birth to true companionship and oneness, not marriage, but love will be the parent.

Ida Cox
One Hour Mama (1920s)

'*O*ne Hour Mama' *was not released on record until 1980 when Rosetta Reitz included the song on the album* Mean Mothers: Independent Women Sing the Blues, Vol I. *Cox's explicit self-assertion is clearly to blame – Reitz described the song as probably 'too rough' for general release.*

I've always heard that haste makes waste,
So I believe in taking my time.
The highest mountain can't be raced,
It's something you must slowly climb.

I want a slow and easy man,
He needn't ever take the lead.
'Cause I work on that long time plan
And I ain't alookin for no speed.

I'm a one hour mama, so no one minute papa
Ain't the kind of man for me.
Set your alarm clock papa, one hour that's proper,
Then love me like I like to be.

I don't want no excuses,
'Bout my loving being so good,
That you couldn't wait no longer
Now I hope I'm understood.
I'm a one hour mama, so no one minute papa
Ain't the kind of man for me.

I can't stand no greenhorn lover,
Like a rookie going to war,
With a load of big artillery,
But don't know what its for.

He's got to bring me reference,
With a great long pedigree,
And must prove he's got endurance,
Or he don't mean snap to me.

I can't stand no crawing rooster,
What just likes to hit a tune,
Action is the only booster,
Of just what my man can do.

I don't want no imitation,
My requirements ain't no joke,
'Cause I got pure indignation,
For a guy what's lost his stroke.

I'm a one hour mama, so no one minute papa
Ain't the kind of man for me.
Set your alarm clock papa, one hour that's proper,
Then love me like I like to be.

I may want love for one hour,
Then decide to make it two,
Takes an hour before I get started,
Maybe three before I'm through.
I'm a one hour mama, so no one minute papa
Ain't the kind of man for me.

I'm a one hour mama, so no one minute papa
Ain't the kind of man for me.

Hélène Cixous

FROM

The Laugh of the Medusa (1975)

I shall speak about women's writing: about *what it will do*. Woman must write her self: must write about women and bring women to writing,

from which they have been driven away as violently as from their bodies – for the same reasons, by the same law, with the same fatal goal. Woman must put herself into the text – as into the world and into history – by her own movement.

The future must no longer be determined by the past. I do not deny that the effects of the past are still with us. But I refuse to strengthen them by repeating them, to confer upon them an irremovability the equivalent of destiny, to confuse the biological and the cultural. Anticipation is imperative.

Since these reflections are taking shape in an area just on the point of being discovered, they necessarily bear the mark of our time – a time during which the new breaks away from the old, and, more precisely, the (feminine) new from the old (*la nouvelle de l'ancien*). Thus, as there are no grounds for establishing a discourse, but rather an arid millennial ground to break, what I say has at least two sides and two aims: to break up, to destroy; and to foresee the unforeseeable, to project.

I write this as a woman, toward women. When I say 'woman,' I'm speaking of woman in her inevitable struggle against conventional man; and of a universal woman subject who must bring women to their senses and to their meaning in history. But first it must be said that in spite of the enormity of the repression that has kept them in the 'dark' – that dark which people have been trying to make them accept as their attribute – there is, at this time, no general woman, no one typical woman. What they have *in common* I will say. But what strikes me is the infinite richness of their individual constitutions: you can't talk about a female sexuality, uniform, homogenous, classifiable into codes – any more than you can talk about one unconscious resembling another. Women's imaginary is inexhaustible, like music, painting, writing: their stream of phantasms is incredible.

I have been amazed more than once by a description a woman gave me of a world all her own which she had been secretly haunting since early childhood. A world of searching, the elaboration of a knowledge on the basis of a systematic experimentation with the bodily functions, a passionate and precise interrogation of her erotogeneity. This practice, extraordinarily rich and inventive, in particular as concerns masturbation, is prolonged or accompanied by a production of forms, a veritable aesthetic activity, each stage of rapture inscribing a resonant vision, a composition, something beautiful. Beauty will no longer be forbidden.

I wished that that woman would write and proclaim this unique empire so that other women, other unacknowledged sovereigns, might exclaim: I, too, overflow; my desires have invented new desires, my body knows unheard-of songs. Time and again I, too, have felt so full of luminous torrents that I could burst – burst with forms much more beautiful than those which are put up in frames and sold for a stinking fortune. And I, too, said nothing, showed nothing; I didn't open my mouth, I didn't repaint my half of the world. I was ashamed. I was afraid, and I swallowed my shame and my

fear. I said to myself: You are mad! What's the meaning of these waves,
these floods, these outbursts? Where is the ebullient, infinite woman who,
immersed as she was in her naiveté, kept in the dark about herself, led
into self-disdain by the great arm of parental-conjugal phallocentrism, hasn't
been ashamed of her strength? Who, surprised and horrified by the fantastic
tumult of her drives (for she was made to believe that a well-adjusted
normal woman has a ... divine composure), hasn't accused herself of being
a monster? Who, feeling a funny desire stirring inside her (to sing, to write,
to dare to speak, in short, to bring out something new), hasn't thought she
was sick? Well, her shameful sickness is that she resists death, that she makes
trouble.

And why don't you write? Write! Writing is for you, you are for you, your
body is yours, take it. I know why you haven't written. (And why I didn't
write before the age of twenty-seven.) Because writing is at once too high,
too great for you, it's reserved for the great – that is for 'great men'; and it's
'silly.' Besides, you've written a little, but in secret. And it wasn't good, because
it was in secret, and because you punished yourself for writing, because you
didn't go all the way, or because you wrote, irresistibly, as when we would
masturbate in secret, not to go further, but to attenuate the tension a bit, just
enough to take the edge off. And then as soon as we come, we go and make
ourselves feel guilty – so as to be forgiven; or to forget, to bury it until the
next time....

Almost everything is yet to be written by women about femininity, about their
sexuality, that is, its infinite and mobile complexity, about their eroticisation,
sudden turn-ons of a certain miniscule-immense area of their bodies; not
about destiny, but about the adventure of such and such a drive, about
trips, crossings, trudges, abrupt and gradual awakenings, discoveries of a
zone at one time timorous and soon to be forthright. A woman's body, with
its thousand and one thresholds of ardour – once, by smashing yokes and
censors, she lets it articulate the profusion of meanings that run through it in
every direction – will make the old single-grooved mother tongue reverberate
with more than one language....

I shall have a great deal to say about the whole deceptive problematic
of the gift. Woman is obviously not that woman Nietzsche dreamed of
who gives only in order to. Who could ever think of the gift as a gift-
that-takes? Who else but man, precisely the one who would like to take
everything?

If there is a 'propriety of woman,' it is paradoxically her capacity to
depropriate unselfishly, body without end, without appendage, without principal 'parts.' If she is a whole, it's a whole composed of parts that are wholes, not
simple partial objects but a moving, limitlessly changing ensemble, a cosmos
tirelessly traversed by Eros, an immense astral space not organized around
any one sun that's any more of a star than the others.

This doesn't mean that she's an undifferentiated magma, but that she
doesn't lord it over her body or her desire. Though masculine sexuality

gravitates around the penis, engendering that centralized body (in political anatomy) under the dictatorship of its parts, woman does not bring about the same regionalization which serves the couple head/genitals and which is inscribed only within boundaries. Her libido is cosmic, just as her unconscious is worldwide. Her writing can only keep going, without ever inscribing or discerning contours, daring to make these vertiginous crossings of the other(s) ephemeral and passionate sojourns in him, her, them, whom she inhabits long enough to look at from the point closest to their unconscious from the moment they awaken, to love them at the point closest to their drives; and then further, impregnated through and through with these brief, identificatory embraces, she goes and passes into infinity. She alone dares and wishes to know from within, where she, the outcast, has never ceased to hear the resonance of fore-language. She lets the other language speak – the language of 1,000 tongues which knows neither enclosure nor death. To life she refuses nothing. Her language does not contain, it carries; it does not hold back, it makes possible. When it is ambiguously uttered – the wonder of being several – she doesn't defend herself against these unknown women whom she's surprised at becoming, but derives pleasure from this gift of alterability. I am spacious, singing flesh, on which is grafted no one knows which I, more or less human, but alive because of transformation.

Write! and your self-seeking text will know itself better than flesh and blood, rising, insurrectionary dough kneading itself, with sonorous, per-fumed ingredients, a lively combination of flying colours, leaves, and rivers plunging into the sea we feed. 'Ah, there's her sea,' he will say as he holds out to me a basin full of water from the little phallic mother from whom he's inseparable. But look, our seas are what we make of them, full of fish or not, opaque or transparent, red or black, high or smooth, narrow or bankless; and we are ourselves sea, sand, coral, sea-weed, beaches, tides, swimmers, children, waves....More or less wavily sea, earth, sky – what matter would rebuff us? We know how to speak them all.

Heterogeneous, yes. For her joyous benefits she is erogenous; she is the erotogeneity of the heterogeneous: airborne swimmer, in flight, she does not cling to herself; she is dispersible, prodigious, stunning, desirous and capable of others, of the other woman that she will be, of the other woman she isn't, of him, of you.[7]

---

[7] Published in *L'arc* (1975). This translation, by Keith Cohen and Paula Cohen, appeared in *New French Feminisms: An Anthology*, ed. Elaine Marks and Isabelle de Courtivron (Cambridge, Mass., 1980).

Adrienne Rich

FROM

Of Woman Born (1976)

'*All human life on the planet is born of woman'. Of Woman Born: Motherhood as Experience and Institution is a scholarly history and a personal memoir. By looking afresh at the assumptions, the superstitions, the laws, the fears and the pleasures of motherhood, Rich probes and heals. This section is taken from 'Afterword'.*

Thinking is an active, fluid, expanding process; intellection, 'knowing' are recapitulations of past processes. In arguing that we have by no means yet explored or understood our biological grounding, the miracle and paradox of the female body and its spiritual and political meanings, I am really asking whether women cannot begin, at last, to *think through the body*, to connect what has been so cruelly disorganised – our great mental capacities, hardly used; our highly developed tactile sense; our genius for close observation; our complicated, pain-enduring, multi-pleasured physicality.

I know no woman – virgin, mother, lesbian, married, celibate – whether she earns her keep as a housewife, a cocktail waitress, or a scanner of brain waves – for whom her body is not a fundamental problem: its clouded meaning, its fertility, its desire, its so-called frigidity, its bloody speech, its silences, its changes and mutilations, its rapes and ripenings. There is for the first time today a possibility of converting our physicality into both knowledge and power. Physical motherhood is merely one dimension of our being. We know that the sight of a certain face, the sound of a voice, can stir waves of tenderness in the uterus. From brain to clitoris through vagina to uterus, from tongue to nipples to clitoris, from fingertips to clitoris to brain, from nipples to brain and into the uterus, we are strung with invisible messages of an urgency and restlessness which indeed cannot be appeased, and of a cognitive potentiality that we are only beginning to guess at. We are neither 'inner' nor 'outer' constructed; our skin is alive with signals; our lives and our deaths are inseparable from the release or blockage of our thinking bodies.

The repossession by women of our bodies will bring far more essential change to human society than the seizing of the means of production by workers. The female body has been both territory and machine, virgin wilderness to be exploited and assembly-line turning out life. We need

to imagine a world in which every woman is the presiding genius of her own body. In such a world women will truly create new life, bringing forth not only children (if and as we choose) but the visions, and the thinking, necessary to sustain, console, and alter human existence – a new relationship to the universe. Sexuality, politics, intelligence, power, motherhood, work, community, intimacy will develop new meanings; thinking itself will be transformed.

This is where we have to begin.[8]

Luce Irigaray

FROM

This Sex Which is Not One (1977)

In analysing woman's use of language, and proposing a theory which counteracts the dominant 'phallic economy' of language, Irigaray takes as her starting point and model the map of the female body.

Thus, for example woman's autoeroticism is very different from man's. He needs an instrument in order to touch himself: his hand, woman's genitals, language. And this self-stimulation requires a minimum of activity. But a woman touches herself by and within herself directly, without mediation, and before any distinction between activity and passivity is possible a woman 'touches herself' constantly without anyone being able to forbid her to do so, for her sex is composed of two lips which embrace continually. Thus, within herself she is already two – but not divisible in ones – who stimulate each other.... Thus woman does not have a sex. She has at least two of them, but they cannot be identified as ones. Indeed she has many more of them than that. Her sexuality, always at least double, is in fact *plural*. Plural as culture now wishes to be plural? Plural as the manner in which current texts are written, with very little knowledge of the censorship from which they arise? Indeed, woman's pleasure does not have to choose between clitoral activity and vaginal passivity, for example. The pleasure of the vaginal caress does not

---

8   From the Afterword to *Of Woman Born: Motherhood as Experience and Institution* (New York, 1976).

have to substitute itself for the pleasure of the clitorial caress. Both contribute irreplaceably to woman's pleasure but they are only two caresses among many to do so. Caressing the breasts, touching the vulva, opening the lips, gently stroking the posterior wall of the vagina, lightly massaging the cervix, etc., evoke a few of the most specifically female pleasures. They remain rather unfamiliar pleasures in the sexual difference as it is currently imagined, or rather as it is currently ignored: the other sex being only the indispensable complement of the only sex.

But *woman has sex organs just about everywhere*. She experiences pleasure almost everywhere. Even without speaking of the hysterisation of her entire body, one can say that the geography of her pleasure is much more diversified, more multiple in its differences, more complex, more subtle, than is imagined – in an imaginary centred a bit too much on one and the same.

'She' is indefinitely other in herself. That is undoubtedly the reason she is called temperamental, incomprehensible, perturbed, capricious – not to mention her language in which 'she' goes off in all directions and in which 'he' is unable to discern the coherence of any meaning. Contradictory words seem a little crazy to the logic of reason, and incredible for him who listens with ready-made grids, a code prepared in advance. In her statements – at least when she dares to speak out – woman retouches herself constantly. She just barely separates from herself some chatter, an exclamation, a half-secret, a sentence left in suspense – When she returns to it, it is only to set out again from another point of pleasure or pain. One must listen to her differently in order to hear an *'other meaning' which is constantly in the process of weaving itself, at the same time ceaselessly embracing words and yet casting them off to avoid becoming fixed, immobilised*. For when 'she' says something, it is already no longer identical to what she means. Moreover, her statements are never identical to anything. Their distinguishing feature is one of contiguity. They touch (*upon*). And when they wander too far from this nearness, she stops and begins again from 'zero': her body-sex organ.

It is therefore useless to trap women into giving an exact definition of what they mean, to make them repeat (themselves) so the meaning will be clear. They are already elsewhere than in this discursive machinery where you claim to take them by surprise. They have turned back within themselves, which does not mean the same thing as 'within yourself.' They do not experience the same interiority that you do and which perhaps you mistakenly presume they share. 'Within themselves' means *in the privacy of this silent, multiple, diffuse tact*. If you ask them insistently what they are thinking about, they can only reply: nothing. Everything.

Thus they desire at the same time nothing and everything. It is always more and other than this *one* – of sex, for example – that you give them, that you attribute to them and which is often interpreted, and feared,

as a sort of insatiable hunger, a voracity which will engulf you entirely. While in fact it is really a question of another economy which diverts the linearity of a project, undermines the target-object of a desire, explodes the polarization of desire on only one pleasure, and disconcerts fidelity to only one discourse –

Must the multiple nature of female desire and language be understood as the fragmentary, scattered remains of a raped or denied sexuality? This is not an easy question to answer. The rejection, the exclusion of a female imaginary undoubtedly places woman in a position where she can experience herself only fragmentarily as waste or as excess in the little structured margins of a dominant ideology, this mirror entrusted by the (masculine) 'subject' with the task of reflecting and redoubling himself. The role of 'femininity' is prescribed moreover by this masculine specula(risa)tion and corresponds only slightly to woman's desire, which is recuperated only secretly, in hiding, and in a disturbing and unpardonable manner.[9]

Annie Leclerc

FROM

The Love Letter (1977)

The frightful prison of love will finally be forced open when all those who know how to talk of love, how to want it and live it, will join together and merge lovingly, bursting with the laughter and the pleasure of being both man and woman, and yet neither; of being both young and old, and yet neither, and yet all else as well. That prison will give way when, branding every place and every text with their subversive love, they cause the downfall, the first death rattle of the haters, the vampires, the zombies, atrocious puppets of our history.

Only then will we know what pleasure, knowledge, activity, language, really *mean*. Are you ready to join us? You, and all the others contained within you, my all-loving ones, I love you.[10]

---

9   Published by Editions de Minuit in 1977. This translation, by Claudia Reeder, was published in *New French Feminisms: An Anthology*, ed. Elaine Marks and Isabelle de Courtivron (Cambridge, Mass., 1980).

10   Published in *Coming to Writing* (1977). This translation, by Isabelle de Courtivron, was published in *New French Feminisms: An Anthology*, ed. Elaine Marks and Isabelle de Courtivron (Cambridge, Mass., 1980).

Rosalind Belben

FROM

Dreaming of Dead People (1978)

Using themes connected to manifestations of the Virgin, Belben constructs a series of reveries on feminine sexuality. This is the second, where 'Mary, Mary quite contrary', contemplates the oppositions of chastity and desire.

Mary, Mary, quite contrary
How doth thy garden grow?
With silver bells and cockle shells
And pretty maids all in a row

I know there is more than colour in my cheeks. 'Like one of those roses you cut and take straight into church,' someone's lovely Granny said, with a face like one of those roses herself.

I am told I shine, I radiate; I'm not sure I want to shine for everyone; some people are not the people I want to shine for. But too many have mentioned it for me to be unaware. It cannot be the sweetness of my nature.

It is the glow of celibacy, I expect; the bloom seen on the scrubbed cheeks of nuns and shining from their eyes; not all, just some nuns; it may be mistaken there as the symptoms of sublimation, holiness. It is not celibacy itself; it is the struggle with celibacy. And not all, not even all nuns, have the same struggle. If you catch that look on a nun's face, you may care to think: beneath her habit, her body, if it had the chance, would lust, and strongly, for it is an ordinary, earthly body; and behind the glowing purity is a mind that has denied itself carnal knowledge. Doubtless there are nuns, spinsters, widows and widowers, wives, husbands, monks, priests who do not have as much libidinous feeling to thwart. A nun, anyway, may sublimate her sexual drive in such great love of God that she rises from the ground and has to be pinned down by the hem of her cloth to the cold and sweaty stones by her sisters singing, kneeling in the quire.

I have not fucked for ten years.

It is a long time. For the whole of the middle of my life.

Ten: one, two, three, five, seven, ten. The first two years are bearable. After that, it feels strange. *Not* fucking is extraordinary, it is the reality and has begun to pall. The seeds of the joke about onions, and getting them.

I have this vague puzzle: that other people fuck, that things happen to them, instead of a blank apathy that is now mine, instead of things seeming to be about to happen and suddenly vanishing, chimerically.

317

I catch myself looking at people's lips; I calculate the history of those lips, in the hours preceding, the night before maybe; the lips are perhaps bruised, are sore from being bitten; I find my hand, palm outwards, covering my own mouth, as if shielding it from nips of jealousy.

It's with a feeling almost of horror that I realise I am not now and never shall be much loved of anyone, especially cared for.

I look at the withered spinsters, twenty years ahead of me, with a new and appalled understanding. Virginia Woolf understood, that loneliness which stretches out and hasn't yet come. Virginia Woolf died two months after I was born.

I am not precisely pitying myself. I am trying to gird my loins.

I am resisting, I want to revolt against being condemned to silence because my life is not valid; because there is a rule against squealing; against pitying oneself; the unthinkable sin.

Desperation can be very quelling. I am shrivelling; so that I am less, I sense, than the air I displace with my body; there is a gap between me and my outer shell; no, it is all shrunk, there is a vacuum; and which surrounds me.

I am aware of becoming dulled, I am afraid of a lessening in intensity, of feeling less. Where do roses go when they fade, where do old roses.

I am quite frugal. Though I am closed in with cold, steel-stiff, and forbidding, more and more each day, week, month, year, don't think I don't ache for it. A word of tenderness, a gesture.

For once again, my expression to be transformed by fucking; for contentment, an hour or two; relief, peace, and tranquillity; not always to have to notice what odd demands life makes; to smell someone else on my skin; for ten minutes, to live on for the next ten years.

Or five minutes. A kiss. To burn in my memory. To remember in order to forget.

To have desire again, to want someone, melting like a snowman at the feet.

There have been moments, many moments, when I want so much to fuck that I can only curl up and lie still. And even my mouth: my lips hurt to kiss. A simple thing, a kiss.

For the sexual charge, the electricity, to run, even through sleeves.

I have woken with breasts swollen and sore, pulsing, the nipples desiccated and peeling; tumbling, falling from the body as it heaves itself to sit on the side of the bed, from lying spreadeagled, supine and confident.

I have woken sopping and swollen, with a devil to suppress between my legs, and with dismay. To the splatter of summer rain.

I have woken with my cunt crying out, lips throbbing and puckering and an empty thumb print pressed into the back of my ear.

It's rather like waking with one's arms outstretched, embracing thin air, an emotional rictus – so that after a while, waking has become the focal point of the day, the point on which the day is hinged, or unhinged.

I want stuffing for the mouth, a cock, a tongue, a rolled-up handkerchief.

A disembodied member: the remembrance of skin, the texture, the unexpected softness and silkiness of penis-skin. And then I imagine that between my legs, clutched in my muscles, at the entrance of my cunt, anywhere. Inside me. The desire is detached, is the sensation alone, is in that one location of my body.

I am half a mouth: the sheets cover half my mouth as I lie on my side; I feel a kiss on half my mouth; half of each lip, the top, the bottom, is alive; the other halves, killed by the white, winding sheet, are dead.

I am balanced on a scream.

Not to float, but to step boldly out of frame, to swim naked in a sea somewhere, to act upon the moment; someone fondles your breasts, and you trot along like a little dog, after the tugging leash of inclination, the flow of feeling, assuming it has a clear, pictorial direction.

It is not that I fear being myself, it is nervousness of the self I shall be in five years, one year, ten minutes. I am husbanding my future self, the person who will reflect, who will have to sit on her life, upon memory; upon a tuffet of memory, eating the cud.

At the present, I am poised on a fulcrum, having to be mindful of future and past and I don't know if, one day, I shall feel relief or regret or not be bothered much either way. I don't know that I have ever really ... adequately ... regretted.

I have a notice of ageing, a wrinkling in the skin between the breasts.

If Venice signifies ecstasy, if she may be acquired as a symbol, there should have been a Venice chapter in all our lives.

If I can look without flinching. I don't believe in atonement.

I turned to nature. To tracks in the snow. To things that lead somewhere. I love rivers, canals, streams, water which holds the mirror up. I love lakes. I imagine swimming very much. The clasp of water, of glittering liquid. I will squat in my imagination by a loch in the Highlands dabbling my toes and watching my own body as it breaks the ripples, stroking the glass face, into the sun or away from it, toward the motionless, invisible heron, stubbing my feet on a submerged tree trunk. I am anxious about drowning; I am out of reach of help, out of my depth; and the long-tailed tits twitter in the pine tree tops. I wait for the osprey which could change one's life but which never appears, forever a possible, and its absence.

I take to the stones; rocks and stones and running water; slabs of rock, flat, and sloping into a river bed; with worn surfaces, rutted and grooved. I have lain, my spine against them; my shoulders on heather, that springs, and bark, that scratches; and on snow, which dissolves.

It is not the wetness of water, it is the darting movement, the staying still, the hand passed through it as if it isn't there. As though it were not real.

I restrict my excitements: to the hedgepig's grunting in the garden; to insects rising on the warm air, transfigured into fluff; to the heat of the sun.

I feel like a Swede at the end of winter.

There is a difficulty in abandoning oneself – head held mutely up to blinding light, mild, feeble light – to nature. In searching the sun and the wind and water, hoping to find hands, fingers, lips and cocks.

But at least it isn't as food is, quite disgusting after a few years' solitude, a disintegrater in the mouth, putrefying before its time, furring the tongue: that loneliness is purely subjective, an illusion, a delusion of the taste buds; my gob is sour with the wrong juices for the meat, fruit, and drink.

I will breathe life into a cheek. I construct a human item, holding the flesh in the hand of my mind: first the colour; filling it with the correct white, pink, pale, and blush; fleshing . . . it out; and then the lying of it to the skin of a pony's neck, or a dog's flank, or a cow's, or a coarse-haired donkey's. I no longer relish the smell of dog.

I am aware of isolated parts of my body which have no feeling: they feel and feel not; such as the hair on my skin.

Or I feel nothing else but cunt, twitching like the nose of a rabbit: and that is all I feel, all I am; the rest is dead; not numb, simply physically not there.

An unfortunate ghost is left clutching her cunt instead of her head, under the arm; where is the expression on a severed head – in ether above the severed neck? – for assuredly such spectres have expressiveness. Can it be the cunt's lips curl into a grin. Smile, cockle, smile. Alas, poor cunt, I knew her well. Alack, O cockle, no teeth, no toothipegs.

In medieval vernacular cockle was a name for cunt.

And pilgrims wore cockleshells in their hats to show the world that cunts were above them, out of sight and mind, and well away from their winkles.

To put winkle into cockle, cock into cunt, is such a *peculiar* thing, if you think about it; and I do think about it; for one part of a human body actually to be fitted inside another's. It's a stupendous notion.

Penis seems feminine; women should have penises, men cockles, raw and red and angry and gripping; the temper of our sexes.

There must have been an Anglo-Saxon word for clitoris, somehow forgotten down the ages; if cockle has got lost, why not mussel; the metaphor will do nicely. I am trying to invent a decent word for clitoris, the ungainliest in the Latin language.

But belonging is not all nameless; it too has flesh, and skin, and stiffening; it is far more than the stiff cock.

The sharing, missing it.

Having a basic need for that, to share experience, which without it has little meaning; wanting to be looked at and to look with. There is a near-imperceptible singing in the voice, in the mind; it says, I am alive; it is vitality. A joyous humming. I lack it. I am not so fragile now, not so hurt; but I should dearly like to be able to say 'we', not everlastingly 'I'. However many years is it since I shared a bath or washed myself in someone else's

bath water. I do long for the sense of someone moving around, breathing, occupying a space, not to be bumped into. Not anyone. I loathe having people here at night unless I am exceptionally easy with them. I am used to houses where visitors can be shut off and avoided.

I am not talking about visitors.

It is that which I don't understand: how it could have happened.

I reject, but cannot escape, the facts, that may have set me on my course. I suppose I am falling back into a predictable pattern of aspirations and emotions; and summoning these with words which have been in service before, the drudges: feeling as others have felt; longing as others have longed; needing what others still need, and have lacked. It's not that I object to being unoriginal, a common phenomenon, or that I mind being lost in the multitude, my individuality no price at all; but that there *is* no escape.

I dispensed with virginity in a house where Admiral Rodney had lived. In the front bedroom: if not upon his actual bed, surely on the spot where he slept; he was born further south, I believe. I was unconsciously fulfilling my lifelong connection – and obsession – with the sea.

Two sweet, gentle, innocent old maids symbolically awaited the departure of my swain, downstairs. There was no blood, no rupture, no pain. The sea was sparkling and green with phosphorus. I had spent my virginity bestriding ponies from early childhood. To spare my landladies, the deed was further done behind the timber dock and in various nooks and crannies.

And so I lived with a man for two and a half years – we have left the seaside and are in London – in a room horribly red like a cave. I didn't regret it; but I wish it hadn't been. It remains my sole experience of living with a lover, as opposed to a friend. It ended awkwardly, and unpleasantly, and it was my fault. He was older than I was.

I flew to Italy, on a wooden seat in a train. I fled. I had some money. I embraced promiscuity, in a lyrical, hilltop Umbrian city; bounded by a wall, with gates, and arches. I slept very high up stone stairs deeply indented with the passion of centuries; the house was fourteenth century; from my window the view was mostly medieval; and far below a 'boy I presently fucked faked antique furniture in his uncle's courtyard, dressed in a suit with a waistcoat, singing or whistling.

I learnt the language quickly. I seemed to be acquainted with every lissome male and, more importantly, with many nubile females who were as I was, from England. For the first time in my life I was popular and gregarious, at the centre of the action. I revelled in it. And it went rather to my head. There *was* a Venice chapter, if such frivolity is acceptable. I enjoyed myself.

Under gnarled olive trees, and the stars; against dark walls; in open fields; in copses; beside the lake, and once, in the lake; beside the river; in tiny cars; in hotels willing to be tipped the wink; in derelict peasants' cottages; in a grand country house; at parties; in a primitive country house; after dancing; after drinking; after lavish meals; on mattress and board, rug and bed; in a

little ancient room down a narrow street, down steps: I fucked. And mildly procured other girls for fucking, for friends. The latter was a mere adjunct to the more absorbing business.

I was 21. It must have done me the world of good.

And then America. Long sprigs of mint, elegant, elongated, spiky leaves, pent up, pressing against the face of the glass, and crushed by splinters, drowned and weighed under in whisky and ice. I have a softness for Americans, those creatures constructed of milk and oysters covered in green spinach and cooked in the shell who swallow Scotch for breakfast. There was only one American but I have been rendered permanently sentimental about them. I lived in New Orleans and worked as a kind of private detective snooping on department store personnel. It was a horrid job. I saw a black funeral with a jazz band, and a little old lady playing the piano in a funny place called Preservation Hall. I rode a bicycle and half starved saving for my fare home. I ate one proper meal a week; a horse collapsed and died outside while I was eating; I was hungry and ate through the agony.

After a tortured two, or was it three, years, during which I had managed to cross and re-cross the Atlantic sixteen times – I worked my passage, I sailed, I went to sea in a big liner. I still have the defunct union card, I have been a member of altogether three trade unions – and he had come to Europe hardly fewer, he and I occasionally coinciding in the same country at the same moment with often a divide of hundreds of miles; after I had stayed two months with friends in Hollywood – that was at the beginning; and after living finally in New Orleans, I withdrew; from America, to Africa. A journey that proved in the end to have been a decisive turning-point, with an Italian ship's captain of dark and brooding complexion, and with whom I went to bed.

There were more, there is more, a little more: but the rest is silence.

I was a woman whom no one had asked to marry.

Mary Swainson knew her at once. As a child she had been very much in awe of her. She reminded herself that she was now grown up and was going to marry Jack, the woodman, as soon as she thought fit, while Miss Turner, poor old thing, had never married at all. Crossing the road, to go through the coppice down to her boat, she smiled at Miss Turner with a queer mixture of kindness, pity and fear.

Then my mother fell ill, and though she recovered, gallantly, to some extent, I imagined I was needed, and I dug in at home, with a sense that there was nothing else I wanted to do. I wasn't needed non-stop, but I couldn't go and come as I pleased, because I surrounded us with animals. I had responsibilities.

If you are told someone has between six months and two years, at the most two years, to live, there is absolutely nothing else you want to do but stay with that someone you very much love. And if she has a terrific will and the energy to live, and lives not for two years but for seven, you still stay,

gritting your teeth, in a paradox of emotions, and with faint, conflicting hope. You are not a sacrifice, the only alternative does not rest in you alone. You are free. It is nobody's fault but your own if you are mouldering. That is how it was for me.

I thought I could resume. It was stupid. A lot of water had gone churning through the mill. I was older. I hadn't the slightest inclination to sally forth metaphorically and look for a fuck as if I had been twenty-one again. I didn't fancy anyone I met, well, hardly anyone. Something had happened to me. I was changed, reclusive, and I daresay unlucky.

Unwanted attentions became the unkindest rub of all, the awful irony. It seems I have been the object of love, or passion, or of both. But I am not so generous I can give myself, my body, to the imagination of other people, unless the tune is called by me. People who have wanted to possess me; to pour their love upon me, except that it feels like piss warm from a chamber pot; to consume me, to ooze unsolicited love upon me; and as if trailing a scent, or a slime like a snail, to sit upon my sofa, breathing and expanding their souls in my own precious space, speaking words I don't want to hear, writing letters with words that simmer in the mind, forcing replies I hurt them by making; it is all too much. I long for a real love, and they sting me with their desire. I cannot be as gentle as I should wish.

I have a neighbour who sweetly offers. I am not tempted. He calls me Lavvy, in the face of hints and pleas, which castrates the notion. I appreciate the gesture. He has repeated the invitation with touching persistence on a weekly basis like hoovering the carpet for ages and ages: we hug each other. It's a habit. He claims he wouldn't be astonished if I succumbed. There is a convenient, uncomplicated cock, and I, I let sleeping dogs lie. Yet I catch myself wondering if I should. If, I think, I have done all my fucking, if I am never to as long as I live, won't I regret not taking the opportunity, no matter what? I feel better for the renunciation, for sticking to a principle. I should be substituting for something sad, something sadder. I observe my tepidness toward him. I dread being one of those females desperate to fit in their last stuffs before the candle flickers. And then I wonder if I'm making too much fuss, shouldn't I relax and take life as it occurs. But he's a nice next-door neighbour, with whom I have a comfortable, totally superficial relationship, and in common, nil.

Irrationally, I feel I can only expose my ten years of denial to a person I know intimately already, and whom I trust. I'm not suggesting it would show, in that I should appear unhandy – it would be as though I had fucked yesterday. It's quite different.

Something did happen to me, had happened to me. I discovered I couldn't come. It may sound idiotic: it shattered me.

I need to be able to explain to that mythical somebody. I can't pretend. I am

not willing to fake orgasm. At that moment I am least ready to be dishonest.
It is humiliating.
It is mortifying.
It is all the more mortifying because for *years* I didn't realise. I thought sex so marvellous I couldn't imagine there was more. I must have known, yet I didn't. I was in that state of knowing and not knowing. On reflection, I can see that of course I knew. But I did not consciously either admit it or know that I knew. I skated over every indication which might have given me the hint. It would have been such an immense admission. I ignored it by turning my head the other way. If I hadn't been a reader . . . no, I read passionately and devotedly and have all my life. If I read books again, which I would have read then, it beats me, how I didn't comprehend. I discussed orgasm with men, without realising what I was discussing.

If someone asked me if I experienced orgasm, I answered yes.

It was confusing. There was the total unreliability of men, and even women, to describe female orgasm correctly, let alone adequately. It is with men I would have talked. I find women difficult; not for a long time have I grasped how friendships with women work, though I must have once. Sexual experience is empirical, and men, even women, tend to assert the general from the particular. That can be a little destructive.

I was ten or eleven when I borrowed a novel from the Boots's library in Ferndown – how different Boots's library books smelt, from public library books today, and how different they looked, with the metal hole in the base of the spine – which was French. The fact that it was French, I thought, explained a great deal. There were descriptions of cock sucking and cunt licking so vivid I couldn't fail to understand precisely what those lovers – so very French – were employed upon. It was dark, and daring, and surprising, but it was clear. I remember nothing else about the book, except its smell; I think I was probably shocked; it must have been an 'unsuitable' book; but it has stood me in good stead. Female orgasm involves intangibles.

There wasn't, it seemed to me, when I couldn't avoid the problem, for someone who had no knowledge of the experience, any inkling of what to expect, any description, whether literary or from lovers' lips, which truly conveyed what it might be like. I felt I had been intensely stupid. I felt my stupidity increase.

I simply couldn't imagine what it could be like. I was misled and diverted in my search of such phrases as 'the little death', and to be 'in the clouds'; I seemed, principally, to be emotionally lacking, with those overtones of swoon; and I concentrated on the deficiencies of my mind. But to be transported by rapture is not really the mother and father, the sole kith, kin, and cousin of orgasm, is it? I'm not sure. It isn't, for me. Orgasm can be an orphan.

I was confused, too, by the non-fiction. A significant proportion of low-orgasmic women have lost their fathers early in life: well, sod that. The fears and failures of women, the ignorance, the reluctance to touch their own bodies, their partners' bodies, the taboos, the therapies, and theories; all that seemed nothing to do with me.

ROSALIND BELBEN

Nor had the men I had fucked with been ignorant, or hesitant, particularly selfish, or brutish, or insensitive. Far from it. It was tragic. It was the Italian ship's captain who told me. You were made to fuck – born to fuck and be fucked, he said kindly, except in one respect. It *still* took a couple of years to sink into my soul. I treasured that remark like a drowning man clutching at a straw.

It seemed it was plastered abroad, on a placard hung from my neck, for all the world, a badge of shame: don't you bother with this frozen person.

Passion is not strictly the point, I thought it was. Passion is possible without orgasm, orgasm is possible without passion. I think if I had been male, I'd have felt castrated.

If you can't come, you are frigid; there is a name for your condition, and it is frigidity. No matter how else you are. The words blur my eyes with injustice, whilst outside the full lips of summer pout irritatingly.

A kind of outraged pride forbids me, ostrich-like, a dignified bird which nevertheless appears foolish, to try. It's as easy to make a fool of a woman as of a man.

I thought I should die without knowing. I wanted desperately, not to be denied another human experience. I withdrew into myself, nursing my secret.

I felt threatened by women in the tube: feminine, neatly painted and scented women, who would cry out at the moment of orgasm, that literary cliché which leaps from the page of every book as if to insult and torment me; like women in movies with contorted faces; and plain, unarresting women, ordinary women who were transformed by sex into writhing ecstasy; if them, why not me? I felt threatened by farmers' wives in country towns, and schoolgirls. As they palmed the hens' eggs and churned their butter and fed their ducks, or did their algebra, they too knew something I did not. They were possessed of the secret. They were real women who satisfied their menfolk, and theirselves. Abandoned females, or inhibited, ignorant, hesitant, passive females, they could all do it. Statistics didn't exist for me; I might as well have been the lone representative of fifty-one per cent of English women, British women, Anglo-Saxon women, for all I was aware.

That Italian bolstered my ego for the years to come. He made me into, for him, a fascinating problem. But at the same time, everything fell into place. I recalled the odd little rejections, the euphemistic questions, gentle probing. I remembered scraps of conversation and segments of the action, the context long gone, which had new relevance.

Nothing had ever so hurt me. Abstract thing.

I was chilled and bewildered.

One day, ripe in age, I picked up my electric toothbrush, touched with the smooth side my clitoris, and the trick was discovered. I was utterly astonished.

I had been reading, actually, an article in a feminist magazine about vibrators. I have never been able to bring myself to buy a vibrator; it's like having clean

325

knickers on to be run over by a bus; what would people think if such an object was found in my flat when I deceased myself; nobody could suspect a toothbrush. I read this article and it came into my mind that in fiction over the years there had been mention, occasionally, of electric toothbrushes and in a spirit of curiosity I stuffed mine up me and got rather scratched; that couldn't be right. Luckily I persevered a second longer. I felt a faint shiver pass through my body.

I became obsessed for a while thereafter, and with practise felt somewhat more than a shiver.

I couldn't have believed it would be so physical. Indeed, with a toothbrush, it seemed entirely physical. It was something the body did, and it would do it though the mind was dwelling on cabbage and potatoes cooking for lunch, or the dog's dinner. It did it better if there was a large penis sticking up before my unseeing eyes, or if I had been thinking or reading erotically, but it didn't make all that much difference if there wasn't and I hadn't. It was completely automatic. How that was a relief!

All those men didn't not know about the clitoris; a poor fellow had pumped away at it so hard it was a pain. I had known since I was at school.

I have very little feeling in my clitoris – that dreary word again; in my oyster, my mussel; hence the expressions 'the world's your oyster', and 'the oyster of your eye'; almost none; and it is diminutive, heavily hooded. It may be a question of nerve-ends. It is, mine is, a useless organ; my feeling all is inside, or at the mouth of the cunt. I cannot come *by hand* for my life. I couldn't save my life if I had to, if I masturbated until kingdom come.

An unassailable, I think, fact. I wish it were not so.

If you examine the cockle, the shellfish cockle, nude and from its shell, you will see – I have been eating cockle kedgeree – the clitoris's likeness. Perhaps we have it all wrong, we have misinterpreted the medieval idiom. It fits, it fits; cock, and little cock its female counterpart. Hey presto: cockle. Our forefathers had already plenty of nomers for the cunt. Is this cockle not cunt but the forgotten lost word?

That is why the shellfish cockle lacks mystery, mystique, and isn't the prettiest of them; the mussel opens its lips; so does the oyster; with force; a raw oyster on the tongue is a taste incomparable to anything else on earth; and it is alive; it palpitates; seems to see you with its single lens; it swims down your throat, is not drowned in your gorge.

The cockleshells of the innocent-oh nursery rhyme could have been scallop shells, any fragile shell; but maids of honour were little tarts with curd filling.

A cockle is no pearl among shellfish, there are others finer and more fair, and more delicious. I want everything for my cunt, and I can't have it. In there would be and must be the sensation I crave, am mad for. The clitoris is fourth-rate, and the toothbrush routine is grotesque and pathetic; how else can I view it?

One might even call breasts whelks: what shape are whelks?

326

The toothbrush is white, slab-shaped, with room for a family of tiny brushes, black red, blue, orange, and is made by Boots; the unfortunate Boots would not have liked his effect on my life; the predecessor was a Ronson, which had greater oscillation, a quality – like a horse – action; the Boots has a stronger motor, and is sturdier – the fat sleek cob of electric toothbrushes; its motor struggles on where other motors might fail; it is the peaky clitoris which has to move, rather than the brush as it would across teeth; it has a long life under trying circumstances, therefore.

I use an ordinary toothbrush for cleaning my teeth. Not from squeamishness. Not at all. To preserve the batteries.

The quaintness of the electric toothbrush renders it acceptable to the mind. It makes a noise like a tractor ploughing along the side of a hill.

In the beginning, narcissistic as a last extreme – what else was there, though not much admiration involved – I would have had a bath. I had a habit then of shutting my eyes as if a painful image had appeared eidetically in front of me. I would scrape at my skin, and mould the muck from my nails into forms which I could destroy, and I was destroying myself. I would pull and tug at my pubic hair. I would stand and let the water run down me. I wrapped myself not in a towel but in my arms. I hugged myself. I was forced to. I would touch each shoulder, holding the knobs in my palms, cupping them. I was holding myself, the hands were mine, the hugger was me. I would be hot, grow cold; I turned my head away and when I looked back I was crying; my lips would ache, my whole mouth ached, first with wanting contact, to touch, to feel, to . . . yet not to devour, not to devour, I did not want to devour myself, I didn't want myself, by myself, at all.

I would lie naked on the bed. I rested my head on my hand; the hairs in the nape of my neck tickled and I thought of centipedes. The sun was shining into the room. It was a lovely summer, as this summer outside my window is. I watched vapour trails break across the sky, their pilots the nearest people to me as I prepared to drag my body from the depths, I thought, of being. I was wet. I was perpetually damp with tears or water. I was wet, I mean, from the bath. I would stroke my breasts, bones, pelvis, flesh. Tracing my wrinkles, the room's lines, ceiling, corners, walls, the light bulb hanging by a thread; curves of walnut, acanthus leaves, mother-of-pearl eyes in the handles of the chest-of-drawers; an oval mirror and columns of curtains; no breath of wind, no breath of anything; the room was part of me; was the red flesh; was the blue skin; in the sun was pale. I opened legs, lips, eyelids, fingers, hooked up my knees . . . to overwhelm reluctance was like pulling on a long rope, or swimming underwater to a distant island; my blood throbbed and I thought I had lain all my life staring at the sky; as I picked up my funny, prosaic old toothbrush.

I don't bother with that kind of nonsense now. It is all a long time ago, and beyond me. It would seem quite foreign to me.

I learnt to place the soles of my feet together and to flatten my knees, which not only increases the intensity but made it even easier. I was a dog with a new trick.

I took my toothbrush away with me – what could be more natural – and had it off in the Little John Hotel in Hathersage, by pure coincidence. Hiding it under the bedclothes, hoping to muffle the genial roar.

I discovered, while it was still a novelty, that I needn't stop. I could come again, and again, and again, and again; once I was up, I seemed inexhaustible. Childishly, then, I attempted the obvious: to see how long I could go on in multiple orgasm. I had tried seven, three and seven being nice numbers. I lay down beside a clock one fine afternoon, when I trusted no one was listening – and if they were, they might think it was my hair dryer or that I was massaging my legs – and carefully counted; if muddled, I made myself discount one; it could have been more, it couldn't have been less; in two hours and ten minutes I had fifty-three orgasms; all good and thorough; I ceased from boredom and because I was a trifle tired; but thereafter I felt better equipped to face strange women in the tube. I held my head up straighter.

I would sometimes stuff a cylindrical bottle, plastic or glass, whatever I had of suitable size, into me, and by touching it, as well as the cockle, with the end of the brush, cause vibrations inside me. But inanimate objects are no substitute.

Those jokes to do with cucumbers and carrots are no more than that: *jokes*. Cruel jokes. The cold and damp of vegetables makes penetration impossible. The cunt shrinks as if confronted with poison. And I am not willing either to purchase or to cover a carrot with a condom.

I had long since turned the toothbrush over and allowed the bristles to grip me. It was as if my body had burst open; and the plastic bristles, they would be streaked with blood where they had bitten in. I wondered if I'd be scarred or calloused, but apparently not. I watched myself in a hand mirror in two ways; my eyes, and the sudden dilation of the pupils; and my cunt's mouth, inner lips, and the sudden spasm, the clenching of muscles, which was involuntary, as I pressed the switch.

I would listen to some music I didn't know, or at least wasn't familiar with, on the radio; and come with a climax of the music, a climax I didn't know precisely when to expect; without effort, with practise, with inspiration, as if the music were my partner and I was attending to its impulse and needs.

One evening, I was abruptly conscious of someone standing at the foot of the sofa, where I lay with my toothbrush, looking at me; since there was no visible person I assumed it was, not a ghost, but a human being out of the body. Whoever it was, with this person watching me, I reached a climax very speedily, and again, and again, immediately I pressed the switch, until I was too embarrassed, under the gaze of the unknown, to continue.

I rather hoped, with tongue in cheek, it wasn't my mother. But my mother was dead, and this seemed to be a living spirit. I am not given to such superstitions. The hair rose on my head.

It would begin at extremities, in my feet, in my hands, and shiver as if through my timbers, my veins and nerves; and my viscera would faint, like shrimps, or eggs; until its warmth collided in my groin. I was a spider with many legs. And depending on the amount of alcohol, hash, in the body, and water in the bladder; upon aspirins, music, sun, rain, storm and tempest, snow and hail, thunder, lightning, and the colour of life; of these, many alternatives; there may have been a fire in my head, in my groin; it may wash upon me slowly, or be abrupt, a disintegration.

If I remove the lyricism.

For up to half a minute, but usually for five, ten, fifteen seconds, there is a – still totally astonishing, absorbing – event in the body. There is a huge jump in the sensitivity of clitoris and cunt both, a stinging sensation, and sharp. The cunt muscles are convulsed by rapid, unstoppable contractions. The cunt, true to its mythological mouth and gullet role, gulps.

I do it for my health.

I think wistfully, from time to time, if only I could try my new-found knowledge with a live cock. I know in my heart of hearts it would be no use. I repeat, the men I have been to bed with were not inconsiderate, or thoughtless, or selfish, or stupid. No matter what ages we fucked for, or touched, no matter how gently, how agreeably I was led on, I doubt if I could come. I am *medically* frigid. It's as if I have learnt two entirely separate responses; and fucking is a very distant relation to masturbation with a toothbrush. I should much, much rather fuck. But I need to come. And never the twain shall meet. The two activities seem as remote from each other as cutting one's nails and . . . cleaning one's teeth. I should like to find out if the cunt can go it alone, but to do that I should have to commit myself to more than a toothbrush.

I am attuned emotionally to the explosiveness of sex, of male sex. I love that, to be whipped up, and to whip up, quickly.

I mind, I mind dreadfully; of course I do; I don't reckon anyone can take that away from me; it would be like trying to deny grief for someone dead; it is as precious to me; as real; as valid.

I meanwhile have to listen in my concrete tower to the simulating moans of the female below, or register the wild orgasmic shriek emanating at midnight hours from the elderly girlfriend in the house next-door, the genuine article I feel sure, and when I spot them holding hands in twin deck-chairs on the lawn I remember how she sounded like a hyena being tickled to distraction, and I pour a drop of affection for her out of my kitchen spy-hole; later in the year I miss her for him, she was so spectacular.

I want orgasm for my cunt, I do, I want it to arise from there; instead of the sense of something being missing, vacant; I want to be filled and then

have an organ, a member, to grip onto, to flex myself onto without being able to help it.

I am bound to mind. To begin to feel otherwise, I should have to have a tangible feedback, a lover, and loving. Day after day after day.

To restore me.

In dreams and fantasies I want cocks in my mouth. In Italy the slang expression *una madonna*, of all things, describes the act of cock-loving in the mouth. I have always liked it. A taste: where words are failing me, are they not? But who the hell am I talking to anyway?

Anne Hooper

FROM

The Body Electric (1980)

*I*n The Body Electric: A Unique Account of Sex Therapy for Women *(London, 1980) Anne Hooper reveals how she encouraged women to analyse the processes and variations of their sexual lives. One of her recommendations was that they keep a menstrual diary. This is an extract from her own diary.*

Saturday 7 January. Day 26 and, as it turns out, Day 1.

We made love last night, not on my part because from a compulsive need to do it, but because we sort of drifted into it. In fact, to begin with I wasn't even sure if I wanted to. But once we'd begun, I was very glad because I was in one of those marvellously physical states where all my sensations were velvet. Anywhere I was touched and any touch I put out to him felt floating and exquisite. Each bit of my flesh was full of tiny air bubbles, all receiving stroking delight. I didn't orgasm in the end, because it would have taken too long. I could have stayed stroked and touched all night. It was marvellous. Discovered in the morning why I'd felt so sensual. My period began, two days early. If someone could market whatever it is that floats

through my body the night before a period, they'd definitely be the world's greatest millionaire.

Penelope Shuttle
Expectant Mother (1981)

In the stillness,
uterine,
hidden from me,
hidden from mirrors,
the foetal roots of wrist
and heart
are coiled within me.
They belong to the child,
to the incast,
a plumage of constellations.

I walk around the house
in bare feet
and a warm rope of blood
links me to my child

Rain falls on garden and inscriptions
but I hold the edge of the rain.
I am a receptacle
in which other rain, amniotic, gathers,
for the one in his official residence
to enjoy.

I think of the quiet use of the unborn eyelids
and the stillness of my breasts that swell up,
a warm procedure of strength.

Already a name suggests its syllables,
but this remains secret,
a fishtail shadow,
a whisper between the night and the day.[11]

---

[11] Published in *The Orchard Upstairs* (Oxford, 1981).

Tee Corinne

FROM

Dreams of the Woman Who Loved Sex (1987)

A mixture of dream and memory, Tee Corinne's erotic fantasy discusses the relation between love and sex by meditating on a series of meetings and partings between the Woman in Love and personified Desire.

The Woman in Love returned from the beach alone, bringing polished bones of wood, blue lupine, pebbles filled with light.

Desire met her halfway with small, hungry kisses, smiles, touches soft as moth wings.

'I've decided to leave my husband,' the Woman In Love said, whispered, sighed.

'Not because of me, I hope,' Desire replied.

'No. No. Because of me.'

Through winter and the following spring they love:

> *When you touch me*
> *When I respond*
> *Joy unfolds*

You have become my text, my love; your body, your words. I have bound your letters into a volume I carry with me, read at night before I sleep, at dawn before I move into the day.

Your love is a fine spray misting my movements, mellowing my colours, lightening what might have been despair. Where your hands have been, I am yours, and your hands have been everywhere. Your words enter my soil like rain. Your memory, Oh love, your memory takes me suddenly, wrenches me from this world into a fairy tale where I am loved the way I always wanted to be.

The Woman in Love dreams and rubs her body against the other's, soft and accessible. She dreams of prairies, wheatfields waving along her torso,

streaming in the wind. She wakens to find her hand between the other's legs. Caressing, she imagines she is the first lover there, that they are 16 years-olds upstairs at her parent's home, holding each other, undressed, their imaginations excited. Everything is new, intense, iridescent.

Younger, she stretches in a sailboat, the sun all over her, salt spray and foam and constant rocking so that the very earth continues to move when she walks on shore again. She tries out different pictures of herself as a grown-up, finds she wants most to be touched enough, a lot, to be made love to all day.

Her skinny friend comes down the boards to help her tie the boat up, younger, graceful, unselfconscious. She wonders about sex with women, between women, will they ever do more than caress each other's breasts?

She dreams again of the boat as a giant padded cradle protecting and nurturing them as they gently go down on one another, liquid and pliant, spotted with spray.

The boat dissolves into a mountain shrouded in fog where they walk, watching the trees and pathways appear and disappear around them. They find a pool and submerge in the streaming warmth, kissing, Oh full lips and hungry loins. Their fingers seek out each other's nipples and rub and squeeze them into exquisite hunger.

They suckle and press, initiating old rituals, reconnecting to a fertile earth where they stretch, slipping fingers into mouths, between their nether lips. They press against the legs and fingers of the other, oblivious. The universe streams out in wisps of foggy thought and sound. Birds announce their coming, cover them with feathers, croon them into dreams within the dreams.

Desire awakens her with coffee, trails fingers along her body, tells her hunger in the touch of her palm. The Woman in Love responds with ardour, pelvis rising without conscious thought. The lover darts her tongue inside, taps excitement's pulse, teasingly withdraws, sustains, intensifies, releases.

Seeking herself, the Woman in Love moves on, awakens as day slowly takes the city, flesh pink, pearlescent, aqua, peach. There appears to be neither cloud nor haze crowding her vision. Alone, nude, she moves against the satin comforter fingering her clitoral peak, her breast, her lips. Moistening her vulva, she works her mons with both hands, commandingly, luxuriously. She arches up to meet her fingers; fantasies being kept by a woman in turn-of-the-century Vienna who enters her room to find the Woman in Love pleasuring herself. The keeper, enrapt, pulls the curtain wider at the window, kneels to watch, touch her legs lightly, make contact without intruding.

The Woman in Love comes as her fantasy self responds to hands caressing her, entering her everywhere.

Nightmares came, dreams in which her fears rose up, enlarged, distorted, embodied in animals, bugs, reptiles, carnivorous plants, menacing, elongated humanoids. She would pull herself awake, sit up throughout the night saying,

'This is what I think. This is who I am. In the dawn the fears will shrink, dissolve. I will endure. I will survive.'
Every morning felt like a new beginning.

The nightmares changed form. She would find her dream self running endlessly, never fast enough. Seemingly outside her body, she would watch the dream self flee from terrors her rational mind could never seem to see.
She learned to stop running, to stand and turn to face her torments, to feel herself grown, able to face the trials of a daily world.

Sometimes she would find herself lost in nightmares of confusion, the substance and context of the material world changing, shifting, offering her no safety. People would alter form and character, laugh at her, tease her.
She learned to look them in the eyes, to believe firmly in herself.

Fragmentary images of magic cities drift across her mind: Montreal, San Francisco, Philadelphia, Paris, Vancouver, Cincinnati, stone buildings, arches, public sculpture. Streets speckled with sunlight. Food artfully piled in store windows.

Riding the train at twilight, her body appears ephemeral in the glass, cruising backward across the winter landscape. Suddenly, entering a tunnel, she becomes volumetric, subtly yet solidly coloured. She flirts with herself, imagines sexual encounters, orgies where beloved hands excite her every sensitivity.

She squeezes her pelvic muscles, considers covering her activity with a coat, seeks out the toilet instead and comes standing, leaning against the wall, her face turned toward the mirror. A long sigh precedes her return to her seat where she sleeps soundly, dreaming of cities.

She camped out by oceans, rivers, on wooded mountain sides, ravine edges, alpine meadows.
Meals became picnics: hard boiled eggs, cold fried chicken, peanut butter and strawberry jam on whole wheat bread, paté, brie, stone-ground crackers, sharp cheddars, apples, dark rye, provolone and corned beef with marinated artichokes, dried figs, sourdough, feta, celery, thin sliced spam grilled on a stick over an open fire.
She did odd jobs for money, staying sometimes shorter, sometimes longer times. Always she moved on.
She stretched herself out along the mountains, savouring the Cascade range, the Olympics, the Siskiyous, glorying in the snow-capped giants, the dark bush of the douglas fir, pacific yew, jeffrey and ponderosa pines.
She learned to be at home in her body, to be her own best friend, her favourite lover. Her dreams became clear and luminous, pearlescent, shimmering.
She began to paint again.

Sweet anticipation, rising warmly into her awareness, the Woman in Love moved on, wiping her past out behind her for shorter and longer periods of time. Opening herself to the world, the Woman in Love reached out with her attention, her intelligence, her curiosity. Time became immodest, a luxury she squandered exuberantly.

Anticipation awakened her, awakened in her, became the subtle tempo underneath her days.

The memory of Desire, going other places, living other lives, the memory of Desire whispered softly to her, a breeze among the cottonwoods, the cypress, jade and acacia trees. The memory of Desire winked at her from small, starry wildflowers, comforted her when lonelineess seemed real.

Sometimes her mind would dream back into the magic words of her childhood: Kissimmee, Lake Okeechobee, the Withlacoochee River, Okefenokee Swamp, Suwannee River, Crystal River, Silver Springs, Apalachicola, Pensacola, Miami, the Everglades, swamp grass, cattails, sea oats, sand between her toes.

She'd awaken to the magic of the present: Klamath Falls, the Rogue River Valley, Savage Rapids Dam, Lake of the Woods, Trinity Forest, Shasta, Sacramento Delta, Monterey, Mount Madonna, daffodils in winter, mimosas in July.

Memory wove into anticipation, washed across her vision each time she entered a new doorway, crossed a threshold, removed a piece of clothing, dipped her brush in paint. Pleasure: anticipated and remembered, cultivated and savoured.

In a glory of late morning sunshine, the Woman in Love sits alone in a Victorian-style bar, waiting for a table in the adjoining restaurant. Yellow mums bloom at her elbow, the glass sparkles, glasses shine upside down in rows. She orders almond wine because it's strange to her, sniffs the scent, turns the glass, amber liquid slowly moving; wooden table, parquet floors glow. A woman with a nose like Desire's slinks by in wet-look pants. The walls are green felt, fern-banked. Well-dressed women of her own age pass with their grown daughters, stately, American.

She imagines everyone undressed, fantasizes body hair, freckles, moles. She remembers a lover's evening touch, warmed with oil, sleek and even, rewarding her anticipatory thrill.

The Maître d' leads her to a seat beside a window. She orders, then reads a magazine: facts, raw material for some other dream.

Later, leaving, she notices the scent of a woman she passes, sweet like the flowers of her past. Then night-blooming jasmine vined outside her window, gardenia waited shyly near her door. Voluptuous magnolia with its lemony air stretched its arms above her, concealed her behind glossy leaves. Honeysuckle and confederate jasmine caressed her summer evenings.

She smells again the twice-blooming orange, heady, pervasive. It touched her earliest, deepest memories. Those blossoms, clustering in celebration

along the rows in citrus groves invaded her tissues with a joy recreated in even the slightest suggestion of their honeyed odour.

Flowers had bloomed inside her as her first lover, very butch, very gentle, held her hand, quieted her fears, taught her pleasure in the heavy, slow-moving air. Her first lover who held her, night after night, barely touching, breathing in rhythm.

She remembers how they didn't even kiss at first, communicating with small sighs and moans. When one night the lover shifted her weight and carefully covered her, the Woman in Love had sighed with satisfaction, felt completed, safe, home. She'd moved against the other. Both moved as ocean waves, as leaves quiver in the evening breeze. They moved against each other, breathed and dreamed. Lying back, she'd flowered within the other's hands, exploded like the night-blooming cereus, unfolding rapidly into the dark, perfuming the air with the odour of her love. Years later she wrote: 'Did you want my heart to stop when you came all dressed in white?'

'Yes,' the other answered. 'Yes.'

Sleeping, the Woman in Love dreams that morning massages her with peach-coloured fingers, nails painted aqua; a fairy silk, midnight garment trailing stars behind her as morning rubs knotted muscles, frees tightened ligaments, realigns her spine.

Morning claims her as her own work of art, painting her in broad strokes, slick with pigment. Outlining her figure, simplifying the background, the structure, the womanly form. She highlights the face, the hands, heart and groin then hands the brush to the Woman in Love, flutters lightly across her face saying, 'Today, reach into the world today.'

The Woman in Love takes her portfolio and fastens pictures to the walls and fences of the city: pictures of women loving, giant flowers, cunts like sea shells, like fish swimming. She hums as she moves, dreaming still, slow dancing through the early streets.

The Woman in Love awoke to autumn, the ginkgo's leaves a yellow skirt around her trunk, floppy bright maple, aspen gold, oak: red and yellow, green and brown.

The Woman in Love awoke and knew her wanderings were over, her roots sunk deep in her own psychic soil. No matter where she went from here, she would always be home.

Autumn spread itself around her, marigold orange and rust, the last of the geraniums, early violets, milkweed seeds in the wind.

Mushrooms dotted the ground, some shouting for attention, others blending, hiding, teasing her.

Cones matured and fell from white and shasta firs, western hemlock, brewer spruce, sugar and lodgepole pine. Golden chinquapin dropped burry nuts among the leaves and scattered berries, madrone fleshed out in anticipation.

The Woman in Love awoke to autumn, specific, extravagant, unique, singing a song of joy.

'You know, I always forget the pungent smell of punk wood trees in bloom, the outrageousness of bird of paradise, salt water in my mouth, salt dusting my skin.

'Memory seems to come so easily to me that I mourn the smells, the images that I know I've lost. I feel pierced when I encounter them again.

'Memory,' she said, 'is an archive, a resource, a library of the senses. Each pattern, taste, smell opening onto others.

'Memories,' she said, 'make noticing in the first place all the more worthwhile. Yet, the older I've gotten, the more I discard by forgetting. And this forgetting seems to be freeing me. It's as if I can finally afford to forget. The monsters, fears, terrors of my past are buried in my past, decomposing, composting, metamorphosed into fertilizer in that slow organic way that living sometimes brings.

'Lighter,' she said, 'I feel so much lighter now and filled with energy.'

She dreams repeatedly of the white flowers of her childhood – fading – the flowered dresses, halter tops, pedal pushers becoming pale, bleached by time, the flowers, pale ghosts of flowers, dissolve into a muted sky, wispy, violet shadows pressed flat within the pages of her mind.

She honours them one final time, then folds the layers of her memory and opens her eyes to a new day.

The Woman in Love met Desire again in London, sitting in a pub, slim, graying, full of stories. They returned to her flat, undressed almost shyly, excited still. Beneath the sheets they continued talking, touched slowly, hesitantly; joked about their mouths being dry.

When the Woman in Love buried her face in the other's shoulder, the hands of Desire were freed to move over her, opening her again.

'So long,' she said. 'It's been so long since we've been together, since it's been like this for me.'

That first coming together, again and again, over distances beyond her imagination, compelled awe. The adequacy of a cheek, a touch, became fire and hunger, sweat and love.

The Woman in Love moaned.

The Woman in Love sighed.

Desire raged and washed over her. This time they both came.

In the morning the Woman in Love woke first, turned to kiss her lover, found her quiet and still. The Woman in Love feared morning would take what the night had given, touched her lover's shoulder lightly and willed herself returned to sleep. She dreamed of beaches, of walking alone on windswept ocean beaches, looking for someone.

She dreams the wind is blowing off the water, reaching through her clothes, drawing the hair from her face. Morning explodes, coral and flushed, exposing multiple horizons. Gulls flash and circle, calling to her, teasingly, to join them. She lifts from the sand, elongating her body, stretching her muscles, reaching out.

Soaring higher, she wants to thank the birds, the morning, but finds she cannot speak. The rosy gilt-edged hands of day encompass her, wrap around her, turn her, mold the furry ravine between her legs. Behind the dreamer's dream eyes, novas explode, the day breaks in two, freeing shooting stars across a velvet sky. The dreamer gasps and twines her fingers in the heliotrope hair of day. An early breeze kisses her cheeks, flutters a curtain lightly across her face. Stretching, she soars again, glides and turns, coupling with the wind.

Nearing Desire, excitement rises, circles within her torso, whistles in her head. Dreaming, she crashes into the other's shore, rolls and turns across her beaches, kites and dips along the other's bony spine.

Desire erupts into a twilight sky to meet her, flowing down her own sides, winking, fiery. Warm breath, lava-flecked, encases her extended body, claiming her.

The Woman in Love awakened to find herself enfolded. Oh, those body smells! warm touch, firm hands. 'Oh, god,' said the Woman in Love. 'Thank you, god,' she said and looked into the other's eyes, liquid, calm and close.

They ate oranges in Valencia and bathed in the sea.

In Barcelona they lived in a small, cool, white room; wandered among the flower vendors until, aroused beyond propriety, they returned to their room and drank each other's bodies, breathed each other's smells.

Their honeymoon lasted as long as they needed. When their work drew them back to America, they returned, alone, together.

Marilyn Hacker
Self (1990)

I did it
differently:
moistened two
fingers in my mouth,
touched
with curiosity,
desire, what I'd
squeezed spasms from before

to get to sleep.
As I would touch an
other's
fullness, blood-ripe
(I was from dreaming
her pleasure
pleasuring
me), I felt
myself, touched
what she would touch me
to, what I
treasured (unexamined),
and ignored.
Velvety, floriform
animal breathes
body-wet like a parched
snail, water;
still, dry,
slicked to a bearing
rolls in place
rooted
where I learned to love
entering; am entered.
Pleasure connects
those parts, nerves whose duty is delight:
a self-contained utopian
dialogue on the beautiful: quintessentially human.[12]

---

[12] From the collection *Going Back to the River* (New York, 1990).

BIOGRAPHICAL NOTES

Kathy Acker was born in New York; in the 1970s Acker was known to a relatively small audience through performance, improvisation and publication with underground houses in America. After the publication of *Blood and Guts in High School* in 1978, her writing was described as 'post punk feminism' and 'post punk porn'. Critics and reviewers have never been quite comfortable with her work; she evades their generalisations. *Empire of the Senseless* (1988) is dedicated 'to my tatooist'. Among students of contemporary culture her reputation as an innovative writer continues to grow. Her other books include *Great Expectations* (1982), *Blood and Guts in High School, Plus Two* (1984) and three early novellas published as *Young Lust* (1989). Her use of the language of sex, erotic and obscene, romantic and clinical, is caustic, painful and tender.

Blessed Angela of Foligno (1248–1309). Angela came from the village of Foligno not far from Assisi and, as a married woman, joined a Francisan order of tertiaries. She experienced a profound conviction of faith in 1285 and, when her husband and children died, made her attachment to the order more formal. In 1291, at the age of 43, she had a vision of God's love while on the path between Spello and Assisi. She dictated the record of her experience to Fra Arnaldo and it was published as *Liber de Vere Fideliam Experientia* (sometimes rendered as the *Divine Consolations* in English).

Anonymous. 'When . . . one reads of a witch being ducked, of a woman possessed by devils, of a wise woman selling herbs, or even of a very remarkable man who had a mother, then I think we are on the track of a lost novelist, a suppressed poet, of some mute and inglorious Jane Austen, some Emily Brontë who dashed her brains out on the moor or mopped and mowed about the highways crazed with the torture that

her gift had put her to. Indeed, I would venture to guess that Anon, who wrote so many poems without signing them, was often a woman,' Virginia Woolf, *A Room of One's Own* (1929).

Aspen. A poet born in Derby, England.

Margaret Atwood (1939–). Atwood is Canada's foremost author. She has an international reputation, and her work is translated into over fifteen languages. She made her name with collections of taut poetry and a novel, *The Edible Woman*, a painful analysis of the disintegration of woman in a consumerist culture. Other works include *Lady Oracle*, *Bodily Harm*, *The Handmaid's Tale* and *Cat's Eye* (1988). Her subjects, in both poetry and prose, are the failure of communication between individuals, the constricting stereotypes of convention, and the falsifications of history.

Jane Austen (1775–1817). In a life uncrowded with incident Austen produced six major novels – *Sense and Sensibility* (1811), *Pride and Prejudice* (1813), *Mansfield Park* (1814), *Emma* (1816), *Persuasion* (1818) and *Northanger Abbey* (1818) – as well as juvenilia, *Love and Freindship*, *The Watsons* and *Lady Susan*. She was working on *Sanditon*, of which only a fragment has survived, at the time of her death. For a long time she has occupied a critical space appropriate to a woman author. That is, she has been considered an expert writer on small subjects, especially to be recommended for never attempting a topic or scene too large for the inevitable limitations of her sex and her consequently enfeebled gift. Only recently has feminist criticism pointed out that Austen's tongue-in-cheek irony conceals a political astuteness and sardonic bitterness – particularly in relation to the social position of middle-class women – which is quite incompatible with the picture of 'gentle Jane'.

Beatrijs of Nazareth (1202?–68). Beatrijs was educated by her mother, at the Convent of the Beguines at Leau (or Zoutleeuw), and at the Cistercian convent of La Ramée where she studied calligraphy. She spent some time in other Cistercian convents but is especially associated with the house at Nazareth where she eventually became Prioress. She wrote an autobiography from which 'The Seven Manners of Loving' is taken.

Aphra Behn (1640–89). Best known as a playwright, she also wrote poetry and prose. Her first play, *The Forc'd Marriage* (1670), was written

after a brief marriage and widowhood, a short career as a spy and a spell in debtors' prison. Successfully earning a living by writing, Behn produced some nineteen plays including *The Rover* (1677), *The City Heiress* (1682) and *The Lucky Chance* (1686). Her best work appears in the comedies of intrigue which unashamedly celebrate the pleasure of sex, and plead for women's right to independent existence and sexual expression. She dedicated *The Feign'd Curtezan* (1679) to Nell Gwynne and *The History of the Nun* (1688) to Hortense Mancini, a lesbian and mistress of Charles II. Behn was also acquainted with the conventional freedoms of male sexuality, being a friend of the libertine the Duke of Rocheester, and lover of John Hoyle, an infamous rake and bisexual. Aphra Behn is buried in Westminster Abbey in London .

Rosalind Belben (1941–   ). Belben is the author of *Bogies* (1972), *Reuben, Little Hero* (1973) and *The Limits* (1974) as well as many short stories and radio plays.

Anne Boleyn (1507–36). The daughter of Sir Thomas Boleyn, she was educated at the French court, returning to the English court in 1522 to attend on Queen Katherine. There she attracted the attention of Henry VIII who arranged a divorce and married Anne in 1533. A figure surrounded by much romance and speculation, it is difficult at this distance to discern how innocent a party Anne was in this. Certainly, extant letters suggest that she was a brave adventurer. In 1536, when the king was tired of her and of her failure to produce a male heir, she was accused of adultery and incest and executed.

Anne Bradstreet (*c*.1612–72). Born Anne Dudley in England, she married Simon Bradstreet and moved to New England in 1630. She bore eight children. Her poems were published in London without her knowledge in 1650, and a second edition corrected by the author was published in Boston in 1678. She is generally considered to be the first poet of the New World.

Margery Brews (b. *c*. 1460). The daughter of Sir Thomas and Elizabeth Brews, she married John Paston in 1477.

Charlotte Brontë (1816–55). The daughter of Patrick Brontë, perpetual curate of Haworth in Yorkshire, England. With her brother and sisters (two other sisters died in 1825), she constructed an elaborate fantasy

world around the kingdoms of Gondal and Angria. Charlotte's own juvenilia was exaggerated, wild and Gothic and her work did not take on its other characteristic extreme ('cool and unromantic as Monday morning') until the 1840s. With her sisters she published a volume of verse in 1846 and wrote *The Professor* while Emily wrote *Wuthering Heights* and Anne wrote *Agnes Grey*. The latter two novels were accepted for publication while 'Currer Bell' (as she had named herself) was advised to produce something with more incident. She did: *Jane Eyre* appeared in 1847. It was followed by *Shirley* (1849) and *Villette* (1853). With the deaths of her brother and sisters (in 1848 and 1849), and with the increasingly autocratic isolation of her father, Charlotte married her father's curate Arthur Bell Nichols in a spirit of resignation. She died soon thereafter of starvation, the result of excessive nausea experienced in pregnancy.

Emily Brontë (1818–48). The sister of Charlotte, Emily spent less time away from home and led an even quieter life. It was the discovery of Emily's manuscript poems which led Charlotte to suggest a joint publication. Contrary to received critical opinion – initiated by Charlotte's own account of Emily's 'untaught genius' – the evidence of the manuscripts shows that Emily was a scrupulous artist, whose revisions and preparations for publication were crafted and precise. Emily's poetry, some of it based around characters and stories taken from the Gondal saga, is notable for its personification of the insistent male muse who importunes the reluctant female poet.

Nicole Brossard (1943–). The author of eleven books of poetry as well as numerous works of fiction and collections of essays, Brossard is an original and inspiring feminist theorist. Much of her work has been translated into English and is published by Coach House Press of Quebec and Toronto. Her work includes *Daydream Mechanics* (1974), *These Our Mothers* (1977), *Surfaces of Sense* (1980) and *French Kiss* (1986).

Elizabeth Barrett Browning (1806–61). Born in County Durham, England, Elizabeth Barrett's family moved to Hope End, an estate near Malvern, while she was still a child. Sharing (or taking over) her brother's lessons, she learnt Latin and Greek and later studied Hebrew by herself. An illness at 15 left her unable to assist with the domestic chores attendant upon a family of twelve and free to concentrate upon her calling as a poet. When her father's fortune

failed the family removed to Sidmouth and eventually to London. Here she made her name in literary circles though clinging always to her invalid couch. Early in 1845 she received her first letter from Robert Browning. They married in 1846, settling in Pisa and then in Florence, and she bore one son in 1849 though she had numerous miscarriages. Her *Poems* (1844) was followed by *Casa Guidi Windows* (1852), *Aurora Leigh* (1857) and *Poems before Congress* (1860). Better known for the romance of her life than for her poetry, Barrett Browning was an outspoken advocate of woman's independence whether sexual, social or professional.

Pat Califia (1954–). A flamboyant celebrant of lesbian sado-masochism, determinedly generating 'lustful electricity' to counteract the drudgery of writing about sex, Califia is also a persuasive and original theorist on the imaginative and materialist sources of women's erotic life. She has written numerous short stories for pornographic magazines and has published *Sapphistries* (1980) and *Macho Sluts* (1989).

Benedetta Carlini (1590–1661). Carlini entered the convent of the Theatine nuns in Pescia near Florence at the age of 9, and she eventually became Abbess. At 23 she began to experience erotic and religious visions which led to the establishment of her reputation as a visionary. Another nun, Bartolomea Crivelli, was required to assist her in her supernatural ecstasies. Later investigations led to Carlini being accused of lesbian practices. She escaped the severest punishments but apparently spent the last thirty-five years of her life in prison.

Angela Carter (1940–). The author of *Heroes and Villians* (1969), *The Bloody Chamber* (1979) and *Nights at the Circus* (1984), Carter maintains a reputation as an innovator. Her essay *The Sadeian Woman* (1979) examines the assumptions of the female role in pornography not as absolutes, but as cultural constructions arising out of specific historical situations.

Elizabeth Cary (1585–1639). Raised in a very strict household, Elizabeth Tanfield early acquired a reputation as a learned woman. At 15 she married Sir Henry Cary, Lord Falkland, and continued her programme of self-education in spite of the disapproval of his family. In 1626 she decided to convert to Catholicism, though she did this secretly in order to protect her husband's position as Lord Deputy of Ireland. When he discovered this subterfuge, he invoked many severe financial

and emotional constraints in order to force her to recant. Her drama *Mariam, Faire Queene of Jewry* (probably intended for reading rather than acting) is the first original drama in English to be written by a woman.

Kate Chopin (1850–1904). She was born in St Louis, Missouri, the daughter of an Irish immigrant. She married Oscar Chopin and settled in New Orleans until his death in 1882. Apart from *The Awakening* (1899) which was received as 'scandalous' and 'morbid', her work largely consisted of essays and short fiction which drew on her memories of life in the South.

Hélène Cixous (1938–). The publication of Cixous's essay 'The Laugh of the Medusa' established her as one of the leading practitioners of modern French feminist theory. She presides over a school of criticism at the University of Paris VIII but has also produced various novels and plays.

Colette (Sidonie Gabrielle) (1873–1954). Forced to write her first novels – the *Claudine* sequence – by her husband who published the work under his own name, Colette established herself as an author with the publication of *Cheri* in 1920. Exact observation and sensuous detail are the marks of her work.

Tee Corinne (1943–). Corinne's *Dreams of the Woman Who Loved Sex* consists of three texts: 'Passion is a Forest Fire Between Us', a narrative of desire; 'The Cream Poems', a sequence of thirty-one poems; and the title fantasy. She has also published the *Cunt Coloring Book* (1975).

Ida Cox (*fl.* 1920s). A popular blues singer who worked the cabarets of the United States with an All Star Band of accomplished jazz musicians.

Joan Crate. Crate was born in the Northwest Territories, Canada. She is the author of numerous publications, including poetry and short stories. She lives in Calgary, Canada.

Anne Batten Cristall (b. c. 1768). Little is known of her life, though she moved in an intellectual circle and was the friend of Mary Wollstonecraft,

Letitia Barbauld, Samuel Rogers and Richard Porson. The names of these people and other eminences appeared in the list of subscribers to her volume *Poetical Sketches*, published by Joseph Johnson in 1795.

Christine de Pizan (*c*.1365–*c*.1430). Born in Venice, de Pizan obtained an education unusual for a woman of her time through her family's close connections with the court of Charles V of France. She was married at 15 to Etienne de Castel who encouraged her learning. He died some ten years later. Christine earned a living to support her three children through her writing. A successful and accomplished lyric poet, she also served as the official biographer of Charles V. She wrote some well-known letters on *The Romance of the Rose*, *The Book of the City of Ladies*, *The Book of the Three Virtues* and a poem on Joan of Arc. De Pizan's portraits of the virtues possible to women in *The Book of the City of Ladies* makes her one of the earliest polemicists for female power.

Elizabeth David (1913–). Born and brought up in Sussex, David began to learn about food when she lived with a French family while studying at the Sorbonne in Paris. Her study of food and cooking began as a personal pleasure, developed when she travelled in France with a friend to write food articles for the magazine *Vogue*, and still continues enthusiastically today. Her numerous books, with their enticing prose, scholarly gastronomy and vivid illustrations, have radically altered British attitudes to the table.

Jill Dawson (1961–). Writer of poetry and fiction. Dawson is the editor of *School Tales*, published by The Women's Press, and is presently editing a book on the self-image for Virago.

Emily Dickinson (1830–86). The American poet Dickinson lived all her life in Amherst, Massachusetts, first as dutiful daughter, later as eccentric recluse. She made one attempt to bring her poetry to an audience, but was discouraged by the unimaginative caution of Thomas Wentworth Higginson to whom she sent some of her work. She did not try again, instead she sewed her manuscripts into tiny 'volumes' and put them away. Her formidable body of work was not published until after her death. Even then, so adventurous was her poetic experiment that it was not until Thomas H. Johnson's edition of 1955 that the poems could be read as they were written.

Hilda Doolittle see **H. D.**

Mary Dorcey (1950–   ). Born in the Republic of Ireland, Dorcey has worked on the Irish feminist papers *Banshee* and *Wicca*. Her first collection of poems, *Kindling*, was published in 1982.

Margaret Drabble (1939–   ). Novelist and critic. Her work includes *A Summer Birdcage* (1963), *The Millstone* (1965), *The Ice Age* (1977) and *The Radiant Way* (1987).

Carol Ann Duffy (1955–   ). *Standing Female Nude* (1985) was Duffy's first collection of poems. It was followed by *Selling Manhattan* (1987) and *The Other Country* (1990). Her voice is strong, hoarding of words, splenetic and discreet. She has also written two plays.

Maureen Duffy (1933–   ). Poet, novelist and critic. Her first novel *That's How It Was* appeared in 1962. She has also published *The Erotic World of Faery* (1972) and *Gor Saga*. Her *Collected Poems: 1949–1984* was published in 1985.

Marguerite Duras (1914–   ). Writer and film-maker, her works include *Moderato Cantabile* (1958), *The Lover* (1984) and the film script *Hiroshima, Mon Amour* (1958).

Sarah Egerton (1669–1722). Born into a land-owning family in Buckinghamshire, in south England, Sarah Egerton was one of six daughters whose mother died when she was 5. After the publication of her feminist satire the *Female Advocate* (1986) she was apparently thrown out of her home by her father. She married twice and nurtured a long lasting passion for a third man which drove her to breakdown. She moved in literary circles and was acquainted with other 'scribbling women', including Elizabeth Thomas and Delarivier Manley. She contributed to *Luctus Britannici* (1700) and *The Nine Muses* (1700), and published a collection, *Poems on Several Occasions, Together with a Pastoral* (1703). Obsessive, angry and forthright, many of Sarah Egerton's poems display a frank avowal of feeling, while others are anti-romantic and cynical, pleading disgust with man and imagining with enthusiasm the (to her, unrealisable) prospect of women's freedom from control.

George Eliot (Mary Anne Evans) (1819–80). A dissenter, an intellectual and a radical, George Eliot was bolder in her life than in her fiction. Choosing to live openly with George Henry Lewes, a married man with

no possibility of divorce, she accepted with fortitude the rejections this entailed. Her novels are *Adam Bede* (1859), *The Mill on the Floss* (1860), *Silas Marner* (1861), *Romola* (1862–3), *Felix Holt: The Radical* (1866), *Middlemarch* (1871–2) and *Daniel Deronda* (1874–6). In some ways the verse drama *Armgart* (1870) is more overtly 'feminist' than much of Eliot's work. More typical however is the gradual and prosaic scaling down which Eliot's revisions make to the 'Finale' of *Middlemarch*.

'Eliza' (*fl.* 1650s). The anonymous author of a collection of verse which is also a spiritual autobiography and a personal testament. *Eliza's Babes: or the Virgins-Offering* (1652) appears to have been her only publication.

Elizabeth Tudor, Queen of England (1533–1603). The daughter of Henry VIII and Anne Boleyn, Elizabeth succeeded her sister Mary to the throne in 1558. Highly educated, she was an accomplished writer of prose and poetry which was much admired by her contemporaries. She was also witty and eloquent – both 'unfeminine' characteristics of great use in her diplomatic life. Her verse was edited by Leicester Bradner (1964).

'Ephelia' (*fl.* 1670s and 1680s). Nothing is known of the life of this pseudonymous poet, though various theories have been proposed. She published *Female Poems on Several Occasions. Written by Ephelia* (1679). The coat of arms that adorns the frontispiece portrait to that edition may suggest that she came from an aristocratic family.

Erinna (*c.* 600 BC). A poet from the island of Lesbos; only a few fragments of poetry are attributed to her.

Mary Fallon (1951–). Born and brought up in Queensland, Australia, Fallon has written for trade publications and advice books. Her creative work has appeared in anthologies and magazines. She has also worked with theatre companies in Sydney. Her novel *Working Hot* (1989) is published by an art press, Sybylla (for Miles Franklin's heroine) Co-Operative Press of Melbourne, and had been reviewed as a 'strong and sensual' work.

Anne Finch, Countess of Winchilsea (1661–1720). Maid of honour to Mary of Modena, wife of James II, she married Heneage Finch in 1684. Finch began writing verse in the 1680s and some of her

work was circulated in miscellanies and collections. She published *Miscellany Poems on Several Occasions* in 1713 but many poems were left unpublished at the time of her death. William Wordsworth and Virginia Woolf are among her admirers.

Foligno, Blessed Angela of see **Angela of Foligno**.

France, Marie de see **Marie de France**.

Kath Fraser (1947–   ). Born in London where she still lives, Fraser is a lesbian feminist and has been a clinical psychologist. Her work has been published in a number of collections.

Marilyn French (1929–   ). The author of *The Women's Room* (1978), *The Bleeding Heart* (1980) and *Her Mother's Daughter* (1987). She has also written *Beyond Power: On Women, Men and Morals* (1985), and two books of literary criticism, *The Book as World: James Joyce's ULYSSES* (1976) and *Shakespeare's Division of Experience* (1981).

Elizabeth Gaskell (1810–65). Brought up by an aunt in Knutsford, Cheshire, England, Gaskell used that feminine world for her well-known novel *Cranford* (1853). Very much a 'womanly' writer, she was dissuaded from the use of a pseudonym on the grounds that, as 'Mrs Gaskell' she could command a very particular, and polite, audience. All the same, she managed to speak some unpalatable truths about the sexual exploitation of the working woman (*Ruth*, 1853, and *Mary Barton*, 1848), and the sexual vulnerability of middle class women (*North and South*, 1855, and *Cousin Phillis*, 1864). Her other novels are *Sylvia's Lovers* (1863) and *Wives and Daughters* (1866).

Emma Goldman (1869–1940). Anarchist. Born in Russia, in 1886 she fled to America with her sister when her father threatened her with marriage. Finding 'free' America as restrictive as Czarist repression, she entered active politics when she conspired with her lover to assassinate the Chairman of the Carnegie Steel Corporation. The attempt failed, but Goldman's notorious career as a defender of violent resistance began. From 1906 onwards she was well known as a lecturer on a variety of topics centring on individual freedom. During the First World War, she opposed conscription, and was deported to the Soviet Union in 1919. She settled for a while in England and later in France, where she wrote her autobiography, *Living My Life* (1931). She died

in Canada on a lecture tour to raise money for the Spanish opponents to Franco.

Elizabeth Grymeston (d. 1603). The daughter of Martin Bernye, she married Christopher Grymeston of Yorkshire. Her only work was the *Miscelanae, Meditations, Memoratives* which was a tract produced for the benefit of her son, Bernye, and published after her death.

H.D. (Hilda Doolittle) (1886–1961). Poet, and a leading member of the 'Imagist' movement. She came to Europe in 1911. Her works are characterised by a spare imagery enriched by mysticism and mythology. Her first collection was *Sea Garden* (1916), and her last *Helen in Egypt* (1961).

Marilyn Hacker. American poet. Hacker's work begins by being unassuming and ends by being compulsive. Her *Love, Death and the Changing of the Seasons* (1986) is a sonnet sequence charting a year long love affair. Her most recent collection is *Going Back to the River* (1990).

Radclyffe Hall (1883–1943). The author of six novels including *The Unlit Lamp* (1924) and *Adam's Breed* (1926), a collection of short stories and four volumes of poetry. Her best known work is *The Well of Loneliness* (1928) – not a cheerful or reassuring book on lesbian choices, but an important one simply because it began to imagine possibilities.

Wanda Honn (1950–   ). Wanda Honn is a pseudonym for Wendy Borgstrom who works in New York City. She is the author of *Rapture* (1987) and *Rapture and the Second Coming* (1990).

Anne Hooper (1941–   ). A professional sex therapist, the author of *The Body Electric: A Unique Account of Sex Therapy for Women* (1980) and *The Thinking Woman's Guide to Love and Sex* (1983).

Luce Irigaray. A psychoanalyst, she is the author of *Speculum de l'autre femme* (1974), *Ce sexe qui n'en est pas un* (1977), *Amante Marine* (1980), *Passions Elementaires* (1982) and *L'Oubli de l'Air* (1983).

Elizabeth Jennings (1926–   ). Although her work has been described as 'good-mannered', Jennings is a poet who can evoke the fret and irritation of desire with cruel precision. Her first collection, *Poems,*

was published in 1955. Her later work includes *The Mind Has Mountains* (1966), *Lucidities* (1970), *Moments of Grace* (1977) and *Celebrations and Elegies* (1982).

Elizabeth Jolley (1923–   ). Born in the Midlands, the daughter of a Quaker family, Jolly trained as a nurse and married Leonard Jolley, a librarian. With their three children they emigrated to Western Australia in 1959. She published two collections of short stories, *Five Acre Virgin* (1976) and *The Travelling Entertainer* (1979) before her first novel *Palomino* appeared in 1980. Other novels are *Miss Peabody's Inheritance*, *Foxybaby* and *The Well*. Jolley's novels often centre on an overbearing woman in her relations with a younger woman. She addresses questions of female sexuality with tact but with determination.

'A Lady' (*fl.* 1770s). The unknown author of *Original Poems, Translations, and Imitations, from the French, &c. By a Lady* (1773).

Letitia Elizabeth Landon (1802–38). Poet and novelist. 'L.E.L.' first came to the notice of the literary world as a pretty young lady with a charming talent for composition. She never recovered. Girlishly dressed and flirtatious when well into her thirties, John Forster broke his engagement to her at a suggestion of improper behaviour. In 1838 she married the governor of Cape Coast Castle, an isolated island off West Africa, and appears to have committed suicide soon after her arrival there. Her most important collections of poetry are *The Improvisatrice* (1824), *The Troubadour* (1825) and *The Venetian Bracelet* (1829).

Annie Leclerc is a teacher of philosophy. Her first novel was *Le Pont du Nord* (1967). Her theoretical works include *Parole de Femme* (1974), *Espousailles* (1976), *Hommes et Femmes* (1985) and *Origines* (1988). She has also written, in collaboration with Hélène Cixous and Madeleine Gagnon, *La Venue à L'Ecriture* (1977).

Julia Lee (1902–58). For some forty years Julia Lee worked as a professional entertainer, mainly in the clubs of Kansas City. She received little recognition during her lifetime but the variety of her songs and their consistent wit made her an accomplished jazz artist.

Mary Delarivier Manley (1663–1724). A difficult but varied and independent life, usually described by male writers as 'colourful', meant that Manley was forced to find a way of earning a living by her wit. Her first

351

plays appeared in 1696; *The Lost Lover*, a comedy and *The Royal Mischief*, a tragedy. In 1709 she published *Secret Memoirs and Manners of Several Persons of Quality, of both Sexes. From the New Atalantis*. Thinly disguised as a series of seduction narratives, this was a satire on a number of eminent Whigs. Manley was promptly arrested, though later released on bail and the case against her dismissed. She succeeded Swift as editor of *The Examiner* in 1711. Her *Adventures of Rivella* (1714) is largely autobiographical. Although no believer in the passions of men, Manley knew how to exploit the myths of sexual conquest for effect.

Marie de France (*c.* 2nd half C12th). The author of the *Lais* which are in manuscript sources in London and Paris is unknown, the title of 'Marie de France' was given to the writer by Claude Fauchet in 1581. Various critics have suggested that she was Mary, Abbess of Reading, Marie de Meulan, or Marie, Countess of Boulogne. She was certainly well educated and acquainted with the life of the nobility.

Mary Stuart, Queen of Scotland (1542–87). The daughter of James V of Scotland and Mary of Guise, she became Queen of Scotland at the age of one week. She grew up at the French court of Henri II, marrying the Dauphin in 1558. At his death eighteen months later she returned to Scotland and her throne. She married Lord Robert Darnley in 1564 and gave birth to a son. Darnley was murdered in February 1567 and Mary married her lover the Earl of Bothwell in May. This last act lost her the support of the Protestant Scottish nobles (always suspicious of her Catholicism) and she was briefly imprisoned before escaping to England to plead for assistance from her cousin Elizabeth. In England she was tried and imprisoned again. For nineteen years she was closely guarded while malcontents centred their plots on her claim to the English throne. In 1587 she was tried for the second time, sentenced to death, and executed at Fotheringay Castle. A serious scholar, Mary was widely read in French, Italian and English, and she also studied Greek, Latin, Scots and Spanish. Some commentators have questioned the attribution of the sonnet sequence to Mary, but the quality and character of the poems are not in doubt.

Charlotte Mew (1869–1928). Living with her sisters and her mother in impoverished circumstances Mew published numerous short stories in *The Yellow Book, Temple Bar, The Egoist* and *The English Woman*. Her two collections of poetry were *The Farmer's Bride* (1916) and *The Rambling Sailor* (1929). A close friend of May Sinclair, Mew was one of the

earliest experimenters with the techniques which came to be labelled 'modernist'. She committed suicide.

Naomi Mitchison (1897–   ). Novelist. She grew up in Oxford, and married a Labour politician in 1916. She produced many works in prose and verse, many of them set in classical Greece and Rome. These include *The Corn King and the Spring Queen* (1931) and *The Blood of the Martyrs* (1939).

Sarah Murphy (1946–   ). She is a translator, interpreter, visual artist, social activist and writer of fiction. Her first novel *Measure of Miranda* was published in 1987 and a short story collection, *Comic Book Heroine*, in 1990.

Nazareth, Beatrijs of see **Beatrijs of Nazareth**.

Anaïs Nin (1903–77). Born in France, she moved to New York with her mother in 1914 and returned to Paris in 1923. She began writing her *Diary* (10 volumes, 1966–83) in 1931. Familiar with the Parisian literary circle, her diary reveals much (not all of it flattering) about the prominent writers of the inter-war years. Her fiction includes *House of Incest* (1936), *The Winter of Artifice* (1939), *The Four-Chambered Heart* (1950) and *Collages* (1964).

Edna O'Brien (1932–   ). O'Brien studied pharmacy before she began to produce the novels about th lives of women which earned her something of a reputation as a naughty Irish girl. The first of these was *The Country Girls* (1960) which centres on Kate and Baba's search for excitement in Dublin. Other works are *Girls in Their Married Bliss* (1963), *August is a Wicked Month* (1965) and *Johnny I Hardly Knew You* (1977).

Alicia Ostriker (1937–   ). Ostriker teaches at Rutgers University in New Jersey. She is the author of an important book on women's poetry, *Stealing the Language* (1986), as well as some six volumes of poetry including *The Mother/Child Papers* and *A Woman Under the Surface*.

Dorothy Parker (1893–1967). American poet, wit and journalist. Parker's first poetry was published in *Vogue* and later work appeared in *Vanity Fair*, the *New Yorker*, and the *Saturday Evening Post*. Her collections of short stories include *Laments for the Living* (1930), *After Such Pleasure*

(1933) and *Here Lies* (1939). Her sardonic humour exhibits an astute consciousness of gender divides and sexual inadequacies, treading a line between the amusing and the painful.

Katherine Philips (1631–64). The 'Matchless Orinda' published her first selection of verse in 1651 as a prefix to a collection of poems of Henry Vaughan. Anxious to preserve her reputation for virtue, and feeling that a name as a writer could not contribute to this, she was much dissatisfied when her poems appeared in an unauthorised edition in 1664. She died of smallpox in the same year. Her friends included many literary luminaries who admired her poetry and mourned her death. Her best known poems are those addressed to Mary Aubrey ('Rosania') and also Anne Owens ('dearest Lucasia'). The abrupt intensity of the desire expressed in these works is still surprising given their context of strict sexual propriety.

Pizan, Christine de see **Christine de Pizan**

Jean Rhys (1894–1979). After a series of early works, *Postures* (1929, reprinted in 1969 as *Quartet), After Leaving Mr Mackenzie* (1930) and *Voyage in the Dark* (1934), Rhys did not publish for some time. Then she produced *Wide Sargasso Sea* (1966) which tells the story of Antoinette Cosway, a Creole heiress who was to become the first Mrs Rochester. A discerning work which embodies a persuasive critical reading of Brontë's *Jane Eyre*, the novel has reached a wide audience.

Adrienne Rich (1929–   ). American poet. Although her first collection, *A Change of World*, was published in 1951, Rich did not find her distinct voice until *Snapshots of a Daughter-in-law* which appeared in 1963. Her resilient feminism, her determined experimentation and her unswerving honesty make her one of the most original of the poets working today. She is tough. She is also tender. Her most recent publications are the collections *The Fact of a Doorframe* (1984) and *Your Native Land/Your Life* (1986), and a selection of essays, *Blood, Bread and Poetry* (1986).

Christina Rossetti (1830–94). The daughter of an Italian father and an English mother, Rossetti spent most of her life at home overshadowed by the artistic exploits of her two brothers Dante Gabriel and William Michael. She began writing poetry at an early age, but seems to have disciplined herself into a contempt for any desire for literary

recognition (see her adolescent story 'Maud', published in 1895). At Dante Gabriel's insistence she published pieces (chosen by him) in *The Germ*, the 'organ' of the pre-Raphaelite Brotherhood, under the name (chosen by DGR) of Ellen Alleyn. She went on to publish *Goblin Market and Other Poems* (1862), *The Prince's Progress and Other Poems* (1866), *Sing-Song* (1872) and *A Pageant and Other Poems* (1881) as well as numerous devotional volumes. Always grudgingly recognised to be a significant voice in nineteenth poetry, Rossetti has nonetheless been relegated to the second class. The determined revising, editing and interpreting of her work carried out by her brother has fostered a reductive academic and popular perspective which denies the adult irony and the covert but pressurised eroticism of her poetry. *Goblin Market* has suffered most persistently from misreading, but other poems are equally in need of rehabilitation.

Vita Sackville-West (1892–1962). The glamour of Virginia Woolf's *Orlando* has overshadowed the literary achievement of the model. Sackville-West was first given recognition with the publication of her long poem *The Land* (1926), a sustained and evocative piece of work, unfortunately little read today. She produced some fifty books of differing kinds, the most interesting of the novels being *The Edwardians* (1930) and *All Passion Spent* (1931). Her life was full and vivid – a fact which rarely appears in conventional biographical summaries which seek to render her talent anodyne and her exploits tidy. They were neither.

George Sand (Amandine-Aurore Lucille Dupin, Baronne Dudevant) (1804–76). Much admired in her lifetime by those who considered themselves liberal thinkers, Sand was 'a brave man' and 'a good woman'. In her work, as in her life, she adhered to a Romantic valuing of the individual life, and her early works (*Indiana*, 1832; *Lélia*, 1833; and *Jacques*, 1834) were especially important for women readers because of this.

Sappho (c. 600 BC). Born on the island of Lesbos, Sappho would appear to have removed to Sicily as a consequence of political strife and to have died there. Her reputed leap to death as a result of thwarted love is generally agreed to be a romantic invention. Some twelve poems preserved on papyrus fragments are all that can with certainty be attributed to her. The acknowledged, and in some senses, the original poet of women's love, Sappho has long been associated with salacious literature – a view rather dictated by conventional fear

of her illegitimate passion for women than any literary content. Tender and exact, her writings still embody a seductive and fiery eroticism.

Mary Shelley (1797–1851). The daughter of Mary Wollstonecraft and William Godwin, she lived with Percy Shelley from 1814 (they married in 1816) until his death in 1823. A friendly competition with Byron and Polidori led to the composition of *Frankenstein: or the Modern Prometheus* (1818). Somewhat embarrassed by her early excursion into the arena reserved for male contemporaries (and Shelley's friends), she allowed her husband to write a deprecating foreword in her name. Her own 1831 introduction to the novel clearly reveals her own 'anxiety of authorship'. In straitened circumstances for some time after 1823, she produced numerous novels including *Valperga* (1823), *The Last Man* (1826) and *Lodore* (1835).

Penelope Shuttle (1947–). The author (with Peter Redgrove) of *The Wise Wound*, a significant re-evaluation of the menstrual cycle. Shuttle has published a number of novels as well as a collection of poetry, *The Orchard Upstairs* (1981).

Elizabeth Singer Rowe (1674–1737). A poet and a dissenting writer on moral and religious subjects.

Stevie Smith (1902–71). Poet and novelist, she spent most of her adult life in the suburb of Palmers Green in London where she lived with her mother and aunt. Of her three novels the *Novel on Yellow Paper* (1936) is best known. Her collections of poetry have sustained steady popular and academic interest. Smith's own witty and irreverent drawings are an essential part of the text.

Gertrude Stein (1874–1946). A prolific author, Stein settled in Paris in 1902 where she was part of a wide and stimulating literary circle. She lived with Alice B. Toklas and wrote her own life in the fictionalised *Autobiography of Alice B. Toklas* (1933). Her first book *Things As They Are* was written in 1903–5 but was not published until 1950. *Three Lives* (1909) was an early example of her intelligent experiments with poetic form in prose. Other works include *Tender Buttons* (1914), *Composition as Explanation* (1926), *Before the Flowers of Friendship Faded Friendship Faded* (1931), *Four Saints in Three Acts, An Opera to be Sung* (1934), *Everybody's Autobiography* (1937) and *Blood on the Dining Room Floor* (1948).

Stuart, Mary see **Mary Stuart, Queen of Scotland**

Elizabeth Thomas (1675–1731). The daughter of Emmanuel Thomas and Elizabeth Osborne, her father died when she was 2 leaving wife and daughter in poverty. Thomas succeeded in educating herself and showed her poetry to John Dryden who was complimentary. She also corresponded with Mary Astell. For sixteen years she was courted by Richard Gwinnet. At first the match was prevented by his insistence that he could only marry when financially secure, and later by the demands of her invalid mother. When Gwinnet died in 1717 he left Thomas £600 but his family litigated and she saw little of this inheritance. Her last years were a long struggle against indigence and she was imprisoned for debt in 1727. Some of her poems appeared in miscellanies (often against hr wishes); she published a collection *Miscellany Poems* (1722) and *The Metamorphosis of the Town: or, A View of the Present Fashions* (1730). Her correspondence with Gwinnet was published in two volumes as *Pylades and Corinna* and *The Honourable Lovers* (1731–2).

Edith Thompson (1895–1923). Edith Thompson was a book-keeper in a milliner's shop and the wife of a London shipping clerk. They lived quietly in a small flat in Ilford, Essex. In October 1922 her lover, Frederick Bywaters, a ship's writer on the *Morea* and some eight years her junior, murdered her husband. The two lovers were hanged on the same day in January 1923 in Holloway and Pentonville prisons in London. The case aroused much public interest and Thompson was turned into an archetypal enigma by many contemporary commentators. Filson Young wrote of her, 'She was remarkable in this way: that quite above her station in life, quite beyond the opportunities of her narrow existence, she had a power of a kind that is only exercised by women possessed of high imaginative talent ... No two photographs of her looked like photographs of the same woman ... She was, to that extent, Everywoman; and she had the secret of the universal woman.'

Marina Tsvetayeva (1892–1941). Beginning to write poetry at an early age, Tsvetayeva had an established reputation by the time she was 18. She married in 1912 and bore two daughters and a son. When revolution and war erupted she lived alone in Moscow for some five years before being reunited with her husband in Prague. An unhappy and hectic life there was ameliorated by an intense recognition of vitality which she never felt again: much of her most poignant poetry, jagged and fierce

in its self-consciousness, was produced during this period. Returning to Russia in 1939 she was consumed by an unequal war against domestic trivia and crises but still continued to write. When war broke out she was evacuated to Yelabuga where she hanged herself after the execution of her husband and the arrest of her daughter.

Tudor, Elizabeth see **Elizabeth Tudor**.

Margaret Watson (?–1645). With Jean Lachlan of the parish of Carnwarth in Scotland, Watson was accused of witchcraft, tried, found guilty, and executed in 1645.

Harriette Wilson (1786–1846). The daughter of a London shopkeeper, Wilson made a career as a courtesan retailing her adventures in her lively *Memoirs* (1825). Her lovers included the Duke of Wellington and the Duke of Argyll, and her acquaintances included many luminaries at the court of the Prince Regent.

Jeanette Winterson (1959–   ). The author of *Oranges Are Not The Only Fruit* (1985), *The Passion* (1987) and *Sexing the Cherry* (1989), Winterson is a writer whose work deals with love, desire, obsession and loss. A vocabulary at once simple and large, combined with an arrogant assumption of privileged vision, allows her narrative a precise and relentless erotic power.

Monique Wittig (1935–   ). Her first novel *The Opoponax* won the Prix Medicis. Her position as an important and exciting writer has been sustained with *Les Guerillieres* (1969) and *The Lesbian Body* (1973).

Mary Wollstonecraft (1759–97). A feminist and a writer on politics and education. Her best known work is the *Vindication of the Rights of Woman* (1792), but she also produced novels, *Mary, A Fiction* (1788) and *Maria, or the Wrongs of Woman* (1797), and *Letters Written During a Short Residence in Sweden, Norway and Denmark* (1796). In her life, as in her work, she insisted on the principle of independence for women.

Virginia Woolf (1882–1941). A dazzling and intelligent writer, Woolf's work still suffers from dull and foolish readers. Her novels are *The Voyage Out* (1915), *Night and Day* (1919), *Mrs Dalloway* (1925), *To the Lighthouse* (1927), *The Waves* (1931), *The Years* (1937) and *Between*

the Acts (1941). The critical inclination to regard her novels as precious and limited grows out of a need to contain her largeness. She escapes all the same. Her other works include polemic (*A Room of One's Own* and *Three Guineas*), fantasy and play (*Orlando* and *Flush*), theoretical speculation ('Modern Fiction' and 'Mr Bennett and Mrs Brown') and opinionated journalism (*The Common Reader*).

Dorothy Wordswoth (1771–1855). The sister of the poet William Wordsworth, Dorothy spent most of her life living with him as his companion, amanuensis and domestic drudge. She wrote some twenty-one poems herself, five of which were published in William's collections during her lifetime. In later life she suffered from much illness and succumbed to senile dementia.

SELECT BIBLIOGRAPHY

Carter, Angela, *The Sadeian Woman: An Exercise in Cultural History* (1979)

Stimpson, Catherine R and Spector Person, Ethel (eds), *Women, Sex and Sexuality* (1980)

Tannahill, Reay, *Sex in History* (1980)

Coward, Rosalind, *Female Desire: Women's Sexuality Today* (1984)

Foucault, Michel, *The History of Sexuality*: vol 1, *An Introduction*; vol 2, *The Use of Pleasure*; vol 3, *The Care of the Self* (1984)

Vance, Carol (ed), *Pleasure and Danger: Exploring Female Sexuality* (1984)

Kaplan, Cora, 'Wild Nights: Pleasure/Sexuality/Feminism' in *Sea Changes: Culture and Feminism* (1986)

Williamson, Judith, 'Sex by Numbers' in *Consuming Passions: The Dynamics of Popular Culture* (1986)

Jackson, Margaret, '"Facts of Life" or the eroticization of women's oppression? Sexology and the social construction of heterosexuality' in Caplan, Pat (ed), *The Cultural Construction of Sexuality* (1987)

Dunn, Sara, 'Voyages of the Valkyries: Recent Lesbian Pornographic Writing' in *Feminist Review*, no 34 (Spring 1990), pp 161–70

INDEX